Blonde & Blue

Book Four of the Alexa O'Brien Huntress Series

Trina M. Lee

Blonde & Blue

Trina M. Lee

Published 2011

ISBN 978-1-463-77319-9

Manufactured in the United States of America

Published by Dark Mountain Books

Editor
B. Leigh Hogan

Cover Artist
Michael Hart

Chapter One

I watched them flock to the dance floor with drinks in hand, a sea of bodies crushed together in a swarm of sexual heat and forbidden desire. The majority of the patrons were human, like usual. But, The Wicked Kiss wouldn't be what it was without the regular turnover of vampire clientele, not to mention whatever else wandered in.

Cymbals crashed as the music came to a crescendo, drawing my gaze to the stage and the burlesque dancers that seduced the crowd. Live entertainment was a relatively new addition to the club, which had recently undergone a bit of a makeover. After killing Harley Kayson, my vampire lover's sire, and taking over the club, I'd been forced to look around and accept the cold hard fact that I ran a whorehouse for vampires. There was no way to sugar-coat it. Just call me, "Madam."

Of course, that didn't mean I had to run a blood whorehouse that looked tacky and cheap. The first chance I got, I made changes, a much-needed therapy. The décor, the entertainment, the security, I'd overhauled everything in my attempt to wipe out any trace of the former owner. To take The Kiss from trashy to classy, hardwood replaced the carpet. A delicious blend of dark colors replaced the garish mix-and-match disaster. Replacing the DJ with a live band and adding the dancers two nights a week had been a key factor in changing the atmosphere of the place. Re-launching The Wicked Kiss had taken a lot of blood, sweat and tears, literally. But, this was worth it, sorta.

"Easy pickings," Jez observed between sips of her bright pink cocktail. "I can see why this appeals to some vampires. Seems like it would take a lot of the fun out of it, though. No thrill of the hunt."

I agreed completely. The rush of the hunt was almost better than the kill itself.

Jez and I weren't vampires. Well, Jez wasn't. I had more than my share of vampire power, thanks to Arys, but I wasn't one, at least not until I died. As Weres, a leopard and wolf respectively, Jez and I desired the hunt. While some vampires shared that need, the bloodlust ruled them.

A few people came through the front entry, and I automatically looked up in scrutiny. I thoroughly trusted everyone working security, especially my mate, Shaz. However, a vampire tried to stake me a couple of months back, and I was a little leery of the patrons.

That had been an odd twist. I'd never been as scared as I was with that stake piercing the flesh just over my heart. The vampire had been pretty clear on his intentions. He believed that someone like me shouldn't exist. I had power that included that of both the wolf and the vampire. It made me more than each of them. Clearly, some people were threatened by that. I couldn't help but look over my shoulder a little more than I used to.

"So where's Kale?" Jez sucked the last of her drink through a cocktail straw, making a slurping sound worse than nails on a chalkboard. "Isn't he usually here, partaking of the goods?"

"Yes, usually. I don't know where he is. It's been a few days since I've seen him."

Kale legally owned The Wicked Kiss due to some string pulling on my end. He'd been a regular patron of the club longer than I cared to think about. When I'd killed Harley, I'd arranged for Kale to take over ownership with me as a silent partner.

"Strange. I haven't seen him lately, either. I wonder what he's been up to." Jez mused, suspicion in her eyes.

Thankfully, Kale's absence didn't affect The Wicked Kiss too drastically. Like a living, breathing entity, it would continue to operate regardless of who was present.

A flash of platinum blond hair moving through the crowd caught my eye, Shaz; every other man in the building paled in comparison to him. With blue jeans and a black staff t-shirt that showed off his delicious build, he was casual but damn sexy.

"Lex, a vampire that Shawn doesn't recognize is trying to get in. He seems sketchy. I don't like him." Shaz awaited my decision, looking down at me with jade green eyes that sparkled with the wolf within. Just twenty-four, he was still so youthful, but he held wisdom far beyond his years.

"Kale's not here to check him out. Tell him to come back another time. Let me know if he makes trouble."

"Yes," Jez added with a sly smile. "I have a pointy little friend that I'd love to use tonight. It's been a while."

Shaz smirked at her. "I hope that means what I think it means."

"That depends on what you think, I guess." Jez winked and waved over a passing waitress for another drink.

Shaz gave her a friendly shove before heading back to the lobby. I was anxious and resisted the urge to follow him. I didn't want to act as if I didn't trust him to take care of an obnoxious vampire. Shaz was an Alpha wolf; he could hold his own. I'm just a control freak by nature.

I gave Jez a quick once over, wondering where the hell she was hiding a stake in tight leather pants and a midriff baring halter top. I was betting on those calf-high, kick-ass boots.

I turned a keen eye to the dance floor. Vampires didn't give a shit about dancing. But, their alcohol-driven donors sure did. The writhing human bodies, most of them scantily clad, were more than some weak-willed blood suckers could take.

I'd seen a lot of crazy shit in this place. Sex and bloodshed were simply the more common occurrences. When Kale and I took over The Wicked Kiss, I had assumed I could change things, make it a place that spawned less death and fewer new vampires. So far, I'd been wrong.

The waitress brought Jez' drink and asked me if I'd like one. I wanted to keep a clear head since Kale wasn't here. Although I could have definitely gone for a Jack Daniels on the rocks, I shook my head. Jez dropped a healthy tip on the tray, receiving a broad smile before the waitress sauntered off to the next table.

"I love that you guys own this place. Free drinks are almost enough to make me a regular here." Jez raised her drink as if toasting the air before taking a large swallow.

"Oh yeah? You stick around long enough, and you'll have vampires crawling all over you, begging for that supreme Were blood."

"I was propositioned the moment I walked in the door. I almost punched the guy in the throat. Now, if he'd been a smoking hot vampiress instead … I might have considered it."

I opened my mouth to make a smart ass remark but was quickly silenced by a woman who threw herself through the entryway, shrieking bloody murder. Blood poured from a ragged wound in her neck and covered her hands. Her words came in a rush, most of them incomprehensible.

It took a moment for me to react. I was stunned by what I saw. Only when Shaz rushed in behind her did I snap into action.

"She just came screaming past me," he shouted over the music. "I don't know what the hell happened."

Many vampires nearby noticed the strong scent of her blood. I reached her quickly, grasping her by the shoulders. She was hysterical, barely focusing her eyes on me. It was obviously a vampire bite, a serious one at that. The blood was pumping fast, and her hysterics were only encouraging the flow.

"Go see if you can find who did this," I told Shaz as I tried to get the woman to look into my eyes. "He's got to be close by."

"Can you speak? You've got to calm down," I said to her, shaking her slightly to get her to look at me.

Instead, her eyes started to roll back in her head, and she said something that sounded like, "I didn't know." I could feel the hungry energy of a few younger vampires that lacked strength and control. This was not looking good.

Everything happened so fast. I sensed the vampire's attack a split second before it happened. He lunged at the bleeding woman in a blur of speed, knocking me aside in his haste to get to her. She didn't make a sound when he bit her, causing another gush of blood to flow.

Jez was suddenly there with stake in hand, trying to find a clear shot. The vampire drank greedily from the gushing fount. A few cries rang out from the onlookers, the human ones. A few weaker vampires backed away from the scene, but the older, more powerful ones merely watched with mild interest.

I grabbed the vampire by the shoulders, but he wouldn't be budged without tearing a nasty hole in his victim. Shifting to an alternate method of attack, I focused on forcing metaphysical power into him, burning him from the inside out. He responded by back handing me hard enough to take me off my feet. Bloodlust empowered vampires the way nothing else could.

Jez took a shot at him next, landing a solid punch to his temple, but he never released his fanged hold on the woman. Jez didn't let up, hitting him again and again. When that didn't work, she plunged the stake into his back, aiming for his heart. She missed. Cursing, she reached for him with fierce leopard claws. Jez grabbed him by the back of the neck, sinking those razor-sharp claws deep into his flesh.

He finally whirled to face her. Blood dripped from his mouth to stain his chin. His eyes were wild, and his pupils were enormous. He moved with inhuman speed, grabbing Jez with both hands. The bleeding woman swayed on her feet. Her eyes rolled up in her head, and she hit the floor.

Instinct said I should help Jez tear apart the crazed vampire, but I couldn't just leave that woman laid out on the floor. As soon as I touched her, I knew she was dead. I was too late. Fuck. This was exactly what I was trying to prevent in this damn place.

Arys was going to love this. He was my biggest skeptic; he doubted I could control my patrons.

I turned back to Jez in time to see her slash those vicious claws across the throat of the snarling vampire. The force took his head right off, and it came straight at me. Without thinking, I ducked, but it burst into ash with the rest of his body. A shower of dust rained down all around me, and I cringed.

The crowd of onlookers quickly dispersed then. Some of them didn't want to end up like our dusty friend, and others just lost interest that fast. The humans were staring at Jez with wide eyes. Bloody claws and wild cat eyes, she was a hell of a vision. She looked far more frightening than the vampires in The Kiss.

I brushed at the dust and ash on my clothes and gave my hair a shake. Well, this was just fucking great.

Then, Shaz appeared in the doorway. His eyes were pure wolf, and blood stained his clothing. And, standing behind Shaz with crossed arms and a smirk was Arys. Fabulous.

I surveyed the mess of vampire remains. That wasn't much of a cleanup. A good vacuum would get the job done. However, that was the least of my concerns. A woman lay dead on the floor of the nightclub I'd sworn to change. So far, things were not going my way. Now, I had to listen to Arys gloat about being right.

He sauntered over to me with a grace possessed only by vampires that had lived for centuries. His sexy, bedroom-messy, raven black hair shone deep blue beneath the dim lighting. The fang-revealing grin he wore irritated me as much as it enticed.

"Go ahead and say it." I threw both hands in the air and glared. "I know you want to. Have at it."

His chuckle stroked me deep inside, and our power sparked when he grasped my upraised hands in his, lacing our fingers together. Leaning close enough to brush his lips against mine, he murmured, "I told you so."

I couldn't help the way my power instantly mingled with his. We were bound by blood, so it would always be this way. Though I'd recently gained more control over my abilities, Arys could always strip me of it with the right touch, look or careful whisper.

"Since you're enjoying this so much, you can clean up the body." I flashed him a smirk of my own and pulled away before the flame burning between us could grow into a blazing inferno.

"I got him." Shaz stepped up beside me with a bleeding gash below his eye. I hadn't noticed it in the chaos. "Pretty easy take down."

I gently touched his face, trying to get a better look at his superficial wound. It looked worse than it was. I couldn't resist letting my pinky finger slide through the blood that ran in a single rivulet down his cheek. He watched as I brought it close, smelling his powerful werewolf blood. I would have tasted it, but Arys intercepted the motion.

Gripping my wrist tightly, he brought my hand to his mouth and slowly licked Shaz' blood from my little finger. His tongue was warm and inviting as he stroked it along my flesh. My breath caught, and I was flush with unbidden desire. Arys' gaze was intent on Shaz, watching for his reaction.

"You are such a dick." Shaz shoved past us, purposely shouldering Arys as he went.

Arys just laughed. He liked to get under Shaz' skin, and Shaz made it far too easy for him.

"Don't start with him tonight," I warned. "If you haven't

noticed, I have enough to deal with here without you playing with him. One of these days, he's going to lose it on you, and then you're on your own."

Arys' smile vanished, but the mischievous glint in his eyes remained. "I wish he would."

"Oh, you do not." I shook my head, exasperated.

Arys' fun with Shaz stemmed from their intense dislike for one another.

They'd gone from fist fights to stubborn acceptance. A *ménage à trois* that resulted in a bite and even a kiss between the two of them had reminded Shaz of what he hated about Arys: everything. Of course, that had a lot to do with Shaz' resentment that he'd enjoyed the bite of the vampire he despised.

"Look, just leave Shaz alone. Help me clean up, and you can rub my total failure in my face later."

I turned away from Arys. People packed the dance floor as if nothing had disrupted them. Newcomers made their way through the lobby into the main part of the club. I had to get this body moved.

Arys swept past me, lifting her easily in his arms and retreating through the rear exit. I caught his eye and nodded my thanks. Ok, so things weren't going as planned, but they could be worse. Right?

Chapter Two

Voicemail ... again. I didn't bother leaving a message. I wondered if Kale wasn't actively avoiding my calls. Foreboding gripped my insides and left me ice-cold. I didn't generally worry about him – if anyone could take care of himself, it was Kale – but something was different this time, all wrong.

Taking a deep breath, I kicked a rock across the parking lot. It was the only sound other than the muffled noise from inside. I needed some air. Escaping outside alone did little to restore my sanity. The Wicked Kiss was one hell of a pain in my ass.

I stared at the back entrance, a plain metal door that led into the back hall where the creepy little rooms were. Vampires brought their meals, er, willing victims in there for a little frisky fun, and Lord knows what else, during a feed. Too many victims had entered those rooms as humans but left as vampires. Taking over The Kiss stopped that, but it hadn't done much to curb the rest of the mindless chaos.

I didn't want to go back in there. Couldn't someone else do it? That someone was refusing to answer his damn phone. With a snarl and a few choice curse words, I yanked the door open and re-entered the nightclub from hell.

I hurried down the back hall, resisting the urge to break into a full-out run. The hall was heavy with the energy oozing from the occupied rooms. The delicious sexual energy, occasionally tinged with fear, drew me like a moth to a flame. Months ago, I would have drooled like a starved dog scenting fresh meat. I had more control than that now, but it still teased my hunger.

A pained whimper caught my attention. It wasn't unusual to

hear cries and shrieks back here. Still, I checked it out. I listened closely, and when I heard a man's voice moan, "More," I was out of there. Clearly, he wasn't fighting for his life.

I jerked back from the door, wishing I would shudder or feel disgust. But, I'd known the intoxicating and powerful bite of a vampire or two, so all I felt was an unbidden rush of pleasure as my pulse raced.

My hate for the place resurfaced, leaving a bitter taste in my mouth. Re-emerging into the club area, that feeling only grew. For the most part, things were back to normal. The dead body was gone, and patrons were drinking and dancing as if nothing had happened.

Arys leaned against the bar, grinning from ear to ear. A woman with bright pink hair sipped a beer and smiled up at him. Oh please. For a vampire that frowned upon the willing victim scenario, he sure was eating up his wannabe victim's attention.

With a scowl, I bypassed the line at the bar and tapped my fingernails on the counter. "Jack Daniels on the rocks."

Without a word the bartender, Josh, slid a glass to me with more than one shot. I thanked him and moved where I could watch everyone. A long swig of the strong whiskey was heavenly. I tried to abstain from booze at The Kiss, but tonight had pushed me past the point of caring. I needed this drink.

I was done. Whatever else happened tonight wasn't my concern, and I wasn't going to do a damn thing about it. The whole damned place could burn down for all I cared.

Jez sidled up to me with a knowing look. "Not worth the trouble, is it?"

"Not even close."

The whiskey burned its way down my throat. A warm tingle started in my stomach and grew to encompass my whole body. That's the stuff.

I glanced in Arys' direction, annoyed at myself for the ugly envy that picked at me. It didn't bother me that he flirted shamelessly with some random human female. It bothered me that he was letting her throw herself at him, knowing she was hoping to end up in one of those back rooms with him.

"She's just food." Jez followed my gaze to where Arys and his new fan were chatting up a storm. "You know that's all he's thinking.

She's drooling over his damn fine body, and he's thinking about bleeding her."

"I know. I think that's the problem. I know how Arys works. I just don't want to see him in action. Not in here."

Everything about Arys screamed sex, so I didn't blame any woman for drooling over him. I couldn't even blame him for taking advantage of it; the man literally fed off it. Now, because of our bond, so did I. Still, I was a little raw from seeing Arys and his sire with a victim.

"I tried Kale again." I steered the conversation in a new direction. I didn't want to focus on Arys being ... well ... Arys. "He isn't answering. I'm starting to think he's avoiding me."

"He hasn't been answering my calls, either." Jez shrugged. "I don't want to over-analyze this, but I have a sick feeling in my gut."

"You're not the only one."

"I'm going to take off. I think I'll stop by the office and see if he's there. Try not to lose your mind. In fact, maybe you should take off, too. You look like you're ready to snap."

I mustered a smile. "Thanks. I might just do that. Let me know if you talk to Kale."

I watched Jez' leopard-golden head disappear out the door. She was right. Why did I bother keeping watch here? It obviously didn't stop people from getting killed, and it drove me crazy. There were other things I could be doing, should be doing, like hunting down the scum that were slaughtering innocents in cold blood.

I could feel Arys' eyes on me. The sudden heavy weight that made me feel like I was in the spotlight. Stubbornly, I wanted to resist the urge to turn and meet his midnight gaze, but I couldn't. I turned to find him standing near the bar alone. The girl with the pink hair was in the lineup for a drink, talking on her cell phone.

Arys crooked his finger and beckoned me over. The sly smile and sexy wink that accompanied the gesture made me weak in the knees. Damn him. Arrogant, deadly and oh so fine, I hated that I couldn't resist him.

I sauntered over to him, ditching my empty glass at a nearby table on the way. "Being here makes me want to hurt people."

"You're speaking my language." Arys slid an arm around my waist and pulled me close. "What about her?" He indicated the pink

14

haired woman. "Me and you. She could be ours. Do you want her?"

I wasn't surprised that he wanted her, but I was surprised that he wanted me to join him. Both vampire and werewolf power flowed through my veins, so tearing her throat out was in my nature.

Instead, I swallowed hard and shook my head.

"No. She's all yours. I can't stop you from killing, but I can't let you do it here."

He raised a dark brow as if he wasn't sure if I was serious. "No problem. No killing here. Just as well. This place is for amateurs." He reached to grasp a strand of my black-tipped blond hair, twirling it around his finger. "Hey, are you okay?"

I found genuine concern in his eyes, and I stroked a finger down the side of his face. "I'm fine, just ready for this night to be over."

A soft kiss had me melting in his embrace. The silver ring in his bottom lip was cold against my tongue. His cologne teased me; everything about him set me on fire. After being involved for almost a year, every touch gave me butterflies as if it were the very first.

Dipping his finger below the waist of my jeans, Arys tugged on my g-string and murmured, "Are you absolutely sure you don't want to tag team that one with me? Last chance."

I laughed and slapped him playfully. "Cut it out."

"But, she's totally asking for it. How can you resist? How can you expect me to resist?"

"I don't expect you to. Just use a little … discretion."

His chuckle sent a shiver down my spine. He grabbed me tightly and nuzzled my neck, grazing my skin with his fangs. The jolt of energy that shot straight to my groin caused me to gasp.

"I can feel it inside you." His whispered words came hot against my skin. "The pent-up aggression. The need to unleash and feed that hunger. Your wolf is frustrated."

I sighed and leaned into him. He wasn't wrong. I should know better than to let the wolf get frisky. It could affect Arys in a pretty ugly way due to our bond. "I'll be fine. I just need to go home and relax."

"You need to stop living in denial. This place is no good for you. You should let Kale deal with it. This isn't your world."

"It is now." I studied Arys closely, curious. "This isn't your world either. You hate it here. So, what's with all the recent visits?"

Arys shrugged and let his gaze wander around the bar. "Well, you're here. Where else would I be?"

"No, really. I know you, Arys. You've been in here a lot lately. That's not like you. What's up?" This was the fourth night in a row that he'd appeared in The Kiss, and I was getting suspicious.

I felt the shift in him as his energy grew defensive. His eyes were still scanning the building, and I began to grow uneasy. What the hell was he hiding from me?

I glanced around, nervous at what I was sensing from Arys. The crowd was starting to thin as most of the vampires lured victims to a more secluded place. Two vampires in a corner booth had a young woman between them. One of them fed from her wrist while the other kissed her deeply. A lone witch at a different table oozed black energy that made my skin crawl. Otherwise, nothing struck me as out-of-place.

Arys pressed a quick kiss to my lips. "I don't want to talk about it here. Later. I promise. I'm sure there's nothing to worry about. I'll be right back."

I was dying to know what had Arys so worried, and patience was not a virtue that I possessed. However, if I could just get through the rest of the night without any further incident, I'd consider it a successful evening.

No sooner had I formed that thought than a loud crash drew my attention to a fight on the dance floor. I couldn't even pretend to be surprised. Since taking over The Kiss, I'd seen just about everything.

Two women were throwing punches at each other. I had to roll my eyes. What could possibly be worth fighting about here? Shaz cast a glance my way. He seemed reluctant to get involved. With a sigh, I waved a hand in their direction and flung them apart. Jerking my thumb towards the door, I made it clear to Shaz that I'd like them tossed out. I wasn't in the mood for this crap.

I'd wanted control of the notorious nightclub because it had such a shady reputation. Paranormal creatures and the stupid humans who sought to be close to them filled The Kiss. I'd assumed I could change the place, but really, it was changing me and not in a good way.

Josh was busy behind the bar so I headed back and helped

myself. I caught myself looking between the whiskey bottle and a glass, wondering if the glass was worth the bother. The Kiss was going to turn me into a raging drunk in no time. I considered drinking from the bottle but poured the glass a little too full instead.

Time seemed to crawl by as I found an empty table and waited for Arys to return. Despite the hard liquor in my hand, my current reality was very sobering.

I sensed a strange vampire's approach before he touched me. I sat up a little straighter in my chair, ready for him to reach for me. Without looking behind me, I grabbed his wrist before his hand could fall on my shoulder. My maneuver soon had him flat on his back blinking up at me in shock.

"What the hell do you want?" I glared down at him. The last thing I needed tonight was another vampire who felt he had something to prove.

His face contorted with pain as I twisted his arm. "Just looking for a playmate. Fuck! Let go of me!"

"Are you new or something? I don't play here. I'm off-limits. All the time." I released him, ready to kick his ass if he tried anything.

I analyzed his energy and decided he wasn't a threat, just a ballsy vampire that thought I was on the menu. It didn't happen so often now that most of them knew me.

"Alright, I got it." He held his hands up in surrender as he backed away. "A simple 'no thanks' would have sufficed, you know."

With a shrug, I waved him off. I had nothing more to say. I was anxious about what was up with Arys. Sitting still was almost impossible. I was restless. After finishing my drink, I took a slow walk around the inside of the building.

Shaz was in the front lobby with Arys. They were speaking quietly to one another, their heads close together. That set off a red flag for me. Arys caught me watching them. He held up a finger in that universal 'one moment' gesture before disappearing outside. I looked expectantly at Shaz, but he revealed nothing.

Now that I was tuned into it, something didn't feel right. It wasn't just the strange way Arys was loitering around The Kiss. The atmosphere within the nightclub felt off-balance, as if something were out of place. My senses honed in on that wariness, focusing until I could feel that vibration that didn't fit in.

I hadn't noticed it before. The metaphysical mojo in the building amounted to psychic noise. Something about the vibe was familiar, and I needed to pinpoint where or who it was. I followed the sensation.

It grew stronger as I drew closer to the doorway that led to the back rooms. It was probably coming from a vampire blood party that would give me the creeps, but I had to know for sure.

The vibe came from the room that Kale claimed as his own. I recognized Kale's energy, but it felt residual as if he were no longer present. I didn't want to acknowledge my suspicions, but I had to see.

Slowly, I approached the door. As I passed other rooms along the way, I shuddered when my senses picked up creepy, vampiric sounds, smells and sensations. A scream rang out, causing me to jump. Thankfully, it dissolved into a series of pleasurable moans.

My senses were on fire. I fought back the intrigue that surfaced within me. I couldn't allow someone else's blood- and sex-fest to distract me.

I stared at Kale's door, knowing he wasn't in there but certain that something was.

I moved fast, before I could chicken out. Trying the handle, I found it unlocked. I gave the door a shove and watched it swing open while I remained in the hallway. The strange mix of Kale's high-strung energy and death greeted me with a slap in the face.

The bedside lamp was on, illuminating two bodies sprawled on the bed, a blonde and a brunette. Each was clad in next to nothing, and both had bloodied throats.

They hadn't been dead long.

My stomach dropped, and I felt sick. Reality crushed the breath from me. Kale had been here recently. And, he was killing again.

Chapter Three

"Don't look for Kale." I barely let Jez get a word out. My hand shook as I gripped my cell phone tightly. "If you see him, you might want to be on your guard."

"What's going on?"

I leaned heavily against the door-frame of Kale's room, staring at the corner of the bloodstained sheets. I couldn't bring myself to look at the faces of Kale's victims again.

"I'm not sure. All I know is that I'm staring at two dead women in his bed right now. He isn't here."

Jez' voice held a note of fear. "Kale's been killing? Oh ... that's not good."

"That's putting it lightly."

"I'll stay alert, but it'll be sunrise in a few hours. I imagine wherever he is, he'll be heading home soon."

I swallowed hard and glanced up and down the empty hallway. "Unless he comes back here."

"Maybe you should leave, Lex. You know how he gets around you. If he's all fucked up, he'll be unpredictable and dangerous."

"Call me if you see him. Otherwise, I'll talk to you tomorrow."

I turned quickly when I felt Arys approach. He wore a frown and hummed with an anxious energy. His attention was immediately drawn to Kale's room, and I cringed.

"You must be so impressed." He grinned. "Isn't this exactly the kind of thing you told me I couldn't do here?"

"Laugh it up." I gave him my best fake, bitter laugh.

Arys surveyed the interior of the room with a nonchalance that only increased my discomfort. "So Kale's acting like a vampire again. It's about time. But, you should tell him not to leave his dead whores lying around like this. It's bad for business."

"I know how much you must love this, but please, let me deal with it before you rub it in my face. I get it, ok? I made a huge mistake thinking I could change anything around here. Ha fucking ha!"

"Lighten up, Alexa. Don't be so uptight about this place. It is what it is." His voice dropped, and he pulled me close. "Look, I want you to take off right away. Go home. Shaz, too. I'll meet you there in an hour or so."

The sudden change in his tone and mood scared me. "Why? Where are you going to be?"

"I will explain everything when I get to your place. Just go. And, please don't decide to be stubborn right now." The worry in his eyes was the only thing that kept me from protesting.

"Alright. I'll head home right away. But, you'd better have a damn good reason for pulling the stubborn card."

"I do." Emotion filled his tender kiss. With a gentle touch, he stroked a hand down the side of my face, and I knew from that gesture more than any other that something awful was happening.

I watched him retreat back down the hall and through the doorway into the front of the club. I hated having to wait for answers. But, I trusted Arys so I'd do my best to be patient. In the meantime, I would head on home.

I was contemplating what to do about Kale's leftovers when the rear entry at the far end of the hall opened and in strode the vampire himself. I turned to face him with a glare, hoping it didn't waver when a wave of his dark energy washed over me. Worse than touching a live-wire, the jolt that went through me felt like I'd just been hit by lightning.

As Kale drew closer I could see that his eyes were solid black. His pupils were so enlarged it was impossible to see that his eyes were really two different colors from heterochromia iridium. He was soaring high alright; no doubt about that. The rush of the kill had many effects. I wasn't eager to see it on a vampire who had kept himself on a short leash until now.

I was relieved when Kale stopped several feet away. I had a feeling he did it more for his benefit than mine. I tried to shield against the pull I sensed from him, but my nature yearned to respond to it. I wanted to taste it, to feel it glide over me like a metaphysical second skin. Kale and I shared the same weakness: each other. My power always wanted him.

"Does 'What in the fuck?' cover it?" I stared into his dark, glassy eyes, hoping to see some semblance of sanity in them. "I can't believe you did this."

"You can't?" Kale tilted his head to the side and looked me up and down. "I'm not an amateur. I was going to get rid of the mess."

Dressed all in black with his leather duster cloaking him, Kale looked as good as he always did, but I was more lured by the flow of power surrounding him. I knew how good it would feel.

"When did you start killing again?" I focused on my irritation, ignoring the honey sweet, coercive vibe that called my power to him.

"Does it matter?" Crossing his arms, he leaned back, against the wall opposite me. The weight of his gaze unnerved me.

"There's no point in talking to you right now, is there? I have to get going anyway. I'm going home."

"Already? But, I just got here." His smile was more than a little evil. The last time he'd looked at me like that, the bastard had bit me.

I regarded him warily. "I've tried calling your phone for hours. Now I see why you were ignoring me. What you do is your business, Kale. I can't stop you. But, this stuff shouldn't be happening in here. You're fucking looped, and you know it. We should talk when you come down off this high. Not now."

"I can tell you right now those two dead hookers are likely among the tamest things you'd find in here tonight if you could see behind every closed door."

I wasn't in the mood to argue. "Hey, it's your club. You own it, and you can do whatever the hell you want here. I'm sure you want to deal with this before sunrise so I'll just leave you to it."

"What's the rush?" Kale stepped away from the wall, blocking my way past him. "You know I won't hurt you."

"I know you want to. Have you forgotten that I've heard this before?"

He reached a hand out towards me as he pulled on my nervous energy. "I won't hurt you. Not unless you beg me to."

The memory his words conjured up brought a flaming hot

blush to my cheeks. Not so long ago, the intoxicating allure of power had led me and Kale into an unplanned intimate encounter. He'd taken my blood, and I'd all but begged him to bang me on the desk in my office. It hadn't happened, thanks to Jez' interruption, but it had come damn close.

He chuckled and took a step that brought him into my personal space. "You're adorable when you blush."

I refused to let him intimidate me. The heady wave of energy that surrounded him like an intoxicating perfume teased my senses. I couldn't shake the feeling that he was doing it on purpose, trying to force me to react to him. That wasn't going to happen. To react would be dangerous, and he knew it as well as I did.

I was tongue-tied as I tried to muster a response. "I got nothin'."

He was quiet for a minute, regarding me with that dark gaze. His power called to me, reminding me of why Kale and I were rarely alone together anymore. It was dangerous. Forbidden fruit always was so much sweeter. I hated how I reacted to him. Combining our power resembled the worst chemistry experiment possible; our uninhibited impulses exploded as my sensuality made me weak.

Nope. Not happening. If I gave in to the luscious way our power felt, even for a moment, I'd find myself begging Kale to bleed me … and Lord knows what else.

"You don't trust me, Alexa?"

Might as well be honest. "I guess that depends what you mean exactly. You're a cold-blooded killer that's had himself on a tight leash for many years. You're about as unpredictable as they come."

"Yeah there's that. But, you think I might try to kill you, don't you?" He took that extra step. My skin grew hot at his proximity, and I drew in a deep breath. Stepping away would only provoke him.

"Can you really blame me for that?"

"Yes. I can." Kale ran a hand through his hair. "Are you going to hold that one time against me forever? It was once. Yeah, you're mortal. You smell and taste so damn good. But honestly, I'd rather make love to you than kill you."

Oh hell. My lungs deflated, and I struggled for air. Stunned didn't begin to cover it. "Oh don't go there, Kale. I don't even know what to say to that." I'd almost prefer it if he wanted to kill me, at least

I'd know how to react.

"Stop with the awkward tension. We should be beyond this." In a bold gesture, Kale danced a hand down my body, careful to never actually touch me.

I could feel the waves of energy as they pulsed under his manipulation. A shiver ran down my spine, and I had to resist the urge to scratch an itch that wasn't physical. He wasn't wrong; I was the one that made things weird with us. I was still carrying around some personal shame for offering myself to him during a moment of extreme weakness.

"How can I not feel awkward? You're practically fucking me with your mind."

His chuckle didn't put me at ease. "It wouldn't be the first time."

"You're going to regret saying that after you come down from this little high you're on. It can't last forever you know."

"We'll see about that."

"You're impossible."

I had to admit, Kale was enchanting when influenced by the power of the kill. It brought out the true nature in every vampire, the killer that always dwelled within each of them. It was delightfully powerful and seductive, and because of that, it was also deadly.

I felt immediately when the atmosphere began to pulse. He was influencing it, trying to coerce a response from me. His expression was carefully neutral, but his eyes were watchful and mischievous.

"I never missed the rush of the kill much until recently. Besides, you got me thinking about what I was starving myself of." Kale's voice dropped in tone. He continued to trail his fingers through the energy surrounding me. It gave me chills.

"Yay me." I pushed back against him, creating resistance, like two opposing magnets. "Can't say I'm proud to be credited for your return to murder and mayhem."

Kale held the resistance between us until I visibly shook from the effort it took to push against him. I almost fell forward when he dropped it suddenly. Taking advantage of my drop in control, he drew on my aura. Pulling my energy to him, he was able to manipulate what I was feeling.

I knew what he was doing. A careful push and pull that created a growing, heady wave that surrounded us. It called to the core of my being, enticing my hunger for his power. Kale knew damn well how strong my desire to consume him could become. He was playing off that, trying to stoke the flames of my hunger in an attempt to lose us both in the fire. Bad vampire.

"It's more than that though." His whispered words were laced with longing. "You made me feel alive again after decades of self-imposed confinement. You set me free."

"Don't forget who you are, Kale. I like that person." The air seemed to grow thick, making it hard to breathe. He was seriously testing my control. All but offering himself to me, Kale was making it difficult to convince myself that I didn't want his blood and everything he offered with it.

He still wasn't touching me, but he might as well have been. As much as I'd mastered control over my power in recent months, it didn't take much to test that. Kale was doing a fine job of it.

"When was the last time you had a really satisfying hunt? Tell me, Alexa. How long has it been since you held down a struggling victim, feeding off the fear, spilling the blood? You know how the power grips you, how it holds you. You know how good it feels when that first drop of blood spills, and there is no turning back." Kale clenched a hand into a tight fist, opening it suddenly to reveal a spiraling silver psi ball that spun several times before dissipating. "It's better than an orgasm."

He was right. What I felt when I killed was very sexual but also very deep and dark, a power that I possessed but never truly commanded. Lost in that power, we became little more than conduits for something bigger, something that wouldn't be denied.

"It certainly is." I dropped my gaze to the floor in a vain attempt to escape his effect. My hunger stirred for the thrill he spoke of, and I groaned inwardly.

"We would be beautiful together, you and I." Kale slipped a finger beneath my chin and lifted my gaze to his. His touch was warm.

I pulled away and in one smooth motion grabbed hold of the pulsating mass of power he had stirred to life. I drew it close, binding it so that it reacted to my manipulations. Absorbing Kale's power into me along with my own and bending it to my will was something I'd learned not so long ago. It worked quite nicely with the right focus.

Kale looked pleased with himself. "So, you do want to play."

"You, my friend, are asking for trouble." I was caught in the intoxicating lure of dizzying energy.

"You know you want to. How long do you think we can keep pretending there isn't something between us?"

"You play dirty, Kale." I shook a finger at him, refusing to answer.

Kale's eyes narrowed when I automatically reached for my keys. "You're going to bail out of here like a bat out of hell now, aren't you?"

"You're dangerous when you're like this. I'm not sure I like it."

"You know that you do." He smirked, and I flipped him off.

"What it means is that I'm going home to pour a glass of wine and slip into a hot bath. We'll talk when being face to face doesn't result in a power play."

"Leaving me with thoughts of killing and you naked in the bath. You're evil, Alexa."

"What can I say? I do my best." I couldn't get out of there fast enough. I didn't trust the darkness in his eyes. Maybe it was my imagination, but it seemed to be growing.

"So um, killing and me in the bath, try not to think about those things at the same time. Ok?" It wasn't easy to slip by him and down the hall without turning my back on him. I must have been incredibly obvious.

He didn't laugh like I'd hoped. His serious gaze followed me. I was painfully relieved when he didn't move. I still had the urge to run. Dammit.

I waved when I was a safe distance away. "Goodnight, Kale. Try not to be the monster beneath anybody's bed for the rest of the night, hmm?"

His jaw clenched, and he forced a smile. "I'll see what I can do."

಄಄಄಄

An old Joan Jett song played quietly on the radio. It was approaching three in the morning, and I was starting to burn out. I could feel the approach of dawn just a few hours away. Once I was on the highway headed for home, the effects of Kale's power games and Arys' fierce insistence began to ebb.

I really was looking forward to that bath.

Shaz had insisted on staying behind a bit longer when I left. We didn't carpool due to our unpredictable schedules.

I was waiting expectantly for him to call so that I knew he was safe.

My phone rang as expected, but it wasn't Shaz calling. It was my best friend Kylarai, a divorce lawyer that kept more frequent daytime hours than I did. She usually didn't call at this time of night.

I hit the hands-free button and was about to say 'hello' when the sound of sobbing filled my car. "Kylarai?"

"Fucking son of a bitch! You were right, Alexa. Julian is nothing but a piece of shit." Her words broke as she spoke through tears. A few more sob-filled curses followed, but I got the gist of it.

"What happened, sweetie? Are you ok?"

She sniffed and took a long, shuddery breath. "I'm not sure. I just caught him with another woman in his apartment. I'm just heading home now. I think I broke my hand punching the bastard out."

"Shit. I'll meet you at your place. Just try to calm down. I'm sorry, Ky."

It was bittersweet news. Julian was a jerk; Kylarai could do better than him. But, the last thing I wanted was to see my dear friend hurt. I shook my head, knowing how protective Shaz was of Ky. Not to mention Kale, Kylarai's ex; he'd sworn to make Julian sorry if he ever hurt Ky.

Stony Plain lay just a few minutes down the highway from the city. It didn't take long to reach the small town we called home. I went straight to Kylarai's, bracing myself. I would be there for her no matter what, regardless of whether I'd approved of her relationship or not.

She was sitting outside on the front step when I got there. Cradling one arm tightly to her body, she sat beneath the glow of the porch light with her head in her good hand. She looked up when I came up the walk. Her face was tear-stained, and her grey eyes were red-rimmed. My heart broke for her.

"I feel like such an idiot. There must have been so many signs. How could I fall for that shit? I'm a fucking divorce lawyer for God's sake. I know all about the cheating type. Fuck!" A fresh wash of tears streamed down her face, and I felt guilty.

I'd known Julian was cheating on her. Shaz and I had caught him with another woman while out one night. I gave Julian the chance to tell her first. He didn't. I'd asked him about it recently, and he'd had little to say. I should have told her, but she knew I hated him. I didn't want to be the one to split them up. It wasn't my place.

"Aw, Ky. I know there's nothing I can say. This is one of the worst kinds of hurt. I wish you didn't have to go through it."

"You all hated him so much, even Shaz. And, I didn't have a clue. Maybe I'm just desperate and willing to settle." She winced in pain.

"You are not desperate. Don't talk like that. He's the bad guy here. Not you."

I reached gently to take her arm, and she surrendered it to me. Her hand was bloody and bruised black. It looked incredibly swollen. I assumed several small bones were broken.

"I should get Arys to heal this, if that's ok with you." I reached for my phone and hit the speed dial for Arys. "That's going to start healing soon. The bones could set wrong."

We had a connection in the city for stuff like this. Werewolves just can't go to human doctors. Our rate of healing and our often extensive injuries would be enough to draw the wrong kind of attention.

"Can't you do it?" Her voice was so soft it was almost inaudible.

I glanced at the blood staining her knuckles. It smelled strong. Pure werewolf. "I wish I could, Ky. I think Arys is the safer bet on this one." With remnants of Kale's influence clinging to the inside of my head like cobwebs, I didn't want to take any chances. Healing wasn't quite my forte, either. It was one area where I lacked confidence.

I kept the call to Arys short and to the point. He was just as clipped when promising to be there soon before hanging up without another word. Strange.

The front door opened, and Ky's roommate, Zoey, stood there looking down at us where we sat on the step. "I thought I heard you out here. What's going on?"

Zoey and I shared a knowing look. She hadn't been Julian's biggest fan either. Kylarai recited the events of her night to Zoey and me. Though she continued to sniff and swear, the tears were slowing.

"Do you want me to separate that boy's balls from his body?" Zoey offered hopefully. "I swear, I wouldn't mind."

Kylarai attempted a halfhearted smile and shook her head. "No. If anyone gets to do that, it's going to be me."

"How's his face?" I asked, wishing I could see it for myself.

"I'm pretty sure I broke his nose. Still, it's not enough."

I shook my head thoughtfully. No, it wasn't enough. To this day I regretted that I'd never been able to make Raoul, the first man to break my heart, suffer the way I had for what he'd done. And now, he was dead.

The three of us sat huddled together with Kylarai in the middle. She leaned into me, and I stroked a hand through her chestnut-brown locks. Her scent was flowery with an underlying hint of wolf. She smelled like home.

It didn't take long for Arys to arrive. I was mildly surprised to see that Shaz was with him. Ky groaned when she saw Shaz. I couldn't say I blamed her. The only reason Shaz hadn't run Julian out of town by now was because Ky had asked him not to.

I gave Shaz a look, warning him not to say anything now that could wait until later. Other than the quiet, knowing fury burning in his jade eyes, he was calm. I moved so that Arys could take my spot on the step. He and Kylarai didn't bother to exchange pleasantries. It wasn't required, and they had a somewhat strained acquaintanceship as it was.

"It'll be easier if I can touch you." Arys was gentle as he held Kylarai's damaged hand.

Zoey sat stiffly, her discomfort with Arys plain, but she watched him with curiosity. Ky wiped at the remains of her tears with her free hand. I could feel the tension in Shaz' stiff posture. I followed his gaze to Kylarai. He wasn't happy. I loved him for caring as much as he did.

"Shaz, please. Don't do anything to Julian." Kylarai pleaded.

"He's not worth it."

I felt it when Arys pushed healing energy into Ky. She gasped but remained still. Arys' fingers lightly brushed the surface of her bruised skin. She would be pain-free within minutes. Arys was a master at healing.

"You know what, Ky?" Shaz paced on the neatly cut lawn. "I won't do anything to him yet, though God only knows why you care. Guys like him deserve a lot more than an ass-kicking. He's definitely getting at least that much."

"I just don't want to think about it now. I need to get some sleep." Her eyes widened, and she looked at Arys. "What in the hell?"

Arys' power had a sensual quality. I hid a smile, knowing she was reacting to him against her will. Kylarai didn't like the power that Arys and I had. It made her uneasy, but right now, it was for her own good.

"Take it easy for a few hours. You'll be fine." Arys released Kylarai's hand, and she stared at it in wonder.

"Thank you, Arys."

He rose and came to me. I noted how he "casually" scanned the street, and it gave me a shock. What did he think was out there?

"We need to go. I don't think anyone followed you, but I don't want to chance leading the wrong person to Ky's house. She has nothing to do with this. Better to keep it that way."

I stared at him in silence, unsure how to respond. He was freaking me out. The darkness suddenly seemed threatening, and I wanted to go home.

Zoey's slight rasp broke the quiet. "Are you guys in some kind of trouble?"

"Nothing that can't be dealt with." Arys sounded confident.

Kylarai met my eyes, and I knew what she was thinking. Just as I had kept my mouth shut about being right about Julian, she did the same. She didn't trust Arys and knew our bond made me a target for power seekers. I couldn't hold it against her, but I hoped like hell she wouldn't get a reason to feel justified in that distrust.

"Call me tomorrow, Ky. Get some rest and try to feel better." I paused to give her a hug before waving to Zoey as Arys ushered me down the driveway.

I paused when we reached my car, but he wouldn't give me a

chance to speak. "Get in your car. Drive home. We'll follow you."

I looked past him to Shaz' Chevy parked on the street. Shaz lingered nearby, waiting to leave. Swallowing hard, I opened my car door and dropped into the driver's seat. I'd find out everything in a matter of minutes. The five-minute drive home would be just enough time to work myself into a nice state of panic.

Chapter Four

My hands shook despite the coffee cup I clutched. I took a deep breath, trying to stay rational. I couldn't believe what I was hearing. I felt like I'd stumbled into someone else's life. Surely, this couldn't be mine.

"This is more than I think I can handle tonight. How long have you known about this?" I stared into the mug of creamy coffee, wishing I could find comfort in it like I used to.

Arys sat across from me, his posture stiff despite his attempt at casual. He wasn't fooling me. "A few weeks. I didn't want to say anything to you two until I knew for sure. I should have stayed in Vegas long enough to tie up loose ends."

"You said that you'd taken care of everything there. Didn't you leave someone in charge?" I was grasping at straws, and I knew it.

"He's dead." Arys ran a hand through his hair and dropped his gaze to the floor. "By getting involved in Harley's Vegas business, I fucked with his involvement in a blood ring. I was too caught up in everything surrounding his death and the conflict here. I knew about this. I just didn't think these guys would take it this far."

Shaz paced around the room, clenching his jaw. He hadn't said much since we got to my place. "So what it really boils down to is that the power you're packing can't protect you from everything. You put Alexa in danger."

"Harley's death put Alexa in danger. And you too, pup." Arys' gaze followed Shaz' motions. "Do you understand what I'm really telling you here? Yes, I was the one who went to Vegas and messed with his business, but you two took him out. And, that left a hole in this blood ring. These guys lost a partner and a supplier, not to mention the most powerful vampire in Vegas. They'll be looking for payback."

I tensed when I felt Shaz' wolf rise to the surface. This was a serious situation. We were all in deep shit. Losing it on each other wasn't going to solve anything though.

"A supplier? How bad is it?" Shaz stopped mere feet from Arys and stared down at the vampire.

"It's bad." Arys met Shaz' eyes evenly. "These guys deal in serious fetish kills. Children, virgins, pregnant women … you name it, they have it. It ain't pretty."

My stomach turned as revolting images flooded my thoughts. "God, that's so friggin' disgusting."

"So now what?" Shaz glanced from Arys to me, worry heavy in his gaze. "What exactly do they want?"

I had to admit, some naive part of me had never entertained the idea of the kinds of fetish kills Arys had described. I didn't want it to exist. I knew I lived in a world of blood and death. But this? This was beyond what I knew. It was vile.

Arys was surprisingly calm. "Retribution, I guess."

"What does that mean?" I forced the question out, afraid to hear the answer.

"They took my guy apart piece by piece before they killed him. They spent all night doing it. This is a dead serious business, one I've managed to stay the hell away from. Until now." The troubled shadows in Arys' midnight blue eyes were chilling. "They'll want Harley's killers to take his place in their circle. Or, they might just want an excuse to stir up shit in our city. It's hard to say really."

"Piece by piece?" I sputtered around a sip of coffee.

"With Harley missing and his Vegas businesses shut down, I can imagine it had a big impact on them. It's anyone's guess what they'll do."

Shaz resumed his slow pacing. I wanted to tell him to sit down already because it was driving me crazy, but it seemed to be keeping him from jumping all over Arys. He was angry though. I could feel it rolling off him.

"So all this power you and Alexa have, enough that she killed Harley … none of this means anything to them? It doesn't protect you or make you a threat to these people?" Shaz' tone was accusing, and his clenched fists shook. "If not, then what the fuck is it good for? It has just put all of us in danger."

Arys made a frustrated noise that sounded a little too close to a growl for my liking. "Look, wolf," he snapped. "Nobody has power like what I share with Alexa, but power comes in many forms. There are others that possess enough to make them a serious force to be reckoned with, and there are a lot of them. The vampires that benefit from a blood ring like this are nothing like the bottom feeders you see at The Wicked Kiss. This is a whole different kind of vampire, my friend, and they are not fucking around."

"Oh yeah?" Shaz snarled with a viciousness that had me up off my chair. "Where do you fit in, Arys? What kind of vampire are you?"

"Ok guys, that's enough." I didn't give Arys a chance to snap back at Shaz. Arys had done some horrific things to his victims in the past. That wasn't the point right now. "Let's try to keep our heads here. This is obviously stressful enough without taking shots at each other."

They both continued to glare darkly at one another though they remained silent. Shaz sat down in the chair I'd just vacated, a major relief. He was quiet when he spoke next.

"So what do we do then? Wait around for these bastards to show their faces?"

"I wish I could tell you." Arys didn't look at him when he replied. "I don't know what they intend to do. All I know is that if they want something, they'll come for it."

I had to resist the urge to take up pacing where Shaz left off. I felt restless and trapped. "So, this is like the vampire mob or something? I don't want any part of it."

Arys actually chuckled at that, and I frowned. "Oh, Alexa. Sometimes I forget how new to this world you still are. These creatures are killers and nothing less. They want the pain and the agony of their victim more than they want the actual death. Dragging out every moment until that final breath, for days even, that's what they enjoy. They are not vampires consuming blood to survive. They are true killers that make death an art form."

"Ok," I murmured more to myself than to either of them. "No reassurance there."

"What is it that makes you so different?" Shaz' question rang with challenge. "You're a killer, Arys."

I tensed, fearing what Arys might say to that. He was a killer, there was no disputing that. But, I'd killed too without reason and would have done so again if Kale hadn't stopped me. Could Shaz judge Arys as a killer without including me in that?

Arys rose and headed for the short flight of stairs that led up to the main level from the sunken living room. He paused at the bottom and looked thoughtfully at Shaz. "Even I know that you're not truly that narrow-minded, pup. You were right there by Alexa's side when she killed Harley. You tore his throat out, did you not? Like it or not, we're in this together. Better get used to it."

I followed Arys to the front door, exhaustion setting in. Sunrise couldn't come fast enough. All I wanted to do was drop into bed. So much for that bath I'd planned.

"This will all blow over. Right?" I could hear the uncertainty in my voice, and it made me cringe.

Arys drew me into his embrace, hugging me close. He deeply inhaled my scent, and I snuggled in closer.

"Of course," he whispered. "We'll deal with it. In the meantime, stay alert. Make sure you're not followed, and try not to be out alone too often until this is settled. Shaz, too."

His kiss was loving and tender. I melted when he slipped his tongue into my mouth. I would have had much more appreciation for it if we hadn't just been discussing fetish kills for vampires.

The pre-dawn sky was beginning to show signs of the coming sunrise. Reluctantly, Arys pulled away and opened the door. I watched him disappear into what remained of the night. I was coming to realize that there was no such thing as a normal life. Not for me. At least, not anymore.

Chapter Five

I didn't expect to see Kale's car in the parking lot when I got to the office. Good. I had a few things to say to him after I was through speaking with Veryl. It had been a while since the bossman had wanted to see me. Our relationship was strained. I had little to say to him these days.

I'm not sure what made me do it, but I cloaked my presence before exiting the car. Neither of them would be able to detect me. Another advantage of being other than human was how easy it was to slip inside unheard. The front door made the slightest squeak, causing me to swear beneath my breath.

Pausing in the entryway, I listened to the sounds of the office. My sensitive ears picked up the low tones of two male voices. The sound of the clock ticking in the kitchen was especially loud as I concentrated. Whatever Veryl and Kale were discussing, it was heated.

I really hadn't intended to eavesdrop when I snuck inside. I was simply curious, and lately, I'd been incredibly suspicious. I was in the dark on too many of the things going on around here. That had to stop.

I slowly made my way down the hall. Veryl's door was at the very end. It was closed. Their voices carried, and I was surprised to hear the absolute venom in Kale's tone. It was a far cry from his usual calm, cool and collected. Interesting.

"She's never going to do it, you know. You need to tell her what's really going on around here. And when you do, shit is going to hit the fan."

There was silence, and I held my breath, waiting for Veryl's response. I had a sick feeling in my stomach that the "her" in their conversation was me. We worked with a few other women. It could be any of them, right? Yeah, not likely.

"It's not that simple. You should know that. I didn't expect her to have as much power as she does. It makes her better for this than I could have imagined. They want her on the big jobs now, but how do I say that to her without getting my head torn off?" Veryl sounded desperate.

"I know that she doesn't take lightly to deception. Can you blame her? Either lay it on the line and let her choose or don't, but I'm not keeping anything from her anymore." Kale's tone was low and deadly.

My pulse began to race. I didn't like what I was hearing. I swallowed hard. Should I keep listening or show myself? I didn't think I needed to hear anymore. I dropped my hold on the power enforcing my shields and waited.

Instant silence. As I'd expected. A full minute passed before the door opened. Veryl stood in its frame, a frown marring his sharp features. "Alexa. Funny. I didn't sense your arrival."

"Good. You weren't supposed to." My wolf stared out at him through my eyes. He appeared unnerved.

"We were just discussing something. Why don't you come in and join us?"

I stepped into the room and took the chair next to Kale. I gave him a pointed look which he ignored. Despite his poker face, I could see the truth in his mismatched eyes: they had definitely been talking about me.

Veryl took his place behind the desk. He turned off his computer monitor before turning his attention to me. "I suppose we should talk. How much did you hear?"

"Enough to know that I was right to be suspicious. Just cut the crap and tell it like it is. Please, don't screw with me anymore."

I'd worked with Veryl for years. He was a former paranormal investigator turned vampire. He had people like Kale, Jez and me work for him, along with a few others. We were pretty much hired guns. We killed other supernaturals, and for the most part, we weren't given a lot of reason for it. I'd always assumed there was a reason to wipe them out, the main one being that some of them risked drawing unnecessary attention to the rest of us. I had known for a while that there were things going on behind the scenes that Veryl kept from us. I had a feeling I was about to discover one of them.

"I'm going to level with you, Alexa." Veryl leaned forward on his desk to pin me with his gaze. "You're a smart lady. You know by now that things aren't exactly what they seem here. I am only one man in a very large and powerful organization. Somewhat of a paranormal CIA, if you will."

That verified some of my suspicions. I'd suspected Veryl's orders came from somewhere else. However, having it confirmed did nothing to ease the sick feeling growing in the pit of my stomach.

"How much of it is human government?"

"The question really is, how much of the government is human? Anyway, that's an entirely different topic."

That was reassuring. "I knew there was more going on than you'd ever say. But go ahead, tell me what it really has to do with me. And, why wait until now to tell me about it?"

Kale remained too quiet for my liking. I wanted to kick him but resisted the urge. I didn't dare take my eyes from Veryl. Whether I could make him squirm or not, I wanted him to feel the weight of my gaze.

"Isn't it obvious? We recruit those with serious power. You have it. You always have. But naturally, we started you out small. Simple vampire kills, something to help hone your skills while reducing the number of vermin on the streets. But now, you're big time."

He let that last sentence hang between us, allowing its true meaning to sink in. Fury crashed over me like a wave on the beach. I was suddenly soaked in it. Deep breaths did little to help.

"And, someone wants to take advantage of that. Right?"

I glared daggers into him. Things had been strained between us since I'd found out that Veryl had taken advantage of a personal situation that had hurt me deeply. He'd kept Raoul's secret from me, hiding the truth about the attack that turned me. The reason why was painfully clear: to gain access to my power.

"Nobody has taken advantage of you, Alexa. Lord knows Kale would never have allowed that." Veryl flashed Kale a dark look. "I assume you heard enough to know he was arguing on your behalf. He believes you will refuse the position you're being offered, and I don't disagree with him."

I glanced between the two of them. Something unsettling lurked in Kale's brown and blue eyes. "And, this would be?"

"Not the pathetic newborn vamps you've dealt with before. There are real powerhouses out there. Like you. Some of them know things they shouldn't. Some of them are spies. And, others are traitors." Veryl gave a dismissive wave, as if the reason didn't really matter. "And, a great many of them are human."

I let that sink in for a moment. This week was really starting to look bad in terms of news and revelations that I'd much rather live without.

Kale shifted uneasily in his chair. "I didn't think that hunting humans was something you would agree to."

As I received more information, I had more questions. "Why are the people on your hit lists chosen? Really. Because I'd been under the impression there was a damn good reason. And now, I'm starting to reconsider that."

"Does it matter?" Veryl asked with a tone that one might use when dealing with a stubborn child. "I'm not at liberty to tell you more than required. In fact, I'm not always given that kind of information, for obvious reasons. In some cases, the less people know, the safer they are."

"I don't like it."

"You don't have to like it, Alexa. You just have to do it. Liking it is just a bonus."

He fixed me with a steely glare that would have intimidated me once. Now, it had me smirking like a rebellious teenager. In recent months Veryl had avoided me. At least, he wouldn't stay in a room with me a moment longer than he had to. He no longer tried to test my power by invasively brushing up against me metaphysically. Instead, he shielded hard when around me so he wouldn't feel my power at all. I still hadn't decided if I was relieved or insulted by that.

"Just be honest with me for once. Why is getting any information out of you like banging my head against a brick wall?" Vampires horde information like its toilet paper in a natural disaster. It's ridiculous.

Veryl fixed me with a look that he meant to be scary. "There are people who don't want to waste your abilities on bullshit kills.

What you have is valuable, and it makes you valuable. Do you understand?"

This was interesting. "I do. Please, go on. I'd like to hear more about these mystery people."

"There's nothing more to know. Information is given on a need to know basis." He shrugged as if there was nothing more to it.

"Well, I need to know why I've gone from killing idiot vampires to humans with power. I smell a rat. Can a human really have enough power to make the big, bad monsters afraid?"

"Yes." Kale spoke up, drawing my attention to him. "You were one once. There are more out there, Alexa, and some of them won't think twice about using that power against us."

I shook my head and frowned in confusion. "Food and foe? Seriously?"

"It's not quite that simple, Alexa." Veryl's expression was bored, as if he couldn't bear to bother with me. "If you really want to push the subject, there are other people you can talk to. Although, I wouldn't recommend it. Not if you want to avoid having them take more interest in you than they have already."

The way he said it chilled me. It set off warning bells in my head, and I wondered what I was really involved in. And more importantly, could I get out if I wanted to? This was something I needed to know more about. Not from Veryl though, clearly.

"Alright. So what's the bottom line here? What is it you want me to do?"

Veryl eyed me like he couldn't tell if I was fucking with him or not. "There's a woman. A traitor. She was one of ours, and now she's working to expose us. All of us."

"So? What are her reasons? Did anybody bother to find that out before issuing a kill order?" I was being a pain in the ass, I knew, but it was impossible to resist.

"She's skilled in black magic, Alexa!" Veryl suddenly oozed menace. "She can drop a vampire with little more than the right words. Do you really want someone walking around with the ability to do that? Someone who believes we should all be hunted down one by one?"

"I won't kill innocents, Veryl. That's my only stipulation. I'm serious."

"I can guarantee you that you've never killed an innocent. No such thing." He sounded pretty much like every vampire I knew. It didn't come as a surprise to hear him speak that way. "Kale will be with you. I wouldn't send you alone, human target or otherwise."

Kale killing humans? Oh, that was terrific. It also explained a lot.

"Fine." I stood up and looked down at Veryl where he sat behind the desk. "I'll do it. But now you've made me suspicious. I don't like that. You'd better not be feeding me another line of bullshit. You haven't quite always had my best interests in mind over the years."

"You see it that way because you refuse to realize that I have withheld some things from you for a reason. For your own good. You're bull-headed, Alexa. That's one of the things I like about you. It keeps you hard enough to do your job, but it will get you into trouble if you aren't careful."

I gaped at him, momentarily flustered. "My own good? How was keeping Raoul's secret for my own good? Seems to me that it was so that you'd have some control over me. Kiss those days goodbye."

Veryl waved a dismissive hand at me. "Whatever. You should go. Call me when it's done."

That was it. He turned his attention to his computer and went about his business as if I wasn't even there. Normally, that would have been enough to push me past the boiling point. My temper was short enough with Veryl that I considered laying into him, again. He was purposely trying to avoid further discussion about hiding Raoul's true role in slaughtering my parents and infecting me. I couldn't blame Veryl; that fight was over, and I'd had a lot of time to say my piece. However, that wasn't what kept my mouth shut right then. No, it was the slightest trickle of apprehension rolling off him.

Spinning on my heel, I left his office with a self-satisfied smile and Kale hot on my heels. Veryl wasn't comfortable with me anymore, and I knew why. My power had grown in the last year, along with my connections. I wouldn't make the mistake of thinking higher of myself than was accurate. I knew I wasn't the big bad that some were. Still, something about me scared Veryl, and that was reassuring. Of course, something about him scared me, too. I didn't trust him, and I didn't know who his, our, employers really were. Something told me I didn't want to know.

I stormed out of the building with one goal in mind: to get out of the place before I blew it off its foundation. Kale didn't let me get more than a few steps ahead of him. I slammed the door open and strode outside, aching to throw a few punches.

"Alexa, wait. I know you're pissed, and you probably have a lot to-,"

I turned on him with a speed and precision that was alarming. Kale might have been taller than me, but my four-inch heeled boots gave me enough leverage to get into his face.

"How many of them were innocent?" I hadn't meant for it to be the first thing out of my mouth. "How many people did I kill with you at my side that didn't really deserve it?"

"Alexa, I-,"

"It's clearly not about good and evil or what someone is. Somebody else is deciding who lives and dies. How could you sit by and let me get drawn into this, knowing how hard it is for me to deal with just being me? And, then you sit there in silence while I'm told that I'm a fucking pawn to some paranormal government! How can you be ok with being a part of all this?"

I clenched my fists so hard my nails cut into my palms. I felt the warmth of the blood trickling between my fingers. Kale's gaze flicked to the blood dripping on the gravel parking lot then back to me. He paused, waiting to be sure I was going to let him speak.

"First of all, I signed on to this for my own reasons. I assumed that you had yours. I have no problem killing anyone who uses their power to abuse others or threaten me. That includes humans." Kale didn't back off. Instead he glared down into my face. "You have no idea how many times I've gone head to head with Veryl because of you. Did I know that he saw you as a fascinating addition to his team? Yes. But, I also happen to know you can take care of yourself."

"Tell me then Kale, how can I do that when I don't even know who I'm working for? The boss I have is a scumbag that has pulled strings in my life since I was a teenager. I thought I was killing the bad guys, you know? The ones that exist only to prey on the helpless, to kill without thought. Now, I'm not so sure."

I had to put some distance between us. Emotion and adrenaline had me vibrating. Taking a few steps back, I pushed my hair out of my face and focused on taking deep breaths.

"You do kill the bad guys, Alexa. You just also happen to work for them."

Those words sunk deep into me, and I swallowed hard. I stared at the empty street, wishing a car would go by to break up the quiet. "The dead women at The Wicked Kiss? Veryl's orders?"

I realized I was hoping he would say something to take the blame from himself, even if it was a lie. Kale wouldn't disrespect me with an outright lie though; that was just wishful thinking.

"No. That was all me."

I knew it but I had to ask. He was a vampire. I would be wasting my time to try to pick apart why Kale did what he did. His past was so horrific that he'd stopped killing and started feeding from willing victims at The Kiss.

I'd known since meeting Kale that this day would come. If it were anyone else, I could have accepted it. But, killing made him unpredictable and dangerous. Sure, he was standing here now, the same normal Kale I'd always known. Yet, the feisty, high-strung killer he'd revealed the other night was always there inside. Only now, I was painfully aware of it.

"How long?"

"A while now."

"... Give me the address. I'll meet you there." After the incident at The Wicked Kiss, I wasn't getting into the closed confines of a car with him.

He studied me with that eerie, dual-colored gaze. I knew he wanted to say something about killing those prostitutes, but I was glad when he didn't bother.

"Look, I don't know all the details, ok? Stick around long enough to find out for yourself how dangerous this woman is. If you're not cool with it, you can take off and I'll handle it. We'll go tomorrow night."

He was trying to smooth things over. As much as I wanted to smack Kale, Veryl was my real problem.

"Fine. I'll be there."

Chapter Six

"Seriously. What do you want for your birthday? There's got to be something."

Sliding a hand through Shaz' soft platinum hair, I smiled and shook my head. "No, there's nothing. I don't want anything. I don't even want to think about my birthday."

"What?" Shaz sat up straighter in the bed, propping himself against the headboard. "We're definitely celebrating your birthday. You're not getting out of it. I don't care what you say."

I groaned and buried my face in my pillow, making a dramatic show of feigned crying. Shaz gave my head a playful shove and laughed. Why did everyone always have to make a big deal out of birthdays? I always had fun celebrating the birthdays of my friends, but I hated being the center of attention on mine.

"I'm boycotting my birthday this year. It's just like any other day. No big deal."

"We're having a party. End of discussion." Shaz pressed a finger to my lips before I could protest. "We can have it at Lucy's Lounge. It's been a while since we've been there."

I could see that it meant more to him than it did to me. With a nod, I sighed and nipped lightly at his finger. "Fine. But no gifts!"

"You know me better than that. You'll get a gift whether you like it or not." Shaz rolled so that he was looking down at me from his raised position. "But, I'm pretty sure you'll like it."

I slipped my arms around his neck as he leaned in to kiss me. The soft sheets slid along our naked skin. Shaz pressed his body close to mine, and I drank in his scent, all male and all wolf. Heavenly.

I welcomed it when he slid his tongue between my lips. Slow and deep, Shaz kissed me with the kind of passion that sent a hot tingle to the tips of my toes. I enjoyed nothing more than waking up beside this man. Pent-up desire filled me, and I looked forward to releasing it with Shaz.

He pulled back and gazed down at me thoughtfully. "I had a dream about Raoul."

"Um ... ok. Not quite what I was expecting to hear." I'd had a dream about Raoul myself not so long ago. One that was extremely vivid. I hadn't mentioned it to anyone.

"He was here, in this house." Shaz went on, glancing around the bedroom as if he expected to see our former Alpha there with us. "He told me to protect you from yourself."

I frowned, confused and irritated by Raoul's message. That bastard never did give me enough credit.

"Is that it? That's all he said?"

"Yep. That's it." Shaz ran a warm hand along my side. "What do you think that means?"

"I think it means that Raoul still thinks he can control me from beyond the grave." I sat up and turned so that I faced Shaz directly. The sheets fell to my lap, exposing my breasts. "Or, it means that you really need to get more sleep."

"Geez, Lex. The guy is dead, and he still can't catch a break from you." Shaz' words said one thing but he reacted the way I wanted him to. Reaching for me, his voice lost that edge of seriousness. "I'd say it's time to let go of your grudge."

I got to my knees and pushed him back against the headboard. Tossing the sheets off, I straddled him with a smile. "And, I'd say it's time for some wake up sex."

Shaz chuckled and ran his hands down my body to grip my hips. "Someone doesn't want to talk about Raoul. Fine then. Whatever you want."

I had been ready for this since I'd got home several hours earlier. Rubbing myself against him, I was pleased to find Shaz already hard. Foreplay was nice, but our sense of urgency made it unnecessary. I just needed him inside me.

I kissed Shaz hungrily, preventing him from any further talk. With one hand I gripped the headboard to steady myself, while with the other I held his shaft firmly. I sucked his bottom lip into my mouth before pulling back so I could look into his eyes. After placing the head of his erection against my warm entrance, I impaled myself upon him in an achingly slow motion.

I watched his face intently, loving how his expression changed as I buried him completely within me. When he hit that sweet spot deep inside, I let out a sigh of contentment. I rose up until he was just barely inside me and plunged back down upon him again. Shaz' gaze dropped to our groins, and he watched as I rode him with slow and deliberate strokes.

He guided my movements by holding my hips, but I wouldn't give up total control to him. Empowered, I controlled our pleasure while he watched with a look of anguished delight on his gorgeous face. I ran my hands through his blond locks, holding tightly when he thrust up into me as I came down. The impact forced a cry from me.

Shaz slid a hand up my back, pressing me close against him so that he could nuzzle my neck. I shuddered when I felt his fierce fangs graze my throat. We clung to one another, moving in unison. He moaned softly, his breath hot against my skin.

I maintained a steady pace atop him, alternating between shallow and deep strokes. I felt a slight sting in my lower back as Shaz' claws pierced my flesh. A growl rumbled low in his throat. He was getting frustrated with the lack of control. I loved that. Wanting to drive him just a bit crazy, I came to a stop with his thick erection throbbing at my entrance. Teasing him, I slipped down just an inch or so before rising up again. I laughed when he snarled in my ear.

I expected Shaz to snap sooner than he did. He actually let me do it twice more before deciding he'd had enough. In one smooth motion he flipped us so that I was beneath him. I stared up into brilliant green wolf eyes. He was wild and demanding when he thrust into me with total domination.

I was thrilled to have my mate possess my body and make it his. Out of the bedroom I wasn't one for being controlled. In the bedroom, everything was different. Shaz' dominant side came out in full force when we made love, and I enjoyed every moment of it.

He moved with fast, slick strokes, filling me over and over again, Shaz moaned my name with a husky wolf growl. A cool wave passed through me. It was Arys. He must be on his way. I often felt his presence before he arrived. Shaz bit at my neck as he drove me toward the brink of climax, and I lost myself in the throes of passion.

The mounting pleasure grew quickly, hurling me past the point of no return. I cried out as I reached orgasm. I could feel Shaz twitch inside me. Warmth filled me as he spilled his seed. The heady waves ebbed slowly, each as delightful as the last. I struggled to catch my breath while pushing the tousled hair back from my face.

That's when I noticed Arys. Leaning in the doorway with his arms crossed casually, he watched us with a mischievous smile. It startled me, and I tried to sit up quickly despite Shaz' weight atop me.

"What the fuck, Arys?" I tried to be mad, but the shock of seeing him standing there was too overwhelming. "Sneaking up on people is not cool. Especially at a time like this."

"You two really should be more aware of your surroundings. Someone could have come in here and killed the both of you while you're banging your brains out." Arys laughed, and I wanted to hit him.

Shaz rolled off me and pulled the sheets up to his waist. "I knew you were there."

"You did?" I studied him for a long moment. That was interesting. Arys always brought out a different side of Shaz, a stubborn, headstrong one. It never failed.

"Yeah. He hasn't been there long. A few minutes or so." Shaz lay back on the pillows with his hands folded beneath his head.

"I felt you." I gave Arys a dirty look. "But, I didn't realize you were here."

Arys gave a fang baring grin and winked. "You were preoccupied. Must have been good."

"Don't even doubt it." Shaz was quick with his reply. I rolled my eyes and shook my head at both of them before getting out of bed.

I strode to the closet, fully aware of the two gazes that followed me. Ignoring them both, I picked through my clothes, looking for something to wear out for the evening. I settled on slim fitting blue jeans and a tight black V-neck t-shirt. I draped a red bra and matching thong over my arm and turned to face my men.

They were watching me in silence. I raised an eyebrow as I crossed the room to the door.

"So that's it, huh?" Arys blocked my path when I attempted to slip by him. "All played out?"

A teasing glint lit Arys' eyes. The look he gave me was almost enough to make me toss my clothes and get back into bed. A glance at the bedside clock nixed that idea.

"Sweetie, I'd love to play with you. But, Kale will be expecting me in an hour, and I need to hit the shower and get ready." I gave each of them a pointed look and smirked. "You guys feel free to play without me though."

Arys kept a perfectly straight face when he turned to Shaz. "Works for me. What do you say, wolf? Up for a little slap and tickle?"

I couldn't contain my laughter when Shaz promptly flipped Arys off. He gave his blond head a shake and tried to muster a glare that fell flat. "I'm definitely up for slapping you, vampire. Not sure about the tickle though. Maybe another time."

I left the two of them to throw verbal shots at each other. My stomach flipped nervously at the thought of hunting down a human with Kale. I wasn't nervous because this hunt sounded especially awful but because I almost couldn't wait.

ༀༀༀༀ

I was anxious as I parked down the block from the address Kale had given me. I didn't know what to expect once we got inside the house. It could be some harmless old lady that knew how to cast love spells for all I knew. How dangerous could a human be? I didn't really want an answer to that. I'd been a human with power, and though it had been minimal then compared to what I had now, it had been the beginning.

"Why are you so tense?" Kale's voice was low as he strolled up beside me. "You've done this before."

"Are you serious? That's like me asking why you're excited."

I followed him down a nearby alley to the back side of the house where no one could see us. There had damn well better be a deadly woman inside this house. I'd killed my share of humans, but it wasn't like this. I didn't do it for somebody else. Not yet anyway.

Abigail Irving. The name meant nothing to me. Putting a name to the woman I was about to kill wasn't making it easier. I didn't know what to expect from her.

Lights were on inside, but I could see nothing through the heavily draped windows. My heart began to race in anticipation. My fangs and claws lengthened as my wolf rose up within me. I wanted this. And God, how I hated that.

With a silent motion, Kale pulled the screen door open. I tensed, expecting him to force his way inside. I was surprised when he knocked instead. I braced when I sensed her sudden fear. I guess she wasn't expecting company at this time of night.

"Why are we both here?" I hissed beneath my breath when I heard footsteps inside. "Is it really going to take two of us to kill one human?"

"Why not? It's fun to share."

I pinned Kale with a wide-eyed stare. The sound of the deadbolt turning was deafening compared to the silence. I sucked in my breath, waiting like a kid on Christmas as the door cracked open an inch. She peered out at us through that tiny space, her brown eyes narrowing. I had to hold myself back, let the moment play out. The scent of candles and incense wafted out to greet us. I wrinkled my nose in distaste as my wolf recoiled against the assault on my senses.

Before either of us could make a move, she blasted me with enough juice to throw me backwards, skidding on my ass. It hurt and I cursed myself for not being ready for an attack. Kale forced his way into the house, and I scrambled to follow him.

The door vibrated on its hinges. I was drawn to her sudden panic. Nothing smelled quite the way fear did. It teased my control, taunting not only my wolf but also the vampire hunger that I now possessed. When I hunted, I was all about the kill. Hunting a human brought out another side, the vampiric one I didn't trust. Bloodlust stirred in me like the forbidden, unnatural hunger that it was.

Abigail didn't act like a victim for a moment. She rushed at Kale with a kitchen knife raised above her head. I reacted without thought; instinct guided me as I grabbed her arm and twisted it behind her back. The knife hit the floor with a clatter. Abigail let out a howl and swung at me with her free hand.

Kale was careful not to touch her, and it took me a moment to realize why. She mumbled a series of words in a language I didn't understand. She smacked me in the forehead, saying one final word. The pain that spread through my head was instant. I went down on my knees hard with an anguished cry.

Abigail shrieked as Kale threw a blast her way.

She was alarmingly skilled in black magic. She could have made deals with demons for all I knew. I had to give Kale a little credit, Abigail Irving had proven to be anything but a helpless victim.

"I'll kill you, bloodsuckers!" Abigail's high-pitched shriek hurt my ears.

Seconds later I felt the atmosphere in the room grow hot as she attempted a metaphysical attack. I felt something burn low inside me, and I tensed, waiting for the pain. Whatever she was trying, it fizzled. She turned to me with eyes wide with horror. She head-butted me right in the face; my own damn fault, I'd hesitated.

I stumbled back a few feet, dazed from the blow. Blood trickled from my nose, and my eyes watered in response. It didn't matter how fast it would heal, a hit in the nose always hurt like a mother fucker. A snarl erupted from me, and I lashed out in anger. My backhand took her off her feet, and she hit the floor hard.

"Not a vampire," she muttered repeatedly as she struggled to get up. "What are you?"

I stood over her, placing a boot on her chest so she remained on the floor. I was shaking with the need to kill her. My eyes strayed to her throat as my wolf encouraged me to tear it out. She was prey. What was I waiting for?

I looked to Kale for some kind of support. I was close to losing control.

Abigail tried again to use her magic. I felt it low inside, trying to take hold of me. I pushed back against her with my own power, forcing hers away from me. She was impressively strong, able to really make me have to work to hold off her attack.

"You were warned, Abigail. What did you think was going to happen?" Kale asked, gazing down at her.

"I did what I had to do. You're filthy, nasty creatures from the bowels of hell!" Abigail stared up at me, venom in her gaze and a litany of curse words poured from her lips. "And whatever you are, you're as tainted as he is."

"Lady, I'm not so different a creature than you are. I think the pot's calling the kettle black here." I tried to get a read on her power, but I couldn't determine if it was more than incredibly strong witch magic. I was sure it had to be.

She was seething. Her fear had faded quickly once the adrenaline kicked in. Thankfully, she didn't seem to be able to take on both of us.

"You're nothing like me. Hurry up and kill me, you heathen! God has a special place for whores like you."

Nothing like being called a whore by a mad woman. The vacancy deep in her eyes screamed 'crazy.' It wasn't worth letting her get under my skin. Regardless, I struggled not to tear her head from her shoulders.

"Alexa? Do you want her?"

I met Kale's eyes, finding my bloodlust mirrored in his gaze. Conflict tore at me, taunting me. If I hadn't been turned by Raoul, if I hadn't become a werewolf, would I have believed my natural abilities to be a tool against the supernatural? Would I have been so different from Abigail Irving?

I shook my head 'no,' but it was a lie.

The bloodlust clawed at my insides. The two predatory natures inside me embraced in an unlikely pairing, sending me spiraling into the black abyss where I always went when I killed.

I stepped back, releasing my hold on the screeching woman on the floor. Kale didn't hesitate. He dragged her to her feet, fighting to bare her throat. She fought hard as I watched, frozen in place. The hum of their power in combat was loud, almost deafening in my ears.

My heart raced in eager anticipation. I waited for that moment when Kale's fangs would pierce her flesh and spill her blood. I could feel her scrambling to re-focus her power, but it was too late. Kale bit deep into her, and I groaned.

I was flushed with excitement. Blood spilled from beneath Kale's lips as he fed, and I stared, transfixed. A frustrated growl spilled from me. I felt myself slipping during that last moment of clarity before the bloodlust claimed me. I moved without thought, crossing the space between me and Kale. I needed to taste her.

Kale surrendered her to me, anticipation gleaming in his eerie gaze. The fight had gone out of Abigail. Kale had drained her quickly. She hung limp in my grasp. Her heart was slowing. Without hesitation,

I ran my tongue over the bleeding punctures in her throat. A roar of thunder echoed inside my head, and fireworks danced in my vision. Blood coated my lips and tongue, but it wasn't enough.

I bit deep, my top fangs slid through her flesh with an ease that made me groan. The wound was ragged, and the blood pumped faster. My wolf fangs didn't pierce as neat and clean as vampire fangs. Right then, all I cared about was the intoxicating crimson nectar and taking everything our victim had left to give.

I could feel Kale's eyes on me. He lingered, close without crossing into my personal space. I knew he wanted to touch me.

Abigail was lifeless when I let her slide to the floor. The urge to howl and drop to all fours was strong. My body vibrated with the rush of the power and the pleasure of the kill. There was nothing like that final moment, when my victim became mine.

"If you kiss me, I'll knock your ass out." I uttered the warning through fangs.

Kale regarded me with a neutral expression. I couldn't read his face, but I didn't need to. I knew what he was thinking because I was thinking it, too. Every time we were in a situation like this, we pushed the limits. How many times could I dance this close to the flames before I set myself ablaze?

"Alexa, just go. I'll deal with this."

"What?" I was flustered, trying to see clearly through the haze in my head.

"You heard me. Take off. It's probably best if you do anyway." Kale gave me a long, lingering look. "Unless you really want to stay."

"Why do you give up so easy?" I snarled. "You don't even pretend to resist anymore! If I lost control, nothing would keep us from doing something we'd regret. Why should I have to always be the one saying no for the both of us?"

Kale stepped in close, forcing me to look up to meet his eyes. "Then say yes, and end the hunger that torments us both."

Staring at the blood that stained his lower lip, wanting desperately to run my tongue over it, logic quickly failed me. It physically hurt to resist the urge. I had to get out of the house; it brimmed with too much power, which exerted far too much influence.

"You know it's not that simple."

I hurried outside to gulp in the fresh night air. The energy that had built up in my core burned like a fire just getting started. But, escaping the strange concoction of power inside the house instantly lifted a weight from me.

"It is that simple." Kale followed me outside but kept a safe distance. "I have done nothing but hold back for months. It's liberating to finally have you know how I feel. You can hide behind the power and blame that if you want to, but you want me, too. It's not always about the power. Eventually, you're going to have to admit it."

I cringed inwardly. Did it show on my face? God, I hoped not. "I'm not ready to do that."

He nodded knowingly, but something remained unsettled in his eyes. It unnerved me. "Go home, Alexa."

It bothered me that he was trying to get rid of me though I knew why. "We'll talk tomorrow?"

He gave me a tight-lipped smile and a brief nod, then turned to re-enter the house. I stood there in the backyard for a minute, wrestling with myself. Conflicted and wired on my kill, I abandoned the notion of picking apart what had just transpired and headed for my car.

Chapter Seven

It was starting to feel like I'd never left The Wicked Kiss. The moment I walked through the door, I asked myself why I bothered. Would things be any different whether I was there or not? Judging by Kale's dead whores the other night, the answer to that was 'no.'

I could feel Arys' presence. I hated that he'd been hanging around so much. It made me think he knew something that I didn't. Knowing him, he did. I assumed he was there because of the Vegas vampires, but I still wasn't sure how concerned I should be about them. Everything Arys had to say about them scared the shit out of me. However, I'd been hit with a lot in recent days, and I could only handle one thing at a time, as it occurred.

It was early yet, barely midnight. The club was busy but not yet crowded. I could still make my way through without having to toss people out of my path. Nothing was amiss, yet. My senses were blazing as I tried to take in everything and everyone. The overwhelming sensation was incredibly uncomfortable at times, but it was better than being caught off guard by the wrong person.

I headed for the back hall with unabashed intentions. The hallway was deadly quiet. I hated that. The silence was unnerving because I knew several of those rooms were occupied. Kale's however, was not. I didn't know where he was, but he wasn't at The Kiss, and that was a good enough excuse for me to snoop around. The door was locked. Just as well. I didn't need or want to go inside. I could sense that nobody was inside, corpses included. That was all I needed to know.

The sound of metal grinding on metal drew my gaze to the parking lot exit at the end of the hall. Arys strolled through the door looking pleased with himself. His energy was running hot, and I gasped when it mingled with mine, merging together the way two separate bodies of water become one.

"I told you not to hunt here, Arys." My glare was wasted on him.

"You told me not to kill here. I followed the rules. Although nobody else seems to have to." With a smirk, he pulled me close for a bruising kiss.

The taste of blood was fresh and strong when he slipped his tongue between my lips. A series of images flashed through my mind, ending with the lifeless body of Abigail Irving. The bloodlust was sharp and sudden. I jerked away from Arys, fighting to clear my head.

"Please tell me you're not feeding from the willing victims here."

He frowned as if I'd suggested something vile. "Hell no. I grabbed a guy in the alley out back. It was just a taste. I didn't kill anybody."

I did my best to roll my eyes, but I ended up giving him a pained look instead. "Kill whoever you want to. Just don't do it in here, and I don't care." As an afterthought I added, "Ok, well not whoever you want to. You know what I mean."

"Are you alright, love?" The humor fled from his expression as he regarded my discomfort. "That's what happens when you feed the bloodlust at first. Rather than feel satisfied, you just want more."

"You knew?" Of course he knew, the same way I'd known the moment he walked in. Hiding it from Arys was impossible.

"Well yeah. You and Sinclair bagged yourselves a human. Nice change. Can't say I mind. Although I'm not too keen on him being your tag team partner."

"I don't want to hear it." I flashed him a vicious warning look, one that he didn't ignore.

Arys held his hands up in mock surrender. "Hey, if you and Kale want to use a job as your excuse to kill shit without a guilty conscience, feel free. But, I can see where this is going even if you choose not to."

"No, you can't. It was one human kill. One." I argued for the sake of refusing to allow Arys to be right. It was useless.

"Just one? Come on, Alexa. You're not that naive, just incredibly stubborn. It's never just one. Not for us." He reached to stroke a lock of my hair back from my face, and I leaned into his touch. "Already it's burning inside you, the hunger for more. I can feel it."

I shook my head vehemently. "I'm not going to be a slave to the bloodlust, not while I still live and breathe."

I knew he was thinking that I was living in denial. Thankfully, he was sweet enough not to say so. It had been a while since I'd killed a human, almost a year, and it felt better than I remembered. I had to shake myself out of that frame of thought. Remembering was not going to help crush the hunger taking root in my core.

I turned to head back into the heart of the club. The Kiss was already busier than it had been just minutes before. Damn blood junkies.

Arys gave the club interior an intense once over. "Do you get a lot of demons in here?"

"What? No. Never." I followed Arys' gaze to the front entry. "Well, there's one."

I'd had little experience with demons, and all of it was bad. I didn't know why one would come to The Wicked Kiss, and I wasn't sure I wanted to.

It hit me all at once. The sinister power that crept towards us was stifling. For a moment I couldn't breathe. It was strong, like cold bitter coffee. Black. It was just so black. I had no better word for it.

The humans were none the wiser, but the vampires in the club quickly withdrew to the farthest corners of the building when the demon entered. Like all of the demons I'd seen, he looked human, Japanese to be precise. Average height with shining blue-black hair, he was quite attractive. I found that most demons presented a handsome façade, but it wasn't their true face.

Even from where I stood I could make out how inhuman his intense red eyes were. That gaze landed on me, and he smiled. Adrenaline crashed through me. *Oh, shit.* He made his way across the room, and I watched him, my mouth as dry as cotton.

Arys stood calmly next to me. His expression revealed that he wasn't entirely unfamiliar with this demon.

The demon stopped a few feet away. I was relieved that he stayed out of my personal space. His power was so unbearably strong that I fought to shield against it.

"Alexa O'Brien." He greeted me with a nod. "I believe we have a mutual acquaintance, Veryl Armstrong." His voice was like a dark, somber melody, immediately mesmerizing. He didn't offer me a hand so much as he helped himself to mine. "My name is Shya. I'd like a few minutes of your time if that's alright."

We all knew the uber polite act was for show. He fully expected me to cooperate. He was one of the people Veryl had said I didn't want to deal with. So much for that. I had no intention of pissing the guy off if I could help it.

His hand on mine was warm as his power slithered up my arm like a snake. I wanted to jerk my hand from his but resisted. "Sure. There are a few tables behind the bar where it's a bit quieter."

Shya shocked me by holding up a hand before Arys. "Sorry, Mr. Knight. I'm afraid this is a private matter. And, since you've turned down our offer, you'll have to sit this one out."

I held my breath and waited for Arys' response. He never told me that demons had asked him to work with them. Why would he choose not to mention that?

Shya never gave him the opportunity to reply. He turned his back on Arys without a second glance and indicated that I should lead the way. I hesitated just long enough to see the fury flash through Arys' midnight blue eyes. Hoping to avoid trouble, I quickly led the way to an empty table behind the bar. I almost laughed with relief when Arys stayed put. It wasn't like him, which told me more about Shya than I wanted to know.

I sat down across from the demon, uncomfortable with the way he looked me over with those creepy red eyes. The snake-like pupils betrayed the lie that his human form projected. I met his gaze directly and concentrated on staying calm but alert. As far as eyes go, this guy had the eeriest I'd seen, including Kale's and my own. I fought hard to keep from falling into their crimson depths.

"I apologize, Alexa. This meeting is long overdue." Shya beamed a pearly white smile at me. "I think it's time we get acquainted."

"Alright." I smiled, hoping it didn't look as wary as it felt.

"I'm going to cut to the chase. I'd like to give you the chance to rise up in the ranks of our organization." He spoke with authority, easily holding my attention with his charming manner. "What we do isn't about good and evil, human or otherwise. It's about power and maintaining an order that was established over thousands of years. I'm sure you understand why a mass public exposure of the supernatural world would be horrific. However, you must know that many beings out there dedicated to just that: full exposure." He paused, giving me the opportunity to form a response.

My tongue felt like a useless slab of meat. He'd just thrown a lot at me. It took me a moment to put a response together. "I'm very aware of how ugly things could get. The last thing I want is to end up on the wrong end of a worldwide witch hunt. I can't imagine why any supernaturals would willingly expose themselves."

"Some believe that by exposing us all, we'll in turn have more control over the human race. I don't agree with this philosophy. We maintain influence over humans when they believe most of us to be a myth. That's where our power lies, especially for creatures like you."

I mulled over what he'd said. Existing in the guise of myth and folklore was necessary. Going public was a suicide mission. "I completely agree."

"It's all so much bigger than what you see with Veryl and his pitiful office." Shya continued, a smile of approval on his handsome face. "We do what has to be done to ensure our freedom and protection. As for those who stand against us, their numbers are large enough to pose a problem, which is where you come in. The more people I can trust to trim their numbers, the better."

"Ok. So someone like Abigail Irving, could just one woman like her really be a threat?" I was already afraid of him. I figured I didn't have anything to lose by asking what was really on my mind.

"She was a feisty one, wasn't she?" He chuckled, and I immediately went cold. "That one knew things. Killing her was the safest way to make sure that what she knew never got out."

"What kind of things?" My eyes were dry. I hadn't blinked in a while because I couldn't pull myself away from his entrancing stare that long.

Shya studied me closely, a simple perusal. He made no attempt to test or touch my power the way so many others had upon a first meeting; he didn't have to. He already knew far more about me than I did about him. Of that, I was certain.

"She knew how to access powers rooted in the pits of hell. I hope her zealous talk didn't convince you otherwise. That woman went mad decades ago. She was a disaster waiting to happen. The demons she was consorting with are now just as dead as she is."

Lilah. One of my coworkers' names popped unbidden into my mind. I'd seen her kill a demon with very little effort.

"I'm always going to be in the dark, aren't I? Never really knowing who I'm hunting or why."

"Oh, you will know. You already do. You know as much as you need to know." The smile suddenly vanished from Shya's face causing his sharp features to seem more pronounced. "You have immense power over vampires and werewolves. You are both and yet somehow neither, all at the same time. The creatures of the underworld are constantly in conflict. The battle for control of both the human and the supernatural world never ceases. You have an opportunity to play an important role here."

I swallowed hard. He really did know an awful lot about me, maybe more than I did.

When I failed to respond, Shya continued. "I like you already. You've proven yourself to be professional and discreet. And, from what Veryl tells me, you have no qualms about speaking your mind." The serpentine smile returned.

"I don't appreciate being lied to or having information withheld from me when it directly involves my personal life and business." I didn't mean to come across as bitchy, but demon or not, he needed to know where I stood.

Shya's expression didn't change. He seemed completely unmoved by anything I'd said so far.

"Understood. You've outgrown working with Veryl. You're capable of so much more. All I want from you is the same loyalty I expect from anyone who works with me. I'm prepared to offer you much more than money." He gave the rest of the club a cursory glance, and I could almost see what he was thinking. He didn't seem to think any better of it than I did.

A waitress dumped her drink tray on a customer with a crash. The tirade she followed up with indicated he had it coming. I shrugged and did my best to tune it out.

"Look, Shya. I can just imagine what Veryl has told you about me, let alone whatever else you might know. You want a fair kill, I'm your girl. All I ask is that you don't ask me to hunt any innocents." I was dealing with a demon. I had to amend that. "What I consider innocent."

He leaned forward, a brow raised. "Tell me, Alexa. What do you consider to be innocent?"

I had no easy answer to that. I didn't need someone like Arys or Shya to convince me that the inhabitants of the earth, both human and otherwise, were far from innocent. That still didn't make them all worthy of slaughter.

"I know that's a trick question. There's no way to answer it without contradicting myself somehow." I paused, trying to form my words in a manner that he wouldn't be able to twist on me. I wasn't a demon expert, but I wasn't born yesterday. "Prove to me a target is dangerous, a threat, anything like that, that's all I ask. Just don't send me in blind. I can't live with a guilty conscience."

Shya didn't miss a beat. "Dangerous? But, even you are dangerous. Some would consider you a threat. It is never so simple."

Dammit. So much for not contradicting myself. "Alright. Point for you."

"I don't claim to understand where your hesitance comes from. You are a killer. It's in everything you are. However, you won't be forced into anything."

"Understood." I knew what he meant. I could refuse a kill, but that wouldn't stop someone else from doing the job.

The weight of Shya's gaze made me fidget. I struggled hard just to sit still. His wicked power was deep and murky, like a bottomless pit that sought to draw me in.

"If you choose to accept the opportunity to advance from hunter to personal assassin, I think you will find there are many perks to having power like yours. That being said, I would like to propose something to you."

The glint of anticipation in his blood-red eyes had me chewing my lower lip anxiously. I wasn't going to like what I was about to hear. He enjoyed that. Fucking demons.

I gestured for him to continue. The noisy din of the nightclub seemed to fade away as I waited to hear his proposal. My heart began to pound. I feared the worst.

Demons were true evil. Despite his professional and almost

friendly demeanor, I didn't forget that. I wasn't surprised that pure amusement shone on Shya's face when he said, "I want you to kill Veryl Armstrong."

I took a few moments to let the echo of that request play in my ears. My reaction was delayed. I was conflicted. Part of me was immediately ready to refuse though something deeper down was intrigued.

"Why?" I deserved to know that much at least. I'd known Veryl for years and this demon for all of a matter of minutes. Did he really expect me to say yes?

Shya pursed his lips and regarded me with a curious expression. "He's taken to meddling in the affairs of others, you included. Of course, I don't have to tell you that. Once it came to my attention that he was blackmailing one of my own, his days were numbered."

Blackmail huh? That didn't come as a surprise. I wouldn't put anything past Veryl. But, did I want to kill him?

"I need to think about it."

"By all means. There are many who would love this opportunity. I offered it to you first. I assumed you would appreciate it after everything he has done to you."

I wasn't an easy enough target to fall for that line, but I knew what he was trying to do. He thought he could get inside my head by going for my personal feelings. I was starting to feel that for everything Shya said, there was something he wasn't saying.

"I might not be the right fit for this. It feels a little too close to home. But like I said, I'll consider it." That's the best he was going to get out of me right then. It became hard to meet his eyes; a magnetic pull seemed to grow and pulse if I didn't look away. It was hypnotizing and intimidating. I wanted him to leave so I could think clearly.

"The wolf's loyalty, it's a lovely attribute." He winked, and though he hadn't done or said anything else, I knew there was a veiled threat in those words. Shya stood abruptly, offering a hand. "We'll speak soon. If you wish to reach me, speak with Lilah."

I didn't want to touch his hand; it almost pained me to do so. I felt the reptilian touch of a snake against my flesh, and I visibly shuddered. Shya was gone before I could fight my way out of the cloak of darkness swirling around him. I watched him disappear through the exit and gradually the suffocating sensation fell away.

Arys was right where I'd left him. With his arms crossed over his chest and a beautiful glare etched on his handsome face, he oozed fury. Shaz stood next to him, a worried frown creasing his brow.

"Got something you want to say to me?" I asked Arys, my tone accusatory.

In the same breath he said, "Please tell me you didn't make any deals with him."

"Of course not. Why didn't you tell me you knew more about who I work for than I do? A little heads up on the big CIA-style demon action would have been nice."

"How could you not have known? Sometimes I think you prefer to be in the dark."

"Why did you turn them down?"

Shaz looked from me to Arys. Curiosity lurked in his jade gaze. As much as I loved Arys, sometimes he really drove me nuts with the secret keeping. It seemed to be a vampire trait, which I could understand to a degree. After several centuries I'd be set in my ways, too. But this was different.

"They approached me about six months ago, after you and I forged our bond. Anything that demon can promise isn't worth what he'll ask for in return, and personally, I want nothing to do with him."

"I wish you had told me."

"Be careful with the demons, Alexa, and you will be fine. You can hold your own. But, think things through before you do anything he asks. Maybe even reconsider what you do. Maybe it's time to get out."

I glanced around for the closest waitress. When I caught her eye, I held up two fingers. A double shot of whiskey couldn't possibly arrive fast enough.

Shaz took the chance to jump in. "What's the point of all this, the whole organized supernatural hit squad? Seems like there's little rhyme or reason to their hit list."

"I've always been under the impression that we avoid exposure by wiping out the bottom feeders and rabid newborns." I shrugged and gave my hair a toss. "It's becoming painfully clear that everything I think I know is something else entirely."

Arys reached for my hand, and electricity crackled when our fingers touched. Shaz winced like he'd felt it, and I looked hard at him.

"The point is maintaining control of humanity by keeping them in the dark." Arys said it with a casual tone that didn't fit the subject. "The Western world prefers to turn a blind eye to most unsavory things. It's easier here to keep a low profile than it is in many older countries where they won't think twice about launching a witch hunt for anything and everything nonhuman. The real risk isn't the newborn vamps and Weres on killing sprees; it's the ones with serious power. Those are the ones that have the potential to blow the world as we know it wide open."

Shaz beat me to it. Clearly we were thinking the same thing. He pinned Arys with a knowing look. "You and Alexa included. Right? You're talking about those with the power to call demons, do magic, manipulate all forms of power. All of it."

"Yes. Alexa and I included." Arys wore that expression he got when Shaz or I came across as exceptionally naive and human.

"Powerful beings controlling others and destroying those that don't play by the rules." Shaz turned that over for a moment. "No different than human government. It makes sense though. I assume you're talking big-time shit."

"From witches who can read minds and vampires who glamour humans to demons and angels that know secrets pertaining to the end of the world itself."

The waitress arrived with my whiskey, and I was so stunned by what Arys had just said that I almost forgot to tip her. I ordered two more. This was as good a time as any to enjoy the free drinks perk.

"Angels?" Shaz and I spoke in unison after the waitress left.

Arys looked amused. "This probably isn't the best place to talk about it."

That was too much for one night. I shot back the whiskey and waited for the satisfying burn that followed. No amount of alcohol could numb out my unease, but I was willing to try.

Shaz leaned in to press a warm kiss to my temple. "I'll see you later. Let me know if you plan on hugging a bottle all night. I'll drive you home."

"Wait." I grabbed his arm, and my wolf was instantly soothed by the contact. "Run with me later?"

His wolf responded strongly to me, making the jade green of his eyes start to bleed across the whites. "Definitely."

He gave me a quick kiss and turned to head back to the front entry. I was almost itchy with the need to shed my skin and be wolf. Arys was watching me with a hungry expression.

"What?" I flashed him a playful smile.

"I want you. Right now. Here." Fire smoldered in his eyes. Nobody could ever say Arys was predictable.

"You're kidding." The waitress interrupted me; I noticed she had brought me double what I'd ordered, in a glass on the rocks. Was I gaining a bad reputation here or something?

No sooner had she left than Arys pulled me into the dark corner behind the bar. I protested, shrieking when he made me spill whiskey down my cleavage.

"Arys!" My protest turned into a laugh when he pulled me against him and kissed my neck. He tugged at the hem of my skirt, and I slapped his hands away.

"Nobody can see us here. Even if they could, I wouldn't care." He sucked hard at the vein in my neck, and my knees went weak. "I need to mark you."

Heat rushed to my groin. His sudden need sparked my own, and I didn't protest when he pulled my skirt up from behind and jerked my panties to the side. A chair at an empty table was the only thing I could hold for stability. I almost dropped my drink in my attempt to set it down.

I expected my inhibitions to surface when he bent me over the chair. The soft touch of Arys at my entrance stole my breath. He thrust into me forcefully, and I gasped. It hurt a little, and I loved it. With one hand on my hip he held tight to me. His thrusts were achingly slow but rough so that I felt the impact deep within. Every slick stroke left me more hungry than sated.

Surreally, the rest of the club operated as normal while we united in violent, physical passion in the shadows. Arys leaned down over me to whisper in my ear.

"It didn't take much to convince you, did it little wolf?"

Finding that sweet spot on my neck, Arys bit deep. My cry was swallowed up by the loud music. I came almost immediately. Electricity surged in my veins as Arys pounded harder into me. Every delicious wave of bliss was just as good as the last. He sucked at the bloody punctures, and my stomach clenched.

His release was sudden and intense inside me. His soft moans in my ear sent a shiver down my spine. I couldn't resist him, obviously. It was impossible to say no to him.

The touch of his tongue felt hot against my wounded flesh. He groaned and pulled away. It had all happened so fast. I was left feeling faint from the head spinning rush.

I tugged my skirt back into place and turned to face Arys. He easily concealed himself back inside his ass-hugging blue jeans. I stared at him, dumbfounded.

"What the hell was that?" It wasn't a complaint. My hand shook when I retrieved my drink from the table. That had been an intense encounter.

"It was a spontaneous urge that I couldn't ignore." He grinned and licked my blood from his fangs and lips. "That was pretty hot for a quickie."

Considering how badly my legs trembled, I had to agree. "That was a little tongue tying. But, let's not make a habit of it. This is not the place for that."

"What's wrong? Don't want the customers to catch you enjoying the place as much as they do?" Arys slipped his tongue into my mouth. Tasting my own blood on him was strangely intoxicating.

"How do I let you talk me into this stuff?" It had been so easy to give in to Arys' whims. The man was the epitome of sex. The rush of having public sex, in The Wicked Kiss of all places, was dizzying and also more than a little risky. The wrong person could have caught us and created an awkward situation. To Arys, that was half the fun.

"There was no talking you into anything. It's not like you protested." He buried his face in my hair and inhaled my scent.

It stung when he ran his tongue over the bite mark. I sighed. "Why the mark? It'll heal by morning."

"Let's call it a vampire thing. It's this place. Too many vampires and any one of them could be one of our uninvited guests."

"I'm pretty sure that every vampire here, welcome or not, knows I'm yours."

Arys scanned the interior of the club, his gaze watchful and deadly. "Let's hope so."

"I hate that you're expecting something to happen. I'm tired of looking over my shoulder all the time." I emptied my whiskey glass, savoring the warmth that spread through my limbs.

"Better get used to it, sweetheart, especially now that you're on a first name basis with your demon bossman."

"That's reassuring, Arys. Thanks." I ignored his smirk. "I'm going to the restroom. Keep an eye on things, will you?"

Every step I took felt light and floaty, like I walked on a cloud. The energy riding me was intense. It felt like I could have spread my arms and taken flight. What a rush!

After retrieving my purse from behind the bar, I headed to the ladies' room. I got halfway there before realizing I'd left my cell phone in the car. Instantly I felt naked. I continued to the restroom, a growing sense of technological addiction eating at me.

A petite brunette stood at the sink, holding a bloody paper towel to her neck. Panic shone in her eyes when she saw me.

"Are you alright?" I asked as the scent of her blood hit me like a slap in the face.

She met my gaze in the mirror and shook her head. "I don't know. There's a lot of blood."

"Can I see?" She was right about the blood. It quickly soaked through the paper towel. I drew her hand away from the wound and cursed inwardly. It was an ugly bite. It looked like the vampire who had bit her didn't know what the hell he was doing. If he was killing on the streets that wouldn't matter much. Here in my club, it was unacceptable.

"I don't feel so good." She was pale and unsteady on her feet. "I'm scared."

The bloodlust didn't sneak up inside me - it burst forth with a ravenous hunger that had me all claws and fangs. She took one look at my eyes, all wolf, paired with my four massive fangs, and she started to shriek. I didn't mean to snarl and snap at her. The scent of fear mingled with blood, and my control slipped.

"Help! Oh my God, somebody help me!" She fought hard, but her strength had already been sapped. Nobody would hear her cries.

"I don't want to hurt you! Please, you've got to calm down!" Blood gushed from the ragged wound in her throat. My every instinct screamed for me to take her down and bury my face in the crimson nectar. I was restraining myself so hard my entire body shook. I couldn't take the temptation. The need was bringing me to my knees.

She threw herself toward the door in a vain attempt to escape me. I reacted without thought, blocking her exit. The growl that echoed through the washroom sounded like someone else.

The struggle was brief. She didn't have the strength. Loss of blood was her undoing, and she fell in a dead faint at my feet. My original intent had been to help her. Now all I wanted to do was taste her. I lost all sense of time and reality. Like a drunken blackout, I was going through the motions without conscious awareness. Her blood was on my hands and in my mouth. I would have killed her if Arys hadn't felt me snap.

Everything was a blur as he intruded upon the scene. The breath was crushed from me when he threw me against the far wall. I slid to the floor but was quickly on my feet. I was stunned by the energy wall he put between us.

"I knew this would happen. It always takes you. There is no fighting the bloodlust once it's in you." He crouched beside the woman, but his eyes were on me.

"Think you can hold me?" I taunted, testing the resistance of his barrier. Sharing power didn't mean we couldn't turn that power on each other. Our bond was a double-edged sword. In a true face off, Arys would be my greatest foe simply because he was a part of me.

"I shouldn't have to, Alexa. I'm intervening because I know if you were in your right mind, that's what you'd want." He concentrated on the unconscious woman, and the room filled with warm, healing energy. "You're no different than any vampire now."

I ran my hands along the energy wall blocking my path. When I focused hard, I could see it shimmering with flecks of gold and blue, the colors of our two auras. Arys was using my own power against me, and it was working. If I hadn't been high as a kite on sex, blood and power, that would have frightened me.

The palms of my hands tingled. I was sure I could manipulate his barrier and bend it to my will, but my concentration was scattered. Arys picked the woman up and, with an exasperated eye roll directed at me, carried her from the washroom. Moments later, the barrier dropped.

A look in the mirror had me shrinking back in horror. Blood

stained my hands and face. Scarlet smears ran around my mouth, up the side of my face and even in my hair. Even as I stood there staring into my unnaturally blue eyes, I licked the blood from my fingers. Seeing my brown eyes all wolf had taken years to adjust to. I doubted that I'd ever get used to seeing Arys' midnight blue eyes on me.

I understood completely why Shaz had such a hard time looking at me like this; I looked like something straight out of a horror movie. My ash blond hair was a wild, blood-flecked mess. I sobered as I stared at my reflection. After what felt like a long time, I turned on the tap and washed the blood from my face and hands.

Arys was right. I couldn't keep fighting this. I needed to hunt, to feast and to kill. The hunger haunted me all the time now. Try as I might to fight the urge, it wasn't going away.

An eerie giggle spilled from between my lips. It echoed in the silence of the washroom. I felt amazing even after just a taste of her. I wanted to run through the forest so fast that my paws barely touched the ground. I suddenly couldn't wait to be wolf. At least in the confines of the forest, I couldn't hurt anybody.

Chapter Eight

I didn't see Arys when I left the bathroom. I kept my eyes on the front exit and forced my feet to keep moving. Shaz was having a heated exchange with a vampire I didn't recognize. He was right up in Shaz' face, demanding entry to the club.

I didn't know or care what reason Shaz had for refusing. That was good enough for me. I held up a hand on my way past and blasted the vampire in the chest with a shot of the tightly wound energy burning its way through me.

"Beat it!" The blow threw him back out into the parking lot. I didn't bother to glance his way. If he made any more trouble, I would kill him.

I needed a few moments alone in the night air to get a grip on myself. I walked quickly through the parking lot to my car, passing Kale's along the way. I did a double take. When did Kale arrive? Thank God he hadn't seen me and Arys getting it on inside.

My hand went to the bite on my neck and Arys' *'Let's hope so'* comment rang in my ears. He'd bitten me for Kale's benefit. That was a whole new jealous low for Arys. He'd never admit any such thing though.

Kale hadn't been in the club, which meant he was in the back, in his personal room. I could just imagine what he was up to, probably with some woman. No imagining! Whatever Kale was up to, I didn't need to think about it, and I didn't want to know.

As I drew closer to my car, I got the feeling that I was being watched. I didn't feel a close presence though. Whoever it was, they were a good distance away. I wasn't in the mood to deal with anyone or anything else tonight. Just to be safe, I cast a power circle around me. Nobody would get close without walking into it and ending up on their ass.

I unlocked my car with the key remote and glanced inside before opening the door, a habit I'd started when I first got my license. Too many late night movies featuring a creep waiting in the backseat had permanently instilled that caution in the back of my mind. The car was clear. Nobody was around. Still, something felt all wrong.

I opened the driver's door, and the white envelope sitting on the seat affirmed my unease. Both my name and Arys' was scrawled on the front in handwriting that was barely legible. I reached for my cell phone first, finding it untouched. Knowing that I was being watched from a distance, I grabbed the envelope, relocked the car and turned to go back into the club. Whatever was inside that envelope, I wasn't looking at it with an unseen audience.

"Take a break?" I whispered to Shaz upon re-entering the building. After a few words to Shawn, another security guy, Shaz followed me through the lobby. I searched for Arys, spotting him near the dance floor enjoying the attention of two women fawning over him. He looked my way almost as if I'd called his name. I gestured for him to join me and continued on to the back hall.

I didn't believe there was anything truly dangerous inside the envelope. I sensed nothing unnatural inside. Still, better safe than sorry. I'd rather open it in a private, quiet area. No matter what it was, it wasn't good. I knew that without a doubt.

Stepping through the door into the back hall made me uneasy. I automatically shielded my presence so that the vampires consorting with their blood whores back there wouldn't sense me, Kale included. Shaz was right behind me, concern etched on his face.

"What's going on, Lex?"

I turned the envelope over in my hands. "Someone was in my car. No damage or any sign of a break in. It was just sitting there on the driver's seat."

His gaze swept over me, and he wrinkled his nose. "Why is there human blood in your hair?"

"I had a little incident in the washroom with a bleeding woman. Nothing to worry about." I was relieved when Arys joined us, preventing me from having to explain further. I held up the envelope for him to see. "Someone left this in my car. They were watching me."

Folding his arms across his chest, Arys nodded. "Open it."

My hands shook slightly when I tore it open. A photo was inside and nothing more. I pulled it out and felt the blood rush from my face. It was a surveillance photo of Lena, the older human witch that Kale and I worked with. I considered her a close friend, family even.

The picture showed her crossing the parking lot of her apartment building, completely unaware that she was being watched. An address and a time were written on the back of the photo. I didn't need it spelled out any more clearly.

"Is this how they get your attention? By threatening innocent people before they've even spoken to you?" Shaz looked disgusted.

Arys shrugged and took the picture from me for a closer look. "I'm actually a little surprised that's all they did. Makes sense that they would use one of your human friends as a way of making sure we'll show up."

Shaz was quickly going from disgusted to livid. "You're not going without me."

"What about Lena?" I looked to Arys for answers. "Will they hurt her?"

A shadow passed behind his eyes, and my stomach dropped. "Not right away. They just want you to know that they can and will if you don't play along."

A scream rang out from down the hall, causing me to jump. It was quickly followed by a high-pitched giggle, and I shuddered. Good Lord, don't let that have come from Kale's room. Shaz frowned, but Arys was completely unaffected.

"What I find interesting is that they want you to meet them in a public place." A small smile played about Arys' lips. "They chose neutral ground because all they want to do is talk. This time. I have a feeling they are looking for ways to deal with us without it becoming a power struggle. Which is why they targeted Lena. They weaken you because of an emotional tie. They don't need to have more power than us to do that."

"Can't argue with that logic." Shaz ran a hand through his platinum hair. "I'd do the same thing."

I nodded and paced a few feet away then back again. "So would I. But, Lena has nothing to do with this. It's not fair."

"Anything to make you squirm, my dear. The biggest mistake you can make right now is to show fear. And, don't even think of rushing over to Lena's. I guarantee they have someone watching her in case you do." Arys glanced at the address on the photo. "We'll meet them and settle this. Don't worry about Lena."

"Shit! That's three days away still." I wanted to punch something. The wall wouldn't be satisfying enough. I couldn't hurt it.

Arys was utterly calm, the polar opposite of the storm of panic and rage swirling inside me. "They want to draw it out so you agonize about it. Don't bother. They won't do a damn thing yet. We'll meet them. They'll toss threats and demands at us, and we'll kill them. Or, something like that."

A door creaked open down the hall, and I knew without looking it was Kale's. Both Arys and Shaz turned toward the sound. I waited, sensing Kale's approach though he moved in graceful silence. I shielded hard, unwilling to touch the metaphysical fire that warmed me as he drew near.

"What's going on?"

Arys passed him the photo, and I held my breath, waiting for Kale's reaction. I was relieved to see that he wasn't strung out on a blood binge. He peered at both sides of the picture, and a frown furrowed his brow.

"I'm coming with you." Kale's tone left no room for argument.

I nodded but said nothing. Instead I called Jez. "Do me a favor Jezzy? Call Lena and make small talk. Just make sure she answers and she's safe. Don't let on that you're checking up on her. I'll call you back in a bit and fill you in."

After hanging up, I let my gaze travel over the guys. I found it easiest to make eye contact with Shaz. "Alright. Monday at midnight we meet them."

"What about Lena?" Shaz asked with a growing fire burning in his jade eyes. "Someone should stake out her place."

"They'll have someone watching her, to make sure you show." Arys was looking particularly smug. I shook my head so that my hair fell over the bite on my neck.

I felt the weight of Kale's gaze upon me. His expression

revealed nothing when he said, "I'll go to Lena's."

That thought didn't sit well with me. I cut the conversation short. "We'll talk about it later. I have to call Jez back, and if I don't go for a run soon, I'm going to lose my mind."

With a curt nod, Kale handed me the photo and retreated to his room. I knew he had someone waiting for him in there, and I wanted to vacate the hall right away. The smirk pasted on Arys' face didn't fade as he and Shaz followed me back into the club.

Shaz headed back to the lobby, calling back to me, "Be careful. I'll see you at home soon. Or Kylarai's. Let me know where you'll be."

I blew him a kiss and turned to Arys with a sigh. "I need to go home. I assume you have other things in mind."

"Go run; I feel your wolf pacing inside me." With a gentle touch, he caressed the side of my face. "I'll stick around for a bit after you leave. I can't take much more of this place. It's painful. So many lovely treats that are to be tasted but never truly feasted upon. It's a tease is what it is."

"Yeah, yeah. Willing victims are such a pain in the ass, huh?" I rolled my eyes and gave him a playful shove.

"Willing victim ... that's beyond ridiculous. Takes all the fun out of it. I thrive on the struggle." He chuckled, and I felt his smooth laughter like the stroke of a finger down my spine. Taking my hand, Arys placed a kiss in the center of my palm. "Come on. I'll walk you out to your car."

జ్ఞజ్ఞజ్ఞజ్ఞ

The breeze was cool against my face as I ran through the forest, dodging stray limbs and jumping fallen trees. As a wolf I was able to maneuver through the thick trees and brush with ease. My body moved with a natural flow, instinct guiding my feet with every step. Lupine muscles and senses enabled me to be one with my environment. I savored every moment of such true freedom.

The sky was clear, the perfect backdrop for the curtain of stars overhead. Unlike the city just miles away, the forest was quiet and peaceful. The scent of rich earth and fresh growth tantalized me. The transition of spring to full-blown summer was full of splendor. Everything was new again, thriving in the circle of life. It was earthly and natural, something the rest of my life was not.

These precious moments as wolf reassured me. No matter how deadly my other side was, as long as I had my wolf to ground me, the darkness wouldn't swallow me whole. As hard as the first few years were after Raoul had attacked me, I couldn't regret becoming a werewolf. The wolf connected me to life in the same way Arys linked me to death. The wolf kept me sane and alive; I believed it with every part of me.

I raced through the forest, ducking a low hanging branch before it could slap me in the face. My ears twitched constantly, ahead then back, listening as Shaz gained on me from behind. I was hoping to reach the clearing ahead before he leaped on me. Once he got me in his sights, he would roll me.

The sound of his pursuit grew quiet, and I wondered what he was up to. I had a feeling he was going to try to head me off before I reached the clearing. Shaz made one hell of a fine wolf. He was stealthy and intelligent. Though I wanted him to have opportunities to make use of those fine qualities, I hated that it put him in danger.

Hoping to throw him off, I veered off my straight path and zigzagged through the trees. I broke through the trees into the clearing and gave a surprised yelp when Shaz leaped out in front of me. He crashed into me hard enough to knock me off my feet. We tumbled and rolled with limbs flailing.

I was quickly on my feet, circling away from Shaz. He sat back on his haunches with his tongue lolling out. I didn't give him much time to enjoy his small victory before I jumped on him, biting at his ears. He whined and tried to pull away.

We fought playfully until we'd both had enough. A wolf play-fight still left real cuts and bruises. We lay in the soft grass for a while, watching the sky change color as dawn drew closer. I caught myself drifting off and decided it was time to head back. As much as I loved the forest, when I fell asleep for the day I wanted to be in my own comfy bed.

Shaz and I trotted back at a leisurely pace. The sun was just barely glowing on the horizon when we crossed the small stretch of field that separated the tree line from Kylarai's backyard. The forest was the one thing I missed the most since I moved out of Ky's and into Raoul's house. Living in a small-town suburb outside the big city made it easy enough to get back to Ky's for a run, but it just wasn't the same as having this lovely forest outside my own door.

Kylarai was standing on the back deck when we approached. She was wrapped tightly in a long, fuzzy robe, and I envied her coziness.

"You two are out pretty late." She greeted us with a wave. "It's four o'clock. Want to come in for coffee since you're here anyway? I put a pot on when I first noticed you out there."

To shift, I disappeared beneath the upraised deck where I'd left my clothes. Shaz followed suit, and within minutes we were sipping from steaming mugs of coffee in Kylarai's kitchen.

"Are you just going to bed or just getting up?" I asked, giving her a serious once over. Her hair was a mess, and she looked as if she hadn't slept in days. "If we'd known you were up, we would have asked you to join us."

She shrugged and stared into her coffee cup. "I've been buried in work lately. Took on a new case that is pretty sticky. They have a lot of assets to split up, and of course they want to fight over every single one of them."

Shaz and I exchanged a glance. Kylarai was a known workaholic. She liked to stay busy with her career as a divorce lawyer, but this was more than that. She was working to escape from her break up with Julian.

"You need more time off, Ky. Regular time off." I didn't mean to scold. She was a grown woman, but she never hesitated to tell me what I needed to hear. I was willing to do the same. Her energy was low, and if I focused, I could feel the distress of her wolf. "Time as wolf."

"I know. Zoey has been saying the same thing." Ky glanced down the hall. The door to Zoey's room, my old room, was closed. "So I was thinking maybe we could do a girl's night out tonight. If you're not busy."

I looked into her grey eyes and saw the pain that she tried to hide. This Julian incident wasn't something she was going to get over easily. I wouldn't have either.

"Yes, definitely. Let's do a girl's night. I could use one, too."

Shaz looked back and forth between us. "What does a girl's night out consist of exactly?"

"If we told you, we'd have to kill you." I smiled and winked.

Kylarai laughed and smoothed down her wild hair. "I promise to sleep and shower first though. I won't make you take me out looking like this."

"Are you kidding?" Shaz let his gaze slowly sweep over her. "You're a knockout, Ky. Never doubt it."

"Nice try, kid. You're not that good of a liar." Kylarai threw a sugar cube across the table at him. "So what's new with you guys? Fill me in on all the latest. Arys worried me with his mysterious danger talk."

Shaz leaned down to retrieve the sugar cube from the floor. "Arys thrives on drama and trouble. I don't think he's happy if there isn't something going on."

"It's nothing we can't handle. I told you about the blood ring Harley was involved in. Seems there are a few people affiliated with him that are looking for a little restitution." I shrugged, hoping I came across as unaffected. I didn't want her to worry.

Kylarai's eyes widened, and she shook her head. "You've got balls, Alexa, more than most men I know. I don't know how you can deal with this stuff and stay so grounded. I'd be a basket case."

"Well thanks, but I'm hardly as well put together as it might appear. This is the perfect time for a night out. I'll have to do laundry when I get home so I have something decent to wear." By that I meant something without bloodstains.

We chatted over another cup of coffee, until the sun was high in the eastern sky. I was stifling yawns like crazy when at last Ky shoved us out the door so she could sleep through the day. I longed for my own bed and my white wolf curled up next to me.

"I'll pick you up tonight at eight," Ky called as we made our way down the front walk. "I can't wait!"

Though I was too tired to show it, I shared her enthusiasm. We didn't spend as much time together since I'd moved out, and I really missed her. As long as I knew Lena was still safe, I'd be able to let myself go and have a good time. Good times were becoming fewer and farther in between. A relaxing night out with the girls was just what I needed.

Chapter Nine

We started in a relatively nice lounge sipping cocktails. When it became evident that the place was full of older couples out for a quiet evening, we began to reconsider. It was a nice place to enjoy a drink, but we needed a venue with a rocking dance floor and sexy man-flesh wandering around. I didn't want to push Kylarai back into the dating scene, but she needed to see how much more was out there.

By the time we headed downtown to a trendy dance club, the place was packed with guys on the prowl. Pushing Kylarai into some silly human fling was not my intention. But if it happened, I sure wasn't going to discourage it.

"Seriously, Alexa?" Ky glanced around the busy club. "Everyone here looks like they're barely legal."

"What's wrong with that? We're here to have some fun. Go grab a drink. I'll stay sober and drive home." I gave her a gentle push toward the bar.

She turned those gentle eyes on me, and I could see the masked pain within them. It hurt me to see that. Maybe this wasn't the road to healing, but staying home buried in legal paperwork wouldn't help either.

"Come on, honey." Jez took Ky by the arm and pulled her along. "Let's go get a drink and hit the dance floor."

I followed Zoey when she pointed out an empty booth in the back. We were hit on twice by guys at the tables we passed. I knew a beauty like Ky would get the same attention. It was wasted on the rest of us; I wasn't interested, and neither Jez nor Zoey were into men. They weren't quite into each other either. I'd tried to play match maker, but ultimately, neither of them seemed interested.

"She's been crying. A lot." Zoey slid into the booth across from me and leaned close so I could hear her over the music. "It's been so hard not to hunt that fucker down and break his legs myself."

"I know. Shaz wants to kill him. Ky made him promise to stay out of it. But, I know if he runs into Julian, nothing will stop him."

"Good. Shaz should kill him. Julian is a waste of fucking space. He hasn't come around since it all went down. If he does though, I'm not holding back."

We fell silent when Jez and Kylarai approached with drinks in hand. Jez took the spot beside me. Damn. I'd still hoped she would have sat beside Zoey. I just wanted everyone to be happy. Was that so wrong?

Jez was quick to avoid an awkward moment by launching into one of her many stories of dating failure. She really did meet some of the weirdest chicks out there. When she got Kylarai laughing, I started to relax. I couldn't help but feel like it would be my fault if Ky had a shitty time out with us.

When a waitress passed by, Jez was quick to grab her and order a tray of shots. That was one way to kick off the evening. Once my companions started on those shots, the mood lightened considerably. We talked up a storm. Girl talk was the perfect remedy for male-inflicted woes. I could see Ky start to shake off the tension that had held her captive. After a few shots, she was visibly relaxed. Ok, so it wasn't the best medicine for a broken heart, but it was better than nothing.

Zoey wasn't much of a drinker. However, Jez and Ky had drunk enough for all of us by the time an hour had passed. Weres could safely hold a lot more liquor than humans. Still, Ky and Jez were giggling like drunken lunatics.

I was happy to sit there and let the massive amounts of human energy wash over me. I was so used to shutting it out, but now that I had better control, I was able to filter out any negativity and just enjoy the lively sensation of so much human energy packed into one place. If I focused, I could hear the sound of hundreds of hearts beating. The noise quickly became overwhelming, exceeding the fine line between enough and too much.

"Let's get this party started. It's time to shake your sweet bits, ladies." Jez tossed back another shot and got to her feet. "Come on. That means everyone."

I exchanged a look with Zoey who rolled her crystalline blue eyes. I shrugged and let Jez drag me out of the booth. Once she got going, there was no stopping her. It was a challenge just to keep up.

We made our way to the dance floor and were quickly intercepted by a group of guys looking for some female company. Jez wasn't so great at polite rejection, so I kept her moving, leaving Ky and Zoey to deal with the guys. I smiled to myself when Kylarai actually paused to talk to them. I knew it was too much to hope she'd take it further than that, but it was a nice start.

"So what do you think?" Jez leaned in close, casting a glance back at Ky. "Do you think she's starting to have fun?"

"It looks like it. I wish there was more I could do for her."

"You're doing all you can. Being there for her is the most important thing you can do right now. It will get better with time."

Would it? I thought about Raoul. He broke my heart years ago, and I felt like I would never truly be rid of the heartbreak. I think many people have that one person, the one they can never escape, regardless of time and distance. I prayed Julian wasn't Kylarai's. She deserved better than that.

Lost in thought, I forced myself to feel the rhythm of the music and dance with Jez. By the time Kylarai and Zoey joined us, I was fighting the ghosts of my past. Zoey made it that much harder. She was Raoul's daughter. She had killed him in front of me. Now, almost a year later, here we were, dancing and sharing concern for our friend. It was almost too screwed up to believe.

Seeing a genuine smile on Kylarai's face made it easy to forget about how fucked up my life was. Tonight was all about her. Everything was going great. At least it was, until a pushy guy decided he wanted to be part of our group, and he wasn't taking no for an answer.

It started when he approached Zoey. She quickly shot him down with little more than a look. Refusing to take a hint, he made a pathetic attempt to grind with her on the dance floor. She gave him a light shove and a warning glare. It did little to deter the drunken fool.

He laughed her off, as if she couldn't possibly be serious. I watched the scenario play out, ready to intervene if necessary.

"Look asshole, I'm not fucking interested. Got it?" Zoey went from calm to seething before I could blink. It alarmed me.

Her admirer appeared confused. The rest of us kept dancing as if we weren't paying attention, but clearly all three of us were taking note of everything. My biggest concern was Zoey throwing a punch and getting us tossed out. She wasn't a full Were. She was a hybrid. Still, she was stronger than the average human, and I knew she could lay this guy out cold. The woman was a damn murderer; this guy had chosen the wrong girl to harass.

"Come on now, baby. Don't be so uptight. It's all good. Let me show you what a real man can do for you." The idiot just didn't know when to give up.

I looked to Jez, half expecting her to get up in the guy's face; she was bad for that. Instead, she seemed to be on the same wavelength as me: avoiding conflict would be best tonight.

Jez motioned to the entry. "I know of a great place to dance a few blocks from here. Let's just take off."

It seemed to be the safest bet. It would be useless to interact with this guy any further. I didn't want that kind of trouble. Now if only trouble felt the same way about me.

We had almost reached Ky's Escalade when trouble caught up to us. This guy didn't seem to know his persistence had turned to obstinate ignorance.

"Give me one chance to rock your world," he slurred as he lumbered toward us.

"Is this guy for fucking real?" Jez laughed at the absurdity of it all.

I had a sick feeling in my gut. Zoey's energy was hot with rage. I fully expected her to verbally tear him a new one, so I was stunned when she lost it completely.

In a flash Zoey was on top of him. She knocked him to the ground and began to land blows that hurt me to watch. I hesitated for just a moment. When I saw that her eyes had gone wolf, and she snarled down at him with fangs, my heart almost stopped.

"Zoey, don't!" I grabbed her from behind. Without taking her eyes off her prey, she elbowed me hard enough to knock me on my ass. I gasped for air, winded by the blow.

"What the fuck?" The sight of fangs bared inches from his face had our drunken friend sounding stone cold sober and terrified.

Everything seemed to move in slow motion when Zoey bit into his throat. Kylarai gave a little shriek, and I began to panic. As a hybrid, Zoey's wolf was trapped inside her. If it got out, she'd be trapped in wolf form again. I'd freed her of it once, but I didn't know if I could do it again.

The scent of blood was strong and immediate. It hit me hard, teasing me even as I watched in horror. The guy on the ground gave a strangled cry that became a horrible gurgle as blood entered his windpipe. Oh God, this was not good.

Jez grabbed Zoey around the waist and threw her. She skidded across the pavement with an angry cry. Her victim was beyond help. He was bleeding out fast. The scent was tantalizing, stirring my hunger. The urge to taste him was almost impossible to resist. I had no real options left. I moved fast. Grabbing his head tightly, I closed my eyes so that I didn't have to watch as I snapped his neck.

"Oh my God!" Kylarai was clearly distressed. Her eyes were wide, and she trembled. "Oh my God! What just happened?"

I glanced around the parking lot. Nobody appeared to have heard the commotion. In downtown Edmonton, it likely hadn't been enough to draw the wrong attention. Regardless, we had to move the body before someone came along.

"We need to throw him in the back of your truck, Ky. We can't leave him here."

"Are you crazy? I'm not putting him in my truck."

Jez held out a hand to Kylarai for the keys. "We have to. Not for long. Just to avoid having anyone find him."

Zoey stood several yards away, watching us in silence. Blood stained her face and clothing. She didn't say a word, but when Jez pulled Ky's Escalade to a stop beside us, she moved quickly to grab the body.

I pulled out my cell phone and hit Kale's number without thinking. I didn't know what else to do. I watched as Kylarai paced back and forth beside the vehicle. *Come on, Kale. Pick up!* Kale's voice had never sounded so good.

"Please tell me you're not busy. I really need your help." I barely let him get a word out. "I'm at a club downtown with the girls. We've had a bit of an accident."

"What kind of accident? Where are you?" The noise in the background indicated that he was at The Wicked Kiss.

"I have a body here that I need to get rid of. You were the first person I thought to call. We're at a place called Dominoes."

"Alright. I'm on my way."

I hung up and took a long look at the situation. Kylarai was swearing at random to nobody in particular. Zoey was silently staring at the bloody spot on the concrete, and Jez was looking at me expectantly. We had a body stuffed in Ky's truck and a vampire on his way to get rid of it. So much for a normal night out with the girls.

ഇരുഇരു

The four of us were quiet. There wasn't much to be said. Zoey had shown me what a liability she was. It had taken very little to make her snap. She was high-strung and dangerous. I knew this already, though. She'd murdered countless people, one being her father. I was conflicted as I stood near the Escalade waiting for Kale.

Not so long ago, I had wanted nothing more than to kill Zoey Roberts. Nobody would let me, not even Shaz. I'd claimed her as my own pack mate out of obligation, hoping for the best. As I stood there questioning that decision, I knew I was being a hypocrite. A killer was a killer, and I was one, too. Hell, I got paid for it.

I recognized the sound of Kale's '73 Camaro before I saw it pull into the parking lot. Good. The sooner this night of fucked up insanity ended, the better.

It didn't occur to me that things could be more awkward until Kale got out of his car. He and Kylarai had dated for a few months before she'd paired up with Julian. They had developed a genuine affection for one another, but Ky didn't want any part of the vampire world. They'd quickly called it quits. Ky didn't know about the strange dynamic that had developed between Kale and me, and I preferred to keep it that way.

"Hello ladies." Kale nodded to the others as he approached me. His gaze lingered on Kylarai who stood at the opposite end of the Escalade.

She took a few steps toward us but stopped as if uncertain. "Hi, Kale. It's nice to see you again."

"It's nice to see you, too. You're looking beautiful, as always." The smile he gave her was endearing. I was relieved to see that he wasn't all vamped out tonight. I should have confirmed that before calling him over here.

"Thank you." Kylarai blushed slightly and ran a hand through her hair in a nervous gesture.

Uncomfortable didn't even begin to describe how I felt. I waited while they exchanged pleasantries, doing my best not to let my discomfort show on my face.

Jez was completely unfazed by everything. In fact, she seemed bored with it all. "Where were you tonight, Kale? We didn't drag you away from anything good, did we?"

"Nothing good enough to make me pass up the opportunity to assist four lovely ladies."

"Oh, please. Your charm is wasted on us. Might as well save it." She gave him a playful smack and pointed to the back of the Escalade. "Our friend is in there. What do you think?"

Kale peered into the truck and immediately looked at me as if he assumed that I'd done it. I shook my head and frowned.

"I'm sorry. You were the first person I thought to call." I shrugged and tried to look apologetic instead of offended. "Things got out of hand here. It happened so fast."

"Don't apologize. I'm glad you called. You know I don't mind." The look he gave me revealed the fire lurking in the depths of his eyes. I tore my gaze away, hoping nobody else sensed the sudden increase in my heart rate. He pressed his car keys into my hand, and I jerked back as if his touch had burned. "Take my car and go to The Wicked Kiss. I'll deal with this and meet you there."

"Really? You're leaving me with your baby? What did I do to earn that kind of trust? Never mind. Don't answer that. I'll try not to get involved in any street races I'm not sure I can win." I winked and gave him a teasing smile.

"I'm going to assume you're joking. And if you're not, I don't want to know about it." With a grin, Kale accepted Ky's keys from Jez and climbed into the driver's seat of the Escalade.

The four of us piled into Kale's car. The scent of leather and a cherry air freshener was faint but pleasant. The scent of blood clung to Zoey, and I had to open the window. I readjusted the seat and mirrors, catching a glimpse of Kylarai's wide-eyed expression in the backseat.

"We're going to The Wicked Kiss?" She didn't sound happy. "Haven't we had enough trouble for one night?"

I wouldn't worry about Kylarai in a place like The Kiss. I knew she could hold her own without losing her mind. I didn't want to take Zoey in there.

"Maybe we can just wait for Kale in the parking lot." I made the suggestion, thinking it would be the safest plan.

"Well if we're going there anyway, we might as well go in." Jez was too busy checking her makeup in her compact mirror to see the dirty look I shot her.

Zoey seemed to know what I was thinking. She spoke up from the backseat, her voice low. "I'm sorry about all this. I fucking blew it tonight. I don't know why I lost it like that."

Well, I sure did. *Because you're the lunatic hybrid daughter of a man with questionable genes.* I kept my mouth shut and thanked God that Zoey couldn't read minds.

"It's happened to every one of us at some point." Jez turned in her seat to give Zoey a reassuring smile, and I cringed. Why was she encouraging this?

Keeping my mouth shut was evidently the best thing I could do right then. I drove to The Wicked Kiss with mounting dread. I didn't mean to be negative, but experience had taught me that a night like this wasn't bound to get any better.

"Let's just go inside, sit and wait for Kale. It will be fine, Ky. I promise." Who was I to make a stupid promise like that? Kale shouldn't be long. As soon as he got to the club, I was going home.

"Yeah, it'll be fine," Jez chimed in. "Just be prepared to chase off several vamps offering you money for a little nip."

"Are you serious?" Kylarai's voice rose in pitch. "They'll pay you for it?"

"Sometimes. They'll do a lot of things. Of course, some people don't care about the money. They'll give it up for free because they get off on the rush." Jez shrugged like it was no big deal.

Kylarai made a sound of disgust. Her opinion didn't change any when we arrived. I was nervous about taking Zoey in there. Not only was she unpredictable, she stank like blood. Despite a wet wipe from Jez, she would still be a vampire magnet.

Shawn was working the lobby. He greeted me with the usual smile and 'hello' before his gaze fell on Zoey. I knew it. As if four Weres in a vampire bar wasn't bad enough, she was going to draw too much attention. *Hurry up, Kale.*

I led the way to the dark corner behind the bar. Only one other table nearby was occupied. I didn't know whether to scream in frustration or laugh with maniacal exasperation when I noticed the vampiress there openly feeding from the wrist of her male companion. Blood, public feeding and a senseless murder so far for the night. What next? A drunken dance floor sex orgy?

"Oh my." Kylarai looked at the couple quickly before averting her gaze. If that was too much for her, she'd never be able to handle what really went on here. It wasn't her world. I resented in many ways that it was mine, but I accepted it.

"This place looks like a riot." The spark of mischief in Zoey's eyes was alarming. Curiosity adorned her fine features as she surveyed the surroundings.

I glanced at my phone to check the time. How long did it take to dispose of a body? Too many things could happen here. Anxiety nagged me as I waited for something else to go wrong.

"Alexa?" A hand on my arm drew my attention to Jez. "Who's the trashy broad hanging all over your man?"

"What?" I followed her gaze, expecting to find Arys with a blood whore again. A shock of platinum hair revealed otherwise.

Shaz was standing in a crowd near the dance floor. A tall, raven haired vampiress was draped all over him. With an arm hooked around his neck, she leaned in close as if whispering in his ear. Her actions weren't casual or friendly. From where I stood, her intentions were pretty clear.

Adrenaline hit me so hard it took my breath away. I was shocked. I was also dumbfounded with jealousy. My body temperature spiked with my pounding pulse, and I felt faint. What the fuck?

"I don't know who that is." I tripped over my tongue as I tried to form words. "I mean, I recognize her from around here, but I don't know who she is personally. And, I don't know why she's so touchy-feely with Shaz." I knew that I didn't friggin' like it though.

"Well if I were you, I'd be doing some finding out. And, I wouldn't be nice about it." Jez was just speaking her mind, like always, but I don't think she knew what an influence she was sometimes.

I wasn't going to go raging over there like an irrational idiot. At least I wasn't until I watched the tramp trail her hand down Shaz' back to his jean-clad behind.

Ky's hand on my wrist stopped me in my tracks. "Wait! Give him a chance."

Like the gentleman that I knew him to be, Shaz grabbed her hand and stopped her mid-motion. He shook his head. I could see his lips moving. She looked amused. Maybe he felt the weight of my stare or perhaps he had caught my scent, but he turned abruptly, meeting my eyes. With barely a word to the vampiress, Shaz made his way through the crowd toward me. She was unaffected. Like any vampire, she simply moved on to another potential playmate.

I took a deep breath, trying to calm my pounding heart. The territorial urge to cut that bitch's head off was tough to combat. My wolf raged at the thought of another woman all over my mate. I stopped and considered how much stronger Shaz must be than I am, to put up with Arys.

"I thought you ladies were going out dancing." Shaz took my hand and gave it a gentle squeeze. "What brings you all here?"

"Didn't expect me, huh?" I nodded in the general direction he'd just come from. "I can see that."

"What? No. It's not like that, Lex. She's a vampire looking for some action. You know how they are. I told her I wasn't interested." Lifting my chin with a soft touch, he kissed me lightly. "Would you have thought the same thing if that had been a male vampire? Because you know those bastards are just as bad."

I fought back the urge to pout openly. "Don't tell me you don't like the attention."

He laughed and ran a hand through his perfect hair. "Of course I do. I'm a hot-blooded man. I'm not dead." He grinned and kissed me again.

I changed the subject entirely. I was embarrassed by my reaction. "Actually, we're meeting Kale here. He's cleaning up a little mishap for us. Zoey killed a man outside a dance club. I panicked and called Kale."

Shaz frowned and glanced at Zoey. I could see him thinking something similar to what I had. She was a loose cannon. "You're sure nobody saw anything?"

I nodded and sighed. I was ready for the night to end. "Pretty sure. As soon as Kale gets back here with Ky's truck, I think I'm heading home."

"Want me to come with you?"

I inclined my head toward the feeding vampire at the next table. "I'll be fine. Someone has to make sure there isn't too much of that going on. You know, I'm starting to consider selling this place to Starbucks or something."

"I doubt that would change a damn thing." Shaz chuckled and pulled me in for a warm hug. I sank into his embrace, wishing I could block out the sights, sounds and smells of my environment.

He was probably right. This place was never going to be anything but a vampire den of sex and blood. Thinking I could change it had been ridiculous. At this point I felt like I was merely trying to survive it. That belief was confirmed when a scream rang out and a loud crash followed. I scowled and closed my eyes, counting backwards from ten.

"That's my cue. Come say goodbye before you leave." Shaz was gone, a blur of blond hair and black attire.

"Is it always like this?" Kylarai was incredulous. "How do you put up with it? It's so … skeevy."

"It really is," Jez chimed in. "If you're not here for fangs or fucking, then it really has little to offer."

It shouldn't have surprised me when Zoey shrugged and said, "It doesn't seem so bad to me."

If she thought for one minute that she was going to delve deeper into the strange world of The Wicked Kiss, she had another thing coming. That would be enough for me to break out the ass-kicking all over her.

"Well, as long as I'm here I'm going to check this place out." Zoey abandoned her chair and perused the crowd eagerly.

I opened my mouth to argue when Jez fell into step beside her. She waved off my protest. "I'll go with her. It's all good."

As I watched the two of them disappear into the mass of

people, I officially gave up. Fuck it. Zoey was a grown woman. If she wanted to play with vampires, who was I to stop her? However, the next time she lost her mind and slaughtered someone, I wasn't doing a damn thing to help her.

I took a seat at the table with Kylarai and focused on conversation with her rather than the circus going on around us. I could only imagine what she was thinking. By the time Kale arrived about twenty minutes later, I'd worked myself into a nice frenzy. I couldn't recall ever being so ecstatic to see him.

He too was accosted by women as he passed through the throngs of humans trotting back and forth to the bar. The difference was that his women were human. Kylarai watched the blood whores with their bitten necks and barely-there outfits, and I could see her grow cold. I don't think she ever realized what Kale was really up to when he was here. Now she was seeing it with her own eyes, and I felt like she was judging all of us. She definitely didn't need to know he was killing again.

After shaking off more than a few admirers, Kale reached our table. My, wasn't he a popular choice among the ladies? I flushed hot at the memory of his bite; I knew one reason why they liked him so much.

He hesitated before taking a seat next to me. I had to quell the instinctive urge to lean away from him.

Placing Ky's car keys in the center of the table, he greeted us both with a smile. "No worries. It's dealt with. But, there is an ugly bloodstain on the floor in the back that's going to need new carpet."

"I guess Zoey can pay for that." Ky's voice was laced with bitterness. "But thank you, Kale. It was nice of you to help."

"I owe you one," I added, flashing him a look that I hoped portrayed my gratitude.

"I'll put it on your tab." With a wink, he nudged me playfully. "Now give me the keys to my baby. I trust you took good care of her."

I had to laugh because I knew him too well. "I'd bet a thousand dollars you examined every inch of her before you even came in here."

"You'll never know for certain."

I passed him the keys quickly, trying to avoid having our hands touch. It didn't work. His fingers grazed mine, and I gasped as his power called to me. His slightest touch had awakened my hunger for him. Sitting there with Kylarai made it hard to deny how right she'd been when she'd told me that I was as power-hungry as any vampire.

I jerked my hand back and busied myself by checking the missed calls on my phone. One from Veryl. No big deal. He could wait. When I looked up again, Kylarai was watching us intently.

Kale stood up, looking flustered. "I'm going to take off. I have something to take care of before sunrise." Kale turned to Kylarai, forcing a smile though he had to feel the tension. "Goodnight, Kylarai. I hope the rest of your night is better."

I was relieved when he bailed out of the club incredibly fast. Before my nerves could settle, Kylarai fixed me with a pensive look and tapped her nails on the table top.

"So, what's going on with you and Kale?"

My heart plummeted like a stone to my stomach. "Nothing. Why do you ask?"

She didn't believe me. "You're all twitchy around him. Like you used to get with Arys before you could admit you were attracted to him. I'm not a vampire, and even I can sense the energy running high between you two. Are you sleeping with him?"

"No!" That was a little too forceful. "No. I'm not. He's my friend. We work together."

Her gaze dropped to the table, and she pursed her lips. "But, you want him. Don't you?"

My mouth went dry, and I struggled to swallow. I didn't know how to answer that without telling a lie. I wouldn't sit there and lie to my best friend. I was many things, some of them pretty awful, but a liar was not one of them.

"Sometimes," I heard myself say. "But it's complicated, Ky. It's bigger than physical attraction. It's deeper than that."

"Power stuff, right?" She looked skeptical.

"Yeah. Something like that." I couldn't make her understand something I had yet to understand.

"It's ok, Alexa. I'm not mad. I just wanted to know. It's not like he and I were a serious item anyway. You're part of his world. I'm not. And honestly, I'm glad for that." She gave the interior of the club a once over before grimacing. "Really glad."

Chapter Ten

I was so lost in myself that it was hard to feel anything but numb. Fear had given way to readiness. I just wanted to get this over with.

My knuckles were white as I gripped the steering wheel. The car wasn't even moving. Arys watched me from the passenger seat, and I could almost hear him wondering how precarious my control was. I needed to remain calm and do whatever it took to keep Lena safe.

After a lengthy argument, Jez and Kale had decided that he would stake out Lena's apartment, and she would join Shaz, Arys and me. Shaz sat in the back with her, the two of them silently watching anyone and everyone who went in or out of the restaurant and lounge that marked the address we were given.

"Ready?" I asked, receiving silent head nods in response. The clock on the dash read five minutes until midnight. Taking a deep breath, I shoved my door open and prepared to face the scum that could threaten someone as innocent and sweet as Lena.

The breeze caught my hair, tossing it in my face. I was dressed for a fight, in jeans and a tank top. I didn't have any weapons other than my own personal arsenal. I felt naked without a little something extra, like a good sturdy stake for a security blanket.

My senses were blazing, running on high alert. I could feel them inside: two vampires. I had a feeling there were more than that. I thought of Kale, alone at Lena's. I worried that we'd left him outnumbered.

At such a late hour, the restaurant was near empty. The real party was happening in the attached lounge. Occupying one large table at the far end of the restaurant were our two vampires. Neither of them were what I'd been expecting.

They sat together facing us, on one side of the table, a man and woman. He was middle-aged in appearance but felt like he'd been a vampire for a very long time. Long, straight dark hair and dark eyes, he was formally dressed. He regarded us with a cool, calculating expression that filled me with ice-cold trepidation.

The woman at his side was tall and thin, a model's body. Her auburn hair was piled on her head and pinned with several gold clips. Her brown eyes fell upon me like I was the main course at a feast. Her off-kilter gaze reminded me of the vacant stare of a serial killer, the look of one truly unstable.

She merely gave me a passing look, though; Arys held her attention. The way she looked him over before licking her lips told me enough. I didn't get the feeling this was their first meeting.

"Arys Knight ... how long has it been? I remember like it was yesterday." She turned a smug smile on the rest of us, but her gaze was locked on Arys.

"Not nearly long enough, Claire. Don't waste time with phony chit-chat. What the hell are you doing in my city?" Arys' tone dripped venom, and when he refused to take a seat, I followed his lead.

"Come now." Claire gestured to the chairs across from her. "We can sit and discuss this rationally, can't we? The faster you cooperate, the faster we can be on our way."

The fury flowing from Arys was palpable. Gripping the back of the chair in front of him, he squeezed so hard that the metal groaned. "Start talking or we walk."

The grin faded from Claire's face, and she became stone. "And, kill your human friend so fast? As much fun as I recall you were to play with Arys, this is business. Don't disrespect me."

Jez and Shaz shadowed Arys and I. They remained quiet, but I felt their tension. They were ready for anything. I wasn't sure what to expect. The vibes I got from the two vampires made my skin crawl.

"Then get to the fucking point." Arys glared down at her with such hate in his eyes. "If you don't want to play, start talking."

Claire's brilliant smile was suddenly pasted back in place. She was genuinely enjoying this whole ordeal. "You let your dog kill

Harley. That put a little damper on business. A blood ring doesn't operate quite so smoothly when one of its founding members and suppliers is suddenly murdered. Maxwell and I are here to give you the chance to make things right."

Did that bitch call me a dog? Or did she mean Shaz? It didn't matter. We'd both killed Harley, and this skank was going to shit talk us like we were common animals. I bristled as anger flooded me.

"What do you expect me to do about it?" Arys was flippant. "Harley's business is none of mine. I want nothing to do with it."

Maxwell was especially quiet. A tiny smile pulled at his thin lips. Something about him just wasn't right. He hadn't done a thing or exerted any power, but I was sure he was the real threat of the two of them. My discomfort grew as a sick sensation crept through me.

"Arys, honey. We just want what's rightfully ours. You'd want the same, would you not?"

"Money?" I asked, struggling not to address the dog comment.

Claire looked at me like I was a child asking a stupid question. "Money is useless to us. We want only one thing." She paused for dramatic effect, and it took all my strength not to roll my eyes at her. Looking from me to Arys, she looked far too happy. "Harley's killers, of course."

Arys laughed bitterly. "Come on, Claire. Be realistic."

"Oh, but I am." She peered at him, wide-eyed and sickly sweet. Leaning in close to Maxwell, she pressed her lips to his cheek and purred, "Isn't that right, baby?"

"Wait," Shaz spoke up, a growl lacing his words. "This is some vengeance scheme because of a dirtbag like Harley? You'd threaten an innocent life over that?"

Claire let her gaze wander over Shaz, but she dismissed him almost instantly. Her eyes found Jez, the only naturally born shifter among us. "Give us the leopard instead, and we'll consider it a fair trade."

I was all fangs. The bitch was crossing the line already. I felt Arys' touch, light on my mind. He wanted me to stay calm. I was trying. Instinct told me that these two were far more dangerous than they appeared. The more of my friends that they threatened, the greater my need to fight back.

Arys leaned down over the table, getting in Claire's personal space. "The leopard is not a bargaining chip. You know damn well that I won't hand my wolves over to you. So get the hell out of my city."

Claire leaned forward on the table, her face a mask of malevolence. "You have something, and I want it."

"Why? Because of Harley? Is this really just business? Because I know there are many people who would love to fill his role. I know you Claire, you'll take any opportunity to buy your way to the top."

She met Arys' challenging glare with one equally furious. "It's a good thing you're pretty, Arys, because love has turned you into an idiot."

The tension in the room became unbearable. It was stifling, making each breath a struggle. I couldn't shake the feeling that somebody was going to snap soon, quite possibly me.

Arys nodded knowingly. "This is about Harley's power in Vegas. You think handing his killers over to the rest of the blood ring will work in your favor. The two of you aren't fit to fill his shoes. You're delusional to think that will work."

Claire laughed openly at Arys, and I felt uneasy. This wasn't going well at all. Something inside me insisted that this was all wrong. Why would these two leave Lena unwatched if she was the only pull they had over us? Even if they had someone else watching her, it just didn't make sense. She was their leverage. Why not bring her? Something wasn't adding up.

"Arys, you have no power here. Our intent is none of your concern." Maxwell spoke for the first time, drawing everyone's attention to him. His voice was low and even, holding the same sense of mystery as the rest of him. He was packing serious power. It scared me.

Maxwell seemed to stare right through Arys. His pupils dilated ever so slightly, and he flashed fang when he spoke. "You seem to be under the assumption that you have room to negotiate. We're not here to bargain, merely to state the terms. Hand over the wolves." To me he said, "Give yourself up willingly, and we don't kill the people you care about."

I couldn't speak. I could barely breathe. This wasn't what I'd expected to hear.

Claire looked spitefully at Arys, but she gestured to me. "Be grateful we're only demanding something you already have in your possession. We could have come demanding virgins and children. You remember how much I like virgins."

A twisted grin crossed her face. With one brow raised, she smirked at Arys. A sudden flash of images moved behind my eyes like a strobe light as Arys' memories swam up from my subconscious. I was battered with visuals of his past, the torturous virgin deaths Claire spoke of. The two of them together ... and so much blood. I fought back a shriek, one hand going to my head. It disappeared as fast as it had come on, leaving me shaky and confused. For a moment I thought I might be sick.

Jez' hand was warm against my back as she steadied me. Claire chuckled wickedly, but Maxwell just watched me in eerie silence.

If Arys was aware of what I'd just seen, he gave no indication. "Go back to Vegas and earn your place, you worthless pieces of shit."

"I was hoping you'd say something like that." Maxwell stood, and power rose up quickly to engulf us.

I was on my knees before I realized what was happening. A shrill, high-pitched sound pierced my skull, and I screamed as pain tore through me. Arys was on the floor next to me.

Shaz grabbed my arm and pulled me to my feet, but I slumped against him. He was unharmed by Maxwell's psychic attack. It had been meant for Arys and me. Jez was by the exit, looking out onto the street. Claire and Maxwell were gone. The searing pain in my head began to subside, but still I gasped for breath like I'd been kicked in the stomach.

Shaz did his best to brush off the waitstaff as they converged on us. Shoving me toward Jez, he hauled Arys to his feet and pushed us all out the door. I tried so hard to get the words out, but they wouldn't come. *Lena. God, no.*

"Are you alright, Alexa?" Jez forced me to look at her as she dragged me along to the car.

I shook my head. It felt like I'd been scorched from the inside out. I coughed, and my lungs ached when I spat blood. Collapsing in the back seat of my car, I was joined by Arys while Shaz and Jez climbed in the front. I handed the keys over the seat to Shaz, though it took far more effort than it should have.

"Lena's," I gasped. "We have to go to Lena's." She and Kale

were in trouble. I knew it. It was too late; we'd fucked up.

"What the hell happened?" Shaz was in Alpha wolf mode. He spoke calmly, but the way he maneuvered the Charger into traffic revealed the urgency driving him. "What did he do to you two?"

Arys sat up in his seat, his hands on his head. Blood trickled from his nose, evidence that he'd taken a serious power hit. "Power push. He shoved more into us than we could channel. Forced overload."

"Did you know he could do that? I mean, why would you walk into that?" Jez glanced back at us, her face a mask of worry.

Arys and I exchanged a glance. Of course he'd known Maxwell could do it. I could do it, too. I'd done it to Harley.

"Not everyone can do what he did." Arys offered nothing else in the way of explanation.

Adrenaline did little to ease the pain. Even as the initial blast slowly faded, the burning sensation remained. I grabbed the tissue box from the back window, taking a few and passing the rest to Arys. Another painful cough brought up more blood, and I groaned in agony.

"This is not looking good." Jez eyed me uncertainly, but I waved a hand dismissively.

"I'll be fine. It's Lena we need to worry about."

"She's as good as dead." Self-blame shone in Arys' eyes. "I should have done something, tried to bargain somehow."

"How? By handing Alexa and Shaz over to be used in a blood ring?" Jez shook her head and swore when Shaz cut off another driver. "They never gave you room to compromise."

Shaz sped through an amber light seconds before it turned red. Under any other circumstance, I would have had a fit over the way he drove my car. With Lena's life on the line, I didn't give a damn as long as he got us there.

Arys slumped against the door and stared out the window. "They demanded something they knew I wouldn't provide. This was their intent all along. Lena was just a pawn to them, a way to make us show up."

"What were we supposed to do? They would've taken Jez as a peace-offering. How fucked is that?" The sound of my own voice made my head throb.

"Julian." Shaz' voice was low, but I heard him clearly. "We

should have arranged to give them Julian."

"I can't believe you just said that." I stared at him in horror. "When did you become so ruthless?"

Shaz met my gaze in the rearview mirror. The ice in his jade eyes scared me. "About five minutes ago, when I watched my mate take a hit that dropped her like a corpse. I'd gladly hand Julian over if that's what it took to make this situation go away."

"You heard them," Arys interjected. "They won't be happy with one inferior werewolf. They want something valuable enough to buy their way into a position of power."

An exasperated sigh came from Jez. "Yep, woke up this evening and asked myself, what's missing from my life? Oh, I know, a run-in with vampires that would love to use me as part of their blood fetish games. Now my life is complete."

The rest of the drive to Lena's was suffered in strained silence. I tried to focus on pulling natural energy into me. From the breeze through my open window to the tree-filled park we passed, it wasn't enough. The moon was washed out by the city. It offered me nothing.

Arys reached across the seat to take my hand. The power of the undead washed over me, and I fell back against the seat with relief.

Power like ours had a few drawbacks, including my mortal body; Arys was able to take more than I could. I was grateful that even as he recovered from the attack, he was able to breathe that healing energy into me.

My apprehension grew when we turned on to Lena's street. No amount of preparation would be enough for what we were about to see.

"Nobody's here," Arys announced as we turned into the parking lot. "They were though."

Kale's car sat in the visitor parking. I almost fell out of the car in my haste. On unsteady legs, I ran as fast as my weakened body would carry me to the lobby door.

It was open, the lock broken. I abandoned the notion of using the elevator and took the stairs two at a time. Shaz and Jez easily overtook me, and I was forced to accept how badly I'd been injured. When Arys and I reached Lena's suite, Shaz was standing in the doorway. I could hear Jez inside, her voice high and panicked.

The look on Shaz' face said it all. "It's bad, Lex."

Though I'd expected that, his confirmation made my heart sink. I had to see for myself. The air inside the small apartment was stuffy and smelled of blood and death. Immediately, the harsh negativity of the energy inside crawled along my flesh as if seeking a way in. It hurt and my shield was weak against it. I was raw in places that had no physical location. The pain echoed like a scream inside my mind.

Rounding the corner from the kitchen to the living room, I jerked to a halt when I took in the scene before me. Kale was on his knees on the floor, his head in his hands. Jez knelt beside him, but her emerald eyes were transfixed on Lena's crumpled form across the room.

She was dead. They'd torn her throat out after slowly bleeding her from every limb. It hadn't been a quick death or even a recent one. She'd clearly been dead for a day already, long before tonight. A pool of old, black blood stained the carpet beneath her. Her limbs were bound. A gag in her mouth had muffled her screams. Her eyes were wide open, frozen in terror.

I thought back to all the times I'd come here for guidance or a visit while she forced tea and baked goods on me. How could I have let this happen?

Tears stung my eyes, crimson drops that blurred my vision. "I shouldn't have left her alone. I should have been here."

"Lex, this isn't your fault." Shaz spoke softly.

I shook my head, unable to speak. I never would have guessed that killing Harley would lead to this. It wasn't fair. Lena had nothing to do with any of it. She was innocent, endangered by association with me. That knowledge weighed heavily, like the weight of the world on my shoulders.

"They pulled one over on you. They killed her long before tonight." Kale looked up at me with pain etched in the depths of his eyes. "One of us should have been here. I should have known."

He looked at Lena's still form, and I saw my own self-blame reflected in his gaze. Kale thought this was his fault. He was wrong.

"We didn't know." I was afraid to speak too loud. The faded essence of witch power lingered in the atmosphere, as if she should still be here.

We could do nothing more. I stared into the living room for a long time, wishing I could do something. I couldn't even close her eyes or cover her up; it was best to touch nothing.

Only my loved ones presence kept me standing. I wanted to sink to my knees beside Lena and sob like a little girl. I felt like a worm on a hook. Sooner or later, we would have another confrontation with Maxwell and Claire. How many more people were going to die because of my actions?

Jez pulled Kale to his feet. Misery clung to him, bitter in its intensity. I didn't want to leave. It felt like I was abandoning Lena, leaving her there alone. I had no choice.

When everyone had left the apartment, I used a dish towel to pick up the phone and punch in 911. The operator's voice came on the line, asking what the emergency was. It wouldn't take them long to dispatch when no response came. I left without looking back. Burying the pain deep inside, I concentrated on what I was going to do to Maxwell and his crew when I got the chance.

"The cops are on their way," I announced when I joined them in the lobby. "We should head back to The Kiss for now."

"I'll go with Kale," Jez swiped a hand through her tears.

Arys was unusually quiet during the ride back to The Wicked Kiss. The vampire that never apologized for his actions was sitting in silence, lost in regret. I stared out the passenger window, watching in the side mirror as Kale's black car navigated the city streets behind us, until a changing light left the others behind.

It ate at me, the knowledge that Lena had been dead before I'd ever laid eyes on Maxwell and Claire. It made me sick. "We can't let them get away with this, Arys. They have to suffer for what they did to Lena."

His voice was low and menacing. "They'll be kissing sunrise when we're done with them."

ଵଵଵଵଵ

Sunrise was quickly approaching. I stood behind the bar, a bottle of whiskey raised to my lips. It did nothing to fill the hole I felt inside.

The club was empty. Last call had been an hour ago. It had taken me that long to convince Jez, Shaz and Arys to go home after Kale disappeared into the night. I wasn't ready to leave yet.

I was in a dangerous frame of mind. I didn't want to think or feel. I just wanted to be numb. The blood hunger carving out my insides promised relief if I would just give in. My weakened state made me an easy target, and I felt myself slipping.

Just let go. The thought whispered through me. I had no strength to resist, not after what Maxwell had done to me. On every level, I was defeated. The emotional distress of Lena's death lurked behind the wall I'd built around it. It too would crash down and swallow me.

I don't remember abandoning the liquor or leaving the bar. I moved automatically, following the deep-rooted vampire instinct that guided me to the back hall. Like every time the bloodlust took hold, I became a rabid mess, moving and acting but not thinking.

I spun in a slow circle, feeling the energy in each of the occupied rooms. A noise drew me down the hall, the sound of a vampire and his blood whore lost in the throes of sexual gratification. Their heady tantric energy was sweet like candy as it rolled over me. A smile tugged at my lips.

The door exploded off its hinges as I entered. Everything moved in choppy scenes, like it all happened too fast for me to follow. Blood was a thick, seductive aroma in the room. Ravenous and wild, I was on them before they could react.

Dragging the vampire off his partner, I flung him aside. Without glancing his way, I held out a hand and drew the energy from him. With the other hand, I grabbed his human lover around the throat and pulled her close. She stank like prey, having been bitten previously. I tore into her viciously so that flesh tore and blood sprayed. She never even got a scream out first.

The vampire tried to fight me off, but it was too late. I had a strong hold on him, and I pulled hard on it. As I sucked him dry of his power, I delighted in the hot crimson fount that ran over my tongue. Blood and power poured into me, and I fell into a state of euphoria. Nothing felt like this.

Letting go and giving in to the bloodlust released me from the chains I'd inflicted upon myself. I drank down the scarlet nectar, delighting in the way it scratched the eternal itch inside me. The rush of blood and power, dancing together around and within me, was thrilling and more importantly, comforting.

It wasn't borrowed hunger anymore. I needed this. As much as I tried to deny that, to escape it, in that moment it was painfully and irrefutably clear. I wanted to savor the magic of falling headlong into the abyss of dark bliss, to feel like this always, free of pain, spiritual and physical ... free from the emotional agony of Lena's blood on my hands. None of that existed as long as that warm human blood passed my lips.

The vampire fell to the floor, drained of everything he had to give. His body burst into dust before it hit the carpet. My victim's heart had slowed, beating its last. I was breathless and exhilarated when I let her drop to the bed.

There was a lot of blood. Such a waste. My fangs had torn a gaping wound in her throat, causing blood to spray and splatter. I licked a smear off the back of my hand and surveyed the mess. I was detached, unable to feel anything about it other than mild acceptance. It was what it was. I stared around at the mess I'd made, and I was at peace.

Drunk on blood and power, I lost my balance and fell on my ass beside the bed. I giggled like a lunatic as I scrambled to my feet. I was on sensory overload, keenly aware of everything. The lights in the hall hummed with an irritating high-pitched squeal. Anxiety rolled off the other vampires in the building as they wondered if I'd come for them next. The scarce traffic far beyond the back exit sounded much too close and far too loud.

I was a disaster. I crashed into the wall on my way out of the room, catching myself before I went down again. Draining a human and a vampire simultaneously had overdosed me. Though I laughed to myself like it was the world's best joke, I was going to have to come down sometime and face reality. But not yet.

I returned to the bar, stopping to stare at the dark, empty interior. It felt so much bigger without the throngs of people littering every square foot. The remnants of their energy still hung on the air, though it was faint now. Catching a glimpse of my reflection in the mirror behind the bar, my jaw dropped.

I was all fangs and bright blue eyes. Arys' eyes. The spatters of blood that decorated my face and hair were deep scarlet in the dim lighting. I was drawn closer to my image, as horrified by what I saw as I was intrigued. I couldn't keep seeing myself like this.

Nothing human remained behind my eyes. The wicked light that glinted in my unnatural orbs was pure predator. Both the wolf and the vampire were present together, something I didn't like to see. It scared me, usually. Intoxicated laughter spilled from me, and I turned away from the mirror before it could become manic sobs. My emotions were all over the place, several hitting me at once.

With the damp bar towel I gave my face a halfhearted wipe. The scent of human blood clung to me. I felt Kale enter the building, and I jerked into action, frantically scrubbing at my face as if it would remove the evidence of what I'd done, but when I pictured him finding the mess I'd left in the back hall, I smiled.

I felt him, every step he took leading him closer to me. Stepping out from behind the bar, I waited for him. Temptation called as his honey sweet energy rolled over me. Kale was a hunger that had never been sated.

He appeared in the doorway, a strange look on his face. "Alexa?"

"That'd be me." I stood there, adorned in the blood of my victim, and I met his gaze evenly. "What are you doing here, Kale?"

"I was going to crash here for the day. Looks like you've been busy. Are you ok?" The concern etched on his face was shadowed by the lust in his eyes. Finding my kill had turned him on, I could feel it.

"Lena's dead. It's my fault." I felt detached from my words and even from myself. "I kill for demons and was naive enough not to know that. I handle the bloodlust like a junkie, and I like it. I am not ok."

He quickly crossed the space between us. Placing a finger beneath my chin, he forced me to meet his eyes. Our auras touched, and I trembled. Kale searched my eyes for something, I wasn't sure what. Sanity perhaps.

"What happened to Lena is not your fault. Don't you dare try to take the blame for this one. Nobody could have stopped this from happening." Pain filled his eyes, and I knew he was hurting, too. We'd both loved her.

I swallowed hard. "It's because of me that they targeted her in the first place. Because Shaz and I killed Harley."

"I know." He stroked a hand down my cheek, pausing to wipe a streak of blood away. "Alexa, you can't bury yourself in guilt. There was nothing else you could do."

I wasn't alone in my personal agony. Kale felt it, too. I refused the tears that stung my eyes. "You don't really believe that. Do you?"

"Yes, I do."

His nearness was teasing my senses, inviting me to wrap that saccharine power of his around me. I pulled away, tearing my gaze from his. I'd swung from giddy drunk to moody sorrow in seconds. I was conflicted by how easily his presence had affected me. What was it about Kale that always broke down my defenses, exposing the raw emotion buried deep inside?

The silence was deafening. All I could focus on was Kale. I wanted to feast upon him as I had with my two victims, but my hunger for him wasn't the same. Whatever it was we shared, it was always there, and I knew I'd never be free of it. Not as long as I tried to fight it. I was just so tired of fighting, but I knew that giving in had never proven to be the better alternative.

"I'm not sure I can do this, Kale. Claire and Maxwell have the drop on us, and they know it. If I don't give them what they want, they'll target somebody else. I don't feel like I have a choice."

"You can't just hand yourself over to them." With a shake of his dark head, Kale gave me a lingering look. "I wish we could turn back time and redo tonight. I really do. But, what happened does not give them power over you. Only you can give that. Don't."

"I wish it was that simple." My guilt convinced me that the situation was hopeless. "I don't know where to begin to deal with this. I just don't want to see anyone else I love get hurt."

Kale's heady energy was strong and pulsing. It reached out to me, and I shuddered. He watched me with intrigue in his eyes.

"You can kill them, and you will. I don't doubt it for a second. Neither should you."

"But who else is going to die first?"

Kale had no answer for that. Despite how little his reassurance did to make me feel better, I loved him for trying.

"You should go home, Alexa. Get some sleep." Kale forced a

rueful smile. "You're growing very hard to resist."

I blushed, my body temperature rising. His energy was running hot. It called to me, bringing forth the laughter that had quelled when he arrived. "I'd apologize but I'm not sorry. I'm so tired of resisting."

Kale's expression grew dark, smoldering. I was suddenly painfully aware of just how close he was. Even in the dim light, I saw his pupils dilate. This wasn't the time or place to play with fire. But, as I watched him react to me, felt it, I reacted too. I had left my self-control in the blood-soaked room down the hall.

"No, Alexa. Don't do this. I told you, I can't do this anymore."

"Then don't." I raised a brow and smiled suggestively. "God, you feel good."

I closed my eyes and breathed him in. He was like metaphysical candy. I gasped when he stepped up to close any remaining space between us. Sliding a hand into my hair, Kale brought his lips to mine, just barely touching.

"You're damn lucky I'm not riding a hell of a high the way you are. I'd have you naked on that pool table already." His lips moved on mine as he spoke, and I melted just a little.

"What's stopping you?"

He kissed me then, a passion pouring forth from him that shook me internally. Kale's soft tongue swept the inside of my mouth. Unlike our last kiss, this was slow and sensual, knocking the breath from me. Disappointment flooded me when he pulled back.

"The only thing stopping me from taking you right here is the fact that your decision is power-driven. When you come to me on your own with nothing to encourage you but the way you truly feel, I promise you, I will love you in ways you can't even dream of."

Kale placed a gentle kiss on my forehead and turned to go. I didn't try to stop him. The weight of his words penetrated the fog in my head. I was shaken and excited but sobering quickly as reality crept in.

He was right. The circumstances, the events of the evening, it was all wrong. If it was to ever happen, it could never be like this.

Chapter Eleven

The hum of voices coming from the television barely kept my attention. As hard as I tried to make myself follow the sitcom, I just couldn't keep up. My thoughts were elsewhere.

I hadn't moved from my spot on the couch for hours other than to refill my coffee mug. Wrapped in my fuzzy black robe, I stared at the moving images on the screen, but all I saw was Lena's broken body. I'd cried myself out of tears hours ago.

A short phone conversation with Jez had provided some comfort. We shared our grief, but on some level, we were alone in our pain. Jez, Kale and I had all had our own relationship with Lena.

To me she was the mother figure I'd needed after losing my own and a teacher that helped to guide and shape the power I now held. She was too good to go out the way she had. Deep in my heart, I knew she wouldn't want me to blame myself. Knowing that made it harder to stop.

I'd been ignoring Veryl's calls all evening. I didn't care what he had to say. I didn't want to hear it. After the third call, he'd left a nasty voice mail saying that feeling sorry for myself wasn't going to bring Lena back and that shit like this happens all the time, especially to humans. That was all I had to hear to know that I would tell Shya yes. I would happily kill Veryl.

Despite my claim that I needed a night alone, Arys had insisted on coming by. He wanted to talk. As I listened to him bang and crash things in my kitchen, I wished he would just say what was on his mind. Instead he'd been fumbling around with the coffee pot and making a poor attempt at heating lasagna.

Another crash came from the kitchen, and I cringed. No wonder I couldn't focus on the cheesy show. "Are you ok, babe?"

"Yes!" His response was frantic. "How many sugars in your coffee? Four?"

"Two. But, you don't need to make more coffee. I still have some." Swirling the murky liquid in my cup, I frowned. It was pretty far from fresh.

"Too late. It's already made. ...Son of a bitch!"

Another crash of dishes got me up off the couch and heading for the short staircase that led to the kitchen. Arys met me at the top, his hands raised as if to block me.

"Don't get up. Just go sit down, and I'll bring it to you." He angled his body so I couldn't see into the kitchen.

"Arys, what did you do? I don't expect you to cook for me. In fact, I think its best that you don't." Standing on my tiptoes, I tried to see over his shoulder. I was sure I'd heard something break.

"Hey, give me a little credit. I'm over three hundred years old. I'm not about to be outsmarted by a stove." His tone was firm, but uncertainty lay in his eyes. "Besides, there's nothing I can do to ease the pain of your loss. I just need to do something. Humor me?"

I sniffed the air, wrinkling my nose. "Is something burning?"

Arys rushed to the stove in a panic. "Shit!"

I watched him pull the blackened lasagna out of the oven and throw it on the counter. Smoke billowed out to fill the kitchen and burn my eyes. Watching the frantic vampire lose his usual cool and calm over a store-bought frozen lasagna was priceless. I laughed so hard my stomach hurt.

"I'll just have coffee. Unless you've managed to burn that, too."

He flipped me off and swore again at the burning mass that barely resembled food. It was just as well; I wasn't hungry anyway.

I descended back into the living room to open a window before settling back into my favorite corner of the couch. I could safely say that the only man in my life I'd be trusting in the kitchen was Shaz. He was a far better cook than I was. Vampires clearly had no business messing around with food and hot appliances.

I hid a grin when Arys entered the room with a fresh mug of coffee. As soon as I caught its bitter scent, I knew I'd have to fake my way through this one. Did he dump a whole can of grounds in there? *Yuck.*

I took the mug with a murmur of thanks, watching pensively as Arys sat on the cushion next to me. He pulled my feet onto his lap, slipped my socks off and began to rub the sole of my right foot. The sip of coffee I took was absolutely vile, but Arys' touch was perfect. I groaned in pleasure. His massage was magic, almost better than sex. Who was I kidding? It couldn't compare to sex, but he hit a few major pleasure points that had me moaning like I was halfway to climax.

"You think that coffee is disgusting, don't you?" He was eyeing me closely, watching the bliss cross my face.

"Yes. I'm sorry. I just have my own way of doing it." Relieved, I abandoned the mug on the coffee table. "But, don't think for a minute that I don't appreciate the thought behind your destruction of my kitchen. I love you for trying."

He frowned, his gaze dropping to my foot. The pressure increased, and I made a sound that could have come from an x-rated adult film. Funny how a great massage can put you in the same state of mind.

"You're not blaming yourself, are you? You know it was for the best that you killed Harley. I hate what happened to Lena. I only met her the one time, and she was lovely. I know she meant a lot to you. But please, don't beat yourself up over this."

I suddenly found the television to be engrossing, if only because it allowed me to avoid meeting Arys' eyes. "I know that, logically. I can't help but feel a little guilty. It's just going to take some time to deal with. I will be fine."

I could see him look at me though I was focused on the television. His stare grew heavy, and I knew he wasn't going to let up. Dragging my gaze to his, I tensed. It had been more than just my guilt over Lena that had him here destroying my house.

"Alexa, I know you share my memories," Arys began as if choosing his words carefully. "I know you saw Claire in my past. I don't want that to be something that haunts you."

"You mean something I'll hold against you?" I asked, taking his silence as a yes. "It's not like I just found out you're a killer, Arys. So you two liked to tag team virgins together. Could have been worse."

Trina M. Lee

I was being a tad flippant but only because I didn't want to discuss this. Arys was a vampire. He loved it. Picking apart a past that existed hundreds of years before I did was pointless. I considered it irrelevant.

"You know what I'm really talking about." He didn't want to say it.

"You mean because you slept with her?" I laughed dryly. "I didn't really think you'd spent three centuries being celibate. What kind of an idiot do you think I am?"

"Come on, I didn't say that." Arys stroked a finger under my toes, and I giggled.

"I know you've had other lovers, Arys. I get that. It was a long time ago. I'd really rather not be forced to think about it though."

He nodded. "Ok, fine. I just felt like I should say something. Especially since I really don't know how much you've seen."

"Enough." I smiled so he would know I really wasn't upset. "Most of it's a blur of random images that move too fast for me to follow. Sometimes I'll see something clearly, as if I'm seeing it through your eyes as it happened. I hate that. But, it doesn't happen much. Your memories are buried deep in my subconscious where I prefer to keep them."

A grin tugged at Arys' lips. "You know your memories aren't a real picnic, either. Some days I wake up screaming, dreaming about your wolf attack. It takes a few moments to grasp that I'm not you."

"Yeah, I'm not sure I'll ever get used to seeing through your eyes like that. I'm just glad it doesn't happen all the time."

We sat in comfortable silence for a while, a comedy show capturing our attention. It wasn't often that we sat in front of the TV and zoned out. It felt good. I didn't spend nearly enough time doing this kind of thing. Normal things.

After giving my other foot the same amazing attention that had me moaning, Arys squeezed in behind me on the couch. He pulled me to him so that my back was to his chest. His arms went around me, and I sank against him gratefully. So maybe a cloud of smoke still lingered in my kitchen and maybe I had more memories of Arys' blood-drunk sexual history than I desired, but I wouldn't have traded it for anything.

Moments like this were blessedly simple. Simple was

underrated. I could use more of this … without the horrible surrounding circumstances.

I snuggled in beside Arys. His body alongside mine was comforting, reassuring in a way that I needed. I was glad he'd come tonight. The moment of calm would be over much too soon.

ഓഓഓഓ

The sun was warm against my face. It felt all wrong. I kept wondering where the clouds were. Today was a day for rolling thunder and sudden rainfall, when the earth, too, cried over the loss of one of its own. Instead, I gazed up at a crisp blue afternoon sky while the sun blazed.

The cemetery was quiet. Those gathered for Lena's burial were small in number. Jez and I huddled together a safe distance from the friends and family neither of us knew. Kale hated that he couldn't be there with us. The sun assaulted my eyes and skin. It burned. Still, it had no further power over me. Not yet.

I recognized Lena's daughter, Brogan. Having met her a few times, I knew little about her other than that she, too, was a natural earth witch like her mother. Despite what authorities might have told her, Brogan would know vampires had been the cause of her mother's death. That was confirmed when she met my eyes across the open grave. Behind her obvious pain was the calm resolve of a witch on the war path.

The minister spoke words of hope and celebration of life. They never penetrated my tough exterior. I was cold with the visual of what had been done to Lena. Personally destroying Claire and Maxwell was all I could think about.

"This is the worst day ever," Jez muttered, fussing with her long ponytail. "I feel like I should say something to Brogan, but I don't know what. Anything that comes out of my mouth is going to be all wrong today."

The past few days had been rough. It showed on Jez. The lack of sleep was evident on her face. Her eyes were puffy, and she had made very little effort to apply makeup. For Jez, that said a lot about her state of mind. She was internalizing, like we all did in these times. Things that usually matter had lost their appeal.

Saying goodbye to Lena was difficult. I fought back tears, fearing they would be blood-red. The pressure built inside me. I wanted to scream if only to feel some relief. We stood quietly through the rest of the short service. When the family began to cry and talk amongst themselves, Jez and I looked awkwardly at one another.

"Should we just go?" I shrugged, feeling out of place.

She held up a bouquet of flowers, waving them so the sweet fragrance wafted to me. As nice as it was, the scent of grief easily overpowered it. "I need to leave these by the headstone first."

Brogan pulled away from the rest of her family to join us. My gaze was drawn to the headstone and Lena's name etched deep into the marble slab. It hurt to look at the headstone, but staring into the pain in Brogan's hazel eyes was worse.

"Thank you for coming," she said, her voice thick with emotion. "My mom talked a lot about you both. And Kale. Please tell him I apologize for the daytime service." She mustered a smile that quickly fell flat.

"Brogan, I'm so sorry." I didn't know what else to say. I had nothing to offer that would ease her agony.

Jez murmured sympathetic words and grabbed Brogan in a friendly hug. I stood there feeling awkward. I shielded against the storm of negative energy rolling from Lena's mourning family. I could feel it battering my personal circle, seeking a way in.

"The cops are passing it off as an unfortunate home invasion." Brogan sighed heavily and tugged a stray lock of dirty blond hair behind her ear. "I smiled and nodded. What could I do? Tell them about the heavy stink of vampire energy left behind? Dealing with the will and everything is proving to be enough hassle. But, knowing they're out there…"

"I'm on it, Brogan." I promised, my temper rising. "I know who did this. I'm going to find them."

"I want in." The determined set to her jaw reminded me far too much of Lena. "I need to be part of this, Alexa."

Jez was already shaking her head. "God no, Brogan. You'll get yourself killed."

We all glanced around anxiously to ensure nobody was within

earshot. Brogan frowned, her expression one of stubborn refusal. The last thing I needed was for something to happen to her, too. No way. Not on my watch.

"I have to do something. I can't just sit by while those bloodsuckers kill more people as innocent as my mom."I understood how she felt. My mother had been murdered, too, by my lover, a man who had gone to bed with both of us. I shuddered at the thought of Raoul touching my mother as a lover or a murderer. The urge to scream built quickly, and I shoved the thought from my mind.

"I promise you, I understand how it feels to lose your mother violently, but putting yourself in harm's way is not what Lena would want. You know that." I could see her forming another protest, so I rushed on. "I might need a locator spell done. You can help with that. But in the meantime, don't get yourself killed. These vampires are ruthless, and if they find out you're connected to me in any way, they will make death seem like a walk in the park."

Brogan absorbed this, nodding slowly. I knew she was wondering now how much hell her mother had been put through before being killed. That hadn't been my intent, but I needed to scare her off the trail. No good could come of Brogan involving herself directly in this.

"Fine. I'll hold off for now. Let me know about the locator spell. I want to help however I can." Her eyes widened, and she reached into the small clutch she held. "I almost forgot. I have something for you. I just started going through my mom's things last night, and I found some stuff she had set aside for you both."

A pained sound came from Jez. "I can't believe Lena was planning for something like this."

"She was a realist if she was anything." Brogan sighed heavily. Producing a small black bag from her purse, she handed it to Jez. "There are two charms in here. The red one is for you, Jez. It's for strength and guidance. The blue one is for Kale. It's for serenity and inner peace. Alexa, there's an amulet for you. I'm actually not entirely sure what it does, but it's strong. I guess you'll figure out what use it could be to you."

"Thank you, Brogan. Please, if there is anything we can do for you do not hesitate to call." On impulse, I pulled her into a quick hug, hoping it didn't come across as awkward.

"And, she's not just saying that," Jez chimed in. "Lena was family. So are you."

Tears welled up in Brogan's eyes, and she smiled sadly. "Thanks you guys. That means a lot. I always knew something like this could happen, but I never really thought it would."

We could say nothing to that. Jez and I faced a similar death every night. It used to seem surreal to me, too, but the cold hand of reality had bitch-slapped that out of me long ago.

Saying goodbye to Brogan was difficult. I wanted to chase after her with warnings to be careful. I was afraid she'd try to take matters into her own hands. She couldn't take Maxwell, I was certain of that.

She made me promise to get in touch for that locator spell before rejoining the rest of her family. Jez and I slipped away, leaving them to grieve privately. We made our way through the graves, out the cemetery gates, and back to my car. Picking my way through the grass in heels proved to be more of a pain in the ass than I'd anticipated.

"I wish Kale could have been here," Jez whispered despite us being alone. "He's always so calming in situations like this. I turn into an anxious mess. ...Or, at least he used to be."

"I hate to say it, but I'm kind of glad he wasn't." I cringed. "Does that make me awful?"

"Of course not. If I were you, I'd probably feel the same. He hasn't been the same lately. I don't like it."

"I've been asked to kill Veryl, Jez. And, I think I'm going to do it." I blurted the words before thinking it through. I hadn't told anyone yet, and I needed to hear myself say it out loud to somebody else.

Jez gaped at me in shock. "What? Are you serious?"

I took a deep breath and told her about my visit from Shya as well as Veryl's attitude regarding Lena. "He's driving me to do it, Jez. And, I can't help but want to."

"You can't trust a demon though, Lex. You know that." Jez fixed me with wide green eyes. "I've never met him, but I've heard enough to know I don't particularly want to."

The Charger was hot inside from the afternoon sun. I wasn't used to being awake at this time of day, and the stuffy interior wasn't helping me stay alert.

"I don't trust him, but I don't trust Veryl, either." I put the key in the ignition but didn't start the car. I faced Jez, seeking some kind of understanding. "I have to admit, I like the idea of taking on bigger kills, people that pose a serious threat. The challenge kind of excites me. Of course, I don't want to make a mistake either. And, with everything else going on, it's all pretty confusing."

Reaching over to grab my hand, Jez gave me an encouraging smile that did nothing to hide the worry in her eyes. "Be careful, Alexa. Remember who you're dealing with and just think things through before you agree to anything a demon says. I don't want you to rush into anything. I don't think I can support you on the Veryl thing. It's just too personal for me. Do what you gotta do. I'll still love you, but I can't condone it."

I gave her hand a squeeze. A swell of emotion brought tears to my eyes. It had been a trying day. "Fair enough."

Chapter Twelve

I turned the small amulet over in my hands, feeling the pure earth energy humming through it. Warm and lively, it felt pure in a way that other forms of power were not. It called to my wolf, and I found myself comforted simply by touching it. I couldn't be sure what Lena had intended in giving it to me. For now, I was content just to have a part of her.

Stuffing the amulet into my purse, I scanned the crowd. The blood whores seemed to be getting younger all the time. I didn't like that. The flash of strobe lights over the dark dance floor briefly illuminated the couple against the wall. The vampiress with the ebony hair held a human male in a firm grip as she fed from him. The scent of blood mixed with sweat, a myriad of perfumes and other human smells was stomach turning.

Several couples were locked in embraces bordering on explicit. The Wicked Kiss was a living, thriving organism of its own. I was quickly accepting that I couldn't control it, I could only survive it, which I had every intention of doing.

I hadn't seen much of Arys in the past twenty-four hours. Every moment the sun was down, he was trying to get a lead on where Maxwell and Claire were hiding out. They'd been lying low since Lena's death. It wouldn't be long before they resurfaced. I fantasized about all the ways I'd break them. I couldn't take back what they'd done to Lena, but I could share her pain with her killers. I itched with anticipation.

Shaz had taken the night off. I'd insisted. He needed more wolf time. I worried that too much time in this place was starting to affect him. Shaz was my wolf, and I needed him to stay that way. I was vampy enough for the both of us.

Neither Shaz nor Arys had wanted me at The Wicked Kiss alone. Sure it was dangerous, but they couldn't constantly be hovering over me. If Claire tried to take a shot at me, Arys would know. I could open the telepathic door between us in a heartbeat.

When my phone vibrated in my pocket, I jumped. No, I wasn't edgy at all. I half expected to see Veryl's number; the guy didn't know when to give up. So when I saw that it was Jez, I was relieved.

Until I answered.

Her words came in a rush, the hysterical shrieking made it hard to understand her. Adrenaline crashed over me, and I hurried through the noisy club to the quieter back hall.

"Jez! What's wrong?"

"Alexa, it's Kale. He fucking bit me! I couldn't fight him off. I tried." Another pained moan followed, and I ran blindly out the back exit into the parking lot.

"Where are you, Jez? Take slow, deep breaths. You have to calm down. I'm coming!" My own voice had risen to the point of hysterical. I almost choked on my panic.

"The office," she gasped. "I'm at the office."

I put my phone on speaker and tossed it on the passenger seat. "Stay with me, Jez. Keep talking." With a squeal of tires I flew out of the parking lot, leaving the stink of burnt rubber behind.

I heard a noise, like her phone had fallen, seconds before the call was lost. I'd given Kale too much credit. Having been so caught up with the Claire situation, I hadn't treated Kale like the threat he was. Unpredictable and self-starved, Kale had been well on his way to snapping. After finding the dead prostitutes in his room, I should have known better.

I feared the worst when I screeched to a halt in the office parking lot. Every precious second was slipping away too quickly. Leaving the engine running and the driver's door open, I skidded on the loose gravel in my haste to get inside.

A bloody handprint on the wall caused my panic to surge. I flung myself beyond the entry, shouting Jez' name. I found her unconscious on the floor in the kitchen. Blood pooled beneath her.

Though her breath came in shallow bursts and her heart still beat, she was fading fast.

"Jez! Talk to me, Jez." I slapped her face, receiving no response. I glanced around frantically, uncertain.

The rich scent of her blood was mouth-watering, but this time it held no sway over me. I saw my friend bleeding to death from a nasty throat wound, and the wolf rose up with a protective snarl to subdue the bloodlust. This was Jez, and she wasn't food.

Vampire blood could heal her. She wasn't conscious enough to drink it nor was there a vampire around. Kale hadn't hung around long after his attack. My blood was still mortal. Could I heal her the way Harley had taught me? I called the energy, but my panic prevented me from focusing on it. I could feel her slipping away. *No!*

"Please, God. Not Jez, too," I sobbed, only realizing then that tears streamed down my face. "Come on, focus!"

I was mad at myself. How could I fall apart when it was the life of one of my dearest friends on the line? I could do this. I had to!

Power swirled about me like a tornado. I couldn't bring it into focus, but the more my desperation mounted, the further it spun out of control. I had the ability to save her, but instead, I was failing her.

The icy touch of vampire power at my back had me whirling, ready to kick Kale's ass. I gasped when I found myself staring into Lilah's flame-colored eyes. Her pupils dilated as she reacted to the wild power encircling me.

"It was Kale," I babbled, all but shoving her toward Jez. "I tried to heal her, and I can't. I just can't." One thing was evident, I was not doing well under pressure these days. Even to me I sounded like the frantic idiot that needed to be slapped.

Lilah was all calm and cool next to my hysterical self. She knelt beside Jez but looked up at me. "I have her; find him." A woman of few words, Lilah turned her attention to the fading leopard and a stroke of fire slammed over me as she called her power. Demon power.

That red-hot power poured forth, wiping out any trace of her usual cool, undead energy. It burned, and I shielded hard against it.

I had to find Kale before he slaughtered his way through the city. How far could he have gotten by now? If I was going to give him the beating he deserved, I needed to gain control of myself. Bad enough, I'd failed Jez. If Kale overpowered me, I might not make it out of our confrontation alive.

The Wicked Kiss. If I had to bet money on it, that's where Kale would go. It was filled with victims he could pick off left, right and center. Leaving Jez was difficult, but I trusted Lilah. Kale wasn't likely to stop anytime soon, which added fuel to my fire. I had to get to him.

My hands shook on the steering wheel as I rushed back through the city. I was filled with dread. I did not want to see Kale on a rampage, and I sure as hell didn't want to be the one to have to stop him. I had no choice. The image of Jez bleeding out swam behind my eyes. How could he do this to her? A little voice whispered in my ear, *He did it to you, too.*

Kale was a killer. The calm, gentle Kale that I knew was only part of him. I could too easily pretend a monster didn't lurk behind those gorgeous eyes. I'd always known this could happen, but I'd foolishly chosen not to believe he really would snap again.

I'd seen horrors in Arys' memory, but I was sure that Kale's past contained worse. Kale had never been one to speak much of his past, but I knew enough to know it was bad. He had a bit of a fetish for the screams of his victims. I shuddered, recalling the night he'd told me that.

I was terror-stricken at the thought of facing him. I would never forget the crazed look in his eyes the night he attacked me.

Raindrops spattered against the windshield, and a boom of thunder shook the night. A thunderstorm was as fitting a backdrop to this night as any. With the press of a button, I closed the sunroof, cutting off the cold, wet spray that hit me in the face. The motion was so mundane and simple, a direct contrast to everything else going on around me.

I didn't think I could possibly be any more afraid than I already was. However, when I approached The Kiss and spotted Kale's Camaro parked haphazardly in the club's "no parking" zone, my stomach dropped. The anger that coursed through me came sudden and unbidden. I was smart enough to fear Kale, but I was also beyond pissed for what he'd done to Jez.

I parked my car so that it blocked his in. I didn't want him getting away that easily, although I had a feeling that he wouldn't try to run when he saw me. Fear fled me when I got out of my car and surveyed the parking lot. It was much too quiet. The noise from inside was muffled. I paused, listening for telltale screams.

I dropped my shields, knowing Kale would feel me regardless. I reached out for his honey sweet energy, sensing him immediately. His energy was buzzing with the bloodlust that drove him. Kale was on a bender, and he wasn't likely to stop any time soon. His energy led me through the parking lot, past the rear exit to the small alley that ran behind the building. How perfectly creepy.

Kale had carelessly tossed aside the bodies of two guys who had the misfortune of being in the wrong place at the wrong time. One of them was still alive, barely. His heartbeat echoed in my ears, and I tried to shut it out. I could do nothing for him now. I forced myself to walk past him without a second look. Unlike Jez, he felt like food.

I hesitated, unwilling to walk into a trap. Kale hadn't already gone inside to terrorize the club patrons for a reason. He was waiting for me. That realization should have frightened me, but I was numb, slipping into survival mode.

The scent of blood and fear was strong. I gazed into the darkness, my wolf eyes re-adjusting to the absence of light. I saw nothing other than a garbage dumpster and some old abandoned furniture some lazy ass had ditched. Wherever Kale was, he was blending into the shadows with ease.

The sounds of the dying man behind me were especially loud. I swallowed hard, struggling to tune it out. Kale could have at least put the guy out of his misery. I couldn't do it. I knew the moment I drew close enough to see his bloody throat, I'd be a goner.

"Don't do this, Kale." I stared into the darkness ahead, willing him to make this easy on both of us.

I could feel him, lying in wait. As each moment dragged by, my trepidation grew. This was a game to him, and I didn't want to play.

I grew frustrated quickly. I didn't appreciate being treated like the mouse in this game. "Here kitty kitty." The taunt sounded like a challenge, and I regretted it as soon as it left my lips. "You don't want to play with me, Kale. You could have killed Jez!"

Thunder crashed overhead, followed moments later by a streak of lightning. The brief illumination lit up my surroundings. If I hadn't been able to feel Kale, I would have believed I was alone out there. Well, me and what was left of his victims.

The air around me never rippled. Not a sound betrayed Kale's movement. He was just suddenly there, right in front of me. I jumped, choking on a shriek, stumbling as I backed away.

The rain came down harder, and I shoved my damp hair out of my face, peering at Kale like it was my first time laying eyes on him. I barely recognized him. His face was stained with the blood of his victims and his hair was matted with it. The solid black of his eyes revealed how far gone he was. Too late, I second-guessed coming here alone, but I wasn't going back now.

Clad in his usual stylish attire, pinstriped pants, a dark shirt and his leather duster, Kale looked like my dreams and nightmares united in one painfully beautiful form. He smelled like blood and death and wore the devilish grin of one mad with bloodlust. His blood-soaked power beckoned to me.

I was instantly defensive, gathering my power tight to me. "Kale, I-,"

I was airborne before I realized he'd metaphysically bitch-slapped me. I hit the ground hard, skidding to a stop next to Kale's forgotten victim. I was on my feet immediately, determined not to let on how much that had hurt. My back and legs stung from scraping along the hard, wet pavement. I prayed that the impact hadn't drawn blood.

Kale advanced on me but made no further move. I stared into his eyes, rife with madness, and I felt despair. I didn't want this to become a violent confrontation, not if I could help it.

"I thought you said you didn't want to hurt me." Appealing to his softer side was my first choice, but I was ready to hurt him if he refused to back down. I knew I could do it.

"I believe I said I didn't want to kill you." Kale regarded me thoughtfully, an amused smile dancing about his lips. "I definitely want to hurt you."

The unspoken promises in his words brought forth my wolf with a snarl. I was all fangs and claws, ready to make him regret whatever he was thinking. Kale reacted with a laugh that shook me to the core. It was pure evil.

"This isn't you, Kale. Let's be reasonable here. You hurt Jez.

She's your friend. I'm your friend."

He scoffed, pushing a lock of wet hair back from his forehead. "This is me, Alexa. This is the side you've always hoped you'd never see again, but just looking at you brings it out of me. We both knew this would happen. You can't save me from myself. You know this. You can't even save yourself. Once it's in you, it is you."

"No." I shook my head vehemently. "That's bullshit. It doesn't have to be this way. You know it doesn't."

"Who are you trying to convince? I get it. You're young and still so new to this. You want to believe there is another way. Try telling that to this poor sap." Kale nudged the body next to us with a booted foot. The man had finally expired. "There is only blood and death. Either that or insanity."

"I guess you'd know, huh?" I was scrambling to put the right words together. Anything to get through to him. "Blood and death doesn't mean hurting the people that care about you. We love you, Kale. We can help you."

I gasped when he stepped in close and laid a finger over my lips to silence me. I battled against the urge to jerk away.

"Be careful what you say, my love. Words can so easily be taken out of context." He smiled down at me, revealing fangs.

My stomach tightened as he pulled at my energy. I pushed back against him, a warning. "So can actions. Don't do something we'll both regret, Kale."

His laughter stoked the fire that always burned between us. "Not to worry. I don't plan to regret anything."

So being rational wasn't going to work. Good to know. What did I have left? Brute force? He'd like that; he wanted it.

"I'm not going to face off with you. Not like this." I steeled myself against the call of his power to mine. He was encouraging it, and though I resisted, my will was weak. It was Kale; I'd always wanted him.

"Then why did you come?" He challenged, his smile vanishing. "You want it as bad as I do. The rush of the power, the struggle of your prey as you give in to the thrill of the bloodlust that you try so hard to deny. Did you come to stop me, pretty wolf? Or, was it to join me?"

"Back off, Kale!" The force that accompanied my shout shoved him back a few feet. I didn't want this to be a clash of metaphysical ability but instinct was guiding my action.

"Too close to the truth for comfort. I understand." His head came up suddenly, and he listened keenly to the night. I listened, too, straining to pick out sounds beyond the rain and thunder.

The faint sound of high heels clicking quickly on the concrete was distant. It grew increasingly louder as the woman drew closer. We were just fifty feet or so from the club's rear entry. I crossed my fingers, hoping that whoever she was, she would go in through the front. Kale braced himself in anticipation, and I held my breath.

She rounded the corner of the building, heading right for us. Clutching a thin jacket and a purse, she hurried to escape the rain. With her head down and her attention on her destination, she didn't even look our way.

"Kale, don't."

We both sprang into motion, but he was faster. She let out a surprised scream when he grabbed her. With a hand over her mouth, Kale leaned in close and breathed deeply of her scent. Her eyes were wide, and she struggled in his grasp. He smiled.

"This is what you came for, Alexa." He met my gaze with delight dancing in his eyes.

I shivered as the rain soaked through my jeans and thin t-shirt. At least I told myself it was from the chill of the rain and not the spark of excitement in my belly. I watched Kale bare her neck and run his tongue over her flesh. She fought to get away, but he easily overpowered her.

"Don't do this," I pleaded. "Let her go. This is between you and me."

"She smells good. Like apples." Kale bit deep into her without warning. I gave a small cry and begged him to stop. There was nothing I could do.

The scent of fresh blood struck me. Kale held my gaze as he drank from her, watching the effect it was having on me. I didn't have the strength to fight the bloodlust. Despite the way I pleaded with him, I enjoyed what I saw. I responded to the scene before me with hunger and intrigue. I wanted to taste her.

I backed away from Kale, forcing my feet to do the opposite of what the bloodlust demanded. I was at a loss, unsure of what to do. A battle waged inside me, one I had to win.

His victim's struggles ceased as she slipped into unconsciousness. Kale raised his head so I could see the blood spilling from the wound. In a dramatic gesture, he swept his tongue over the punctures in a languorous motion that almost brought me to my knees.

His tone was deadly wicked when he murmured, "Tell me you don't want just a taste."

"I want you to stop this fucking nonsense before you drive us both crazy. You're being an idiot." I spat the words through a mouthful of fangs. My fury was growing, and the urge to tear a strip out of Kale was strong.

Letting the woman fall to the ground without a second thought, Kale advanced on me. Panicking, I lashed out with a warning shot, just enough to let him know I was ready to defend myself. He continued forward, unfazed. This was going to get physical.

"And, you're being the challenge that I'd hoped you'd be." Moving inhumanly fast, Kale grabbed me in a vice-like grip and kissed me before I could form a protest.

The passion in his kiss momentarily left me stunned. The blood in his mouth was delicious and tempting. My resistance quickly came undone as the bloodlust found victory. Kale's tongue was persistent against mine, and I caught myself kissing him back before common sense took hold.

Pulling away, I hauled off and punched him right in the face. It knocked him back a foot or two but otherwise resulted in nothing but a smirk and a cut lip. Spilling Kale's blood could never be a good thing, not when I wanted him the way I did. Still, I found some gratification in hitting him with my fist instead of my power. It gave me so much more satisfaction.

My wolf was ready to kick his ass, and I followed up with a kick intended to take his legs out from under him. However, his undead reflexes were stellar, and he caught my leg and gave it a twist. I yelped in pain, fearing the worst. He didn't really hurt me though, not like he could have. Instead he gave me a shove that sat me down hard on my ass.

I glared up at him, a growl rumbling in my throat. He stood over me, waiting for me to get up. "Come on, Alexa. You need the violence to justify your feelings. So if it makes you feel better to throw punches, I'm happy to take them. You can beat me black and blue, but it won't change the way you feel."

I came up off the ground snarling and swinging. It wasn't the knowing look in his eyes that unleashed my fury but the truth in his words. Kale was more than happy to give as much as he was taking. I ate more than a few hits that would have knocked any human out. It would hurt later, but I was running on adrenaline and lupine wrath.

In a move that both surprised and satisfied me, I flipped him over my body so he landed hard on the ground next to me. Maybe you couldn't wind a vampire, but that had to hurt. If only it had knocked some sense into him. All it seemed to do was encourage him. Holding tight to my forearm, he followed through with my momentum, using it to pull me off balance while getting to his feet. Since I was the one with functioning lungs, I had the breath crushed from me.

Kale pulled me to my feet. His touch stirred my power, encouraging it to devour him. "Have you had enough yet, my love? I can do this dance with you all night."

Despite gasping for air, I bared my fangs at him. "You're sick, Kale."

Stroking a hand down the side of my battered face, he smiled, almost sadly. "And, you are my disease."

"What do you want from me? Really." I drew a shaky breath and slapped his hand away.

Looking into Kale's drowning orbs was like falling into an abyss, so deep and so endless. He leaned in too close for my comfort, inhaling my scent.

"Are you sure you want the answer to that question?" His lips lightly brushed my ear, and I trembled. "I want to explore what it is that draws me to you. I want to discover why it binds me, why everything in me longs to be yours. I want to be able to look at Arys and not die inside with envy. I want to bring you to your knees and make you scream. And, sometimes, I just want to be free of you altogether."

So much for a simple answer. A storm of thoughts and emotions pummeled me. I was at a loss for words. A wall deep inside me began to crumble and with it, my own resolve.

He jerked away from me so fast I jumped, startled by the sudden motion. Kale paced a few feet away before whirling to fix me with a deadly stare.

"Perhaps the real question isn't what I want from you, Alexa, but what do you want from me? You're pretty back and forth on that. You beg me to bleed you one day but tell me to back off the next. I'm starting to think you're trying to drive me mad."

My heart raced. Kale's energy was erratic, pained and tempting. It called to me, and I felt the wild vampire power rise up inside me with intrigue.

"I don't know what I want from you! Is that what you want to hear? I don't fucking know." That was as close to the truth as I had for him. "Sometimes, I want to devour you, just take all you have to give until there's nothing left. And sometimes, I want to fuck you senseless while doing it. Then there are the times I want to wrap myself in the comfort I find in you and just ... be."

My words hung between us, heavy and honest. It felt good to get it out, but I still didn't know what it all meant. I'd never felt as confused over anyone as I did with Kale. Was it wrong? Or, was it just circumstance?

The silence was thick with tension. The power crackled around us, creating sparks in the rain. Rain had soaked my hair, and I pushed it out of my face. I waited for Kale's response. The hard glint in his gaze was unnerving. I was afraid of him right then; I couldn't judge his state of mind.

I sensed his inner turmoil, his struggle. He quickly closed the distance he had put between us, and I braced myself for anything. Sliding a hand into my wet hair, he vibrated with pent-up energy. His hand was even warm, despite the cold rain that poured down, and I caught myself leaning into his touch.

"I can't go on like this much longer. One of us is going to end up killing the other. I fear that might be the only way you can set me free."

"Shut up, Kale. Don't talk like that."

His hand tightened in my hair, just enough to become painful. "God, I want to hurt you right now. Anything to make you stop saying my name like that."

The shock of fear that slammed through me was paired with excitement. Part of me was eager to see what he would do. It was ludicrous. We were both so far gone.

"Can you do it? Make me a victim? Kale?" I taunted as his sweet energy rolled over me. It would be so easy to give in, and I was so tired of resisting.

"You'd like that, wouldn't you?" With a sudden pressure, he pushed power into me. It burned just enough to blur the line between pain and pleasure.

The pain increased as Kale forced me back against the building. The stone was cold and wet against my back. I gazed up at him, and he reached to stroke a finger beneath my chin as he contemplated me. I wanted him to do it, to give in to whatever he was feeling. Something inside me was waiting for that second when he went too far.

I gasped, a smile tugging at my lips. Grasping his power, I drew it in to me, making it mine. Five centuries of undead energy was a heady intoxicant. The rush that spilled over me was enough to make me dizzy. Kale was like a fine wine, stronger and better with age.

"I'd like to see you try." I was like a kid playing with matches. The very real possibility of how badly I could get burned didn't seem like a good enough reason to play safe.

"I know what you're doing. Taunting me isn't the way to make me back off. You are just pouring gasoline on the flames. I can't resist you, and I'm done trying."

He claimed my lips in a kiss that was wild with untamed need. At the same time, he released his hold on the energy within him so that it sought to get to me. It crashed over me like a wave, and I was left struggling to stay afloat in a sea of power and desire.

I delighted in the taste of blood on his tongue as he delved into my mouth. I breathed him in like his kiss was air. The boundary line was suddenly so far away it couldn't be seen for dust. I fell into Kale, and I fell hard. Kissing him back with total abandon was so liberating that it was dizzying.

When Kale realized I wasn't fighting him off, a sense of urgency overcame him. He kissed me hungrily, as if he feared that at any moment I would come to my senses and throw him another punch. I was too far gone to climb up out of the abyss I'd fallen into. The scent of rain mixed with Kale's leather kept me buried under a veil of desire that would no longer be denied.

I tasted blood as his fangs scraped my lower lip, just another sensation to add to the rest. The fading warmth of his body against mine contrasted with the cold rain pelting us, and I pressed closer to him. Slipping my arms around his neck, I clung to him with a desperation I hadn't known that I possessed for him. It could shock me later. Right then, it was freedom.

Kale's hands were on my waist, sliding up under my shirt to caress my bare flesh. I ached for more. It wasn't enough. When his mouth came warm against my neck, I sighed. The scrape of his fangs on my skin held the promise of danger and bliss. I needed it.

When he peeled my wet t-shirt off, I didn't stop him. He paused just long enough to gaze into my eyes. I saw myself reflected in the drowning black of his pupils. And more than that, I saw his agonizing need.

Pulling me close, Kale pressed his lips to the swell of my cleavage, and I melted against him. I grasped his wet hair in my fingers, amazed at how soft it was. His tongue was warm and moist on my chilled flesh. We'd come this far before. That's where it had ended. Not this time. Lord, not this time.

Perhaps the back alley behind The Wicked Kiss wasn't the most ideal setting for such an encounter. The lightning flashed overhead, followed by thunder, and I found it perfect. Impatience drove me to know more of him, all of him. I sensed magic in Kale's touch. I guided him back up to my lips so I could taste him again.

He touched my breasts through the restrictive, damp bra, but I didn't want that. It wasn't enough. The insistence in my kiss drove him, and he ran his hands low down my body to relieve me of the clingy, wet jeans. Anticipation had me growling. I was eager and ravenous for Kale.

I barely noticed when he stripped me of my skimpy underwear. Cloaking my body with his, Kale sheltered my nakedness with his long duster, providing me with warmth and cover. I reached blindly for him, seeking his skin on mine. He was already moving to free himself from the restraints of his pants. I gasped when he lifted me in his arms so that my weight was divided between the wall at my back and his embrace.

The warmth of his hard shaft against my entrance was sudden and startling. I peered into his eyes, finding him watching me intently. He gave me one last split second to stop him. I never did.

Kale slipped inside me with a slow, steady motion that knocked the breath from me. Our gazes were locked, and I felt vulnerable as every wall I'd built between us crumbled into dust. Buried deep within me, Kale gave a sigh that echoed what I felt. I watched as some semblance of sanity crept back into his mismatched eyes, but we weren't turning back now.

"Alexa." My name was a whisper as he kissed and bit at my neck.

With firm but unhurried strokes, he filled me again and again. A swell of emotion rose up to shatter what remained of my denial about my feelings for Kale. I wasn't going to attempt to define them, but I could no longer refute their existence. He shared with me weaknesses and vulnerabilities that nobody else did, like the constant battle with the bloodlust and the reasons not to give in. I felt safe with him. Kindred.

The crackle of energy sounded loud despite the storm. A silver and gold sphere of power encircled us. The colors of ours auras rolled together like the colors in a candy cane, never joining but twisting and turning together just the same. It was mesmerizing.

We moved together, hidden in the shadows, two souls united in passion and longing. Kale's every touch was intimate. His every movement burned with the flames of sensuality. I'd never dreamed he could make me feel this way. He forced throaty cries from me with each thrust. I was lost in the spellbinding sensations of having him inside me. It felt like a dream.

Kale sucked at the vein in my throat, and I bared my neck to him in invitation. I wanted it as badly as he did. His fangs were sharp against my sensitive flesh. He bit deep, and I gasped. My heartbeat pounded loudly in my ears. Rather than withdraw his fangs right away, he left them buried. It burned until I wanted to scream, but the pain was bliss. I didn't want it to stop. Kale was making me his in every way, and I wanted it.

When at last he released his hold on me, my blood rushed over his tongue. I felt myself hurtling toward climax as he sucked at the wound. Kale's pace increased, and he groaned when I tensed. His body responded to mine, and I felt him fighting the release. Our release was stronger than we were, though, and it smashed into us with a head-spinning impact.

He held me for what felt like a long time after. I clung to him, unwilling to let go yet. He pulled back just enough to meet my eyes, and a frown creased his brow. I realized then that hot tears rolled down my face. I shook my head, trying to calm his concern but unable to form words.

Unwilling to break the spell by speaking, he settled for holding me close and pressing soft kisses to my face. It did little to quell the ridiculous flow of tears. I felt betrayed by them.

We stayed there in the rain, each of us unwilling to break apart. Nothing would ever be the same between us again. I had felt the love that burned inside Kale for me, and I'd been forever changed because of it.

I reached out to stroke a hand down his jaw. I had always adored Kale. Now, I knew just how deep it went. Maybe I'd always known.

At long last, Kale pulled away, and I was left standing nearly naked in the rain. I felt no chill though. I was numb to everything except what I now felt inside. Kale slipped out of his jacket and wrapped it around my shoulders.

"I'm sorry." He kissed me, gentle but deep. "Don't hate me for this. I have to go. I can't stay. Not right now."

He disappeared into the night before I could reply. I struggled into my soaking wet clothes, and then I stood there, clutching his jacket to me while the rain slapped my face. The remnants of our power hummed around me.

I waited for the numbness to creep in, to wipe away the raw, agonized emotion that racked me now. It never came.

Chapter Thirteen

Leaving the dark confines of the alley meant returning to everything I thought I knew. I refused to think about what had just happened. I couldn't for fear I might break. Turning the corner into the parking lot, I gasped as the part of me that was all Arys was awakened. He was here.

Dread washed over me, and I felt faint. I headed for Kale's car, easily manipulating the door lock with slight focus. I held my breath, hoping the alarm wouldn't go off. I pulled the door open. Silence. I tossed Kale's jacket into the backseat, relocked the door and slowly made my way to the front door of the club. I didn't want to go in there.

The sudden warmth of the club was stifling. I felt torn from the natural beauty of the rain, thrust into this artificial world. My wolf hated it. Ignoring the questioning look from Shawn, I made my way inside, leaving a wet trail behind me. I likely looked like something spawned in a B-rate horror movie.

Arys was leaning on the bar, engrossed in conversation with Josh. He looked up at my arrival, and I swallowed hard. Would the rain have washed away Kale's scent? Did the truth shine in my eyes like a beacon?

"What in the hell happened to you? You look like something the cat dragged in." Arys scanned me from head to toe, his gaze narrowing. "You've been crying."

I kept my distance, afraid to touch him. "No. Why? Is there blood on my face? There was an incident at the office. Jez has been hurt. I can't stay. I need to check on her."

"Where's Kale?"

Arys' tone was sharp, and I cringed inwardly. I fumbled to form a response. I was tongue-tied, knowing the truth was clear in my eyes.

"I don't know. He attacked Jez." I could offer nothing more. I wouldn't directly lie to Arys.

He reached out to shove the mess of wet hair off my neck, exposing Kale's bite. "Let me rephrase that. Where in the fuck is Kale?"

"Arys, don't. Please. It's not what you think. He didn't hurt me."

Rage rolled off him with a scorching heat. "It's exactly what I think. I knew this would happen. I knew you'd never be able to resist him."

The lack of surprise in Arys' eyes bothered me. He'd been expecting this? I wasn't sure if I should feel ashamed or insulted.

"I guess you're always two steps ahead of me, huh?" I snarled, spinning on my heel to go. I had no right to be angry, but I wasn't going to have this conversation inside The Wicked Kiss while Jez was injured and Kale was God knew where.

Arys stopped me with a hand on my wrist. His grip was tight enough to hurt. "You and I need to have a little talk. Go and see to your friend, but after sunrise, I'll be expecting you."

"If you hurt Kale-,"

"Then what, Alexa? You'll do something about it?"

I stared into his cold blue eyes and watched as they bled to wolf. I shook my head, knowing there was nothing I could say or do now.

"It will hurt me, too."

Arys released his hold on me and stepped back. "Get out of here, Alexa. I'll see you at sunrise."

I left without a backwards glance. My cheeks burned with humiliation. I was tired and confused from being pulled in so many directions. I didn't know how to be so many things, to have so much expected of me. I finally found peace, short-lived as it were, in the loss of control. The rest of the time, I was a caged animal, longing for freedom, but that surrender always came at a price.

Lilah had left a message on my phone. Jez was at home. She would be fine. The news brought tears of relief to my eyes. Lilah concluded the message by asking me to return to the office before dawn if I was able. She wanted to see me.

That was something I didn't anticipate. I was curious but wary. What could she possibly want to see me about? I had a few hours yet before the sun would break over the horizon. If the rain continued, it would be an overcast morning with little to no real sunlight.

Being a shifter had some perks, for instance, the clean sweat pants and hoodie sweater in the trunk of my car. I kept extra clothing on hand for those unexpected shifts to wolf. I changed in the backseat, grateful to shed the last of my rain-soaked clothing. I tried to squeeze the excess water from my hair. It hung in disheveled chunks that dripped down my back. I would have loved a hot shower right then.

I couldn't help but worry as I drove mechanically back to the office. I doubted Kale would step foot inside The Wicked Kiss tonight, and I sincerely hoped I was right about that. Whatever Arys was feeling, it was justified, but hurting Kale wouldn't change anything for the better.

I wanted to see Jez but decided it was best to let her get some rest. Knowing she was safe and alive made everything else seem a little less important. Maybe everything was going to blow up in my face at last. I'd crossed a line, and it was going to hurt everyone involved. Yet, Lena's death, the close call with Jez and the lingering presence of Maxwell and Claire made my personal drama pale in comparison.

Only Lilah was present when I reached the office. The scent of pure Were blood still hung on the air though she had cleaned up the mess. She came out of Veryl's office, sensing my arrival. Dressed simply in jeans, a tank top and sweet army boots, she wore no makeup. Not that she needed any, Lilah was a simple beauty. Strong cheekbones and sharp features made her flame-colored eyes seem to glow. Her wavy locks were just a few shades darker, a deep burnt orange.

She snapped her fingers as she approached, and a circle formed around the building. A wave of demon magic swept through me, throwing me off-balance. It left me feeling nauseous.

"Sorry about that. Better safe than sorry." Lilah gestured for me to join her in the kitchen.

I followed her in, suddenly aware I hadn't cleaned up the blood on my face or neck. Her gaze went to the vampire bite I wore, and I thought I saw her hide a smile. Could she tell it was Kale's?

"No worries. What's up? Jez is ok?" I sat down after she did though I would have preferred to stay on my feet.

"She was knocking on heaven's door, but I was able to bring her back. She'll be fine in time." Her choice of words struck me as strange. Before I could respond she continued. "I wanted a chance to talk with you, one on one. I know we rarely get the opportunity. Things are changing. I thought it was time."

I was uneasy. Lilah had never given me reason to fear her, but she was a demon. I didn't know if I could trust her.

"Alright. What's going on?"

Lilah sat casually in her chair, one leg crossed over the other. She regarded me with a serious expression. "You've spoken to Shya. He wants you to act as one of his personal assassins, a position that is not handed out to just anybody. I know you're headstrong and temperamental. I believe you're a perfect fit. But, what he's asking of you is dangerous. More so than anything you've faced or done. I can guarantee it."

"I haven't had much time lately to consider it. There's a lot I'm not sure of."

"I'm not here to convince you either way. Your choice is your own. I will give you one word of advice though. Don't agree to anything Shya asks of you unless you're committed to it." She blew a lock of hair out of her eyes and flashed me what was supposed to be a friendly smile. "You have power over vampires and werewolves. Naturally, Shya finds that appealing. I'm not sure he's ever seen anyone like you. Be careful."

When other creatures took an interest in me because of my power, it never seemed to go well. Shya was different, he wasn't a power-hungry vampire seeking a fun toy to suck dry. He was a demon, and what he wanted from me was probably far worse.

"Easier said than done." I picked up a sugar packet off the table and began to fidget with it. "I don't trust anyone anymore, but the fact remains that I need to do more than I've been doing. Staking newborn vampires has lost its appeal."

Lilah nodded, watching my nervous fidgeting. "I imagine. A challenge definitely does keep things exciting. As the decades pass, that's essential to sanity."

"Sanity," I scoffed. "Who needs it?"

"Rough night?"

I searched her eyes, finding genuine interest. "You could say that."

"Well, whoever he is, he's not worth it." A wry grin lit up her face, bringing an amused light to her eyes. Lilah was stunning in her own way. "Anyway, I have something for you."

I couldn't help but be curious when she left the room. I managed to keep my butt in the chair and wait. I heard a door open and close down the hall. What could Lilah possibly have for me? She re-entered the kitchen holding a long, thin box.

Placing it on the table between us, she reclaimed her seat and flipped the lid open. Inside was the most elaborately made, dangerous looking dagger I'd ever seen. The blade shone in the fluorescent lighting. It was longer than my forearm and designed in a gentle curve. Notches were cut out at the base of the blade, allowing it to cut through the air with little resistance. From where I sat, I could see the symbols etched into the metal. Whatever it said, it wasn't in any human language. The handle consisted of a series of coils of what appeared to be black jade. It was a magnificent weapon.

I could feel the power that emanated from it. Like a kid presented with a shiny toy, I immediately wanted to touch it. Instead I stared in wonder, my curiosity growing.

"It's called the Dragon Claw. I'm sure you can feel its power." Lilah turned the box so I could get a better look at it but made no move to touch it herself. "It was created to destroy those with a physical demonic form. That means earth walking demons and vampires. It doesn't even have to hit the heart. Once it pierces their flesh, it's all over."

"Wow." I gazed from the dagger to Lilah in wonder. "That's amazing. Where did it come from?"

"Would you be reluctant to take it if I told you it was forged in the fires of hell?" Her expression was dead serious. No joke there.

"Take it? Really? Me?" I sounded like a moron, but it was just so unexpected.

"You're still mortal. And, I sure as hell can't use it. One nick of that blade, and I'd be dead." She shoved the box even closer. "Here.

Check it out."

My hands were surprisingly steady as I lifted the Dragon Claw from its velvet bed. It was solid and heavy, but it felt good in my grasp. The jade handle was smooth but easy to grip due to the raised coils. The dagger spoke to my power, molding its own as if to fit me. Warmth radiated up my arm, but it felt right.

"It feels like it was made for me." I stared down at the gorgeous weapon in my hand, awestruck.

"It was."

Lilah's simple admission startled me, and I had to do a double take. "Seriously?"

"Yes. Shya had it made. All he needed to bind it to you was a strand of hair, easily taken from the hair clip left in your office." With a shrug Lilah picked up the sugar packet I'd dropped and began to fold down the edges. The casual gesture contrasted the weight of her words. "Sorry if that sounds creepy. It's demon magic. He needed a part of you. So now it's yours."

I didn't know how demon magic worked, and I didn't think I wanted to. It was very presumptuous of Shya to make such a thing for me. It raised warning flags.

"Why? What does he expect in return for it?" Suspicious, I laid the dagger back in the box, going so far as to close the lid.

Lilah chuckled. "Smart girl. Always ask that exact question before accepting anything from a demon, especially Shya. This time he only wants your assurance that you will kill Veryl."

Ah, so she knew about that. "Why is it so important that I do it? Can't anyone else? Why can't you?"

My question had been petulant though it hadn't been my intent. She was unfazed.

"Because I'm the one he's blackmailing. If I kill him, everything he has on me leaks to the people I want it kept from. He's assured me of that."

That was not what I'd expected. I turned that tidbit of information over in my head. Veryl was a scumbag. I didn't know what he had on Lilah nor did I need to; he was out of line.

"How do you know it won't still leak if I kill him?" It occurred to me that at no point since being asked had I really intended to turn down the hit on Veryl. What did that say about me?

Lilah met my gaze, and I saw in her eyes that she trusted me, something I was sure didn't come lightly. "I don't. It's a chance I'll have to take. The cocky prick has been using it to manipulate me for long enough."

Silence descended as I contemplated everything I knew. It was none of my business, but I couldn't help but wonder what Veryl had on Lilah. She herself was an enigma. I'd been dying to know more about her since we'd met. I'd never known anyone like her. Though she'd scared the crap out of me a few times with her power over demons, I had no reason not to help her.

"Lilah, please forgive me if I'm overstepping my bounds here, but what are you? I mean, I know vampires are rooted in darkness, demons in their own way. But, they aren't demons the way you are." There. I'd taken my chance and given words to the question nagging me.

I feared a negative reaction, but it never came. She didn't appear to mind my inquiry.

"I'm a demon. One of the highest in rank. Or, at least I was. I was cursed. Forced into a corporeal form. A vampire." The sugar packet in her hands suddenly exploded in a burst of white powder. "Veryl knows my true identity. That is information that could end my entire existence if it should fall into the wrong hands."

She was shut up very tight. I couldn't get a feel of her energy at all. The shadows in her eyes spoke loud and clear though. If I thought I had problems, Lilah's would likely blow mine out of the water.

"Thank you for sharing that with me." My gaze dropped to the box, and I thought of Maxwell and Claire. A weapon like that could be an advantage. "I'll do it. I'll kill Veryl. Just make sure Shya knows I don't owe him anything else."

"No problem." Lilah stood up and offered me a hand. "Let me know if you ever need anything. I mean it. Oh, and when it comes to Shya, watch out for the pretty words. He has a way of saying things that makes them sound better than they are."

"Gotcha. Word games with demons. I'm on it."

I smiled to lighten the mood. It didn't help. I'd gone from vampires to demons and from friends to lovers all in one night. I was ready to hide out in bed for a few days and will it all away.

That same hot wave of nausea passed through me when Lilah dropped her circle. Her demon power was heavy and thick. It felt like metaphysical molasses. I didn't like it.

I sat in the car after Lilah left, watching the night slip away. The rain had let up, but it hadn't stopped. Placing the Dragon Claw box on the passenger seat, I couldn't resist opening the lid to slide my fingers along the smooth expanse of the blade. It felt like a part of me. Knowing what Shya had done to create it should have bothered me more than it did. Touching the magical dagger and knowing it was mine, I was smitten.

ళళళళ

Coffee in hand and heartbeat erratic, I made my way up Arys' front walk. His neighbor, Mrs. Olson, sat on her front porch reading a book in the sunlight. The rain had stopped, allowing the sun to break through. It was a lovely morning.

She waved when she saw me. Her little dog came barreling across the lawn to bark at me, something he always did. He had no problem with the vampire that lived in this house, but he sure hated werewolves. The dog had been a gift to Mrs. Olson from Arys, after he'd killed the last one.

"Beat it, Frankie." I hissed beneath my breath. "You can't take me, and you know it, you little ankle biter." To Mrs. Olson I beamed a big smile and waved.

I felt Arys' heavy energy inside. Standing in front of the door, I sucked in my breath and knocked. In a sinister motion, the door swung open, revealing nobody on the other side. Arys was feeling cryptic. Fabulous.

I closed the door behind me and turned to find Arys looming in the darkened kitchen. I jumped, spilling hot coffee over my hand and on the floor.

"Holy shit, Arys. Are you trying to give me a heart attack?"

He retreated into the living room, expecting me to follow. Ignoring the coffee spill on the floor, I did follow, squinting as my eyes adjusted to the lack of light. The windows were so heavily draped, not a sliver of light made it through.

"How is Jez?" With a dark brow raised, he fixed me with a pointed look. Instead of sitting down like I'd expected, he remained standing in the center of the room.

I shifted my weight from one foot to the other, feeling awkward. "She'll be ok. I didn't get a chance to see her yet. I ended up talking with Lilah at the office."

"You'll be happy to know I never saw Kale. Your illicit lover remains alive to tempt you another night." His tone dripped venom, and I cringed.

I couldn't say anything to that, so I sipped my coffee, seeking comfort in the simple act but finding none. If he was going to rant and rave, maybe even lash out at me, I'd stand there and take it. He had every right.

When Arys saw that I wasn't going to offer an excuse or protest, some of the fire in his eyes burned out. "Dammit, Alexa! I want to ask you why, but I already know. I've been there. And, I gave in every damn time, too. But, it makes me sick with jealously, and I hate that I feel something so trivial and human."

"Is it human though? Why are all negative feelings simply human in your eyes, Arys? I saw pain in the eyes of a demon tonight, and I know damn well she's never been human."

His jaw clenched, and his gaze fell to the floor. "I want to kill him. Part of me wants to do it just to hurt you. And, then this little voice, this little fucking annoying voice reminds me that would make me a hypocrite."

"I'm not going to try to justify what happened. I know I can't, and I'm really not sure what to say here." Honesty seemed like the best policy. Arys was freaking me out a little.

"I have been where you are, Alexa. The power and the attraction, how it draws them to you, and they just can't get enough. It's what we are. And, it's in our nature to take advantage of that." Crossing his arms over his chest, he turned away from me. "I've been around a long time. Some might say too long. I have been with many lovers, though I have loved very few of them. Do you love him?"

Arys turned that drowning blue gaze on me, and I sputtered coffee. I knew what he was saying. Sexual energy was part of the feed.

Arys expected that the allure would at times cross into a full physical expression. He was separating this into two categories, feeding and love. And, I knew what he wanted to hear.

"I don't know." Wrong answer. "I mean, I care about him. He's my friend. But am I in love with him? I just don't know."

I fought to maintain steady eye contact with him. It was near impossible. He stared into me, and I felt like he was seeing parts of me I couldn't even access.

A few steps brought Arys painfully close to me. "If you were in love with him, you'd know. So either you're deluding yourself from your true feelings, or you're using him. It makes sense. He shares your weakness, your pain. It unites you. And, for a few minutes, that brings you peace."

White noise roared in my ears. Images flashed through my mind of Kale's agony and his need when he took me outside The Kiss. I'd shared it, every emotion. Together we had sought escape. Maybe Arys was right.

I sat down hard on the couch, spilling my coffee again. I stared at the splash of creamy brown liquid on the back of my hand, wondering when everything had gotten so complicated.

"It won't happen again." It couldn't. Kale was in love with me, and whatever it was that I felt for him, it could never be what he needed.

With an exasperated sigh, Arys picked up a photo from the mantel and put it back down. He was restless. The photo was of me. Shaz had taken it the summer before, when I wasn't looking. It was a profile shot with the sun setting in the background. It had been taken at Kylarai's.

"It will." Arys sat on the opposite end of the couch. He didn't glance my way. "I understand what you're going through, Alexa, the bloodlust and the power. It's so much to handle. But, I'm not where you are. Not anymore. I can only do so much to help you. But please, give me the chance to try."

"Arys, I do need help." My voice cracked with emotion. I willed him to look at me. "Things are changing. I'm changing. I'll never get through it without you. Please, don't let me self-destruct."

Reaching across the center cushion that separated us, he took my hand. That small gesture meant a lot. "Ah, my wolf. If only it were that easy. Self destruction is a choice one makes. I'd assumed you'd be a vampire before it got this bad. I was wrong."

"I don't think anything goes the way we expect it to. Not in our world." I abandoned what was left of my coffee on the glass top table beside the couch. Caffeine wouldn't help me now.

"Certainly not as far as you're concerned." He laughed dryly. The sound was hollow. "You can't make yourself a victim to the weaknesses anymore. It's time to take control."

"I know." Fighting the bloodlust and its urges was taking a toll on me. I couldn't keep doing it. "Resisting just makes it so much worse."

"If you weren't so damn stubborn, you wouldn't suffer the way you do. Feeding on life, it's what we do. Look at the rest of the world. Everyone is feeding off each other in this big, sordid mass of broken energy and fragmented souls. What makes us any worse than the rest of them?"

He wasn't wrong. The line between black and white had long since blurred to grey. Good and evil danced together, each unable to truly exist without the other. Humans had proven themselves to be just as evil as any of us. Still, the need to know I wasn't like the vampires burned in me. I was surrounded by creatures that thrived on the lives of others, and I couldn't accept that I was one of them. Not entirely.

"I feel like every night is a fight. All I want to do is give in, but I feel like letting myself is admitting defeat." Sharing this inner truth with Arys lifted the weight of it. I didn't want to constantly feel like I was fighting a losing battle. I just wanted to be.

"The only way to control it is to stop fighting. Otherwise, you risk driving yourself mad." His expression was haunted.

I remembered enough of his early memories to know Arys had put up the same fight I had. That side of him ceased to exist. He was all vampire now and more than happy to be. Would I, too, one day look back at this and be glad I was rid of this part of myself? The thought was overwhelming.

"I hate Raoul." The admission came unbidden as I sought a source to blame. "If he hadn't attacked me, if I'd never been anything other than human …"

Arys released my hand, but he moved closer, his action demanding my attention. "You wouldn't be here with me right now.

Nor would you have anyone or anything you now hold dear to you. Don't play the 'what if' game, Alexa. Life was never meant to be any way other than how it is. That's one thing I promise will be proven in time. Living in regret is not living at all."

"Listen to you and your centuries old wisdom." I gave him a playful shove. "I don't want to be like this, Arys, a slave to the power and bloodlust. I don't want it to tear apart my sanity or my relationships with the people I love."

"It's a drug." Arys nodded knowingly, reaching to touch a dreadlocked chunk of my disastrous hair. "As long as you resist the call, it will make you its slave. It's only when you finally accept that it's a part of you that you realize it's really not so bad."

Spoken like a true junkie. Arys had long since made his peace with it. I had yet to do the same.

"I'm not ready to let it become part of me yet." My voice had dropped to a whisper. Constantly fighting the many hungers I possessed was draining. I needed to escape, if only for a while.

"It already is. It's too late for that." Arys turned the matted lock of blond hair over in his hand, but his eyes were on me. "You're stronger than you think you are. Nobody can help you – you can't even help yourself – until you believe that."

The urge to crawl into his lap and find comfort in his embrace was strong. I didn't do it. I feared his rejection. Fatigue began to set in as the previous evening caught up with me. I longed for sleep, the only place where I might find a brief reprieve.

Arys' touch was gentle when he pulled me close and pressed his lips to my temple. "Go home, Alexa. Get some rest. There's nothing more to say right now." When I gazed up at him, wide-eyed and fearful, he brushed a soft kiss across my lips. "I love you."

Stepping out of the comforting darkness of Arys' small bungalow into the bright morning sun was disorienting. It burned my eyes, and I reached for the sunglasses that should have been perched atop my head but found none. I must have left them in the car. Scatterbrained and exhausted, I avoided home and instead headed for Kylarai's side of town.

I needed to be alone in the comfort of the forest. I needed to be wolf. Sometimes I went there and believed everything would be right with the world if I never left. This was one of those times.

Chapter Fourteen

Despite the craziness of the previous night, I woke up at sunset in the mood to kick some ass. I needed to burn off the pent-up frustration and aggression. The approach of the full moon was causing my wolf to stir restlessly. It was less than a week away, and I could feel it singing in my blood.

Avoiding Shaz was harder than I'd anticipated. I knew I had to come clean with him about Kale. I wasn't ready yet. During a brief phone call I told him I was spending the night prowling for something ugly to kill. I needed to pay Jez a visit as well. I felt relief when he said he was going to run with Kylarai. He'd be safe with her in our small town instead of in the city where assholes like Claire and Maxwell were waiting for the right opportunity to cause more chaos.

After spending the day in the forest, a hot shower felt like heaven. I tied my hair back in a ponytail and dressed for a hunt in leggings and a black top that said, "Suck it." I was hoping to find a vampire or other big nasty up to no good. I was eager to try out the Dragon Claw, and a good kill was just the therapy I needed.

Veryl would have been an ideal target. I contemplated it many times during the short drive from Stony to Edmonton. It didn't feel right though. Not tonight. I wasn't in the right head space for him. Tonight I wanted a mindless kill, something I could just have fun with. Veryl was different. With him, it was personal.

The bloodlust lurked, rising up to claw at my insides before slipping back into the recesses of my mind. Eventually I'd have to accept that it would always be with me. Ignoring it had proven to be careless and stupid. Sating the bloodlust was going to have to wait, though. The need to kill something that could fight back was dominant.

Finding vampires had grown easier since blood bonding with Arys. If I concentrated, I could feel them like a blinking beacon in my mind. I couldn't pinpoint the exact location of every vampire in the city, but I could get pretty close. The Wicked Kiss lit up like the Las Vegas Strip when I tuned into the energy that way. It was mentally blinding, crawling with vampires.

Did Claire know I could do that? Anyone who did would be smart enough to cloak their presence. I thought about Maxwell's blast of power, hoping to feel it out there. Nothing. Their time was coming. Claire and Maxwell would make their next move, and Arys and I would be ready.

I parked in the seedy section of town. Typical, new vampires would come here for an easy kill. The place was littered with drug dealers, prostitutes and random homeless people. Easy pickings. When I considered what went on here, the activity at The Wicked Kiss didn't seem quite so bad. At least there, the victims usually enjoyed it.

Striding down the street with the Dragon Claw clutched firmly in hand, I let all other thought blow away on the warm night air. Unfortunately, the dagger was far too big to safely secure it anywhere. The curved blade made it hard to fit to a sheath. I'd have to find a way to conceal it for future outings. A jacket could always help with that.

Two vampires lurked a few blocks ahead. I could sense their high-strung energy and hunger. They couldn't be very old. Cloaking my presence, I clung to the shadows as I silently approached. They were following a prostitute.

I saw her before I saw them. She dragged on a cigarette while ambling along as if she had no real destination in mind. A car sped by, slowing long enough for the occupants to shout something derogatory at her as they passed. She gave them the finger and continued on. I tried to imagine living her life and couldn't. Some would feel the same about my life. Funny how that worked. The grass really wasn't always greener on the other side.

The vampires didn't stalk her as I would have. Instead they callously leaped out at her from between two buildings as she passed. Like starving dogs, they were on her with little thought or tact. I was glad I'd decided to come out tonight.

I sprang into action, excitement thrilling through me. With a perfectly timed body check, I knocked one of them off his feet. Their victim shrieked and flailed wildly as she fought back. Everything happened so fast that it took a moment for the vampires to realize I'd crashed their party.

The one I'd knocked down was already on his feet, and I was ready for him. I swung the dagger, narrowly missing when he dodged the blow. He counter attacked, but I was ready for it and easily avoided contact. I could feel their lack of real power. All they had was inhuman strength.

Their victim was momentarily forgotten as they made the unspoken decision to tag team me. She'd already been bitten, but she was conscious and able to run as fast as her stiletto heels would carry her. My attention was on the vampire closest to me. He was circling me, trying to get me moving so my back would become unprotected at some point. I trapped his buddy in a circle, smirking at his sudden outrage.

"It's you. Goddamn werewolf bitch." My target snarled at me as I advanced on him. A newbie who'd heard of me? Interesting.

"Am I ruining your evening?" I smiled, revealing wolf fangs. "I get bored sometimes. This should give me a minute or two of excitement."

He looked uncertain, his gaze darting from the dagger in my hand to his buddy trapped in my circle. I could see it in his eyes. He was thinking about running. What a damn coward. Every step I took toward him had him dancing backward like a boxer. He had no way out of this, and he knew it. I quickly grew frustrated and without a second thought, flung the dagger so it spun end over end as it sliced through the air.

It struck him in the chest. Pity. I'd been aiming for his neck. The blade plunged through his flesh, and no sooner had blood burst forth than he dropped into a pile of dust. The Dragon Claw clattered to the asphalt with a sharp, metallic sound. I quickly retrieved it before dropping the circle that held the other vampire.

"Look, I don't want to tangle with you. Ok?" His hands were held up in surrender as he backed away slowly.

"Are you kidding me?" I stood in the middle of the quiet street, watching him flee. Disappointment filled me.

I was more than satisfied with the dagger. It did exactly what Lilah had promised. However, this was a failed attempt at working off some aggression and angst. Newborn vampires didn't have what I wanted. My thoughts strayed to Shya. Working for him could be incredibly dangerous and maybe even stupid. But, it might be just what I needed.

I quickly lost interest in the lesser vampires creeping the night. The dagger test was a success. It had killed that vamp without piercing the heart. Uncanny. It would taste Veryl's blood soon. I was eager for it.

After storing the dagger safely in the trunk of my car, I headed for a late night grocery store to buy a few things for Jez. She was a huge fan of chocolate, making it easy to find something she'd like. As an afterthought I grabbed a tub of cookie dough ice cream. It couldn't hurt.

She was alone when I arrived at her swanky apartment on the south side of town. I wasn't sure I'd ever seen Jez look so rough. She was beyond pale. Her skin was so white it appeared translucent. It caused her green eyes to stand out in startling contrast. Clad in soft flannel pajamas with hearts on them, she didn't look anything like the bad-ass cat I was used to seeing.

"Go ahead and say it." With a roll of her eyes, she took the bag of fattening food from me, going for the ice cream right away. "Yes, I do feel as bad as I look."

I followed her through the small but impressive kitchen where she paused to grab two spoons before continuing to the living room beyond. For an apartment, the ceiling was especially high. The furniture was simple black leather, all of it matching. The sound of vehicles on the street below drifted in through the open balcony door. I took a seat beside her on the couch and glanced at the television. She was watching *Jeopardy*.

"I'm sorry I couldn't help you, Jez. I should have been able to. I tried, but I just couldn't focus." I accepted the spoon she held out to me. Drowning my recent worries in ice cream really paled in comparison to the booze and blood I'd rather be drowning them in.

"It's ok, Lex. I'm fine. And, Kale is the one that tried to kill me. Don't you go feeling all guilty about someone else's mistake." Jez shoveled a spoonful of ice cream into her mouth and sighed. "Thanks.

I totally needed this."

Jez needed a sugary treat, and I would have gladly traded it for warm, lively blood. I frowned as I turned that thought over in my mind. It made me feel like a monster. The irony was that she was the one who had never been human.

"Have you heard from him?" I hid a wince when I asked. I could only imagine what Jez was feeling toward Kale right now.

"He's called. I've ignored those calls. I have nothing to say to him right now." Crossing her legs and settling back into the corner of the couch, she met my gaze. "I just can't believe he tried to kill me. Kale. Of all people. I get it: the guy has issues. But really? I would have expected it from you first. No offense."

I took a bite of ice cream, finding that my stomach instantly rejected the sweet substance. "None taken. How did it happen?"

"I walked into the office, and he was there. I knew he was a mess just from the looks of him. It all happened pretty fast." Emotion swam behind her eyes. She must have relived it so many times already. "How many people did he hurt after that? Do you know?"

I nodded, suddenly finding it hard to maintain eye contact. "A few. It was bad. I tracked him down at The Wicked Kiss. We had a bit of a confrontation. I haven't seen or heard from him since."

Jez' spoon stopped halfway to the ice cream container. Staring at *Jeopardy* as if it was suddenly the most fascinating thing I'd ever seen did nothing to help me escape the moment. She might have been recovering from her dance with death, but the leopard was as sharp as ever.

"Alexa? Did you do something?" She studied me hard, and I shrank back until my back was pressed against the opposite side of the sofa. "You finally fucking did it. You screwed Kale. And, after what he did to me?"

"It wasn't like that, Jez. I didn't go after him with that kind of intention. You know that. Things got carried away. There was a confrontation. He hurt me. I hurt him. Something changed, and the next thing I knew ..." It was hard to say it out loud. She gestured for me to spit it out. "The next thing I knew he had me up against the side of the building in the rain."

"I can't believe you fucked the guy after he tried to kill me. You're lucky I love you so much, or I'd claw your damn eyes out."

She shook her head and mustered a glare. "Well, go on. You have to tell me about it."

"What? Oh no. That's not necessary. Besides, there's nothing to tell."

"Yes, there damn well is. Start talking. If you can do it, you can tell me about it."

I found some relief in the fact that nobody in my life would ask for details except Jez. However, I wasn't sure I was ready to relive the encounter with Kale. I'd done my best to shove it from my thoughts.

"It was sudden and out of control. We were idiots to let it happen. I can barely think about it." I met her scrutinizing feline stare and felt like a mouse. With a sigh, I gave in and recounted the events of that night, omitting the really candid details that nobody but Kale and I needed to know.

When I finished, she wore a strange smile. "I knew it would happen. Gotta say, I think it's only going to make you both crazier than you already are."

"Yeah well, you're not the only one." With a groan, I told her about Arys' quick discovery of my little indiscretion and the talk we'd had after. "The worst part is I think he's right. I love Kale so much. But, I'm not in love with him, and I can never be what he needs. Even saying that, part of me still wants that connection. He shares something with me that I can't share with anyone else. It's so selfish, I know. I'm totally ashamed of myself."

Jez looked thoughtful as she continued to feast on ice cream. "What is liquid nitrogen?" Her response momentarily threw me until I realized she was responding to the television. Alex Trebek confirmed her answer to be correct.

"Sorry," she said to me. "I don't think rushing to believe what Arys tells you is the wisest move. This thing with you and Kale, it didn't happen overnight. He's not on my list of favorite people right now. But, he's still Kale, and we care about him. Whatever it is between you two, don't be too quick to write it off because of what Arys said."

"You're not helping, Jez." I slumped in my seat, turning the spoon over in my hand. I had no appetite for ice cream. "This is confusing enough as it is. I haven't told Shaz."

Her jaw dropped, and she reached out as if to slap me. I warded her off with my spoon. "Don't be an idiot, Alexa. Don't tell him! Especially not if it was a one time thing that's never going to happen again. Why hurt him for no reason?"

This reaction from Jez didn't come as a surprise. I didn't share her opinion. "I can't hide this from him. He would find out somehow anyway, and it would be so much worse. No. Shaz is one person I will never hide anything from."

Jez frowned. "Well, let me know how that goes."

My stomach turned at the thought of confessing my sin to Shaz. Tomorrow night. I had to do it. Putting it off any longer would be pushing it. It would look like I was hiding it.

"Enough about me." I rushed to change the subject before she could persist. "How are you really feeling? Do you need anything?"

"Nothing I can't obtain through a phone call for takeout. Really, I'll be fine. I think I just need to sleep for a few days."

Despite her weak energy and pale skin, the spark in her eyes reassured me that she would be fine. Kale had gotten lucky this time. He would never forgive himself for this. It would have destroyed what fragment of sanity and true-self Kale still possessed if he'd killed her.

"Lay low for a while. At least until those blood ring vamps are dealt with. You'd never stand a chance against them in this state." I studied her closely, sensing the breaks in her aura. She felt weak like prey. "And, stay away from Kale, too. Don't be alone with him for a while."

Jez laughed bitterly. "You don't have to tell me twice. You'll probably see him before I do. Can you tell him something for me? Tell him I forgive him. I just can't be around him right now. Maybe not for a while."

"Of course. I'll pass that along though, honestly, I'm not sure I can be around him right now either."

The conversation took a more casual turn, and I happily used the chatter as a temporary escape from my thoughts. It didn't take long to tire Jez out. Though she begged me to stay for a movie, I insisted on letting her rest. Nocturnal or not, Jez needed sleep. And, I needed to scratch the itch of bloodlust growing in the pit of my stomach.

"Call me if you need anything," I repeated like an annoying mother hen. "I mean it."

"Does that include some tender loving?" she teased with a grin.

145

It was nice to see her smile. It banished the image of her lying there on the floor bleeding out.

I pulled her close for a hug before heading for the door. "I'll see what I can do."

All jokes aside, Jez had come frightfully close to death at the hands of someone she trusted. I had to admit that I was glad that I wasn't the one who had attacked her. I'd tried once. Ironically, Kale had been the one to stop me. If only I'd been there to do the same for him.

Every creature, human or otherwise, was driven by some kind of hunger, some dark desires. Knowing that didn't make me feel like any less of a monster. As a naive newbie to the supernatural world, I'd truly believed using my abilities to hunt others was doing good, making it all right somehow. Now I saw the other side. My job was no more than a way to ease the urge to kill while reducing the risk of public exposure. Even that was no longer enough for me.

The bloodlust rose up to remind me that I would have no relief. Between the hunger for human blood and the yearning for more than what hunting newborn vampires could give me, I was like a junkie in need of a fix. I was sick of being a slave to my desires. Something had to give.

Flirting with the idea of finding my own willing victim, I, like many others, was drawn to The Wicked Kiss. If the source of the blood I desired was willing, how wrong could it be? It seemed so simple, like a twisted bloodlust booty call. Yet, I couldn't bring myself to do it once I got there.

As close to a vampire as I was, I still was not one. Letting myself come to their feeding ground seeking a fix made me feel more like a junkie than anything else I'd done so far. I couldn't do it. The wolf and the woman that I was refused to allow it. I found relief in that. The vampire inside could only push me so far. I was wolf, and I'd been born human; I had to hold tight to that.

It wasn't the first time I'd stared around the inside of the nightclub and felt the shadow of regret. Binding myself to Arys wasn't what I wished I could take back. I feared the future I'd created for myself. Rising as a vampire had seemed like some far off event that might or might not happen. But, it would happen. I would be one of them, and that knowledge sickened me. The deeper I sank into their world, the more I realized that I didn't want to belong to it.

Leaning against the wall in the dark, I crossed my arms over my chest and stared at the floor. I couldn't stand to watch the human donors throw themselves around. I'd never understand why they wanted to flirt with death in such a way. Surely some of them held to the hope they would be turned. They were all fucking crazy.

I was torn up inside and frightened by some of the thoughts and future scenarios playing out in my head. Bound by blood to a vampire, I was destined to rise as one after my death. It sounded pretty cut and dried, but was anything ever so simple? I could never voice these feelings to Arys. He would take it personally when it had nothing to do with our emotional attachment at all. This was all me.

I sensed the presence of a werewolf seconds before Shaz strode through the door separating the club from the private area. My heart skipped a beat when my gaze landed on the black-haired vampiress at his side. The wolf within rose up with a vicious snarl, and it was all I could do to contain myself.

The shock on his face when he saw me mirrored my own. All sense of rationale went out the door with what was left of my sanity. I was halfway across the room in seconds. The power swelled inside me so that I felt like a bubble about to burst. The bite on Shaz' wrist taunted both my jealousy and my bloodlust.

"Alexa, let me explain." Shaz held both hands up in a gesture of surrender. His companion merely regarded me with curiosity.

Enraged and crushed, I flung out a hand, casting enough power to throw the vampiress off her feet as well as several others in the vicinity. I wanted to slap him. Hell, I wanted to throw him across the room. So, Shaz had a dirty little secret of his own.

"This is running with Kylarai? You lied to me? So you could come here and be a blood whore for a vampire?" The truth was harsh. It hurt me to see it in his eyes.

I spun on my heel and rushed out of the club. I felt sick, like I might vomit. Shaz was right behind me, grabbing my arm in an attempt to stop me. I shook him off, determined to escape the sudden and ugly situation. I shoved past the people making their way inside and hurried through the parking lot. My power was massive and wild, triggering a chain reaction of car alarms as I passed.

"Alexa! Just hold on a damn minute!" Shaz easily caught up to me. He forced me to stop and, with both hands on my shoulders, held tight so I couldn't pull away. "Can we talk about this?"

I looked at the bite on his wrist, and my stomach flipped. I tried to shove him off me, but he held firm. "Talk about what? Your recent decision to become a donor? I don't even know what to say."

"Just let me try to explain. Please. I know how bad it looks. I was going to tell you, but I didn't know how." Anguish filled his jade green eyes, and I choked on my own guilt. "I've been kicking my ass over this. I wanted to tell you, Lex."

I sucked in a deep lungful of summer night air. I felt like I couldn't breathe. "So tell me. Tell me how long this has been going on. Is it just blood? Do I even want to know?" I was flustered and panicked. It showed.

It was never just blood. That's what Arys would say. To vampires, the exchange of blood is more intimate than sex, especially when both parties are willing. The thought of Shaz sleeping with her was like a knife twisting in my guts. My breath came fast, and I felt faint.

Shaz gazed deep into my eyes, forcing me to look at him. "I tried to resist. I really did. Since that night with Arys, it's been in the back of my mind. It fueled the curiosity and the temptation. I couldn't help it. I know that's no excuse. I should have told you."

Shock washed over me like a cold bucket of water in my face. This was my fault. I'd drawn him in, and like that first hit of heroin, the rush had claimed him.

How could I not have known? Vampire bites heal quickly on a werewolf, but there should have been some other sign, something I missed.

"Are you having sex with her?" I didn't want to know, but I couldn't not know either. "Is she the only one?"

When he was sure I wouldn't run off on him, Shaz released me but didn't step away. "There have been others. No intercourse."

Short, simple and painfully clear, an image flashed through my mind, the vampiress on her knees before my white wolf as she pleasured him. A pained sound came from me, rough like a growl. No intercourse. Yeah, I knew what that meant.

"Alexa, I'm so sorry." His voice broke, and I had to look away.

"Don't be too quick to apologize. I guess I couldn't have asked for a better way to tell you that things went too far with Kale." The urge to cry was strong. The certainty that I didn't belong in the vampire world grew. They were ruining everything and everyone I loved.

Shaz was silent for a moment. His energy was roiling with guilt, pain and now fury. It hurt, and I had to block it out.

"That isn't as much of a surprise as it should be." With a heavy sigh, he ran a hand through his platinum hair and stared at the traffic that passed on the street.

"I'm sorry I ever dragged you into this godforsaken world, Shaz." I sat heavily on a concrete parking curb, staring at my feet. "It destroys everything."

"I don't blame you for anything, Lex. You've never forced me into a situation I wasn't willing to be in. We're not human. Not even close. This world is ours, vampires and all."

My heart sunk. "You like it. And, I hate that."

He joined me on the curb. We didn't look at each other or touch. It was too awkward to pretend that everything was ok.

"You like it, too. What do you expect? We can't go through the motions of what normal life used to be. There is no nine to five job, no minivan full of kids and no picket fence. Not for us. I don't know about you, but I need more than that anyway."

I nodded, bitter with the truth he spoke. I was a mess of jealousy, hurt and guilt. "I don't want to be one of them." The confession slipped out, but it felt good to give voice to it. "The thought terrifies me, and I can't tell Arys."

Shaz did look at me then. Guarded concern shone in his eyes. "You're not going to do anything stupid, are you?"

"How much stupider could my actions possibly get right now?" I laughed bitterly.

"I'm serious. Don't you dare do anything to put yourself in danger, or worse. If you do something drastic, if you leave me here without you ..." He didn't have to finish that thought. The fear that gripped him was palpable even though I tried to shield his energy.

The wolf in me wanted to nuzzle him, to adorn him with wet wolf kisses. "Honestly, right now, I feel like throwing myself in front of a train, but I'd never do it. You know that. I've come too far to go out like that."

His expression was scrutinizing. I wasn't lying. Werewolves can detect a lie, an advantage that even vampires didn't seem to have. Finally he nodded, and some of the tension he'd been holding slipped away.

A particular question was floating around in my head, demanding that I spit it out. It was there, on the tip of my tongue, but I bit it back repeatedly. With a frustrated growl I blurted it out. "Why here, Shaz? With the vampires and blood whores that are nothing but junkies. Why not with Arys and me?"

I watched his eyes go wolf, and anger had his beast glaring out at me. "Wow. That's selfish, Lex. You know how I feel about Arys. He's not the easiest guy to deal with. I love you. You have to know that. But, just like you can't get everything you need from me, there are things I can't get from you either."

That hurt. It was brutal in its truth, and like they say, the truth fucking hurts. I heard a roar in my ears, like the sound of an entire ocean crashing over me. With my cheeks burning and pulse racing, I got up and walked away. One foot in front of the other, I walked down the street with no destination.

Shaz' words rang in my ears. He was right. I was being selfish because I didn't want to hear that. He deserved to find his own way, too. I knew that. I just couldn't accept it yet.

I could hear him calling my name. He would come after me because that's who he was.

I wanted to fall to all fours and run blindly through the streets seeking escape. But, nothing would make this all go away. I could run, but my past would be with me. Always.

I reached the end of the block when Shaz caught me. He was aggressive, grabbing me with clawed fingers that cut into my flesh. I yelped from surprise more than pain.

"You don't get to walk away from me! I'm sorry if you don't like what you hear, but we have to be honest with each other. You can't stand to hear it? Well, how do you think I feel?" Shaz bared fangs at me as his wolf pushed to break free. "How do you think it makes me feel to see those vampires crawling all over you? To have to share you with them? It makes me sick."

I recoiled in horror, wanting to escape both Shaz and his awful words. "So running off to get a few vampires of your own is the solution? Isn't that a bit hypocritical?"

His voice dropped suddenly, soft but deadly. "Maybe you're not the only one with a dark side."

Before I could fire back a retort, a sharp pain shot through my skull, blinding me. Maxwell stepped out of the shadows flanked by two lackeys. His assault on me was fierce, and I dropped like dead weight hitting the ground. With a commotion, the vampires quickly took Shaz down. I fought to see through the agony tearing through my brain. I was helpless.

Maxwell was a blur when he crouched beside me. The black veil of unconsciousness began to steal over me, and I struggled against it.

The last thing I saw was his mocking smile as he gazed down at me. "I've got to say, so far it has been a real pleasure doing business with you, Bitch."

Chapter Fifteen

I drifted in and out of consciousness. It felt like my head was in a vice. Maxwell clearly felt he had to keep me incapacitated which was a dead giveaway that he felt I was a threat. It was too soon to tell if that was a good thing or not. It might just get me killed that much faster.

Despite the pain that racked my brain, I was aware that we were being transported by vehicle. I could sense Shaz near me. My wolf paced inside me, anxious to burst forth and tear out some throats. I had a bad feeling that wasn't going to happen.

The scent of car exhaust mingled with cigarettes. Some vampires clung to old, useless habits. The smoke made me feel ill.

It was hard to tell how far we traveled before coming to a stop. I concentrated on gathering my power and forming a circle, but Maxwell had stripped my power. Opening the mental door between me and Arys was painful but possible. Forming thoughts enhanced the mind-shattering agony.

I sensed Arys' panic right away. He knew that if I was opening this link between us, it was bad.

'They have me and Shaz. I don't know where we are.'

'I can find you. Don't shut me out, beautiful wolf. I'm coming for you.'

I breathed a sigh of relief, finding restored strength in our connection. 'Don't walk into a trap. They'll be ready for you.'

We were in a Hummer. Shaz was slumped against the opposite door watching me with a confused frown. His face was bruised and battered.

The door was suddenly jerked open, and he almost fell out of the vehicle. We were dragged out roughly by the lackeys who shoved us along to an old two-level house. I couldn't tell what part of town we were in, but the lack of nearby dwellings was not reassuring.

The scent of blood and death hung heavy on the air. Whoever had called this house home was likely dead. Maxwell stepped up beside me, and I shrank back against the lackey crushing my arms behind my back. I didn't want another taste of his power, not unless I was the one controlling it. As long as he had the upper hand, I was only wolf.

"You didn't think we were going to stop with the witch, did you?" His calm tone and neutral expression conveyed a nonchalance that was carefully constructed. In his warped mind he was making casual conversation.

I bit back a series of curses that threatened to explode forth. Freaking out was not going to help. I kept my mouth shut, refusing to look at him. I guess Maxwell didn't like the silent treatment because he gave me a shove as we ascended the few steps leading up to the porch. The vampire holding my arms let go, and I hit the old, creaky, wooden planks hard. My upper fangs dug into my lower lip from the impact, and I tasted blood.

Shaz' growl was low and menacing as he struggled to come to my aid. They wouldn't let him. Maxwell waited for me to get up before opening the door so his flunkies could usher us inside.

The heavy aroma of potpourri wafted into my face, a cloying cover for the death and fear that lingered.

Directly in front of me was a staircase with old, worn carpet. To the left was a living room with an older model television and very few gadgets or electronics.

I had the distinct feeling an older couple had lived here. It pained me to think of Claire and Maxwell killing them and taking over their home. If only the old myth about vampires needing an invite was true. As it was, they could enter any building they damn well pleased.

To the right of the stairs was a dining room that appeared untouched, as though it hadn't been used in years. It was simple enough. A large table that had once seated an entire family paired with a cabinet filled with fine china and ornamental items. A plaque among them caught my eye. Praying hands were carved into the wood with the words: One Day at a Time.

Before I could take in more of the house I was pushed into the living room and forced down on the couch. The scent of perfume rose up to haunt me, flashing images of the aging woman who had worn it. Searching the end tables and bookshelf, I found a photo of her – it had to be her – with her husband at her side. They were beaming at the camera, arms around each other. They had to have been well over sixty.

I fumed, angry with what had happened to them. I shot Maxwell a glare, but he was too busy keeping Shaz separated from me to notice. They sat him down in an armchair on the opposite side of the room. I could see into the kitchen behind him but just barely. I kept expecting Claire to appear. I couldn't sense her, but I'd had no awareness of Maxwell before he took me down either.

Maxwell grabbed Shaz' wrist and sniffed at the wound. "Someone's already been at you, hmm? Pity. I like to have the first bite." Shooting me a warning glance, Maxwell inclined his head toward Shaz. "Try anything and this one dies."

I glowered at him. "Is there a point to this? Because I'd like to get to it."

Forgetting about Shaz completely, Maxwell glided across the room to stand before me. I braced for the hit, knowing it was coming before his hand collided with my cheek. My face stung, and it took all of my inner strength to take it. If I didn't, he would hurt Shaz.

My white wolf was being restrained by two of the three lackeys. He was snarling and straining against them. If he shifted he would have an advantage, but with a powerhouse like Maxwell present, it could get him killed. I tried to meet Shaz' eyes, to will him to calm down. He was already past the point of calm.

"You," Maxwell pointed a finger at Shaz. "Sit and shut up." A slap of energy had Shaz sitting whether he wanted to or not. "And you," Maxwell grinned down at me from where he stood. "Keep flapping that pretty yap of yours. I love a woman who doesn't know her place."

"Is that so?" Claire's voice rang out as she descended the stairs. "Careful, Maxwell, some women don't take kindly to chauvinism."

His eyes flashed with something close to anger before he turned to her with a big phony smile plastered in place. "Of course, my dear."

Claire stopped in the entrance to the living room and surveyed us. She wore a long black cocktail dress and held a goblet of blood in one hand. I was dying to roll my eyes at her. Like Maxwell, she was drawn to Shaz because of his wound. If I got out of this alive, I just might have to kill that black-haired vampire bitch at The Wicked Kiss.

"Oh my, you're a gorgeous thing." Claire fawned over Shaz much in the way one would admire a perfect holiday meal. "I can't wait to taste you."

"Oh, fuck no." I risked another slap from Maxwell. The bitch wasn't touching my mate.

The slap never came. Instead, Maxwell stepped away from me. Though he had all the power, Claire was the one pulling the strings.

Eyeing me with interest, she came to sit next to me on the couch. As if we were old friends, she smoothed a few tendrils of hair back from my face. I shot her a look of pure venom.

"You know, Alexa. This never had to happen. You could have played along and given us what we want. Now we have to torture it out of you." She smiled so sweetly as she spoke.

The word torture set off every survival instinct I had. My heart pounded despite my best efforts to remain calm. She would sense it and know she had me right where she wanted me.

"I prefer it this way." This from Maxwell who stood in the center of the room watching the door. They had to be expecting Arys.

"Really?" I was feeling better. Stronger. As long as Maxwell didn't slam me again, I might be able to draw on Arys' power to reinforce my own. "You honestly expected me to hand myself over to you just so you can take over where Harley left off?"

Sipping from her goblet of human blood, Claire pinned me with an appraising gaze. "This is business. It's all about supply and demand. And, you are in demand. I'm sure you understand that. You run a little business of your own built on the very same foundation. Do you not?"

I growled beneath my breath, hating that she'd caught me on that one. "It's not the same. The supply in my business is willing, not forced."

"I beg to differ. Willing victims are there because they want something, too. That's how it works. Supply and demand. In your case, the supply also demands." She made a face at her glass but continued to drink from it.

"Why do you need us? You're not powerful enough to earn your own place? You need me to do it for you." I was hoping to keep her talking until Arys found us. I could feel him there in my mind, a silent presence offering me strength and comfort.

"Werewolves are a hot commodity, and the werewolves that murdered Harley, even more so." Claire crossed one leg over the other, flashing a glimpse of thigh to the room through the slit in her skirt. "And, whatever you really are, people want a piece of it."

I looked at Shaz, finding assurance. "I'm a werewolf, Claire. Don't try to define me beyond that."

Maxwell scoffed. "A werewolf with enough power to be a hell of a trouble maker. It's your own actions that brought us here. If you hadn't interfered in the first place, we'd still be in Sin City grabbing tourists and virgins."

"Virgins in Sin City," I muttered. "Lovely paradox."

Claire waved a hand dismissively at us. "If anything, she did us a favor by killing Harley. It saved us from having to do it."

I groaned inwardly. I never would have dreamed that Harley's death would come back to haunt me like this. By wiping out one damn vampire, I had endangered myself and many others. It was a harsh truth to swallow.

Maxwell grumbled and shot Claire a dark look. "Enough talk, Claire. It's clear that we'll have to convince Ms. O'Brien to play along. The hard way."

The blood drained from my face, and I felt faint. I'd rather be dead than be part of what he'd described. Shaz was staring at the floor. I was sure he was waiting for the right moment to make a move, but I prayed he wouldn't do anything to get himself killed.

Claire shocked me by leaning in close, invading my personal space. She breathed deeply of my scent. "She smells good alright, but she's not pure werewolf. I think I'd rather keep her for myself." Before I could cuss her out for talking about me like I wasn't there, she drifted back over to Shaz.

The urge to pull on power through Arys was strong, but I knew it would be a mistake if I couldn't pull enough to take on Maxwell. He had weakened me. I was mortal, and he was not. The odds were not in my favor.

When Claire leaned in to sniff Shaz, he pulled away with pure disgust etched on his face. She huffed, clearly offended even though she was the one holding us against our will. She swallowed the contents in her glass, watching him as she licked the rim. In a blur of motion, she grabbed Shaz' injured wrist and bit deep.

He didn't even flinch. I came up off the couch with a snarl, instinct driving me. Drawing on Arys, I lashed out at Maxwell with a blast intended to keep him from stopping me. I just wanted Claire. The other three vampires sprang into action. One of them dragged me down to the floor where I fought to be free of him.

Maxwell's snicker as he watched was infuriating. It took all three vampires to hold me. I was forced to watch as Claire held her empty glass so that Shaz' blood would flow into it. She spared me a smile.

"You fucking bitch!" I spat. "I can't wait to tear your throat out."

Though my wolf raged, my inner vampire was surprisingly calm. My power immediately sought out a source, finding the three vampires holding me immobile. I grasped their energy and pulled hard on it. I could have drained all three of them like I'd done with the vampire at The Kiss if Maxwell hadn't been so quick to react.

I threw up a circle just in time to block his expected attack. However, I was momentarily stuck. I wasn't at full strength. Either a physical or a psychic attack on Claire would compromise my circle and make me vulnerable.

"Clever." Maxwell eyed me with a renewed interest. "So, you have a few tricks up your sleeve for a self-professed werewolf. Too much trouble."

"She's going to give us what we want. If she doesn't, we'll take it out on her little friend here." Claire's eyes sparkled with malevolence. She ran a hand through Shaz' hair with excessive force and raised the glass to her lips. Her pupils dilated as she tasted the blood of my mate. "You certainly are a divine thing. I could just take you home and keep you as a pet."

Watching her touch him made me crazy. Shaz pulled away from her, but she held tight to his hair, earning a growl from him which she ignored. After finishing the wolf blood in her glass, she roughly jerked his wrist to her mouth and ran her tongue over the bite. Her eyes were glazed as the heady werewolf blood affected her.

"Play along, Alexa. Let's make a deal, and we can all go our separate ways." Maxwell spoke to me, but he watched Claire with perverted intrigue.

"I have nothing to give you." I also watched Claire, waiting for the right moment. I couldn't stay trapped inside my circle. I had to do something.

"Help us get what we want. Nobody else you love has to die."

"If you want me so bad, you'll have to take me against my will."

A burst of power shattered my circle. Maxwell grinned. "We just did."

He was on me in a heartbeat. I found myself flat on my back, staring up at the ceiling as I gasped for breath. Maxwell straddled me, his perfect composure gone as he wrapped his fingers around my throat. Smacking my head against the floor a few times seemed to please him. Adrenaline prevented me from feeling any pain. I tried to strip his power, but he had a tight shield in place. I couldn't breach it.

I felt him digging deep inside me, tearing at the energy I'd just consumed. He wanted me helpless. I couldn't blame him for that, but I had to stop him from succeeding. I resisted, throwing up every metaphysical wall and barrier I could muster. He punched holes through them all.

In my peripheral vision I saw Shaz snap at Claire. She shoved him back in the chair and climbed on his lap while I watched helplessly from the floor. Old and strong, she didn't have much trouble pinning Shaz in place. The empty goblet in her hand became a weapon, and she smashed it against the side of his face. The sound of glass shattering was met with a yelp.

Maxwell dragged me to my knees, forcing me to watch as Claire fought for Shaz' throat. Bloody cuts marred the side of his face. I was desperate to get to him. Fire scorched my insides as Maxwell's power burned through me. I might have been powerful, but he had centuries of experience on me. Once again, I was at his mercy.

Only when I sat motionless and fighting for every breath did he release me. "That's enough, Claire. Take it slow, sweetie. We don't want to kill them yet."

"Fuck you." I coughed out. Oh God, where was Arys?

"I won't kill him," Claire purred as she licked the blood from Shaz' face. "I just want to play with him. He's so strong and silent. I want to see what it takes to make him scream."

All the ways I wanted to kick her ass flashed through my mind. I willed myself to get up. I thought of Shya and his claim that I held power over both wolves and vampires. How could he believe that? And, if a demon saw that in me, why didn't I see it in myself?

"I'll never scream for you, bitch." Shaz snarled. "I'd rather die first."

Dragging a long fingernail over the vein in his untouched wrist, Claire watched the blood rise to the surface. "Honey, you will be begging for death before I'm through with you."

The scent of Shaz' blood taunted my bloodlust. Weakened as I was, it came on strong and demanding. My hunger for the destruction of both vampires was greater.

"Such pretty eyes," Claire cooed, gazing into Shaz. "I'd love to add them to my collection."

My stomach twisted, and a heavy sensation settled in my guts. She stroked a gentle hand along his arm. In a swift motion, she grabbed one of his fingers and snapped it back with a *crunch*. Shaz grunted but didn't cry out the way I would have. He was holding his own against her, an impressive feat. It killed me to watch her hurt him.

"Stop, please!" I looked to Maxwell for help, but he was enjoying it.

"I need you alive, Alexa. Dead werewolves are useless to me. Help me get what I want, and if you can survive it, you can walk away free and clear." Maxwell shrugged as if he found it to be a great offer and I was the one being unreasonable.

I knew what they were doing. They couldn't simply drag us all the way to Vegas against our will. We would have too much time and space to put up a fight. They thought they could break me by forcing me to watch them torture Shaz. They were right. I couldn't take much more.

'I can feel you,' came Arys' voice in my head. 'So very close.'

Relief flooded me. I got to my feet though my head protested the move. Maxwell's fingertips crackled with energy, alive and ready. The room spun for a moment, and I struggled to see clearly. Being stripped of personal energy had left me feeling like I was barely contained within my body, a horrible sensation.

The door exploded, pieces of wood and metal flying. Arys burst through in a storm of power and wrath. His presence strengthened me in ways our mental connection hadn't. My power reached for him, finding that familiar bond. Arys wanted Maxwell, but anticipating the attack, Maxwell was already dragging me against him. With one hand on my throat in a crushing grip, he sneered at Arys.

"I'll kill her," he warned. "You might take me out, but she'll die first, Arys."

From her place atop Shaz' lap, Claire leaned her head back and laughed. "Now, it really gets fun. I was waiting for you, Arys."

Arys was livid. The energy rolling off him was hot enough to burn. "I can't believe you were stupid enough to bleed my wolf."

Claire began to pet Shaz as if he were no more than a common stray. "I can't believe you thought I wouldn't."

Arys moved suddenly as if to physically pull her off Shaz. She simply nodded, and her three minions jumped to restrain Arys in a brutal assault. Amusement danced in her eyes. This really was a game to her, but I sure as hell wasn't having any fun.

Arys turned his venomous gaze on Maxwell. "Is this really necessary?"

The two vampires glared daggers at one another. The power in the room was thick, almost dizzying. Arys had come here ready to face off with Maxwell. After the way the bastard had hit us both during our last encounter, I was wary.

"It is. We want something. You have it." Maxwell's power burned inside me. Something about Arys made him ruthless, ready to destroy me without a second thought despite the fact that he needed me.

"Bullshit. You came to make sure Harley was dead and decided to take advantage of it. But, you never expected Alexa to be everything she is, did you? So you thought you could use her for leverage in your own city."

I gave a small cry when Maxwell pushed enough power into me to serve as a warning to Arys. It felt like a scorching hand gripped my heart. Claire watched from where she perched on Shaz' lap, holding a tight handful of his hair. A smirk danced about her lips, but there was a shadow of uncertainty in her eyes.

Arys fought against those holding him back, and Maxwell forced my head to the side, exposing the artery in my neck. "How long do you think it would take her to bleed out? Care to place a wager on it?"

"Not as fast as it would take to turn Claire to dust. Are you really willing to risk your other half?" Arys cast a casual glance at the female vampire, and immediately she grabbed her head and shrieked. "You know you'll never be able to fill Harley's shoes. It's a little like playing dress up, don't you think?"

"Perhaps. It's just business, you know." Slashing a hand across the side of my neck, Maxwell opened a wound that was just deep enough to have the effect he wanted. I yelped when he tightened his grip on my throat.

Taking advantage of Claire's momentary distress, Shaz shoved her violently to the floor. He was off the chair and next to Arys, who held him back with a warning look. The vampires holding him got rough, shoving Arys to his knees. Shaz' eyes were pure wolf, but he waited, knowing a sudden move could be a mistake.

Even with my life on the line, I found reassurance in their ability to be a team when it mattered. I'd remember this next time they were tossing insults at each other … if I lived to see it.

I shuddered at the chill of Maxwell's tongue as he tasted my blood. I felt him react to me as he drew on my energy as well as my blood. I cringed inwardly, expecting the piercing pain of fangs, but it never came.

"Werewolf blood be damned," he murmured. "This alone was worth the trip. I understand why you're so protective of her. I would be, too. Dangerous, though, addictive."

He didn't taste me again. I couldn't be sure, but he seemed apprehensive. *Addictive.* I flashed back to the night Kale confessed to me that he hadn't stopped thinking about me since tasting my blood. I was walking, talking vampire heroin. It explained a lot.

Arys inclined his head, pinning Maxwell with a studious gaze. "Someone's after you, huh, Max? You reek of desperation."

Maxwell's energy grew frazzled. "You know how it goes. It's all about who has what and who wants it most."

As if to emphasize his point, Maxwell hit me with a power

push that had me screaming. Stars burst in front of my eyes. I pushed back against him, but even with Arys present, I was too weak. Blood began to drip from my nose, and I coughed painfully.

Recovered from Arys' psychic assault, Claire gravitated closer, curiosity and hunger gleaming in her eyes. "I want to taste her."

"I'll drop you where you stand, Claire." Arys looked from her to Shaz who stood tense but ready. They paid him little attention, a mistake in my opinion.

"No, you won't."

She struck me hard enough to throw Maxwell off balance.

Bright light burst behind my eyes, and I spat blood. The raging wolf inside me took the hit and enjoyed it. A smile crossed my face when I snarled, "You hit like a bitch."

Unable to hold back anymore, Shaz rushed her. Together they crashed into a coffee table, smashing it to pieces. Finding a jagged piece of broken wood, Shaz aimed for Claire's heart, but the vampire had already moved clear of the blow. She was on her feet again, delivering a swift kick that caught Shaz in the jaw, sending him into the shattered remains of the table.

She sprang at me, but I was ready. I brought a foot up into her gut with as much force as I could muster. She hit the opposite wall hard enough to knock picture frames down around her.

Everyone snapped into action at once. Arys lashed out with enough power to throw off all three vampires holding him. Two of them burst into dust.

Slamming my head back into Maxwell's face, I heard the crunch of bone and felt it give beneath the impact. He loosened his hold on me, and I followed up with a well placed kick between his legs. Arys was just suddenly there, stopping Maxwell with a hand before he could recover. The two of them glowered at each other, and the tension in the room grew unbearable.

"You shouldn't have come." Arys spoke through gritted teeth.

They were testing one another, seeing who would break first. The power in the room rose to a suffocating level. I felt a twinge in my gut as Arys drew on the earth through me. Undead, he couldn't tap into the earth without a living conductor.

"I told you. I'm here for the wolves that killed Harley." Maxwell jerked away from Arys, shock on his face. Seeking to escape the lively earth magic, he quickly encircled himself.

"You're out of your league." Arys laughed, a cold malicious sound. "Harley came for her, too. And now, he's dead."

"He really came for you, and you damn well know that. He knew that the way to get to you was through her."

Something in the atmosphere shifted. Even Claire remained where she was; we all watched as Arys and Maxwell shared something unsaid, something the rest of us weren't in on.

Arys was tightly wound, ready to break. My wolf looked out from behind his eyes. "Yeah well, he failed, didn't he?"

Maxwell regarded Arys with astonishment. With wide eyes, he almost took a step toward Arys before catching himself. "She's the one. The one you've been waiting for."

"Shut up!"

Before Maxwell could utter another word, Arys smashed through his circle. It jerked hard on the earth magic running through me, and I stumbled under the pressure. Sunrise wasn't far off. We were running out of time to safely escape.

Maxwell and Arys grappled with both fists and metaphysical fury. With a deafening smash, they hit the big picture window. It cracked in many places but didn't give way. Sparks of red and blue rained down as their energies collided, throwing each vampire in opposite directions.

I grabbed for Shaz, pushing him out of the trashed living room toward the front door. He still clutched the shard of table leg, ready to use it. I drew a circle around us, but it was weak.

"I want those wolves, Arys. The blood of the killers of Harley Kayson would make Vegas mine. As it was meant to be." Maxwell wore the crazed expression of a man seeing a way to secure himself a stronghold.

Arys slowly made his way toward us. "It was suicide to come here."

"I'm not leaving." Standing his ground, Maxwell watched with narrowed eyes as we fled the house.

"Then I guess we'll be doing this again real soon." Arys hesitated before tossing a parting shot. "Remember Max, you just fucked with two day-walkers. Sleep tight."

Inside, Claire demanded that Maxwell stop us from leaving. I was already dragging Shaz down the front porch, unable to hear Maxwell's reply.

I didn't appreciate being a pawn in his attempt to gain control of his city. Harley had a reputation in many places. It made sense that the one capable of killing him would be of interest to others. How would they react if they knew Harley had taught me how to kill him?

Arys' old Firebird looked like a godsend sitting in front of the house. I couldn't possibly get in fast enough. The last few hours of the night had been a gong show, and I wanted nothing more than to hide out at home until I was at full strength. Though I didn't usually trust Arys' driving, it was of no concern to me then.

We drove through the city, headed for The Wicked Kiss, in a strained silence. There had to be less than an hour until sunrise. I knew Maxwell and Claire would use that hour to vacate the premises and find a new haunt. They wouldn't stick around for me to come back for them when the sun was high in the sky.

"Here." Shaz leaned forward from the backseat. He held his hand out, but I didn't see anything. "Careful, don't drop it. It's just a few strands."

I turned on the interior light, and the auburn hairs in his hand glinted beneath the dim light. I turned to him with excitement. "Claire's hair? Amazing. You're a genius, Shaz."

He shrugged and turned his attention to the scenery flying by outside. Now that we weren't in a fight for our freedom, the awkwardness of our prior conversation came back to haunt us with words neither of us were ready to say.

Turning in my seat to face forward, I gingerly held the hairs, fearing I would lose them. This would enable us to track Claire. A good enough witch could do it regardless of the shields Maxwell used to hide their presence. We had a part of her; it had to work.

With a screech of tires, Arys decided last-minute to stop as the light turned red. I didn't have the energy to be worried about his chaotic driving. If we got there in one piece, I'd consider the night to have had a silver lining.

"Arys, is there something you want to tell me?" A bitter edge crept into my tone.

"No. Should there be?" He didn't even so much as glance my way.

I sucked in a deep breath and held it until my lungs threatened to burst. My stress quota had been reached hours ago. "Fine. Have it your way."

I wasn't up for a fight with Arys on top of everything else. Fuck it. Maxwell had revealed enough to make me suspicious. Whatever Arys was hiding, it already lived in his memories housed in my subconscious. It would come out one way or another.

Chapter Sixteen

I drove down the highway for home with the beam of Arys' headlights in my rear-view mirror. Being alone with my thoughts was exhausting. A dull throb in my temples served as a reminder of how easily Maxwell had stripped my strength and power. That wouldn't happen again.

We were cutting it close to sunrise, but after more than three hundred years, Arys knew how far he could push it before endangering himself. Ten minutes down the highway, we reached the Stony Plain exit. I wanted to go home, to bed, where I could hide beneath the covers and cry. I was relieved when Arys turned off to go to his own house. I needed to be alone.

What a night. If I'd known how it all was to play out, I'd have just stayed home. Too late for that. I'd heard Maxwell's strange comment about me being the one Arys was waiting for. I'd discovered Shaz' little secret. The recent memory was enough to make me cry. Maybe if I hadn't been so damn tired.

The darkness was thinning. As I navigated the small town streets toward home, the stars overhead disappeared from sight. The sun was coming, and with it, the promise of payback. Arys had a point. Nocturnal as werewolves were, nothing stopped us from walking in the sun. Now that I had a way to locate Claire any time I wanted, a daytime attack seemed like the best way to exploit their few weaknesses. Unfortunately, it wouldn't be today.

Turning the corner onto my street, I was surprised to see Shaz' car parked in front of the house. After his fast exit from The Wicked

Kiss' parking lot earlier, I had expected him to head for home. Or, wherever else his desires took him. Though he had a key to my house, he sat on the front step. He stood up when I pulled into the driveway. My stomach clenched.

"Hey, babe." I was sick with worry but greeted him as if everything was fine. My legs felt like jelly as I walked across the yard to him. "I didn't expect to see you again tonight.

True to his most common nervous habit, Shaz ran a hand through his hair once then a second time. "I think we both need some time alone right now, but I didn't feel right leaving it this way. There should be no secrets between us. I'm sorry you found out the way you did."

Shifting my weight from one leg to the other, I crossed my arms over my chest, unsure of what to do with myself. I wanted to tenderly touch his bloody, bruised face. "If anyone should apologize, it's me. I brought you into the chaos of vampires and everything that goes with them. I feel like it's consuming us both, and it's my fault."

"You can't take all the blame for this, Lex. It is what it is, and we both play our part. We deal with it, or we let it break us. I'm not ok with letting this come between us. Our bond was built years ago, before any of this came into play. That's worth fighting to protect."

In this house, I easily flashed back in time to several years ago when I'd been a foolish idiot fawning over Raoul but always finding my comfort in Shaz. Back then I hadn't realized why I always gravitated to him, but Shaz had always been the one.

"It scares me. I can't help but fear that this is going to tear us apart. If not now, eventually." It was a confession that stung, one I wanted to wish away rather than validate with words. "It feels like the only time I know who I am anymore is when I'm with you."

Without hesitation, Shaz pulled me into his arms. I crumbled against him as tears pricked the back of my eyes. Despair taunted me, encouraging a few hot tears to slip down my face. They were pure and clear, void of blood. I inhaled his scent, finding the heady mix of wolf and pine to be cleansing.

"Lex, you're the one that helped me hold it together when the wolf was new and I wanted to tear every living thing I came across to shreds. You helped me remember that I'm a person and not just a predator with a human face. I've always adored you, and nothing is going to change that." His hand was warm against my forehead as he smoothed back my hair. "We're both in a really fucked up place right now. But, when haven't we been?"

I shook my head and choked back a sob. "Not like this. It's never been this bad. I know it's wrong but the thought of her touching you, feeding on you, it makes me want to die. I'm sorry. I hate myself for making you feel this way."

His deep sigh resonated with unspoken emotion. We stood there on the front lawn, clinging to one another like the desperate kids we'd started out as. Those days were long over and yet, I felt just as young and naive as I had then.

A car engine down the block started, breaking the quiet of early dawn. One of the neighbors was on her way to work, just a general part of everyday human life. A relatively mundane event that I was suddenly madly envious of.

"Hey, we're not doing that." He murmured into my hair. "No blame and guilt. It won't do either of us any good. I want you to know, I understand things better now. I'll never know exactly what it's like for you, but I've gotten a taste of the temptation you deal with. And, it's a bitch."

I pulled back to gaze up into his eyes. His expression solemn, Shaz clasped my hand in his. I could feel his unease. He was as shaken up about this as I was.

My gaze dropped to our joined hands, straying to the bites on his wrist. "I don't want this to break us."

He nuzzled me, a gentle brush of his cheek against mine, the soft touch of his lips to the side of my nose. "Nothing will break us."

It was exactly what I wanted to hear. So why didn't I believe it?

I wanted to say so much, but none of it seemed right. Demanding that he stay away from The Kiss and especially away from the vampire bitch who bit him wouldn't be proper. Jealousy ate at me, and I had no choice but to take it. As it was, I was dying to beg him not to fall in love with her. The irrational request slowly died inside me, fading as the night did.

The faintest trace of morning light peeked over the horizon. As dawn rolled in to the east, the night continued to linger in the west. The sun and moon shared the sky, the rulers of day and night meeting for the briefest of moments before they were forced to part. How many people paused even just once in their lifetime to witness this flash of short-lived beauty?

I couldn't give it up. How Arys ever managed to find contentment living always in the dark, I would never know. I lived for the night, but I always knew that the morning would come, that I would see it should I choose to. To have that choice stripped from me … I couldn't bear it.

"Tomorrow after sunrise, I'm going back for Claire and Maxwell. They want werewolves, I'll bring them werewolves." A smirk twisted my lips as I envisioned how I hoped it would all go down.

"Bring the pack?" Shaz nodded approvingly. "Great idea."

"Anyone willing to come, anyway. I think it will give us a huge advantage. I plan to be at full strength, and this time I will be ready for Maxwell."

"I'll be by your side. Don't even consider going after them without me. You know Arys will have a fit."

"I don't doubt it. But, I have a secret weapon, something those vamps won't see coming." I gestured for him to follow me to the trunk of my car. I lifted the velvet lined box from its place under the spare tire. It was the best location I'd had to hide it.

Opening the lid, I released the breath I'd sucked in when I caught sight of that gorgeous blade. The Dragon Claw took my breath away as it had the first time I'd laid eyes on it. Shaz was immediately intrigued. Reaching to glide a hand over the flat side of the blade, he seemed to fall under its spell.

"It's amazing. Where did you get it?" He stroked it almost lovingly, lingering on the jade handle. "It feels like you. Like its part of you."

I met his confused expression with one of my own. "You can feel that?"

"Yeah. It's strange, but I get this wolf vibe from it. Your wolf."

"It was made for me, with a piece of my hair. By demons." I paused. What more could I really add to that? "It will kill a vampire with just a cut. Doesn't even have to hit the heart. It works like a dream."

"So I take it this means you'll be working with him. The

demon that came to see you at The Kiss." His response was guarded, but I knew he didn't like it.

I shrugged and closed the dagger box. "The only thing I've agreed to do for Shya is kill Veryl. Beyond that, nothing has been determined. I don't trust Shya. I can't."

"Kill Veryl? Wow. I knew you were pissed at him after the whole Raoul thing, but I didn't realize you were that pissed at him."

Slamming the trunk closed, I clutched the dagger box tightly. "He's blackmailing Lilah. I can't help but feel I don't owe him any alliance. Not anymore."

Shaz walked me to the door, and though I wished he would stay, I knew it was best for both of us if he didn't. His eyes filled with longing, and he touched a hand to my face when he said, "Be careful."

I smiled, glancing away to hide the shadows of pain I didn't want him to see. "I will."

A soft touch of his lips to mine had me fighting tears again. I was astounded that I had the energy for tears at all. Shaz lingered, kissing me again, tender and affectionate.

"Get some rest, Lex. You need it. I love you."

I watched him go, wishing I could say everything I'd held back and knowing it wouldn't change a damn thing. "I love you."

The house felt especially large and quiet. I was seldom home alone. Without the sound of Shaz banging around in the kitchen or Arys offering random commentary on television shows that he simply had to pick apart, it seemed so vacant and lifeless.

Drained and exhausted, I hurried through a shower and slipped into a silk bathrobe. The delicate material felt good against my battered skin. Despite how fast I healed, stiffness had set in to make every bruise and ache excruciatingly pronounced. Soon, I would be healed and rejuvenated, one advantage of being inhuman. I'd had worse. I'd survive.

I climbed into bed with the remote in hand. Spreading out in the center, I had a moment of enjoyment at having the whole bed to myself. It wasn't something I'd like to get used to, but it was perfect right then.

After channel surfing my way to a standup comedy special, I half-listened to the crude comedian. Though sleep was waiting to claim me, I couldn't stop thinking about what Maxwell had said to

Arys. I wanted answers.

I searched my memory, fighting to break through the barrier that kept Arys' several lifetimes of memories locked away from my conscious mind. I should have been grateful for that barrier; it kept me from being overwhelmed by Arys' past. It kept me sane. But, there had to be a way to break through, to pinpoint the one memory that would reveal to me what Maxwell meant. Besides, occupying myself with Arys kept me from obsessing over Shaz.

Settling myself comfortably amid the pillows and comforter, I let the haze of slumber creep in. My angle was to fall into that lucid semi-conscious state between awake and asleep. I knew I was slipping, and true sleep would claim me any moment. Fighting it, I focused on Arys, letting my mind wander over some of the memories of his that I had already seen clearly.

Most of them made little sense to me. They often came in random bursts of visions and feelings. When we'd first bonded our power, his memories haunted my dreams often. Now they were repressed, hidden away inside my mind where I generally preferred them to stay.

I drifted in and out of Arys' past, seeking Maxwell. It was there; I knew it was. I just had to tap into it. I kept Maxwell at the front of my thoughts, hoping it would pull him out of the dredges of my mind.

'What, pray tell, are you doing, my wolf?' Arys' voice boomed through my head, scaring me out of the hazy lull I'd fallen into.

Jerking upright in bed, I swallowed hard and gasped for breath as my heart pounded. 'Nothing. Just trying to fall asleep.'

'Fall asleep? Or dig through my memories for answers I'm not ready to give you?'

Tapping Arys' thoughts was not part of the plan. I kicked myself, glad he couldn't see me. I knew he'd be giving me *the look*, the what-the-hell-are-you-thinking look.

'You weren't supposed to know.' Sometimes, censoring myself was for the best, but this wasn't one of them.

'I gathered.' Even telepathically his cynical tone came across just fine. 'Go to sleep, Alexa. You'll know when I'm ready for you to know.'

That chauvinist attitude ticked me off, and I let him feel my anger. It was just like him to boss me around because he wasn't in control of a situation. 'Don't tell me what to do, Arys. You'll have a fight on your hands.'

His low, velvet smooth chuckle floated through my mind to touch me intimately. 'Do what you will then, you feisty little pain in the ass.'

He was gone, closing the door between us with a force I felt. He didn't think I could do it. If Arys believed I could sift through his memories like rifling through a file folder, there's no way he would have laughed it off. Cocky vampire.

Sleep came and with it the deep dreamless slumber that often accompanied extreme fatigue. If I was going to get the information I felt entitled to, it wasn't going to be easy.

Waking just past sunset, I felt momentarily disoriented. As much as I would have loved to stay in bed, I had things to do. Once Maxwell and Claire were dealt with, I was having a movies in bed weekend come hell or high water.

Rather than attempt a last-minute wolf pack meeting, I decided to call select members one by one. The town pack was small and for the most part, tightly knit. However, a few pack members had a family, children from before the change. I wouldn't call them. I wouldn't risk anyone's mother or father.

I didn't want to ask Kylarai because I knew she'd say yes. Endangering her was not what I wanted. Yet, she was my beta wolf, and she would be insulted if I didn't call her first. While I peered into the bathroom mirror and applied smoky black eyeliner, she returned my call.

"Julian wants to come," she informed me as soon as I picked up. "I think you should let him. Zak's coming, too. How many do you want to bring? That will make five altogether, us included."

I leaned in close to the mirror to double-check the liner framing my brown eyes. "Four. I don't plan on shifting. Four should be plenty. I don't want to drag too many innocent pack members into this either. Julian has dues to pay. I'll gladly let him put his life on the line. I guess Zak's a big boy. But, are you sure you want to come, Ky? Don't feel obligated."

"Of course I feel obligated. We're pack. You know I've got your back if you need me. I want to back you up, Alexa." She paused, and I heard papers rustling in the background. "Besides, I could use a little excitement."

Kylarai had been itching to break away from the same old routine for a while now. I couldn't blame her in the least. It was hard enough to see how my world had affected Shaz. I wasn't letting it happen to Ky, too.

"Excitement that could get you killed isn't necessarily the best way to break away from the everyday." I recalled the utter horror and disgust on Kylarai's face when we were in The Kiss.

"Trust me, Alexa. It will be good for me to help you kick some vampire ass. Just say when, and I'll be ready."

Ah. It made sense now. Kylarai saw a chance to sink fangs into some vampires, and she wanted to take it. Since Arys and I had bonded through blood, Ky had been less than enthusiastic about my relationship with him. If tearing a strip out of Claire and Maxwell made her feel any better about it, then so be it. I was suddenly relieved. She could handle this.

It would be several hours yet before sunrise drew near. Perhaps it would be smart to lay low until then. I had no such intentions.

"I have some things to do. I'll call you later. Be ready by dawn."

Chapter Seventeen

A vampire lover with something to hide, a wolf mate with his own dirty secrets and a birthday in less than a week. If I lived to see my twenty-seventh birthday without losing my last shred of sanity, it would be a miracle. By that time I might be hard pressed to find a reason to celebrate. If I didn't self destruct by then, I'd drink to that.

The bloodlust that had me currently stalking the slums was just the icing on the proverbial cake. I was giving in on my terms. Hunting down my own victim had to be better than letting the hunger choose one for me. By starving the bloodlust, I only weakened myself. I was through with that shit.

I knew exactly what I wanted.

A few blocks away from Chinatown, the real street people showed their faces. A couple of crackheads harassed a prostitute for money half a block away. I watched from the shadows as she lipped them off while threatening them with a can of pepper spray. She was young, too young to be selling herself for drug money. Perhaps what she was about to see would be enough to get her off the streets.

I didn't want her nor the junkies ambling away, chased off by the sight of the pepper spray. Some vampires might not mind some illegal narcotics in the blood, but to me it just stank of toxicity. I was counting on stereotypes to deliver me a victim I could sink my teeth into.

The need to satisfy the hunger was constant, but I was content to wait. It would be worth it. I didn't have to wait long before a simple beige sedan rolled to a stop beside her. Excitement thrilled through me. Any john that was willing to pick up a streetwalker as young as her was fair game as far as I was concerned.

She leaned down near the driver's window to speak with him. He looked like your everyday guy. Short, dark hair and glasses, he was clean-cut with a professional appearance. He could have been a doctor or a banker, a regular professional with a regular life. But here he was, stopping off for a piece of underage action on his way home. So now, he was mine.

After exchanging a few words, she walked around the car to the passenger side. With preternatural stealth and speed, I attacked. I sprang at the car like a rabid cat, easily dragging the driver out. His eyes widened in sudden fright as he drank in the sight of me snarling down at him.

The girl shrieked and jumped away from the car as it rolled along, still in gear. It came to a stop against a nearby light standard. The john put up a good fight. He flailed like a victim in a horror movie during those last few seconds before the axe falls. I loved it. Every panicked motion and high-pitched, pathetic scream fed the hunger burning inside.

The prostitute was forgotten as her shrieks echoed in the distance along with the click of her high heels. A small, twisted part of me said, *take it slow*, but I couldn't resist. I tore into him with a frenzy of fangs and claws. His blood was hot against my face, and I sighed when it hit my tongue.

Everything in me that was vampire cried out in victory while my wolf was strangely content with our choice of victim. I barely left him in one piece. Wolf fangs did a hell of a number on the throat of a human. He was a mangled mess when I decided I'd had my fill.

Fed by his fear and my lust, my ears buzzed with high-running energy.

My body vibrated with exhilaration and an erotic heat swept me. Looking at the remains of my victim, I knew I had to act fast, but part of me didn't give a damn if anyone else happened to come along. Really, what were they going to do about it?

That kind of thinking was going to get me in shit. With a euphoric giggle, I dragged the body over to the car and stuffed it in the trunk. Yeah, this one was going to give a detective something to ponder. I should have at least dumped him in the river, but there was no time for that. This was exactly the kind of kill that would have had

Veryl jumping down my throat. Somehow, I had the feeling Shya wouldn't feel the same way.

Veryl. Yes, that was something coming up quickly on my to do list. Licking the blood from my lips and fingertips, I slipped back into the shadows and made my way back to my car. The rush of what I'd just done had me soaring, and I regretted how quickly it had all happened. I recognized the vampire's need to draw it out, to enjoy every second. My victim had gotten off lucky, this time.

I knew I should have been afraid of how close I was walking to the blood madness I found so repulsive in the vampires of The Wicked Kiss. I wasn't. I had too many other things to fear.

As I basked in the metaphysical ecstasy, I was numb to the emotional turmoil that I'd sought escape from. Perfect. Turning my emotions off was the only way I could get through the next day or so without coming apart. Telling myself things could be worse did nothing to make me believe it. If I let myself think about it, I saw Shaz with that vampire bitch, and it threatened to bring me down.

The afterglow of the kill enveloped me in a safe, warm circle of energy that danced with the promise of sanctity. Nothing could hurt me if I stayed wrapped inside this feeling. It made sense when I applied it to both Arys and Kale. They sought escape from the pain of raw emotion in their kills. But, if that soon became the only way to find freedom, was it not just a different form of imprisonment?

Muttering a few obscenities under my breath, I decided pondering the depth of it all was a waste of the amazing power high I was riding. My limbs felt light and floaty. My keen senses were finer tuned than usual if that were possible. The sounds of the city's dark side was filled with the occasional squeal of tires, loud voices and far off shrieks. The creatures of the night wore many faces and forms. I was just one of so many.

As I drove through the slums, watching it slip away to better neighborhoods, I expected to feel guilt or shame. I felt nothing. By the time I sat in my car in The Wicked Kiss parking lot, I was certain I'd just rid myself of the last part of me that had been human.

I wrestled with the decision to go inside. The black Camaro a few spaces away taunted me as surely as it had my adrenaline pumping. I wasn't ready to confront Kale. I knew I never would be. If I didn't feel such obligation to this hell hole, I would consider leaving and never coming back. If only.

The moment I crossed the threshold into the club I felt Kale's gaze land upon me, and I just needed one stiff drink. I headed straight for the bar. I waited for Josh to slide me a whiskey, doing all I could to avoid looking when I felt Kale sidle up beside me.

The whiskey hit my bloodstream and quickly paled in comparison to the rush of blood and death. I shoved the empty glass away and turned to Kale, expecting to pass out from the nerves.

The burning emotion in his eyes said more than words. It tested my resolve and urged me to give in to the promise of the comfort that I knew I could find in him. Wanting someone this bad wasn't right. Not when you couldn't really have them.

"I shouldn't have run out on you the other night. I hope you can forgive me for that. I've been kicking myself ever since. It was selfish." The atmosphere grew intense. Kale's energy was running hot.

I fidgeted with a strand of my hair, feeling the anxious need to keep my hands busy. "It was smart. I don't blame you. Really."

"It was chicken shit. I should have stayed." Kale grabbed my hand and slipped his fingers between mine. The undying hunger I had for him flared to life. "I didn't want this to happen, Alexa. I didn't mean to fall in love with you. But, it's too late for that now."

"Kale, don' t... we don't need to do this right now." I choked on my guilt; I seemed to have so much of it these days.

"I know you'll never love me the way I want you to. But, I know you feel something for me. And whatever that is, I need to know. I think you owe me that much."

What was it about Kale that brought me to my knees? He was one of the strongest people I knew, having survived more than most could dream of. All he had to do was turn those passion-filled eyes on me, and I became weak.

"I owe you more than that. I'm so confused ... so much is going on, and I'm starting to feel like I've reached my limit on how much I can take. I want to escape, and the only way I know how is by giving in. Giving in to you, to the bloodlust ... I see everyone around me doing the same, and I can't take anymore."

The emotion burst forth as the place deep inside where I tried to bottle it up reached capacity. I wanted to cry, but I refused to let the blood tears fall. Screw that.

Kale touched the faded bruise outlining my left eye. With a shuddery breath, I drank in the comfort of his soothing touch.

"Sometimes fighting so hard to make everything right is what brings you down in the end." Pulling me against him, Kale murmured into my hair. "Some things have to happen, and you have to learn to let them."

Breathing in his heady scent of leather and soap, I found the solace he always promised me. I longed to believe that there would be meaning in all of this. It was hard to think that such horror as the bliss I knew when I killed and the indiscretions of both myself and Shaz could have any kind of purpose.

"I just want to be free from it all." The burning in my veins was driving me crazy. Kale was as much of a drug to me as the bloodlust was.

Slipping a hand into my hair, his voice dropped to a whisper. "Let me love you the way I should have when I had the chance."

I gazed up at him, smitten and conflicted. I wanted to say yes. It was on the tip of my tongue, but what came out was, "I can't. It's not that I don't want to..."

"It's that you never let yourself feel anything other than pain and agony. Really, Alexa. That's getting old." In a brazen move, he claimed my lips in a tender kiss that left me dizzy.

I groaned and pulled away, but he held tight to my hand. "Why do you always have to be right? Maybe that's what's getting old."

I shook my head and stared at our joined hands. How did I make it clear to him what I felt when I didn't really know? From moment to moment it changed. Overwhelming desire became mind racking guilt, and somewhere in between was what I really wanted.

Before I could utter another word, I gasped as the cold undead power of Arys rose up with an icy blast inside me. He strode through the door with eyes blazing in anger.

I jerked my hand from Kale's and immediately felt like an ass. Kale merely regarded Arys' approach with indifference while I quaked with tension and fear.

My dark vampire was fuming. As he drew closer I felt it burning inside me, hot and bitter. I drew myself up and faced him, ready for the fit of temper I could tell was coming.

Arys cast a furious glare Kale's way before turning it on me.

"What the hell are you doing here? Last night's torture session wasn't enough for you. Fuck, Alexa! When did your death wish get so bad?"

"Excuse me?" I looked up into Arys' gorgeous face, finding myself torn between defensive anger and nervous laughter. "I'm not a child, Arys. Don't talk to me like I'm incapable of taking care of myself."

"You mean like you did last night?"

Kale regarded us both before his pensive gaze settled on me. "You were tortured?"

"Not really." I shrugged as if it was no big deal. I didn't want the both of them all over me with the scolding. To Arys I said, "I don't have a death wish."

"Like hell you don't," he scoffed. Turning his midnight blues on Kale, he scowled. "Funny how you weren't around last night when she could have used you, but when there's a chance of getting some tail you show up."

My stomach dropped. I opened my mouth to spit out a panicked reply, but Kale beat me to it. He was more prepared for this moment than I was.

"Ah yes, here we go. Say what you will, Arys. I don't owe you an explanation, and if it's an apology you're expecting, you'll be disappointed."

"That doesn't surprise me in the least. You've been after Alexa for a while now. So now that you've gotten a taste, I know you'll be backing off." The threat was there, spoken in low tones. Arys' menacing calm was more frightening than his temper tantrums.

Kale reclined against the bar, fixing Arys with a disaffected stare. "Alexa can make her own decisions. Sounds to me like you have bigger worries right now than whether or not I have a thing for your girl."

"Yes!" I interjected quickly, angling my body so I stood between them but could see them both. "We do have other things to worry about. Things that I plan to take care of after sunrise."

"What?" Arys' attention was quickly diverted as I'd hoped it would be. "Oh, hell no. You are not taking them on without me."

"Yes, I am. I'm going in with four wolves as well as the dagger Shya gave me. I'll be fine. Let me draw on your power if I need it, and they won't stand a chance. Give me some credit. These aren't the first vampires I've hunted."

The atmosphere grew stifling. Arys was seething. "You took something from Shya? A demon? See, I told you. Death wish. If Maxwell overpowers you…"

"I killed Harley just fine without you. I think I can handle this." It was a low blow, and I immediately felt bad.

Harley's death hurt Arys more than he would ever admit. I understood well the love/hate relationship he'd had with his maker. I'd had my own with Raoul.

Arys eyed me with an unreadable expression. He hid it well, but I'd hurt him. "So you did. A night hasn't gone by when I haven't thought about what it felt like to feel him die. Forgive me if I don't care to relive it with you."

I cringed inwardly and gave myself a mental bitch slap. How did I even begin to back-pedal on this one? "I shouldn't have said that. I'm sorry."

"Don't be. Just don't get yourself killed. Unless you're ready to join the fang club."

"I have no intention of that happening. Not yet." Did my tone sound too rushed? I hoped not. I didn't want either of them to know just how much the thought of turning terrified me lately.

I felt Kale's scrutiny. If anyone would figure me out, it would be him. He crossed his arms over his chest and studied me. "I know you can kick-ass like nobody's business, but are you sure you want to take a risk like this?"

Despite the fact that Kale was backing his opinion, Arys shot him a dirty look. I couldn't look either of them in the eyes. The interior of the club was sweltering from the heat of so many bodies, along with my own growing discomfort. I needed some air.

"I'm sure neither of you would be saying this if you were able to come with me. Four wolves backing me are more than enough to kick some vampire ass. Would either of you really want to face that?" I challenged. Neither of them responded, leaving me feeling validated. I knew what I was doing, and they would just have to trust me on this.

Reaching for my hand, Arys regarded me with an unsettling darkness. His gaze strayed to Kale, and he grinned. "I would much rather be at your side, as I should be, but if you insist on going during daylight, I understand. I will eagerly await your return."

Turning that sexy smirk on me, Arys gripped my hand tight and bit deep into my wrist. I gasped and gave a small cry of pain and surprise. In a dramatic move that stirred our shared power, he swirled his tongue leisurely over the bloody wound. A shock of heat pooled between my legs, and a blush stole across my cheeks.

Despite the way my body reacted to him, I was mad. That was nothing but a territorial show, marking me in front of Kale. It made me feel like a possession to be claimed, and I was livid. It was in Arys' nature to claim me as it was in mine to refuse to allow it. As much as I wanted to pummel him right then for such a cheap move, I had responded the way he'd known I would. Though my conscious will defied the idea of belonging to him, the rest of me responded in full. We were bound and, like it or not, I was his.

With a low growl, I broke his hold on me and stepped away. Glancing furiously from Arys to Kale, I was mortified. Kale's eyes widened as he reacted to my spilled blood, but there was pain in their depths. Instead of smacking Arys, I shoved past him and stormed outside.

Blood dripped down my hand as I fumbled with my cell phone. I scrolled through my contact list for Brogan's number. Pain shot up my arm from my bleeding wrist, and the urge to throw my phone in a fit of anger was strong. Before I could either throw it or hit send, Arys was there, pulling it from my hand.

"I'm not going to apologize for marking you. I have every right."

I glowered up at him from beneath lowered lashes. "Everyone's doing whatever they want and clearly feeling little remorse. That's fine. Let's all just run amok. We can self destruct together."

Arys grabbed me by the shoulders before I could turn away and searched my eyes. "That wasn't really a reply to me. What's going on with you?" When I pursed my lips and shook my head, he persisted. "Is this about Shaz?"

"You know about that?" My accusatory tone was thick with suspicion.

"Yes."

"For how long?"

"A few days. And, don't look at me like that. It was the pup's place to tell you, not mine. Just like I didn't inform him about your recent indiscretions. It wasn't life or death, Alexa. It was personal. Therefore, not my place."

I wanted to argue with that but couldn't. His logic was sound. Sticking Arys in the middle wasn't going to change anything. The Shaz incident was eating at me, lurking in the back of my mind. I just kept seeing him with her, and I felt sick.

The crimson droplets staining the concrete at my feet brought my attention back to the immediate issue. "This," I held my injured wrist before me, "was not necessary. It's the vampire equivalent to pissing on me, and I'm not cool with that shit. I'm already part of you. Permanently. There isn't a damn supernatural being in this city that doesn't know it. Rubbing it in Kale's face is low, Arys. Even for you."

His dark gaze held no hint of repentance. "It was nothing compared to what I'd really like to do to him. Live with it, Alexa. It could have been worse."

This territorial vampire nonsense with Kale was heads and tails beyond the tension Arys shared with Shaz at times. Arys enjoyed the conflict with Shaz, and ultimately, he always conceded to my wolf, acknowledging Shaz' place as my Alpha mate. It was different with Kale. It scared me because I didn't really know if I could trust Arys not to take it to the next level.

Slipping an arm around my waist, Arys pressed close and brushed his lips across mine. I couldn't stay mad when the touch of his tongue to mine had me melting. The burning heat of my power mingled with the icy cold of his to encase me in a rousing warmth. This man would always be my kryptonite. Dammit.

I bit his lower lip aggressively. "You're a real pain in the ass sometimes, you know that?"

"I do what I can." His soft murmur was accompanied by a mischievous smirk. "If Sinclair was just a toy to you, I might feel differently. But, I know what he wants from you, and I can't help but remind him that I got here first."

I'd done the same thing with the snooty chick that lived in Shaz' apartment building. "Yeah, yeah. That'd better be all you do."

I tensed when Arys brought my bleeding wrist to his lips. Placing a soft kiss to my injured flesh, he breathed in the scent of my blood and sighed. "You've been killing."

"Yes." It wasn't something I'd want to freely admit to anyone else. "Fighting it makes it so much worse."

His shoulders slumped, and when he looked at me, there was guilt in his eyes. "I can't watch the bloodlust drive you mad. Because it will, and you will grow to hate yourself."

"What choice do I have? Fighting it breaks me down until I lose control. I'm already hating myself." Turning off my emotions during the kill didn't make them cease to exist. It simply locked them away in a place where I could pretend to forget. For now.

Arys shook his head. "No more of this. We deal with it, you and I. You can't be killing humans. Not while you're still mortal. It will take away the last of your humanity, and as selfish as this sounds, I'm not ready for that yet."

I slipped a hand into his glossy black hair and nuzzled him. "Neither am I."

His lips were warm against my face as he kissed the side of my nose. His concern meant the world to me. I wouldn't have to fight this battle alone. I could have wept with relief.

My reassurance was short-lived. A chill crept through me when Arys said, "Then it's settled. We hunt together."

Chapter Eighteen

I sipped from a Tim Horton's coffee, watching Brogan form a salt circle on the pavement. It was just past dawn. The Wicked Kiss' parking lot was almost empty save for a few vehicles, one of them being Kale's Camaro. Any vampire who hadn't left yet would be trapped in one of the back rooms for the day.

I knew Kale was alone in his room. His lingering presence spoke louder than his earlier invitation. As I watched Brogan prepare to cast a locator spell, I tried not to think about Kale's admission of love. My focus had to be on finding Claire and Maxwell. Everything else could wait.

At such an early hour, the traffic passing by the club to go downtown was scarce. It wouldn't pick up for a while yet. Every time I heard a vehicle, I glanced up expectantly, looking for Shaz' car. He would be arriving any moment with Kylarai, Zak and Julian. Arys had left an hour before dawn but not before making me promise to maintain an open mental link with him until I was finished with Maxwell and Claire. I was confident that we would take them down. It might not play out the way I envisioned, but it was going to happen.

Sitting in the middle of the salt circle, Brogan pulled four blue candles from her bag and arranged them around her at the north, east, south and west points. She placed a goblet of water before her. Taking a stick of jasmine incense from her bag, she glanced at me expectantly.

"I'll need that hair now. And, as much quiet as possible. Do you think they'll be here soon?"

"Any minute now. We can wait so they don't disturb you." I pulled my wallet out of the back pocket of my jeans and retrieved the auburn strands of Claire's hair. I'd taken extra care not to lose it.

"I'd rather do it now, before they get here. I'm not quite as good at this as my mother is. Was." Brogan's face fell, but she quickly hid the emotion that I could sense building within her. "Anyway, I need to concentrate. The fewer people here, the better."

"No problem. I'll give you some space and tell them not to arrive yet."

Crossing to the opposite end of the parking lot, I perched on the hood of Kale's car and sent a text message to Kylarai telling them not to come until I got back to them. Then I reclined against the Camaro's windshield and watched Brogan work the spell.

I couldn't help it when my mind strayed back to Kale, so close but so far. Was he thinking of me, too? Did I really want the answer to that? I could just imagine his reaction if he knew I was reclined on his prized possession with thoughts of him swirling in my head. I owed him an explanation and an apology. It wasn't going to come easy.

A cool wind picked up suddenly, ruffling my hair. Brogan sat in a meditative state, her lips moving fast. I could only catch bits of what she said. None of it was in English. The candle flames flickered and the scent of jasmine carried to me on the breeze. With eyes closed, she dropped Claire's hair into the goblet and stirred it with a finger in a clockwise motion.

Brogan's blond hair lifted gently as the wind whipped around her. Goosebumps rose up on my skin in response to the power she called. It felt pure, earthy, but strong. She was underestimating herself if she didn't think she was as good as Lena. I was willing to bet otherwise.

I was intrigued by the power a skilled witch could call. It was not unlike my own. However, the manner in which they accessed it was much different.

Watching Brogan reminded me of all the times I'd done the same thing with her mother. I hadn't let myself truly feel Lena's loss. It was too hard. But, it would come. It had to. I didn't want to let her go. Though it wouldn't bring her back, today there would be retribution for what had happened to her.

A satisfied but sad smile crossed Brogan's dainty features, and her eyes snapped open. Motioning me over, she called, "I've got a location."

Hopping off Kale's car, I almost skipped over to her. The wolf inside me was readying for a fight. I was almost excited.

"You were right." Brogan began blowing out the candles before extinguishing the stick of incense. "They moved pretty far from the last address you had for them. They're on the outskirts of town, a farmhouse to the east. I'm coming with you."

I paused during the text I was typing to Ky. "Um, no way. I can't risk you, Brogan. Your mother would never be cool with that."

"Well, she's not here, and these are the people who killed her. You have to let me come. Would you have it any other way if you were in my position?" Her jaw was hard set, and a challenge was in her eyes. "I know they're dangerous, Alexa. I'm not powerless. I'll let you call the shots. Just … let me be your backup."

I finished typing the text before answering. I was torn. I would refuse to be left behind if I were her. She did have power. It's not like she'd be defenseless. *Shit.*

"Fine. But, you follow my lead, and don't you dare get yourself killed. This is completely against my better judgment."

She nodded solemnly, but there was a glimmer of light in her small smile. "Thank you."

It wasn't long before Shaz' car turned into the lot. A small thrill of anticipation shot through me. It wouldn't be long now. Any remaining doubt I'd had was fading fast.

For a moment, I felt heavy discomfort when Shaz stepped out of the car. I swallowed hard and pushed the negative thoughts aside. Whatever was up with him, with us, it was irrelevant right now. It had to be if I was going to stay focused.

Much of the awkward apprehension slipped away when he pulled me into his arms as if nothing had ever happened. Was I making it out to be more than it was? If he could put it aside, then I could do the same.

"Are you ready to do this?" His jade orbs shone with enthusiasm. He was eager for this.

"I think so." I glanced over at his car where the others waited. "How's Julian? He's not going to be a liability is he?"

With a shake of his blond head, Shaz grinned. "Not on my watch."

"Then let's go."

ဢဢဢဢ

Brogan had been right about the farmhouse. The evidence of the death of the occupants verified that our vampires were inside. The sun shone down brightly, trapping them effectively. The golden light stung my eyes but, otherwise, didn't harm me.

We had to drive two cars to fit everyone. It was also safer, in case some of us didn't make it out, the others could still leave. If Maxwell was as clever as I thought he was, he would know we were coming for him. He'd be ready. Yet, he wasn't smart enough to skip town. Typical.

With the Dragon Claw in hand, I faced the four wolves that sat ready and keen before me. Both Shaz and Julian wore matching expressions. They were looking forward to this. Somehow, I didn't entirely find that reassuring. Their eagerness to kill vampires was helpful for the current fight but alarming in its implications. There was no love lost between vampires and werewolves.

"You guys know the drill. Don't leave anyone alive, and don't give them a chance to fight back if you can help it, especially the male with the power. He's extremely dangerous. But, if you can incapacitate him without dusting him, leave him alive. I have a few questions for him."

I had nothing more to say. We had three vampires to kill, one who was deadly. Hesitating would weaken us. It was time to do this.

I could feel Arys in my head, observing the only way he could. He was thankfully quiet, allowing me the illusion of being alone with my thoughts. Knowing he was there enhanced my concentration; I would think of nothing while he was in my head but the task at hand.

Striding up to the front door of the old but well-kept farmhouse, I kicked the door open. I wasn't surprised by the angry swarm of energy that greeted me. I was ready for the attack. Drawing on my bond with Arys, I absorbed what I could of the blast and deflected the rest.

I paused in the doorway, the dagger in one hand and a psi ball in the other. The windows had been boarded up haphazardly, preventing the light from penetrating the interior of the house. Maxwell stood in the open foyer right in front of me, his face absent of any real expression. I couldn't see either Claire or their remaining vampire lackey yet.

The wolves swept past me, two on either side. The sound of snarls and growls quickly filled the eerie silence. Both Shaz and Julian lunged at Maxwell who quickly lashed out at them with a blast of power which I intercepted with my own. The two wolves almost collided in their frenzy to get to him. He was fast, moving to avoid them in a smooth motion that left them scrambling to regain their footing.

"I knew you'd come. I didn't think it would be so soon after we broke you though." Maxwell smirked and pulled his power tight to him, forming a circle.

From deeper in the house a scream rang out as Zak and Kylarai found Claire. She wouldn't stand a chance. Brogan hung back near the door, but I could feel her readiness.

Something told me that the Dragon Claw would cut through Maxwell's barrier as if it wasn't even there. It would be over too fast. Perhaps it was stupid to hold out, but I didn't want him dust, not yet. Not until I could get some answers from him regarding Arys' little secret, something Arys wasn't going to be happy about.

"Is that what that was all about? You didn't break me, asshole. Not even close." This was already going better than I'd hoped. With Maxwell trapped inside his own circle, he wasn't much of a threat.

I advanced on him, testing the dagger by swiping it boldly through his bubble. It dispersed immediately. The shock that adorned Maxwell's face was priceless. Grabbing him by the throat, I threw him up against the foyer wall so hard the windows in the house rattled.

Shaz paced close by. I saw no sign of Julian though the sound of conflict reached me from the back of the house. A series of snarls and snapping jaws were followed by a yelp I recognized as Kylarai. I fought hard to tune it out. Losing my focus would put us all in greater danger.

Maxwell pushed against me with fiery hot power that burned. I smiled because this time I was ready, and I knew I could take him. The direct connection to Arys infused me with enough power to knock me breathless. It burst through me from head to toe, using me as a living vessel to channel it. I wasn't sure how much I could take before it overwhelmed my mortal form, but I guessed I'd find out.

I pressed the dagger to Maxwell's throat, careful not to let the blade bite into his flesh. Not yet. "Ready to do a little talking, pal?"

"Screw you, wolf." He was putting on a tough front, but the heavy sense of apprehension slowly trickled from him.

"I have questions, and you have answers. Play along, and I'll kill you fast. If not, I can really drag this out."

A strained cackle poured forth from Maxwell. "We'll have plenty of time to play twenty questions during the trip back to Vegas. Still not willing to make this easy on yourself? I told you. Help me get what I want, and then I let you go."

"I'm not an item to be bargained with. Especially for power and prestige you don't have the balls to earn on your own. If anyone deserves Harley's place, it's me. I want to know about Arys. Tell me why you said I was the one he's been waiting for. What does that mean?"

'Alexa.' Arys' tense silence was shattered by the vicious warning in the back of my mind.

Intrigue swam in Maxwell's inky gaze. "Let me go, and we can talk this out like the professionals we are. I'm sure we can strike a deal of some kind."

"The only deal on the table is how fast I kill you." I snapped, baring fangs at him. Instinct demanded I kill him. Small talk and bargaining was for vampires. I was wolf, and I wanted his death.

"What's wrong, Alexa? Is Arys keeping secrets from you?" A gloating grin lit up Maxwell's pinched features. "Help me get what I want, and I'll tell you anything I know."

Infuriated by his cocky attitude, I slammed my power through him. He grunted, stiffening as it burned within his core. I felt his sudden alarm as he tried to grasp my power and strip it from me. That wasn't going to work this time. I was prepared for that.

I lashed out at him again, forcing him to go into defense mode. As long as he was focused on protecting himself, he wouldn't have adequate strength to take me down. I followed up with a knee to the groin. Cheap shot? Maybe. Effective? Yes.

He grunted, and a small whimper escaped him. "Look bitch,

this is bullshit. I'm not going to trade blows with you. If you're going to kill me, then do it."

"So you're only content to beat me and torture my mate? If I fight back, you lose interest? That's fucking pathetic."

"I didn't come here to torture anybody. What can I say? One thing led to another." His expression grew cold, and he regarded me with hate shining in his eyes.

The dagger blade was dangerously close to piercing the skin of his throat. Part of me wanted to take his head off. Maybe it wasn't worth it to attempt to get information from him. Maybe this was a confrontation better reserved for Arys.

"Last chance to tell me something I want to hear." My hand shook in my effort to keep from slicing into him.

"Would that help? If I tell you that Arys knew you were out there somewhere, his metaphysical other half. That he was informed of your coming over a hundred years ago? And what it would mean for him? Would a little elaboration make you willing to give me what I want?"

Stunned didn't even begin to describe what I was feeling. It was hard, but I maintained a steady poker face. "No. If you were worthy of taking Harley's place in Vegas, you wouldn't need me."

"Your loss." Unable to affect me, Maxwell targeted Shaz.

The yelp that my white wolf emitted hurt to hear. I concentrated to keep from turning my back on Maxwell to go to him. Brogan's soft tread could be heard on the hardwood floor as she ran to him. I wasn't going to get my answers. Not today.

I plunged the Dragon Claw into Maxwell's guts with pleasure. My only regret was that it had been too soon. For a moment he simply stared at me like I was an idiot for missing the heart. I held tight to the handle and watched as realization sank in.

Panic caused his eyes to widen, and he reached for the dagger, clawing at my hand. It was too late. It happened slower than it had with the young one. His body began to collapse in on itself as he crumbled to dust. His mouth moved, but no sound came out. Jerking the dagger free, I stepped back and watched him fall to pieces at my feet.

Warmth spread from the dagger's handle up my arm as it thrummed with demon magic. It was dizzying and a little frightening. I gazed at what was left of Maxwell and wished I'd made him suffer. Dead wasn't good enough after what he'd done to us and to Lena.

Shaz padded over to me. He was fine but winded. Brogan stood hugging herself near the doorway.

"Stay here," I told her before following the sound of commotion in the living room at the back of the house. She gave a slight nod, her gaze transfixed on what remained of the vampire.

A gunshot rang out, deafening in the confines of the house. Two fierce snarls followed. I ran down the hall and skidded to a stop when I almost tripped over Zak's fallen form. His sides heaved as he struggled for air. Blood seeped from an ugly wound in his chest.

Kylarai and Julian were engaged in a face-off with Claire, who shook violently as she grasped the shotgun. It came as no surprise that a farm family would keep a gun around. If Claire had had any real power, she wouldn't have needed it.

She whirled to face me, the barrel of the gun drifting from me to the two wolves baring deadly fangs at her. A pile of dust in the corner indicated what was left of the remaining lackey. I'd have never guessed that a woman with a gun would have been the biggest threat we'd face here.

"Back the fuck off!" Claire's voice was high and desperate. She waved the gun wildly, and I braced, expecting an erratic shot to go off. She didn't know how to use that thing.

I held up a hand and concentrated on tranquil energy, hoping to calm her. "Take it easy, Claire. We don't all have to die here."

"Tell that to your wolves. I'm not letting those bastards tear me apart. I won't die like that!" She swung the gun back to Ky and Julian, aiming at Julian's face. Whatever they'd done to kill her vampire minion, it must have been ugly for her to react this way.

I felt Shaz tense beside me as if bracing to leap. I angled my body to block him. We faced supernatural threats every night of our lives. It was not going to be a friggin' gun that killed him.

"Come on, Claire. You've lived how many lifetimes, and now you want to go down fighting with a gun as your defense?"

In my head came Arys' worry. 'Let her go, Alexa. She's not worth taking a bullet.'

I ignored him. He was right, but I couldn't let her just leave, not after what she did to Shaz and Lena. If I hit her hard and fast with a solid strike, it might be enough to disable her before she could get off another shot.

'Are you willing to lose Kylarai or Shaz over this? Don't take stupid risks.' Arys was growing angry. I was relieved that he wasn't physically present to fight me for control of the situation. 'You don't have control of the situation! You have a wolf dying on the floor.'

'Stop distracting me!'

Claire emanated fear, a tantalizing scent that instilled the need for the kill in every one of us. I had to make a move quickly. I couldn't be certain that I could take her down faster than she could pull the trigger again. Arys was right. It wasn't worth any of our lives if I tried and failed.

Before I could make a decision, Julian snapped. He lunged, his strong hind legs launching him swiftly straight at her. The gun sounded, and he dropped in a heavy thud that shook the floor beneath my feet. It all happened faster than I could blink. My hands vibrated with the power I held ready. Taking advantage of Claire's momentary distraction, I hit her with enough metaphysical force to drop an elephant.

It was more than I'd anticipated. It flowed through me like a wave that could be neither seen nor touched, forcing me to my knees. I could feel Arys behind the massive wallop, guiding it when I ceased to have control. For a split second my skull felt like it might blow. The pressure eased, and blood dripped from my nose.

Claire hurtled through the air to crash through the draped window in an explosion of glass. I scrambled to my feet and rushed to the gaping hole. The wail that came from her was horrifying, so inhuman I quaked. Yet, watching her burn was harder than hearing her die.

Her skin sizzled audibly, blackening at the sun's lethal touch, but death didn't come immediately. The sickening stench of burning flesh was overwhelming. My stomach turned, and I fought the urge to vomit.

I turned away, unable to watch anymore. A quick look at Julian's destroyed face was worse. He was dead. I couldn't save him. Tearing my gaze from the brown wolf's corpse, I rushed to Zak, finding him struggling to hold on.

'Help me,' I begged Arys. The high level of power we'd raised would be enough to heal Zak, I knew it. I just didn't have the mental clarity and calm needed to do it. Killing was easy. Healing was hard. One might think it should be the other way around.

Kylarai's high-pitched whine was mournful, and my heart broke for her. Scumbag or not, she'd loved Julian. Shaz went to her, nuzzling her face with wolf kisses. I focused on tuning out everything but Zak and what he needed from me.

'Concentrate.' Arys' guidance was stern but gentle. 'Make him all that you see, all that you feel. Envision the brokenness inside him. Push the energy into him as you would in an attack but direct it. Give it a purpose. You can do this.'

He fell silent, leaving me to save my wolf on my own. I didn't ask much of my pack. I did all that I could to leave them out of stuff like this. They'd proven their loyalty by being there when needed, even Julian. My wolf rose to the surface, straining for release, seeking a way to comfort her own. It hurt to deny the need to shift. Right now, I had to be the vampire.

Closing my eyes, I held my hands over Zak's wound, close but not touching. The harsh sensation of pain rolled off him. I could feel him slipping away.

Tuning out my surroundings was near impossible, but once I fell into him, aligning Zak's broken energy with my own, it came together much smoother than I expected. I honed in on the wound, seeing it in my mind. With a deep sigh, I pushed my positive, vibrant energy into Zak, seeing his wound as healed. I held that vision as the current connecting us grew strong and warm.

I felt disoriented, as if the room was spinning and I didn't know which way was up. A roar of white noise filled my ears. It was exhilarating.

The power fell away, and I opened my eyes to find Zak lying naked beside me on the floor. He'd shifted back to human form. The wound in his chest was healed, only a faint trace of pink scar tissue remained. A handful of buckshot lay beside him.

He blinked up at me with glazed eyes. "Alexa?"

I exhaled slowly, realizing at some point I'd held my breath. I felt drained. Good thing I'd killed Maxwell when I had because I didn't have the energy to take him on now.

"Come on." I helped Zak to his feet, supporting his weight

when he leaned heavily on me. "Let's get you out of here."

I didn't want him to see Julian. They were best friends. Zak had been through enough. I cast a glance back at Shaz and Kylarai. Shaz was nudging her along, urging her to follow me out. She resisted, her gaze locked on the body of her fallen former lover. After a few moments, I heard her paws pad along behind me.

Brogan looked up in shock when we appeared. She took in the naked werewolf at my side and averted her gaze. I would have laughed if the situation hadn't been so somber. Werewolves got used to being naked around other people. It came with the territory.

Once I got Zak settled in the backseat of Shaz' blue Cobalt, I turned to go back to the house, but Zak grabbed my arm and held on. "Alexa. What happened? Did Julian make it out?"

His jaw was clenched, and he studied me knowingly. I wasn't going to insult him by lying or sugar-coating the truth.

"He's dead, Zak. I'm sorry."

With the barest of nods, he turned away from me and began to pull his clothes on. I tossed the Dragon Claw into the trunk of my car before turning to Kylarai who was doing her best to hide her tears as she slipped into a long blue summer dress. I felt awful for her.

Before I could say as much, she waved me off. "I'm not ready to talk about it, Alexa. Sorry." Falling heavily onto the passenger seat of Shaz' car, she stared out the window at the field beyond.

"Hey, don't look so defeated." Shaz was a hell of a vision. His face was bruised, and he winced in pain as he tugged a black t-shirt over his head. "Julian was an idiot to attack her the way he did. What happened to him wasn't your fault, Lex."

"I'm not sure they'd agree with you." I ran a hand over his bare ribs as he pulled the shirt down. "Are you ok? You didn't break anything, did you?"

"A cracked rib, I think. No worries. Really. It'll be fine." He captured my hand in his own and gave it an affectionate squeeze. "So what do we do with the remains? I imagine the bodies of the home owners are in there somewhere, too."

I nodded absently, studying the property. "There's got to be some gasoline in the shed or the garage. You guys take off, and I'll deal with the rest." My voice dropped to a breathy whisper. "And please, don't leave Kylarai alone, no matter what she says. Stay with her a while."

"Of course." Shaz kissed me softly, a brief but tender touch. I was reminded instantly why he meant so much to me. Too much to let anything, even The Wicked Kiss, come between us. "I love you."

"I love you, too, babe."

I watched until his car disappeared from sight. Then I turned to Brogan who stood uncertainly near my car. "So, how do you feel about arson?"

Chapter Nineteen

I stood outside The Wicked Kiss for a long time before mustering the nerve to go inside. I smelled faintly of smoke from the fire, and my hair was a mess. Neither of those were good enough reasons to put this off.

The club was deadly quiet, foreign. I rarely saw it empty and silent. The back hall felt eerily calm. I could feel the energy of those occupying the rooms. There weren't many of them.

Following the hall to room thirteen, I grew increasingly edgy with each step. Was he sleeping? Would he feel my presence? My pulse quickened. *Steady breaths.*

After taking care of things at the farmhouse, Arys had silently slipped away, closing the mental door between us. I was grateful for that because it saved me from having to do it. I knew he was upset with me for pumping Maxwell for information. However, I could only deal with one vampire at a time.

I hesitated outside Kale's door. I could feel him in there. What if he was sleeping? Maybe it was better not to disturb him. I reached out to knock, but before I could, the door swung open.

Kale stood in the doorway, casually dressed in track pants and a plain white t-shirt, a rare look for him. I liked it. He regarded me with an expression of relief and intrigue. I gazed into his mismatched eyes and felt myself falling.

Tearing my gaze away, I glanced nervously at the floor, my feet and finally past him into the room. "Did I come at a bad time?"

"Not at all." He swung the door open wider and stepped back

to allow me in. "Come on in."

"I think we need to talk."

"How did everything go? I assume by the soot in your hair and the fire in your eyes that you kicked some ass."

"I guess you could say that. I lost a wolf. Julian, to be precise."

Kale swung the door shut, locking it as if he expected an interruption. "Can't say I'm sorry to hear that. How's Kylarai taking it?"

"Not so well." I stood awkwardly in the middle of the room. I could either sit on the bed, bad idea, or at the small bistro table in the corner. I chose to stand.

"Well, I'm glad the rest of you made it out ok. I was worried." The depths of his concern was there in his eyes. He'd been afraid for me. It warmed my insides in a silly, high school crush kind of way. It was so wrong.

I tried to lighten the mood by laughing off his worry. "Hey, I told you I'd be fine. You shouldn't underestimate me."

"Never." A lazy grin lit up his face. "I give you more credit than you know."

A strange silence descended. I studied the diamond pattern on his black and grey bedding, the tile on the ceiling and the plush carpet beneath our feet. Anything to avoid eye contact.

"Kale, we have to talk about this. I'm not even sure where to start. Since the other night … in the rain … I've been so confused. What I get from you I can't find in anyone else. But, what we share is weakness, and we both know misery loves company." I fumbled with the words, wishing they would come out perfect. "It's selfish of me to seek comfort in you when I can't return what it is you give me."

He seemed to contemplate what I was trying to say. Leaning back against the door, he crossed his arms and pinned me with a piercing stare. "You are my weakness, Alexa. It isn't the bloodlust or the thrill of the kill. That's all part of what I am. It has been for centuries. The appetites of the vampire are not a weakness. If anything they are strengths to be mastered. It's you that brings me to my knees."

I groaned and paced the length of the small room. I glanced at the bed, knowing that he'd taken many human women there, for their body and their blood. I was glad our encounter hadn't been in this room.

"Is it me? Or, are you drawn to the power that makes me its bitch?" It was a challenging question, a potentially loaded one. I had the distinct feeling that I wasn't going to get the answer I wanted.

"How can you ask me that? Of course it's you. The power is part of you, part of your thrall. I won't deny that. But, if this was based only on power, I'd be throwing myself at Arys." Kale spat Arys' name like it was something bitter in his mouth. "Somewhere along the way, over the years we've been friends, I fell for you. Hard. But, that's not what you want to hear, is it?"

No amount of distracted gazing around the room could keep our eyes from locking. The look he gave me was direct, daring me to tell the harsh truth.

"Kale, this is difficult for me. I do feel something for you. I'm just not sure I can call it love. I have two men in my life that I constantly feel torn between. This," I motioned between the two of us. "This just isn't right. It can't be."

"Why? Because Arys got to you first? That means you can't possibly love me too? Correct me if I'm wrong, but from what I've seen over the past year, he has been less than great for you. Or, maybe I just think that because I'm the one you run to every damn time he lets you down."

That stung because it was true. Guilt washed over me, and I bit my lower lip until I tasted blood. "Alright. That's fair. I won't argue that. Arys and I do have issues. Big ones. But doesn't everyone? This is about you and me right now."

"There is no you and me. Isn't that what you're saying?" Kale stood stiffly. His energy was harsh and pained. It burned a little if I focused on it intently.

"I don't want it to be this way between us. I can't lose you, Kale. And, I don't know how to keep what we have now without ruining it." I took a step toward him but stopped, unsure of what to do with myself. "What we did the other night, I'm afraid it's changed everything. It never should have happened."

He shoved away from the door in a fast, smooth motion. With the grace only a vampire could possess, Kale swept me into his arms and kissed me. It was deep but gentle, with the sweetness that I'd come to associate with his kiss.

"But, it did happen," he whispered against my lips. "And, you loved every minute of it. Of course it changes things. God, I can't stop thinking about what it felt like to finally be inside you."

"Stop that."

"No. You want me, too. I can feel it. Playing this right and wrong game isn't doing a damn bit of good." His lips were warm against my skin as he kissed his way down my neck.

"I can't be in love with three people. That's too fucked up, even for me. I feel so torn between all of you. It's selfish. And, *that* is wrong."

Putting my hands on his chest, I pushed Kale away. I was a mess of emotion. From shame to desire, a storm brewed inside me. I did want him, but none of it made sense to me. How could I feel something so different for all of them?

Kale didn't let me put space between us. He was determined to get out everything he had to say while he had the chance.

"Alexa, not once in the time I've known you have you given yourself to any man that you didn't somehow feel for. Look me in the eye and tell me that you don't love me."

When a friend becomes a lover, they already know so much about you. I fell into Kale's amazing eyes. He waited for my response with a forced calm. I could sense the tension he held.

He was right. I had never slept with a man I didn't have genuine feelings for. Four of them, each so different from the others. And, I loved them all. Even Raoul, despite everything he'd done. Sure, many people loved more than one person in their lifetime. But me? I was clearly a classic case of fucked up beyond all repair.

I couldn't bring myself to lie to him. It would be easier to walk away from this with a clean break, but it wouldn't be fair.

"Don't make me do this. Please." I pleaded. "I can't."

"Say it, and I will go on as if nothing ever happened." He grasped a lock of my disheveled hair, sliding it between his fingers. "Tell me you don't love me."

I let out a frustrated growl. Why couldn't I damn well say it? "I don't love you, Kale." There. That was excruciatingly hard. The moment the words left my lips, I knew it was also a lie.

"Liar," he hissed before kissing me again, a bruising crush of his lips to mine. "I wish you were telling the truth. It would make it easier to walk away. I know that's what you want."

The raw emotion in his voice cut deep. Kale was in agony. Over me. It was all wrong because he was so far above and beyond me. As self-deprecating as it was, I couldn't help but feel he was cheating himself of something better.

"What I want is for you to be happy with someone who can give you what you need. I want us to be the way we were … before that night in the rain." I reached to lay a hand on his face, surprised when he turned his head to avoid my touch. "I don't want to be the one who hurt you."

Capturing my hand in his, he pressed a chaste kiss along my fingertips. "It's too late for that. I don't live in a fantasy world. I'm fully aware that you're spoken for as wolf and vampire. But what about the woman I've watched struggle and suffer? The one that shares with me what can never be shared with the men that claim her? Where does that part of you belong?"

The words tumbled forth before I realized what I was saying. "That part of me belongs with you. But, it isn't that simple. If there were ever a time for us, Kale, it wouldn't be right now."

He nodded solemnly, but there was relief in his eyes. "I know. I just need to hear you say it. Tell me what I am to you."

I was overcome by the flash of melancholy energy that bound us. His emotions were running high as were my own. It was impossible not to vibe off each other as we were tossed by a tornado of passion and pain.

I was tired from days of stress and overwhelmed by the betrayal of my own heart. When had I fallen for Kale? And, why did I feel so certainly that walking away from what we had was the right thing to do?

"You're everything to me that I wish I could be for you. You bring me comfort when I need it, and you set me free from the restraints I impose on myself. If things were different somehow, you'd be the one." I almost choked on the words as I watched the shadows darken his expression. "I'm sorry. I don't want it to be this way, but there is just no other way it can be. Not right now. It's better for both of us. You know it is."

Kale was silent, studying me so intently that I felt itchy and uncomfortable. Just when I thought he was going to push me away, he pulled me tight against him. The sensation of his arms around me was bittersweet. I stood stiffly for a moment before melting into his embrace.

He ran a hand through my hair as if he didn't notice what a mess it was. "I'm the one with centuries of experience. Why do you get to be the one that's right about this?"

"Just lucky I guess."

His soft laughter was forced. "If it makes any difference, I fought it every step of the way until there was just no denying it anymore. I didn't want us to end up this way."

With a heavy sigh, I held him with a fierce grip. "I adore you." Maybe it wasn't the right thing to say, all things considered.

Time passed as we stood there clinging to one another. I would have been happy to drag the moment out far longer than was realistic. If I didn't disentangle myself from him soon, I might never leave his room. The peace that I found in Kale engulfed me, tempting me to surrender to him fully. I couldn't.

A physical ache started in my stomach when at last I pulled away. *Just one last kiss,* I told myself. Then it was time to close the door on what Kale and I shared. The thought filled me with anguish, and for once, both the wolf and the vampire within me lay silent. Their influence was absent, leaving me feeling bare and vulnerable. I couldn't blame my feelings on either side.

I kissed him with everything I had. My hands shook as I held his face. The soft touch of his tongue on mine was dizzying. I drank him in, savoring the heat that rose up between us. My power came alive, reaching for him. Falling into him was like stepping off the edge of a cliff. The freefall felt amazing, but I feared the impact I knew was coming.

Right when I knew I should have broken it off, Kale deepened the kiss. His hands were in my hair and tension thrummed through his body. He explored my mouth with a hunger I couldn't help but respond to. When I was with Kale, everything else ceased to exist. The danger of what we shared lay in the illusion that the rest of the world fell away.

The urgency that gripped us was the same determined need that had driven us in the alley behind The Wicked Kiss. I felt the sudden need to rush, to join in that sacred but forbidden union.

"We can't do this." A sob escaped me, and I broke away from

him, turning away so he wouldn't see the tears that spilled down my cheeks. "I have to go."

"Alexa, wait." Kale grabbed my arm. "Are you alright? I don't want to see you cry."

"Well, you weren't supposed to." I faced him, quickly swiping at the blood-red tears.

His shoulders sagged as if he held the weight of the world. The sadness in his lovely eyes hurt me to see. He reached to capture one of my tears on a finger. "I can't watch you leave here in tears. Please, don't cry. Not because of me."

"I'm crying because the only time I feel safe anymore is when I'm with you. And, I know that I can't hide away here inside that feeling forever. Even though I wish I could." I took a deep, shuddery breath. This was harder than I'd anticipated. "Thank you for being who you are. You have no idea what it means to me. Maybe we've already gone too far to go back, but I don't want to lose our friendship."

A frown creased Kale's brow, and he shook his head. "I know it's better for us to deny what we feel. I know you might never love me the way I wish you would. But, don't ever worry about us. I'll always be here for you."

What could I possibly say to that? I had to get out of there before I turned into a blubbering idiot. The powerful emotion in the room hugged tight to me like a second skin.

I clasped his hand in both of mine for a brief but heart-breaking moment. "I need to go. I'll see you soon?"

"Certainly." Kale's gaze was on our hands as I pulled away. When I reached the door, he said, "Hey, Alexa. It's ok that we are what we are instead of what we should be. Believe that."

ଚ୦ଚ୦ଚ୦ଚ୦

It was mid-afternoon already, and the sun was high in the sky. I couldn't stop yawning as I drove through the quiet streets of Stony Plain. I desperately wanted a hot shower and some quality time with my bed, but my best friend needed me. So, I was on my way across town to Kylarai's.

Shaz' car was parked in the driveway, and I breathed a sigh of relief. I'd been afraid that Ky would have chased him off so she could be alone in her grief. I understood that she'd need that time to herself, but right now, she needed us.

I clutched my takeout coffee cup and made my way up the front walk. I paused to admire the flower garden near the door. Kylarai really had a way with things like that. I envied her. I could only keep plants that could handle a little neglect.

I knocked firmly on the door and entered, glad to escape the sun's harsh rays. Shoving my sunglasses on top of my head, I blinked a few times while my eyes adjusted to the dimmer lighting. The sound of voices drifted from the kitchen where I found them sitting at the table across from one another, drinking coffee.

They both looked up at my arrival, and I suddenly felt uneasy. Shaz' eyes narrowed as he caught Kale's scent, and I wished I could tell him that it wasn't what he was thinking. I hesitated, unable to decide where to sit. Kylarai glanced up at me with red-rimmed grey eyes, and my heart broke for her.

"I'm not going to insult you by asking how you're feeling." I slid into a chair at the end of the table, purposely not sitting right next to either of them. It was so obvious. "I'm sorry, Ky. I never wanted this to happen."

She shrugged and squeezed a crumpled tissue in one hand. "It happens. We knew it was dangerous. I just wish I'd had a chance to say something to him before it was too late."

I knew that feeling very well. I reached across the table to give her hand a friendly squeeze. "I understand."

"So you saw Kale?" She kept her expression neutral, but I could see the suspicion in her eyes. "You kind of smell like him."

"Yeah, I saw him. I stopped by to tell him what happened. To let him know we were ok." I looked from her to Shaz, peering intently into his jade eyes. "That's all."

Shaz cleared his throat and leaned back in his chair, but he didn't remark on Kale. His silence bothered me more than if he'd been openly angry.

"Is there anything we can do for you?" I asked, changing the subject. "We can make you something to eat, run some errands. Anything."

With a shake of her dark head, she tapped a fingernail on the side of her mug and stared into the remains of her coffee. "No. Thank you. Honestly, I just want to be alone. I don't mean to be rude or anything."

"Of course you're not." Shaz stood up and began to clear the cream and sugar off the table. "I'd want to be alone, too, if I were you." He met my eyes briefly then, and I felt some of the tension between us slip away.

"I have something to ask the two of you, if you don't mind." A nervous rush caused my heart to race. I hadn't planned to bring this up now, but it seemed to be just as good a time as any.

Shaz dropped back into his seat, and they both turned to face me. I sipped from my coffee and readied myself. This wasn't going to be easy.

"Alright," I continued, feeling the weight of their gazes. "There's no real good way to say this. I hate to even have to bring it up, but if I don't do it now, I might never get another chance. This is about my bond with Arys. You both know what it does to me. But lately, it's gotten worse." I paused, mustering the courage to spit out the real point. "I've been killing. Nothing crazed or incessant but it's happened. What I need from the two of you is a promise. When I die, when I become a vampire … if I'm nothing but a blood crazed monster, I want you to promise that you'll kill me."

A moment of quiet passed, so intense that I could hear the buzz of various electronic devices in the house. They stared at me, Kylarai in calm contemplation and Shaz in stunned silence.

"Are you serious?" He asked after a long moment of thinking it over. "Do you realize what you're really asking us?"

"There's nobody else I can trust to do it. Other than maybe Jez." My stomach turned, and coffee didn't seem so good all of a sudden. "Arys would never do it. And, the way I've been feeling lately – the loss of control and sometimes not even knowing who I am anymore – I just want to know that if things get bad – if I'm not me anymore – when the time comes, that someone will stop me."

Shaz gave a frustrated growl and leaned heavily on the table with his head in his hands. "Dammit, Lex!"

Kylarai didn't share his reaction. She was nodding thoughtfully. "What about Arys and Kale? They're not maniacal blood junkies tearing apart every human that crosses their path. Why would you be so different? If anything, they would help you through it."

"They'll do their best. I'm just asking you in a worst case scenario situation." I hated the position I was putting Shaz in. His anguish at my request was heavy on the air. "Shaz, I asked the two of you because I know I can trust you to do it. Arys would never do it. And, I'm not sure I trust anyone else enough to ask it of them. I'm sorry."

"Don't be," he groaned, running both hands through his short platinum hair so it stood up in disarray. "I'm glad you came to us. I'm just praying it never really has to come to that."

I squirmed in my chair, finding it hard to sit comfortably. "I don't plan on dying any time soon. Not if I can help it. I just need to know I can count on you guys if it comes to that."

"You can. I promise." Kylarai offered a reassuring hand pat and a small smile. "I strongly believe you have more inner strength than you know. And, when the time comes, you will realize that. But, if we have to do this, we will."

"Thank you. That's all I needed to hear." Looking to Shaz, I raised a brow in question.

He slammed a hand down on the table, causing my coffee cup to jump. "I'm sorry. I just really need to hit something right now."

"I think the two of you should probably talk." Ky shoved her chair back and stood. "I'm going to take a bath and try to get some sleep. Thanks for coming by. And Shaz, thank you for staying with me. I'll be fine. I know you have a birthday party coming up, Lex. I wouldn't miss it for anything."

She mustered another smile, but I saw right through it. She was doing her best to put on a good front so we would leave without worrying about her. I knew Kylarai. She was strong. Strong enough to have killed the wolf that attacked her as well as her abusive prick of a husband. This woman was a delicate flower on the surface, but underneath she was a rock. I knew she could handle the loss of Julian. Hell, she'd just agreed to kill me herself if she had to. Kylarai would be fine.

I got to my feet and pulled her into a warm hug. She smelled like wolf, and I held on a little longer than necessary to revel in that familiar scent.

"Alright, we'll take off and let you have some time alone. Speaking of alone," I glanced around curiously. "Where's Zoey?"

"Apartment hunting. Now that she has the money Raoul left her, she's striking out on her own. She's even talked about getting a job." Ky rolled her eyes. "Though I can't imagine her working a regular job. Should be interesting to see what she gets herself into."

"I guess that's all good as long as she stays out of trouble. I can't handle a repeat of our girl's night out."

I turned to leave, waiting while Shaz said goodbye to Kylarai. Pressing a kiss to the top of her head, he hugged her close. "Call us if you need anything. Even just to talk. Anytime, ok? I mean it."

Shaz followed me from the house to the driveway where I stopped by his car. He looked as tired as I felt. I watched him run his hand through his tousled hair a few times, and I had to smile. I would never stop being grateful for him. He was a blessing.

"So you were with Kale." His tone was careful, like he was trying to keep accusation from creeping into it.

I met his gaze evenly, having nothing to hide. "Yes. I needed to see him. I went to tell him that what happened with us that night can never happen again."

"Oh." He seemed surprised. "I see. I don't know what to say to that. I'm relieved I guess."

I nodded and kicked a pebble near my foot. I wanted to tell him that now it was his turn to do the same and call it quits with this whole vampire donor nonsense. It didn't work that way. He had to do it on his own.

"Well, it was a mistake. It shouldn't have happened." As much as I regretted the pain it had caused, I couldn't regret what Kale and I had done. Not entirely. I was glad to have that memory. Though the only person I was likely to admit that to would be Jez.

"Lex, you and me, we're all good. Ok? I could be upset about Kale, but I'm not in the position to point fingers. And honestly, right now, I'm a little more concerned with the request you just made inside. What the hell was that all about?"

Leaning against his car, I tugged my sunglasses back into place, using the sun as an excuse to hide my eyes. "It was just a backup plan. Worst case scenario. No worries? Ok."

He shook his head, a determined set to his jaw. "Don't bullshit me. You're being less than forthcoming here, and I want to know what you're not telling me."

I attempted to stifle a yawn. It had been a long couple of days. Before I could respond Shaz was turning me toward my own car.

"You look beat. I'm not feeling so hot myself. But, you're not getting out of this. I'll meet you at home."

Chapter Twenty

Two nights had passed since we had killed Maxwell and Claire and had lost Julian. I'd had a chance to speak with both Shaz and Arys one-on-one about where I stood with Kale. Though Arys was still keeping secrets and Shaz had his own issues, I felt relieved of some of the recent tension among us. I didn't expect perfection in our relationships. In the world we lived in, I knew better than that. However, I did expect closeness and a willingness to work through our problems. So far, so good. Of course, I still had every intention of getting Arys' secret out, even if it killed me. Knowing me, it just might.

It was the first night of the full moon. It would be at its fullest tomorrow when I would run with the pack. Usually, I'd be running as a wolf tonight, too, which I was counting on to throw Veryl off. He wouldn't be expecting me.

I left Raoul's Jag a few blocks from the office and walked. Driving right up to the door might give me away. Cloaking my presence, I stole through the night with ill intentions.

I glanced back at the sleek black car with a shake of my head. Poor Raoul. He'd have kittens if he could see how I drove that thing. I sure didn't baby it the way I did my own car. The Jaguar was my stealth machine, the car I used when I didn't want to announce my presence with a loud, red muscle car.

My right hand was wrapped firmly around the handle of the Dragon Claw. It felt good. Empowering. Burning deep in my core was as much power as I could possibly hold inside my mortal body. It strained for release, and I had to concentrate to make sure it didn't escape me.

I kept waiting for the nerves to creep in. It didn't happen. I was rock solid and ready for this. It occurred to me that this might be a mistake, but I didn't truly believe that. Veryl had hidden my own past from me and then acted like I had no right to be pissed about it. Now he was blackmailing Lilah, someone who had never done anything to make me think she deserved it. Yep. I was ready for this, maybe even a little eager.

I slipped inside the office building with little effort. A couple of locks weren't going to keep me out. A very weak energy barrier lingered just beyond the doorway; I wasn't sure if it was meant for me or Lilah. Regardless, Veryl's power was minimal compared to mine, and I walked right through it.

This wasn't going to be a showdown; I wanted it to be quick, as fast and clean as possible. At least that was the plan. I didn't even plan to enjoy it. Though try as I might to resist it, an element of excitement was creeping up inside me. Hunting humans was driven by my weakness and in turn it made me weak. Hunting a creature of the night was a whole different ball game. It made me feel strong and powerful, which I preferred to the former.

Veryl might have been an asshole, but he wasn't a fool. His door was ajar, open just enough to give him a glimpse of anyone approaching. I could see him from the end of the hall where I stood. He was typing furiously, his eyes fixed on his computer screen. He glanced up with a start, cursing when he saw me.

"You shouldn't have come, Alexa," he called as I made my way toward him. "You don't want to do this."

"Don't I?" I gripped the dagger just a little tighter and smiled.

He knocked his chair over in his haste to get up. Reaching under his desk, he produced a well-sharpened stake. Not a trace of fear came from him. Veryl had been expecting this.

"You're a pawn, Alexa. Playing right into Shya's hands by doing his dirty work for him. You're better than this."

I stood just inside the door to his office. It wasn't all that big, and the massive desk in the center left little room for a good fight. I had to make this quick.

"Don't talk. It's only going to waste time." I held my free hand up, moving it in a counter-clockwise circle. Power went out from me, pasting Veryl up against the far wall. The stake in his hand was useless.

He glared at me, still unafraid. "We've worked together for years. I did all I could to keep you from him. Now just that fast he has you brainwashed? Think this through."

"You did what you could to keep a lot of things from me. You get your hands on information, and in some cases people, and you do all you can to make it work to your advantage." I advanced on him, the dagger warming in my hand. "Now it's caught up to you."

"Alexa, please! You don't know what you're getting yourself into. He's a demon for God's sake! Do you think he gives a damn about you? He has plans for you. Once you stop playing along, he'll abandon you. Or worse. Eventually, you'll have to make a choice, and I doubt it will be his side you'll choose."

That made me hesitate, but I tried not to show it. I didn't doubt that Veryl knew things about Shya that I didn't. But, I also knew he'd do anything to save his own ass.

"You know what? I don't care. I don't want to hear it."

I raised the Dragon Claw and only then did panic seep into his eyes. He fought to get free of the power holding him.

"What did he offer you? What did he tell you to get you to do this? Whatever it is, it comes with a price. You can't trust a demon."

"Actually, I was more than happy to do this. You're making it easier by the second." I wasn't letting him plant doubts in my head. He'd done enough damage over the years. "I don't trust demons. And, I don't trust you. Not anymore."

I saw myself reflected in his eyes. My mane of ash blond hair was sleek and smooth, a direct contrast to my wild blue eyes. Arys' eyes. It was still startling. But, what struck me was the ruthless glint I saw deep within them.

"He'll drag you into the pits of hell if you let him. You have no idea what you're getting involved in." Veryl glared at me with a growing hate. "Don't do something stupid that you'll regret."

Unwilling to hear another word, I slammed the dagger into Veryl with enough force that we both grunted. His mouth gaped, but no further sound came out. He simply stared at me in horror before dropping in a pile of ash at my feet. A puff of ash rose up to choke me. I glanced at the bloody dagger blade, shaken and wound up. The rush of what I'd just done hit hard, and I sat heavily in Veryl's chair.

After letting it all sink in, I turned to his computer and thought, *Why the hell not?* I clicked around through his documents, finding most of them to be password protected or encrypted. A series of documents with various names caught my eye. My own name was part of the grouping. I cursed my inability to do much more than stare at the password prompt. After trying several possibilities, I gave up. Hacking into protected files was not my forte.

I was itching to know what was in the files with my name on them. The bastard sure made it hard to regret what I just did. *Sorry, Veryl. Payback is a bitch.*

So maybe I couldn't open the folders, but I had no problem emailing them to myself. Veryl might have been secretive, but he wasn't as technologically savvy as one might expect. I didn't know anyone who could get into those folders, but I'd sure as hell find someone.

I shut down Veryl's computer and called Lilah to let her know it was all over. As I left a message on her voicemail, I busied myself turning off the lights and locking up. The moon was thrumming in my veins, calling my wolf forth. My dirty work was done for the night. I had a pack run to get to.

෨෨෨෨෨

I ran through the forest, kicking up the earth beneath my paws. I pushed myself hard, reveling in the exertion of every muscle. Raising my nose to the wind, I searched the night air for the scent of my wolves.

I could smell them deeper in the forest. The scent of pine and earth mingled with the faint aroma of rain. The ground was still dry, but it was coming. I could feel the approaching rainfall. Of all the wonderful smells in nature, rain had to be among my favorites.

Gradually, I slowed my pace until I trotted along leisurely, slipping through the trees with grace and ease. I was lost in thought, pondering my upcoming birthday party. In just a few days, I would be another year older, something I considered a success. Every year was worth celebrating, but I wasn't sure I agreed with Shaz' idea of a celebration. I wasn't sure about having a big party. For the most part, I was going along with it because I couldn't bring myself to crush his enthusiasm.

Twenty-seven wasn't all that old; however, I couldn't help but wonder how many years I would have before it all caught up to me, before I died and rose as a vampire. That concept seemed so foreign as I moved through the forest as wolf. I could no longer readily accept that fate. I possessed a deep inner fear that when that time came, my wolf would cease to exist. It had taken so long to accept that I was the wolf. To think of losing that side of me was like losing myself.

It terrified me because I didn't know what would happen. Werewolves don't become vampires the way humans do. Biologically, it just didn't happen. Our bodies don't process anything the same way a human's does. Though Arys insisted my mortality ensured the blood bond would cause me to rise again as a vampire, I had my doubts. If it were to happen the way he thought it would, I would be the only shape-shifting vampire in existence.

Shoving the thoughts from my mind, I turned my attention to the moment at hand. I cleared a fallen tree with a bound, landing lightly on the other side. A few stray twigs snapped beneath my feet. Such simple sounds, but I loved them. The wolf was in me all the time, but only in these moments did I appreciate it fully.

The stress and pain of recent events slipped away as the night wind carried me along. I made my way through the trees to the clearing where the pack gathered on nights like this. I could feel the tiny eyes of small critters watching me from the safety of the treetops. The scent of new life was everywhere as summer flourished. It was entrancing.

I broke through the trees into the clearing with an extra bounce to my step. Abandoning my human form didn't happen often enough, but nothing felt so good, so truly free. I gazed at the moon overhead, drinking in the silver light it cast upon me. The blanket of stars stretched as far as I could see. Wistful and happy, I lifted my voice to the sky and howled, a long gut-wrenching sound that echoed all around me.

The chorus of howls that filled the night in response stirred a warmth in my belly. My wolves answered my call, and I knew they were coming. Kylarai emerged from the opposite side of the clearing, her muzzle coated in deer blood. Her grey eyes fixed me with a calm stare, but I could feel the pain she tried not to convey. Without Julian at her side, she was lost.

Shaz appeared right behind her, his white fur also bloody from their kill. He had a goofy wolf grin as he trotted over to nuzzle me with his wet nose. I sat back on my haunches, giving in to his playfulness. We wrestled and nipped at one another until the others began to fill the clearing.

When every wolf was present, watching me with attentive gazes, I embraced the change and resumed my human form. I wasn't ready to let the wolf slip away, but I needed my voice for this. Like usual, there was a brief burst of excruciating pain as my body reformed itself, and then splendor when I was whole again. It happened fast, faster than it had when I was a new wolf. For that I was grateful.

Letting my hair fall over my breasts, I positioned myself behind Shaz' sitting form so that for the most part, my nakedness was minimal. I had nothing these people hadn't seen before, but it made it a little easier to look them all in the eyes.

"I'm sure you all know that we recently lost one of our own." It was easier to claim Julian than I'd thought. He was no less of an asshole in death, but the reality of it was, he was ours regardless.

I took a few deep breaths, hoping the right words would come to me. For so long I had kept this side of my life separate from the rest, but that had changed when I decided to take wolves on the hunt for Maxwell and Claire. I owed it to the rest of them to let them know what was really going on outside of our town and our pack.

I scanned the group of wolves sitting so patiently, waiting to hear why I'd called them together. Our pack had shrunk over the past year. Currently there were nine wolves calling this town home, myself included. Each of us so different as people and animals.

I knew danger could find them through me on a grander scale than most of them realized. I couldn't leave them in the dark, especially if one day they, too, would be faced with the choice to fight by my side.

"I'm also sure that most of you know there is more to me than human and wolf. I can do things that tend to set me apart. Things that attract attention from creatures of all kinds. It's time for me to tell you what that really means to the rest of you."

Chapter Twenty-One

It felt strange to be back at Lucy's Lounge after spending so many nights at The Wicked Kiss. It was a foreign world, a primarily human one. It was nice to sit in the large corner booth with my friends and be able to enjoy the setting instead of being on the lookout for serious trouble.

Lucy's Lounge was smaller than The Wicked Kiss, but it had an upper floor. There was nothing special about the small town club. It had somewhat of a country feel to it even though top 40 music pumped out of the speakers and everyone was dressed in club wear. I loved something about the small town vibe; it felt like home.

I was having a hard time relaxing despite the easygoing atmosphere. I glanced down at my attire, second guessing it even though it was too late for that. It was the fourteenth of June, my birthday, so I'd gone all out. It seemed like as good an excuse as any to go shopping.

The black and white knee-length dress encased my body like a glove. Nearly all white with a stripe of black that wound diagonally across the bodice and around to the hem of the skirt, the dress had caught my eye from a shop window. I had to have it. Jez had talked me out of my usual knee-high boots and into a pair of four-inch stilettos. With my long hair pinned up, I was feeling more feminine than I had in a long time.

"Aw, Jez, no. I told you guys not to get any gifts." I protested when she slipped a box across the table to me.

"Too bad. You know I don't do what I'm told. Besides, I made it myself so you have to accept it." She shrugged and tossed a golden lock of hair out of her eyes. "Open it."

I'd never been so happy to see Jez looking like herself again. She had recovered from Kale's attack physically, but the emotional scars were there. In a tight leather skirt and a black bustier with those amazing red-painted lips, she looked great. But, I knew she was holding a grudge, and I couldn't say I blamed her. I'd invited Kale to the party, but he had a tendency to avoid these things. I couldn't help but think that might be best tonight for several reasons.

Kylarai and Zoey watched me untie the ribbon holding the box closed. I felt like I was being put on the spot. I'd specifically told everyone that I didn't want any gifts.

I lifted the lid of the box, finding the most magnificent stake inside that I'd ever seen. It was made of cherry wood and had my name etched into it. It brought a smile to my face.

"Thank you, Jez. This is so cool of you. I can't wait to use it."

"I'm sure you'll get your chance sooner than you think." She smirked and reached for her glass, finding it empty. "Dammit. Where's that wolf with our refills?"

I scanned the crowd near the bar for Shaz. "I'm sure it won't be long. Calm down booze hound."

"We got you something, too, Lex. It's back at the house. Too big to carry in here. Want to know what it is or should we keep it a surprise?" Kylarai's smile lit up her whole face. The pain was still there, in the depths of her eyes, but she wasn't letting it define her every moment. I was glad to see the strength that I knew was inside her.

"No, don't tell her," Zoey interrupted. "It's one of those things she just has to see."

I was curious to see what kind of gift those two would come up with together. I sensed Shaz' approach and looked up to find him juggling a tray laden with drinks. My heart skipped a beat as I drank him in.

His hair was stylishly spiked so that it went every which way. He was casual but sexy in blue jeans, a black t-shirt and a leather jacket, my favorite look for him. Watching him glide through the crowd, deftly maneuvering the tray to avoid any spills, I might have swooned a little. He could still make my heart race.

"It's about time," Jez proclaimed when he set the tray before us. She wasted no time setting tequila shots in front of each of us. With a wry smile she raised her shot in a toast. "To Alexa, for making it longer than I ever thought she would. Bottom's up, my friends."

I slid over in the booth so Shaz could sit beside me. His musky wolf and pine scent hit me, and I savored it. I still felt ill when I thought of what he'd been up to at The Wicked Kiss, but I knew I had to deal with it since I had gotten him wrapped up with vampires in the first damn place. All that mattered was that I needed him. We'd overcome so much already. We were strong enough to survive this, too.

I wrinkled my nose and grimaced even before the tequila hit my tongue. Drinking bathroom cleaner had to taste better than this. A slice of lime took the edge off, but it didn't stop me from cursing at the empty shot glass.

"I don't know how you can drink that shit, Jez. It's a slap in the mouth." Shuddering, I reached for a double shot of whiskey instead.

Jez helped herself to another tequila. "Don't be so weak. This is the stuff that'll show you what you're made of."

The table dissolved into a debate over the nastiest alcoholic drinks in existence. I was content to drink my whiskey and listen to them compare everything from moonshine to absinthe. It all sounded nasty to me.

Shaz leaned in close so I could feel his breath on my ear. "So, no Arys yet?"

"Not yet. He'll be the last to arrive. Like always." I couldn't help but look toward the front entry even though I'd feel his arrival before I saw it.

I observed our fellow patrons with casual curiosity. I think I almost missed the place a little. At least I did until Casey walked in.

The tall, skinny brunette was Shaz' neighbor. She was also interested in him, or she had been at one point. I watched her saunter through the club to the bar. She looked our way briefly, her gaze locking on Shaz. Oddly enough, I felt no real animosity toward her. All it took was remembering the vampiress that had sunk fangs into my white wolf to make Casey look like a child in comparison. All those times I'd felt threatened by her seemed so pitiful now.

Pretending not to notice Casey, I turned my attention back to the conversation. Somehow a body shots reference had steered the topic to sex and drunken one night stands. I didn't have any one night stand experience myself.

"This one chick had a full dominatrix dungeon in her basement." Jez said between shots. "But, I told her, no deal. I don't play the submissive for anyone. If there's going to be a top, it'll be me."

Though Shaz might never say so, I'm sure he would have been happy to listen to her sexcapades all night. Kylarai's eyes widened slightly, and she blushed. This kind of blatant discussion wasn't quite her style. I laughed, having heard far crazier stories from Jez than that. Zoey regarded her with a smirk. Her intense blue eyes showed intrigue.

"Oh, come on you guys." Jez slapped a hand down on the table. "I can't be the only one with crazy one night stand stories. Fess up."

"None here," I said truthfully.

"No," her green cat eyes flashed with mischief. "But, I know you have some wild three-way stories. Do tell."

I laughed, embarrassed as heat rushed to my cheeks. "Hell no. You're doing a great job of entertaining us on your own."

Shaz squirmed beside me. He was feeling the burn of being the only male in attendance. "Good Lord, I never thought I'd say this, but I almost wish Arys was here." He laughed uncomfortably and sipped from his beer. As an afterthought he added, "And, don't any of you dare tell him I said that."

Kylarai tossed a lime wedge at him, aiming for his head. She missed. "I can't believe you just said that. Never thought I'd see the day."

"Trust me. You haven't seen anything. Nothing has changed." With an eye roll, Shaz downed the last of his beer and reached for a tequila shot. At the rate the booze was going down, this was going to be a hell of a birthday.

"Wait a minute." Jez held up a hand, her grin growing wider. "Nothing? Are you saying you and the vampire don't get a little kinky when you're both with Alexa? Because I find that hard to believe."

"Believe it." Shaz spoke quickly. Maybe a little too quickly. "No kink. Ever."

I was pretty sure he was stretching the truth on that, but I wasn't going to say anything. It wasn't at all what Jez was thinking, but there had been some intense moments between Arys and Shaz. Despite the fact that Shaz got off on a vampire's bite, he clearly wasn't ready to admit that it had all started with Arys.

After few more shooters, I was laughing off Jez' playful harassment of Shaz. Knowing she was making him uncomfortable only made her eager to continue. He shot me a questioning sidelong glance to which I just shrugged. He thought I had told her the dirty details of our encounters with Arys, but I hadn't. She was just a clever cat.

The newest Lady Gaga song started, sending flocks of people to the dance floor. Jez was determined to be one of them. "Come on, Alexa. You have to dance with me. Anyone else coming?"

Zoey and Ky shuffled around to let her out of the booth. When I stood up to join her the tequila hit me, creating a warm tingle in my limbs. I waited for the others to join us, but they all shook their heads, happy to stay put.

Jez frowned at them, shaking her head. "Ok then party poopers. I expect to see a new batch of drinks at this table when we get back."

Dancing with Jez felt so good after the recent chaos in my world. The dance floor was crowded, filling my nostrils with the scent of alcohol, sweat and a myriad of perfumes and cologne. Once I got moving to the rhythm of the music, I let go of everything that had happened over the past few weeks and just danced.

I hadn't fully realized how much tension I'd been carrying around until it slipped away. I could always count on Jez to help me focus on having fun and letting loose. She was a dream. If I didn't have her, I'd be so tightly wound that I would have spontaneously combusted long ago. I'd never been so grateful for my friends as I was right then.

We were having a great time, dancing and turning down advances from the few guys that dared to approach us. The evening was full of laughter, music and more booze than even Weres should consume. Though it wasn't anything fancy or elaborate, our little party was a lot of fun. Until Kale showed up.

Jez stopped dancing the moment I sensed him. She stood stiffly beside me while the flailing bodies of other people bumped into us.

Her smile vanished, a fierce glare in its place.

"What the hell is he doing here? Did you invite him?"

"Of course I did." Taking hold of her arm, I led her off the dance floor to avoid getting trampled. "I didn't expect him to show up. He never comes out with us."

"He tried to kill me, Alexa. I'm not sure things will ever be the same between us." Anger burned in her eyes.

I didn't know what to say to that. I let my gaze roam over Kale, appreciating the sight of him dressed head to toe in black, his leather duster flowing behind him. I was relieved that the loud music muffled my small whimper.

"Well..." I zoned out, unable to tear my gaze from him.

His short brown hair was gelled in the front, just a little. It was simple and stylish without being overdone or dramatic. He stood near the entry, surveying the bar's interior. No sooner had his gaze landed on us than Jez was stalking angrily across the room toward him. *Oh, shit.*

I hurried after her, knowing that a tequila-fueled Jez was likely to say or do something she'd regret later. I was right. Before I could stop her, she slapped Kale with enough force to make me wince. Her hand connected with his face hard enough to be heard despite the loud music. I caught her wrist before she could land another slap or decide to turn that open hand into a fist.

"What are you doing here?" She demanded as her fury burst forth.

Kale looked her evenly in the eye while lightly rubbing his jaw where she'd hit him. "I was invited."

"Jez, come on," I pleaded. "This isn't the time or place for this. If you have something to say to Kale, it can wait until you're sober and not about to ruin my birthday. Why don't you go back to the table?"

I didn't have to look at our table to know both Kylarai and Shaz had taken notice of Kale's arrival. Geez, this was awkward for so many reasons.

"You shouldn't have come, Kale," she hissed, her tone filled with venom. Rage emanated from her, hot and tempting as it danced along my skin.

"Jez, go back to the table and turn all that hyped-up energy into something useful. Like getting to know Zoey a little better. Hmm?" I wasn't suggesting; I was demanding. She had every right to be pissed at Kale, but she wasn't going to take it out on him at my birthday party.

She looked at me with those flashing cat eyes, and I stared her down. Jez was feisty and daring, but she wasn't stupid. She held my gaze for a moment before scoffing, "I don't do crazy broads like Zoey."

Stifling the urge to sigh, I gave her a gentle push toward the table. "Yes, you do. Now get your ass over there before I go a little crazy-broad myself."

After a moment of consideration, she turned to go, but not before leaving Kale with one last remark. "You tried to kill me, Kale. I owe you an ass-kicking."

He watched her go, a pensive look in his eyes. "I completely expected that. Actually, I expected worse." Meeting my eyes, he shrugged and offered a forced smile. "I'm sorry. I shouldn't have come. She's right. But, I'm not staying. I just wanted to give you this."

From a pocket he produced a small box, covered in colorful birthday gift wrap. I was suddenly nervous when he pressed it into my hand. Our fingers touched briefly, and a spark of electricity passed between us before he pulled away.

"Oh, Kale you didn't have to do this. Really." I stared at the box, curious but tentative.

"Open it later. When you're alone. And really, it's no big deal. Just something I wanted you to have." His gaze strayed past me to where Shaz watched from the table. He hesitated then pulled me into his arms. Holding me close for just a moment, he pressed a kiss to my forehead. "Happy birthday, Alexa. I wish you nothing but happiness."

He turned to go, and though I wanted to stop him, I didn't. Instead I turned the box over in my hands, certain that whatever was inside, it meant a lot to Kale. I returned to the table, hoping to avoid questions as I slipped the box into my purse. No such luck.

"A gift from Kale?" Kylarai inquired, her tone carefully neutral.

"Uh, yeah." I didn't want to look at either her or Shaz, but I didn't have much choice. "It's nothing, I'm sure. I'll open it later."

Shaz said nothing, but I didn't miss the way his wolf seemed to creep up behind his eyes. I knew Kylarai well, and it was apparent to me there was something more she wanted to say, only Shaz' presence stopped her.

I dove into another whiskey, seeking escape from the sudden discomfort. To my surprise Jez had slid in next to Zoey, and the two of them were leaning in close together so they could converse over the loud music. Soon Jez, with a bright pink drink clutched in one hand, dragged Zoey out to the dance floor. I was relieved to see that Jez hadn't let Kale's appearance ruin the whole evening.

"I'm going to reload the liquor supply and grab us a pool table. Sound good?" Shaz stood up to leave, and I moved to let him out of the booth.

Pool sounded like a good way to keep busy without awkward silences. I nodded my agreement and swallowed hard, knowing what was coming once he left. I sat there alone with Kylarai expectantly, but she only stared at me with stormy grey eyes.

"Ok, Ky. Just spit it out. I know there's something you want to say."

She tapped her long nails against her beer bottle, eyeing me thoughtfully. "Alright. I don't want to make this weird, but I know about you and Kale. Shaz told me. Don't be mad at him. He just needed someone to talk to. It came out the other day, after … after we lost Julian."

I savored the taste of the whiskey, using it as a way to buy myself a few seconds before responding. I couldn't be mad at Shaz. He had every right to confide in Kylarai. We were a tight-knit group. I just hated that he'd been the one to tell her. It should have been me. I should have had the guts to do it myself.

"I should have told you, Ky. I'm sorry. It was just once, and it won't be happening again."

She looked skeptical. "But he's in love with you. I thought as much that night he helped us out after Zoey lost her mind. Seeing the way he looked at you tonight, I'm sure of it. So I have to ask, do you love him too?"

Choking on whiskey tends to hurt a little bit. I coughed it out, feeling embarrassed and completely put on the spot. Kylarai tried to hide a smirk as I regained my composure.

"That is not a yes or no answer. I wish it was. I feel something for Kale that is rooted in our friendship, in things we share. It's confusing and hard to define, but it's real. I don't think I can give you a straight answer."

She nodded knowingly. "So, that's a yes." I grimaced and she laughed. "It's ok, Lex. I'm long over Kale. What we had was short-lived and never really got the chance to become more than deep affection. I just want him to be happy."

Guilt rolled through me, and I sighed. "So do I."

"Come on, let's go kick Shaz' ass at pool. We can team up against him."

Doing something as mundane and human as shooting a game of pool was just what I needed. I'd been leery of Shaz' insistence to celebrate my birthday. I didn't think I could have an outing that wasn't one supernatural incident after another, but this was nice. It was uneventful, for the most part, and I couldn't have been happier with that.

It was well past one in the morning when I felt the thrilling rush of Arys' presence. I was momentarily breathless, excited just by the sight of him. His hair was messier than usual, but it was no less sexy than any other time. I couldn't wait to run my fingers through it. I couldn't help but ogle his bare, muscular arms and the way his shirt defined his firm body. The dim lighting glinted off the silver rings in his nose and lip. The lusty urge to nibble the one in his lip was strong.

Arys swept past Shaz on his way to me, pausing long enough to smack the end of Shaz' pool cue as he lined up his shot. Shaz' cue slipped, knocking one of Kylarai's balls into a nearby pocket. He whirled around to glare into Arys' smirking face.

"Fuck you." Shaz' eyes flashed with a deadly light. Then a small grin broke over his handsome face, and he gave Arys a shove.

I couldn't help but grow tense as I watched them. Though I'd never say it to either of them, part of me found it to be a bit of a turn on when they went at each other, as long as there was no real chance of anybody getting seriously hurt.

"What took you so long?" I demanded as Arys swept me into his arms.

He kissed me before I could utter another word. It stole my breath and left me weak in the knees.

"Happy birthday, my gorgeous wolf." He chuckled, a low sensual sound that got my blood pumping. "You'll get your gift later, back at your place. Which is what took me so long to get here."

"Gift?" I raised a brow, suspicious and curious. "Why does nobody honor the no gift rule?"

"Trust me. You want this gift. Me and the wolf pup are even going to play nice tonight. Just for you." The wink and the fang-revealing smile he gave me spoke volumes. "Are you ready to abandon the drunken human festivities yet? Looks like Shaz is about as drunk as I like him to be."

Arys was in a devilish mood. It practically oozed from him. He didn't even sound angry when he said, "Sinclair was here. I can smell him on you."

"He was only here for a minute. Don't you dare bite me in here."

"No. I'll save that for later." Arys' rare eagerness was refreshing and infectious.

Shaz and Arys locked eyes, sharing a look before Shaz turned back to his game. They had something planned. That much was apparent. I was intrigued. This didn't happen often, not with Shaz' personal issues regarding Arys and the intimacies that arose when the three of us were together. I was certainly looking forward to the rest of my evening.

Kylarai sunk the eight ball, and there was a whoop of boastful shouting as she celebrated her victory over Shaz. "You owe me a drink. I kicked your ass just like I told you I would."

Shaz tossed his cue down on the table and feigned a dirty look. "No fair. My game was sabotaged by the asshole."

"I'm almost ready to call it a night, Lex." Ky sidled up next to me, nodding in greeting to Arys. "I'll take the two crazies back to my place for the night. I assume you have plans with these two."

I followed her gaze to where Zoey and Jez were challenging a table full of guys to a shot-for-shot contest. Those guys had no idea what they were up against. Jez would drink them all under the table and still be able to walk a straight line in her heels.

"Thanks for coming out, Ky. You're a good friend." I hugged her close, sensing the inner pain she was masking so well on the surface. What I wouldn't have given to take it from her. "I love you. And again, I'm so sorry about Julian."

"Forget it." She waved me off, keeping that strong outward

facade firmly in place. "I love you, too, Lex. I'm so happy to know you. You're an amazing person. Even if you are a little scary sometimes." Her laughter was musical, bringing a smile to my face. "I'll go round up the rowdies. Come by tomorrow for your gift."

After being forced into a few last birthday shooters and a series of last drunken birthday wishes, goodbyes were said, and my intoxicated friends made their way out. The DJ shouted that it was last call, sending a flock of people rushing up to the bar.

Arys turned to Shaz and me with fire in his eyes. "Now, if you two are successfully liquored up and finished with the meager entertainment," he gestured to the dance floor and pool tables, "let's go get the real party started."

Chapter Twenty-Two

As I pushed open the door to my house, I was greeted by the warm glow of dozens of carefully placed candles. The front sitting room walls were decorated in shadows that danced with the flames from floor to ceiling. I paused to admire the welcoming warmth. It was serene and more than a little romantic.

A vase of wild flowers sat on the table near the door. I leaned in to smell them, savoring the heady scent. "Aw, did you guys do all this? It's so sweet."

"Arys did it, but it was my idea." Shaz grinned and gave me a light smack on the rear.

I dropped my purse on the table and reached down to pull off my heels. Arys stopped me with a hand on my arm. "Leave them on."

The desire in his midnight blue eyes made it impossible to deny his request. Leaving the stilettos on, I followed the candles through the house. It must have taken Arys hours to arrange them all. The aromatic concoction of cinnamon and vanilla was tantalizing. I had a weakness for the scent of vanilla.

The glow of the flames lit up the path to the bedroom downstairs, leaving everything outside the immediate area dark. It created an eerie contrast of light and dark that left me wanting to search the darkness though I knew nobody lurked within it.

In the doorway to the bedroom, I stopped and surveyed the mass of candles adorning every table top and dresser in there, too. The bed was layered in red, pink and white rose petals. Two bottles of champagne sat in a tub of ice on the dresser. The ridiculously cliché setup would normally have me laughing at the sappy romanticism of it.

But, I seldom got the chance to be silly and cliché, so I was going to enjoy it.

"It's totally cheesy, isn't it?" Shaz slipped an arm around me from behind and kissed the back of my neck.

"Yes. I love it though."

Arys swept past us, entering the room with a smooth glide. He regarded me for just a moment before reaching to free my hair from the pins that held it. Tossing them on the bedside table, he nodded his approval as my blond locks tumbled down around me.

"Much better." With a hand under my chin, Arys lightly kissed me, the briefest touch.

Standing between the two of them, the sensation of their bodies against mine taunted me. The promise of what was to come stirred the longing low in my core. It was good to be the birthday girl.

Sharing an intimate encounter together, the three of us, didn't happen as often as Jez would like to imagine it did. It was a mind-blowing experience, to have them both at the same time. It was one of the few times the tension between Shaz and Arys slipped away completely.

"Champagne?" Arys was across the room popping the cork on the bottle before I could reply.

"No way," Shaz shook his head and steered me toward the bed. "You're not getting me drunk."

"You're already drunk. Besides, you process it fast." Arys held a glass out to each of us. "Humor me."

I hid a smile as I took the glass. Arys did prefer Shaz to be loosened up. It gave him greater allowance to push Shaz' boundaries.

"So, do you want your gift now, or later?" Shaz sipped from the champagne glass, pointedly looking at Arys before abandoning it on the table.

"I thought you two were my gifts." I glanced down at Shaz where he knelt at my feet. He ran a hand up the inside of my leg, toying with the ribbon from my heels that wound around my ankle.

"We are." With predatory poise, Arys plucked the glass from my hand and watched Shaz slowly slide his hands further up my leg. "Just relax, Alexa, and let us celebrate you."

I stepped carefully out of my dress, sliding it down my legs. My gaze met Arys'. He watched with dark desire, looking me over like

I was something to be feasted upon. It was a dangerous look, one that had me quivering. Anticipation built quickly.

With a small growl, Shaz nipped at the inside of my leg. I gasped when the warm flick of his tongue followed. His fingers found the soft stretchy material of my pink G-string. In an aggressive motion that sent a shock through me, he drew them aside and pressed his mouth to my most private region.

My fingers slid through his hair, and the sudden surprise of his tongue knocked me off-balance. Arys chuckled and came to stand behind me, encouraging me to lean back against him. Happy to allow him to support my weight, I felt the sharp touch of Shaz' fangs, and I moaned.

Arys gazed down my body, watching Shaz. The wolf glanced up to lock eyes with the vampire, and there was an intensity so deep in his jade green eyes that I almost lost myself. I couldn't read his expression, but I had a feeling that Arys could. Their best communication came in the form of silence and deep stares. I often felt like they were sharing something I wasn't in on, but it never bothered me. Only in those times did I feel they were united.

Sweeping my hair off my neck, Arys bit lightly at the exposed vein there. A pleasurable tickle shot down my spine, making me giggle in a way that I hated but Arys loved. Gently, he reached around to cup my breasts. It didn't match the aggressive attention I received from Shaz as he kissed and licked me with undeniable hunger. I groaned when Arys caressed my nipples until they stood firm, my fingers tightening in Shaz' hair.

It didn't take long for them to bring me to the brink of climax. Though when I expected to plunge over into that amazing abyss of ecstasy, Shaz denied me that glorious fall. Instead he pulled away, teasing me lightly with his tongue, ignoring my frustrated growl.

He slowly slid my panties down my legs before rising to his feet. Arys followed his lead, stripping me from the confines of my bra. I reached for Shaz, wanting to feel the silk of his hair between my fingers again, but he stepped just out of reach and began to disrobe.

His eyes were all wolf. It wouldn't be long until he was all fangs and claws, just the way I liked him. Tearing my gaze from his, I appreciated his fine form, admiring the curves of his muscles, the way that little smattering of hair below his belly led to the finely sculpted organ that I ached for with anticipation.

The power between Arys and I flared to life with a staggering strength as he reacted to my growing passion. It flowed through the room with an almost audible *whoosh*, followed by a small gasp from Shaz as he felt it. I studied him, curious to see how it affected him.

Shaz reached for me with clawed hands that left faint bloody scratches where they touched my skin. Sliding one hand under my leg, he lifted it so that he could step in between my legs and easily slip inside me. In time with his thrust, he kissed me with a bruising ferocity that left small cuts on my lips and tongue from his fangs.

I could feel Arys' growing intrigue as he stood behind me, his face just inches from Shaz' over my shoulder. The press of his erection against my back was exciting. I reached back to play in the soft hair at the nape of his neck.

For one interesting moment, Shaz and Arys stared into one another, each of them on opposing sides of me. For just a second, I thought Arys was going to close the distance between them, but Shaz pulled away before it could happen. The memory of the one and only kiss they'd shared lingered in my mind. It had been extraordinarily sexy.

It had also been something that had pushed Shaz across his own boundary line. He would never give himself fully to Arys, whether or not the vampire desired such a thing. I knew that much. But, how much of himself was he willing to give? That remained to be seen.

As Shaz slowly loved me, Arys warmed until the heat rolled off him. He was feeding off of us, basking in our heady werewolf energy. I could feel him getting off on the spicy sexual energy we were creating, and I longed to feel it as he did.

Arys pulled away, leaving me void of his warmth. Shaz took the opportunity to turn us so the bed was behind him. Holding tightly to me, he fell back on the bed, pulling me down on top of him. For a humorous moment, I sprawled haphazardly atop him. We both laughed while Arys merely rolled his eyes at our drunken idiocy.

He stood near the foot of the bed, gazing down at us. He waited until my attention was on him before revealing his nakedness one piece of clothing at a time. I felt like a starved woman at a feast. I wanted him close again, so they both touched me. I craved it.

Shaz gave me a light slap on the ass, and I returned my attention to him. Guiding me carefully, he repositioned us so that we both sat facing one another on the bed, with me in charge as the one on top. Impaling myself along his hard length, I stared down into his beautiful eyes, seeing myself reflected in them.

The sitting position was nice. It forced us to press close, maintaining a deep level of intimacy as we moved together. It should have been a perfect moment of love, but an image flashed unbidden through my head, the black-haired vampiress with her lips on my white wolf, her fangs buried in his flesh. It stunned me, and I felt myself pulled from the magic of the moment.

"Lex?" Shaz whispered my name and pushed the hair back from my face. "Is something wrong?"

"No," I said quickly, fighting not to let it show in my eyes. "Nothing wrong."

Arys watched me with a peculiar certainty, and I was sure he'd seen the vision that had just flashed through my mind. He never said as much, just prowled closer to the bed with a sly, unnerving ease.

Shaz pressed his face to my throat, his lips warm against the pulsing vein there. I looked to Arys for help, seeking escape from the ugly images swirling in my thoughts. He slid onto the bed, coming to embrace me from behind.

Pressing soft kisses to my shoulders and the back of my neck, it surprised me when I heard his voice whisper through my mind, 'I'll kill her.'

Tension filled me, and I closed my eyes, focusing on their scents, refusing to allow this night to be ruined by my own insecurities.

'No, Arys. That won't help anything. She isn't the real problem.'

The musky wolf scent of Shaz mingled with Arys' hair products to create a comforting aroma that was just the two of them made one. It stirred a ravenous response that I could feel in the pit of my stomach.

Arys knelt behind me, stroking his hands over my body as I moved with Shaz. As Arys manipulated the powerful energy the three of us called, I was able to fall deeper into the two of them. Nothing else mattered right now other than this current moment. I had to let myself believe that.

Shaz twitched inside me. A tingle filled my belly as his approaching release encouraged my own pleasure. With Arys' metaphysical guidance every sensation was heightened. Their hands were all over me, in my hair, on my breasts, gripping my hips. My breath came faster, and I clung to Shaz so tight my clawed nails left bloody trails in his skin.

The scent of his blood hit me, and the bloodlust crawled up within me, threatening to burst forth. A throaty snarl escaped me as Shaz pushed me over the edge of climax, and I was suddenly caught in the throes of ecstasy. Mixed with every amazing wave that rocked my body was the hunger, the desire to bite into the wolf beneath me. I wanted him.

Sensing my hunger, Shaz gazed at me with a yearning that almost matched my own. He wanted it, too. I'd gotten used to seeing wariness in his eyes when the bloodlust raised its ugly head. Finding his expression full of intrigue left me conflicted. I loved it as much as I hated it.

My lungs heaved as I caught my breath. I slid out from between them and collapsed in the middle of the bed. This left them staring at one another with a strange, even look. Shaz quickly put some space between them by reclining back on the bed and rolling onto his side next to me. However, his gaze remained fixed on Arys.

"You want something, wolf?" Arys' pupils dilated as he taunted Shaz.

Shaz reached out to touch me, a gentle hand on my leg. He continued to watch the vampire, a darkness settling into his wolf eyes. My heart raced as I waited for Shaz to give voice to his wish.

Instead of replying, Shaz pushed himself up on his knees and reached for Arys. Though I couldn't take my eyes off them, I groped blindly for the nearest champagne glass on the table. All the booze in the world wasn't going to take the edge off. I knew what I was about to see, and it twisted my insides in a mass of confusion.

Arys wore a look of devious satisfaction as Shaz slid his hands into the vampire's jet black hair. He curled his fingers into fists, holding tight to Arys' locks. He leaned in close, his mouth hovering just inches from Arys'. I held my breath, waiting and hoping, but for what I wasn't sure.

With the barest brush of their lips, Shaz spoke softly. "Don't turn this into a game. You know what I want." For just a moment he nuzzled Arys, a strangely affectionate gesture for two men who couldn't stand one another. Then Shaz tilted his head to the side, offering his neck to Arys.

I sat upright, a glass clutched in my hand. The intensity of the scene before me was rife with lust and power. It took concentration on my part not to shatter the glass with my grip. I watched my white wolf offer himself to Arys, and I was both horrified and madly turned on. As much as I wanted to watch Arys feed from Shaz, I knew that this more than anything showed how far into our world Shaz had fallen.

I didn't expect Arys to look to me for permission. I saw the question in his eyes, and I stared back at him, giving no indication of what I preferred. This was between the two of them. And honestly, I didn't know. I was merely a bystander.

Arys would never pass up an offer like this from Shaz. Though Shaz was taking a dominant stance, Arys was always the one in control. With a slight smirk, he bared his fangs and bit hard and fast into my wolf.

Shaz grunted slightly as he relaxed into the bite. His knuckles were white from gripping Arys' hair so tightly, and the energy that rolled off him was thick with wanton desire. It struck me like a slap in the face, and I couldn't help but respond with my own hunger for blood and sex.

The champagne in my hand quickly lost all appeal. I held the glass forgotten and watched as Arys tasted Shaz, his tongue gliding over the bloody wound. The sound of my heart pounding in my ears alerted me to the fact that I'd stopped breathing, frozen in the moment.

Goosebumps rose up on my skin as a rush of power crashed over me. Arys drove it, sweeping Shaz up in its thrall. His eyes closed, and he leaned into the vampire's dizzying allure. Arys was carefully in control. He pulled back before taking too much. I tensed, waiting to see what would happen next.

For a brief, heart-stopping second, I thought Arys would push it further, as he had once before. Expecting that very thing, Shaz' eyes opened in a glare, and he growled. His hands slipped from Arys' hair, and he turned his head away before Arys could kiss him. Instead, my beautiful vampire leaned into Shaz and boldly ran his tongue along that soft spot beneath Shaz' ear.

Shaz pulled away. His eyes were wild, pupils huge. He breathed hard, almost panting as the power in the room pulled him under like a deadly undertow. Soaring high on lust and werewolf blood, Arys was on me before I could blink.

Knocking the glass out of my hand, he pushed me down on my back and forced himself between my legs. It was rough and even a little painful when he reached one hand into my hair, pinning my head to the bed. Adrenaline burst through me. I was eager for him, crying out when he forcefully thrust inside me.

Pressing his lips to mine, Arys kissed me hungrily. I tasted Shaz' blood in his mouth, and my pleasure was instantly heightened. White noise roared in my ears as our power flowed freely.

Arys rolled us onto our sides, so we lay facing one another. This allowed Shaz to align his body to mine from behind. As Arys pumped into me with an aggression that pleased my wolf, Shaz held tight to me from behind.

With a clawed hand tightly gripping my waist, he bit the back of my neck with those four massive fangs.

I yelped and felt the telltale warmth of blood. Wolf fangs hurt worse than vampire fangs. They were fierce, made for shredding and tearing.

Even as careful as he'd been, the burning pain was shocking. The wolf inside me loved it. The savage touch of my mate was stimulating, banishing the human fear of pain and instead finding joy in it. The gentle touch of his tongue on the wound was as intimate as when he'd licked between my legs. Shaz tasted my blood, and it made me crazy.

Wrapped up in the two men I loved with all my heart, there was nowhere else on earth I'd have rather been. The give and take of love and pleasure was a rollercoaster of power, emotion and acceptance. Time ticked by as we all sought something in one another whether it be gratification, affection or simply acceptance. It was long after dawn by the time we lay sprawled on the bed in exhaustion.

My body was decorated in bloody scratches, bites and bruises. I didn't attempt to get up; my heart hadn't returned to its normal pace, and my breath still didn't come easily.

Shaz fetched a pair of sweat pants from the drawer in my

dresser where he kept some of his things and disappeared upstairs.

I lay in the disarray of the blankets, snuggled against Arys. He stroked a hand through my hair while we listened to Shaz slamming doors upstairs. It sounded like he went into the garage.

"That wolf needs to be careful." Arys broke the silence with words that made me apprehensive. "He was far too willing to give his blood to me. That kind of behavior can lead to addictive tendencies."

"What about you?" I countered. "You wanted him. I didn't see you turn him down."

Arys looked at me like I'd said something ridiculous. "Of course not. He still has a very firm guard up when it comes to me. If I see it fall for even a minute, I'm taking advantage of it."

"I'm worried about him. He gets off on the rush. I don't want to see him become a junkie for it."

"Try not to worry about him too much. We won't let our wolf become a blood whore. Besides, I think it's you that stands the greatest risk of forming addictive tendencies."

It was soothing to hear him call Shaz "our" wolf. But, that was overlooked when I heard what he had to say about me. "Hey! I do not have addictive tendencies."

"Don't you?"

Before I could toss a defensive retort back, Shaz entered the room carrying a shiny, black chrome rim with a big red ribbon tied around it. I sat up quickly, reaching to touch the smooth metal.

"Happy birthday, babe." Fangs now absent, Shaz kissed me warmly. "The other three are in the garage. I hope you like them. I think they'll look awesome on your car."

"I love them! I can't wait to get these on my beast." I let out a girlish squeal. Brand new rims for my car might not seem like the most romantic gift, but coming from Shaz, it was perfect.

Arys propped himself up on an elbow, his hand under his head. He lay there on the bed in all his nude glory. "Nice choice, pup. Those will look great." To me he added, "My gift to you is in the nightstand."

I sprang at the nightstand like a rabid dog, eager to see what my vampire would choose to give me. I almost upset a few candles in my rush to get the drawer open. I had to dig through a pile of blue tissue paper before I found it, an incredibly old book. The leather cover was worn and thin; the pages had yellowed with time, and it had that musty book smell that all old books eventually have.

Lifting it carefully, I set it on my lap and opened it. It was a journal, Arys' journal. The dates written in faded ink on the pages were shocking. There were journal entries from more than a hundred years ago.

"I know you have all of my memories," Arys watched me flip through the pages, "but they're mostly a mess of random images in your head. Yours are for me, too. I thought this might help. I wanted you to have it."

I gazed at Arys in wonder. I never would have expected something so deeply personal from him. "Arys … thank you. This is so thoughtful. I don't even know what to say. I really appreciate that you would be willing to give me this."

I reached out to grasp his hand, hoping he saw the gratitude in my eyes. I gently replaced the journal back into the nightstand drawer. Arys smiled and pulled me back down on the bed beside him. I reached for Shaz who quickly joined us.

As tired as I was, I didn't sleep. I waited for each of them to fall asleep, and then I carefully disentangled myself from their grasps and left the bed. Wrapping myself in the black robe that always hung on the back of the door, I glanced back at the two of them.

Shaz clutched his pillow, snoring softly. He was facing away from Arys, far enough out of reach to avoid accidentally touching. Arys had an arm up over his head, hiding his face from view. I wondered if he really was asleep at all. He didn't sleep much, and when he did, it was light, like he was always partially alert.

Though they were only a few feet apart on the bed, it was like they were worlds away from one another. I linked them, and without me, they were nothing. I didn't particularly want them to be close, but I didn't want them to always be at odds either. I really didn't think that would ever change.

I stepped lightly on the stairs as I made my way up to the main floor. Many of the candles had long since burnt out. I blew out the ones that remained lit as I followed them back to the front entry. My purse sat right where I'd left it, with Kale's gift inside. My curiosity climbed.

I sat in a chair near the front window, my purse in hand. The blinds were drawn, but the brilliant glow of the sun beyond cast shards of light upon me. Taking the carefully wrapped box out, I turned it over a few times. Maybe it was nothing of extreme value. Perhaps I was over thinking this.

With a deep exhalation of breath, I tore off the paper and opened the box. A small note fell out into my lap, but before I could read it, my gaze landed on the silver cross pendant displayed on a bed of cotton. It was breathtaking.

It was old, possibly Elizabethan old. It had a slightly medieval look to it. There was a small black diamond in the center. It was unlike anything I'd ever seen. It had to be the oldest, most valuable item I'd ever held.

I picked up the note, finding it scrawled in Kale's careful handwriting. It said only: *It used to be my mother's. Now it should be yours. Happy birthday.*

Stunned didn't even begin to cover it. Tears pricked the back of my eyes. A swell of emotion quickly overwhelmed me, and I choked back a sob. Kale had just given me his heart in more ways than one. I hadn't asked for it, but here it was, lying in a box on my lap.

He had asked nothing in return, knowing that I couldn't give him what he so freely gave to me. Staring into the box, running my fingers over the sleek silver cross, I knew with my whole being that I couldn't love him. And yet, I knew that I did. So why did it feel so bad?

Chapter Twenty-Three

I couldn't lie to myself. I was totally freaked out. As I got out of the car and stared across the street at the old church, an uneasy feeling gripped me. A shiver slithered down my spine. I didn't like this one bit.

Shya had asked me to come. He was elusive but indicated he had something he wanted me to see. I shielded hard, hoping to avoid any unwanted attention. Some things inside that church had never been human. I could feel them.

I glanced at Kale, seeking some kind of reassurance. His presence was a great relief. I wasn't sure I'd have had the courage to walk in there alone.

In the car on the way over, I'd tried to thank him for his gift. I wanted to say so much more, but none of it was right for the situation. He'd waved me off, effectively keeping the conversation from taking a personal turn. That was likely for the best.

"Remember, we're just here to observe." Kale fell into step beside me as we crossed the street. "No matter what you see here, don't get involved and don't draw attention to yourself. Trust me. The less anyone knows about you, the better. Oh, and shield tighter than that. I can feel your apprehension."

"Why did I agree to this again?" I muttered beneath my breath.

"Because you have power that puts you in a class all your own. It's a good thing. It gives you leverage. Just use it carefully."

I fell silent, slipping into stealth mode. The wolf inside was on full alert as I paid keen attention to my finely tuned senses. The scent of car exhaust lingered on the air. I saw no obvious sign that the church was occupied. As we drew closer, the atmosphere grew stifling with a strange energy I couldn't identify.

I toyed with the idea of turning back before it was too late. Once I stepped foot through that door, I wouldn't be able to change my mind. I couldn't shake the feeling that what I was about to encounter inside was going to strip away the last of my remaining illusions regarding the world I lived in.

Kale was calm, his walk confident. This wasn't new to him. He cast one last look my way before reaching for the handle of one of the large, double wooden doors. A brief shadow of uncertainty flickered in his eyes, and then it was gone. I got the distinct feeling that he would have preferred me not to be there. It did nothing to ease my concern.

The inside of the church was smaller than it looked from the outside, almost cozy. It was dark, the only light provided by the glow of the moon beyond the stained glass windows and one lonely light over the altar.

I followed Kale's lead, slipping into the darkness at the back of the church near the door. He was deathly still. I stood close, leaning into him more than I meant to. I might have been a bad-ass with the vampires and werewolves, but when my gaze took in those at the front near the altar, I was scared.

Shya loomed over a human man who knelt before him. Dressed in a simple dark suit, Shya didn't so much as glance our way though I knew without a doubt that he was keenly aware of our arrival. He was intent on the man at his feet. What really stole my breath were the massive black wings extended behind him. I had to tear my gaze away.

Even from where I stood I could see that the man on the floor was trembling. He was also clearly a man of the cloth, a man of God. The stench of fear emanated from him, strong and inviting. I took shallow breaths, refusing to react to the taunting scent.

Aside from Shya, one other demon was present. He had no visible wings, but the dark power rolling off him gave his nature away. He stood off to the side, hands clasped, just watching the scene before him. Another human man stood next to him, his face revealing no emotion or thought. He had a poker face like nothing I'd ever seen. He was also dressed like a man of the cloth. The way he watched the man on the floor whimper without reaction made me go cold inside. What the hell was going on here?

"We don't have to kill you, Jon. In fact, I'd honestly prefer not to." Shya's smooth, low voice was sinister. The air seemed to grow cold as he spoke. "But, I need to know where you found out about my little arrangement with your friend Evan here, because I think we have a traitor. And, I'm sure you understand that's something I just can't allow. Don't you, Jon?"

Nodding his head, Jon stared at Shya's feet, as if he couldn't bring himself to look the demon in the face. I had no idea what was going on, but I couldn't help but feel bad for the guy. I sure as hell wouldn't want to be in his place.

"I can't," Jon stammered, tears streaming down his cheeks. "I can't. They'll kill me."

Shya stared at him, red eyes glinting with malice. "So will I. Make your choice."

This was hard to watch. My palms were sweaty, and I fought the urge to fidget nervously. Kale stood stiffly next to me, watching with disinterest. I couldn't help but wonder how many times he'd witnessed something like this.

I watched with uncertainty. Jon's lips moved but no sound came out, a silent prayer. Then he looked up at Shya with venom in his eyes and spat, "Do what you will, demon. I don't serve you."

It was so quiet I could have heard a pin drop. I was tense, my focus on staying calm, hoping my shaky breaths didn't sound as loud to everyone else as they did to me.

In a sudden swell of dark fury, Shya freely exuded the power of his anger. Despite how hard I was working to shield myself, the demon's energy cut through me. I choked on a gasp as I tried not to react. It was unlike anything I'd ever been slapped with by a vampire. This hurt. Bad.

I was aware of how small of a wave I'd been hit with, and that nobody else seemed affected by it but me. If I hadn't been afraid of Shya already, I would have been then.

Kale barely moved from his rigid stance, but with the slightest of movement, he slowly slipped his fingers between mine. I stiffened at first. Then almost instantly, the searing sensation left by Shya's power dissipated as Kale added his strength to mine. It felt nice, strong, but it was missing that sense of true unity that I shared only with Arys, that sense of being one.

For a long, strained moment, Shya stared down the man who dared to defy him. It lasted only seconds though. Shya gave the barest nod, and an unseen figure stepped out from the darkness beyond the altar light. It startled me. I hadn't seen nor sensed him. The dim glow of the light fell upon him, and I was stunned.

The angel moved swiftly, an upraised sword clutched in both hands, a blur of motion. The immense silvery grey wings cloaking his tall, darkly clad frame distinguished him from the demons. The faintest iridescent shimmer was visible in his wings as he brought the sword down with enough force to make the blade sing as it cut through the air. It sliced clean through Jon's neck, taking his head off before I could look away.

This had to be a dream, a really ugly dream. The angel glanced at the remains with cold indifference etched in his fine features.

Shya turned away, directing an order to the other demon present. "Get this cleaned up."

It all happened too fast to process. Before I could take it all in, Shya was heading our way, his face grim. Kale dropped my hand, and I faced Shya with a confidence I didn't entirely feel.

"As you can see, there is a lot more to this than rogue creatures running amok." With a dismissive wave of his hand, Shya gestured to the headless body near the altar. "Normally, I wouldn't bother to deal with something so trivial myself; I would have one of my people do it. However, this time it was personal."

The scent of blood and death grew heavy on the air. As horrified as I was by the entire situation, I couldn't stop the bloodlust from rising. Though I was looking only at Shya, I could feel the watchful gaze of the angel upon me. It set loose a handful of butterflies in my stomach.

I forced myself to maintain steady eye contact with Shya. Looking into his intense red eyes was difficult. "Can I ask what this was all about?"

"Of course. You're an important part of the team. You have every right to a few questions." His interest was solely on me. Not once did he look at Kale or anyone else present. The undivided attention was unnerving. "Let me tell you one thing, Alexa. The most valuable power someone can possess is the right information. Jon had it. And, since he wouldn't share that information, he had to be taken out of the equation."

I wanted to ask how taking a man's life could be so simple, just part of an equation that I didn't fully understand. Instead I said, "But why? What could he have known that was worth his life?"

Shya eyed me appraisingly. He nodded slowly, as if in approval of my desire for an explanation. "I understand that in some ways you're very much still human. You need to be able to justify death. Well, tell me, would you be able to justify it if you knew that the information he harbored could expose you? That it could land you in a lab where you'd be picked apart by human scientists in a vain attempt to find out what makes you what you are?"

My mouth went dry, and the blood drained from my face. What Shya described had always been one of my greatest fears. He had put me in a tough place. I didn't believe that my life was more valuable than anyone else's, but I did believe that mass public exposure of the supernatural was in nobody's best interest.

"Point taken." I nodded, having nothing else to offer. I was in no position to either condone or condemn what Shya had just done. I wasn't sure what I would have done if it had been me. I hoped to never be the one who had to make that call.

"Don't worry your pretty little head about it, Alexa. I want you for the vampires and werewolves. For now anyway."

That pretty little head comment would have earned anyone else a bitch slap or at least a seriously tongue lashing. I took it from Shya simply because I had to. He towered over me with those scarlet eyes and wings that went from shoulder to ankle, and I was overwhelmed.

"I'm not making any deals with you." My voice wavered, but I meant it.

A grin lit up Shya's face in a way that should have made him appear friendly but really just made him predatory. "I like you. You're young yet, but you know what's best for all of us. Kale assures me that I can trust you. Prove him right, and I'll be happy not to have to kill the both of you."

The way Shya spoke was so casual, like he was discussing the weather rather than threatening to kill us. All I could do was play along with a smile and a nod.

"So," Shya clapped his hands together and smiled. It shone in his eyes, and he was suddenly a whole different persona than seconds ago. "State your terms. I assume you have some. You have genuine potential, and I will do anything to make you happy to work with me."

My lips curved into a smile, but it didn't feel natural. "Let's start there. I work with you, not for you. I won't be forced to do anything I don't believe in."

"Certainly."

"I do things my way. And, my personal life stays personal. I won't have my actions watched or judged." I didn't mean to sound bitchy, but I felt the need to show a little backbone. Something told me that with Shya, if I gave him an inch he'd take more than a mile. He'd likely take me to hell and back if he could.

"As long as you never betray me, Alexa, I really don't give a damn what you and yours do." Matter of fact and somewhat flippant, Shya shrugged.

"Fine. Thank you." I wasn't going to push things further. I'd address everything as it occurred. What mattered to me right then was that Shya knew I wasn't going to be controlled.

The angel glided up next to Shya, but his pale silver gaze was on me. Blowing a shaggy lock of fair hair out of his eyes, he openly glowered. "So this is the one that will lead vampires and wolves. Doesn't look like much. Kind of small. Cute I guess."

My jaw dropped. He was an enigma, a being so enchanting that I was both in fear and awe of him. Unlike Shya, I couldn't feel the angel's power. I had a feeling it was simply because he didn't want me to. But angel or not, who the hell was he to talk about me like that?

A retort burned on my lips, but before I could get it out, Shya cut in. "Piss off, Falon. Give Ms. O'Brien some respect. There is much more to her than it might appear."

I was completely offended. Not only did I hate being spoken of as if I wasn't present, I also hated being underestimated. Anyone who chose to use "cute" and "small" to describe me was immediately on my shit list.

Falon looked me over, his glower becoming a sneer. "Well, I should hope so."

My wolf came snarling to the surface, and I growled. Satisfied with my reaction, Falon turned on his heel. Cloaked by his ethereal wings, he slipped through the large double doors and into the night. *What an asshole.*

"Pay no attention to Falon. He doesn't think very highly of anyone." Shya wasn't apologetic, just matter of fact.

"That's fine. I don't think very highly of him, either." It wasn't often I developed a sudden dislike for someone within just minutes of being in their presence.

Shya cast a fleeting glance back toward the altar. "I won't keep you any longer. I have some business to take care of here with my friend, Evan. We'll speak soon. Please, both of you, have a lovely night."

Just like that, we were effectively dismissed. Turning his back on us, Shya left us standing by the door. Kale snapped into motion, guiding me outside with a hand on my back. I saw no sign of Falon outside. He was long gone.

"What in the fuck was that?" Glad to be free of the confines of the church, my disbelief exploded out in a blast of incredulous diatribe. "He asked me here so I could watch a man be murdered and have an angel talk shit to me?"

"Fallen angel," Kale corrected. With a jingle of keys he unlocked the passenger door of the Camaro, holding it open for me. "Only a fallen angel would be seen in the company of demons."

I reached over to unlock Kale's door, waiting for him to get in before continuing my rant. "Fallen angel? Are you kidding me? What makes him any different from a demon then? And, what's with his attitude?"

"Whoa, one question at a time." Kale laughed as he started the car and put it in gear. The engine roared, and we were on our way, leaving the church behind. I couldn't possibly get away fast enough. "Demons are fallen angels. At least, they were once. But a fallen angel isn't always a demon. They choose to fall. They don't all choose to take it all the way."

"They just linger in between? What's the point? Why even fall if they aren't going full demon with it?" I rolled down the window to let the summer night air caress my face. Now that I was out of the blood-filled building, the bloodlust was waning.

"You're asking the wrong person, Alexa. I don't know much about angels. It's rare to even see one, especially one that hasn't fallen."

Like I didn't have enough to occupy my thoughts these days. I had so many questions after what I'd just seen. Questions that would mostly go unanswered.

We rolled to a stop at a red light, and I glanced over at Kale. The glow of a streetlight fell upon him, illuminating his pale skin and sharp eyes. I wondered if he'd been killing recently, but I didn't want to offend him by asking. I liked him better when he wasn't.

"What's wrong, Alexa?" He met my eyes briefly before turning his attention back to the road. "Is it Shya? You don't have to worry about him. Keep your distance, don't get tricked into anything, and it will be fine."

"I wasn't thinking about Shya, but now that you mention it, I'm more afraid of myself right now than I am of him. I killed Veryl, without a second thought, and I don't regret it. Now, I've made an agreement with a demon, and I'm not even sure what he wants from me." Suddenly panicked, I stared out the window at the dark storefronts and office buildings as we passed. "I'm afraid of turning into the same thing I've been killing all these years."

Kale's energy grew warm as his mood shifted. "That won't happen. That's not what you are. Shya believes you have power over both werewolves and vampires, and judging by the way your power can manipulate me, I'm inclined to agree with him."

I flashed back to an incident at The Wicked Kiss a few months earlier. A vampire had attacked me with a stake, swearing to never bow down to me. *I'm nobody's slave,* he'd said as he pressed a stake between my ribs.

"I feel like I'm living in denial, like everyone else knows more about me than I do. I'm not sure I know who I am anymore." The confession fell from my lips. I doubt I would have said it to anyone else.

Kale reached over, and I thought he was going to take my hand. He seemed to think better of it and instead smoothed a strand of my hair back behind my ear. "You'll find out. We all do eventually. Even if it takes five hundred years."

Closing my eyes, I concentrated on the way the breeze streaming through the open window felt on my face. I wasn't sure how to feel about Shya and the role he wanted me to play, his personal assassin, the one who would keep the vampires and werewolves in line. It sounded huge.

I was wary. However, I did believe that creatures of the night needed to stay in the dark. Much of our power lies in the myth that we don't exist. It had to stay that way. Otherwise, all hell would break loose. I was willing to do my part to keep that from happening. All I could do was pray that I never had to become a monster to do it.

Too late. I ignored the ugly voice of guilt that taunted me. Kale was right. Things to come would show me who I really was, one day at a time. Still, I couldn't help but wonder if I was just another one of the bad guys.

Chapter Twenty-Four

"Are you sure about this?" I couldn't sit still. Squirming on my seat with discomfort, I started to question my decision to listen to Arys.

He sat next to me, an untouched martini in front of him. He kept trying to slide it in front of me, and I slid it right back. I wasn't touching a drop of alcohol, not with what he had in mind.

"Relax, Alexa. Enjoy the buildup. It's like foreplay. No need to be impatient."

"I'm not impatient. I'm nervous and starting to change my mind."

Tearing his gaze from the interior of the martini lounge, he fixed me with a daring stare. "Oh no, you're not. I told you, I'm not going to let you be bloodlust's bitch anymore. It doesn't have to be all or nothing. You'll see."

He hadn't let go of his intent for us to hunt together. It made me uncomfortable in more ways than I could count. I'd seen Arys in action. It was both thrilling and frightening. But, to accompany him? It didn't sit well with me.

"You damn hypocrite." I ran a finger along the top of my sparkling water glass. I felt too nervous to drink it. "You live by the rule of all or nothing. Isn't that why you look down on the vampires that feed at The Kiss?"

"This isn't about them. It's about you. You try to hide that it drives you crazy, but then you break down and slaughter someone. You're not cut out to live my lifestyle. The guilt would eat you alive." He offered me the olive from his drink, and I grimaced at the smell. "Besides, I don't take the kill every time. Just more often than not. Every now and then, I like the tease of resistance."

I didn't know what to expect from a hunt with Arys; I'd half expected to stalk helpless victims in dark back alleys. When I'd voiced that very thing to Arys, he'd both scowled and laughed at me. Instead we'd ended up in a martini bar on the main floor of a five-star hotel with a key to a room upstairs. It seemed like excessive work to me though Arys shrugged it off as no big deal.

I watched Arys as he scanned the lounge for the right victim. I was impatient and wanted to get this over quickly if I had to do it at all. But, he was calm, like the fox in the hen-house, deciding which one he liked the most.

"So, what are we waiting for? Can't we just do this already?"

He frowned and ran his tongue over his lips. Just watching him perform the casual action made my stomach tighten.

"Patience, my wolf. Don't be so quick to act. If you're stuck with the bloodlust, you might as well learn to enjoy it. It doesn't have to all be bad."

"That's the problem. I want to hate it, but once I'm caught up in the moment, there's nowhere else I'd rather be. And, that's what I hate."

Arys took my hand and lightly ran a finger over the back of it. His touch stirred my longing. The bloodlust was running high. Arys had wanted me to be at its mercy. I couldn't say I was loving it. My senses were on fire. Every touch and smell was amplified. All I could focus on was the tingle in my loins as he stroked a finger up my bare arm and the thick scent of human blood. It begged for my attention, making it hard to acknowledge any other smells in the lounge.

"That one, right there." Arys drew my attention to a woman sitting alone at a table on the opposite side of the room. "She's perfect. Do you want her?"

She was a leggy brunette in a designer dress, staring intently at her cell phone. Nothing distinguished her from any other woman in the lounge except for the fact that she was alone.

"A woman, huh?" I teased. "I guess that's fair considering I'm usually the only woman present."

Arys grinned, but his eyes glinted seriously. "Alexa, I don't mind sharing you with the wolf pup. You seem to think I do, but sharing you with him means not having to share you with anyone else. Simple logic but it works."

I thought it over, finding his logic to be a tad skewed like usual, but somehow, it made sense this time. "Alright. You want her, that's fine with me."

I was uneasy, but Arys had promised me that we weren't killing anyone tonight. This was about finding the balance I needed to appease the bloodlust without taking the kill.

Tipping my head up with a hand under my chin, Arys kissed me lightly. "Stay here until I give you a signal."

He slid off his stool and was gone before I could change my mind. The sound of my heart beating was suddenly deafening in my ears. I clutched my purse tightly and fidgeted with my short skirt. I couldn't tear my gaze off Arys as he sauntered through the room like a wolf stalking prey. As I watched him go, the nerves melted away, replaced by a hungry anticipation.

Arys was a vision of sensuality. He moved through the room with dark intentions, drawing the attention of several women as he passed. It was impossible not to look at him. From head to toe the man oozed sex. It didn't come as a surprise that the majority of other women thought so, too.

At his approach, his intended victim glanced up from her cell phone. She looked wary, but once Arys started talking, she smiled. I would have loved to hear what he was saying. The grin he beamed at her was downright seductive. I was falling for it from where I sat. So when she gestured to the chair next to her, I wasn't surprised. Actually, I was a little turned on watching Arys work his magic, although a little part of me wondered if I was as easy a target as this woman was turning out to be.

Watching Arys seduce our victim made me ache for satisfaction. My growing hunger was testing the limits of my control. I'd questioned his intent to lure her upstairs to the room, but my patience was slipping. Now, I just wanted to make it happen.

The brunette leaned into Arys as they talked. Something in her eyes, a strange glazed look, indicated Arys' influence over her. That had been easy. Not many vampires had that ability to make people want to surrender, happily accepting that he would drain their life away. I was painfully aware that, because I loved him, I often forgot how very dangerous Arys really was.

Catching my eye, Arys nodded ever so slightly toward the

door. With eager anticipation, I picked the olive out of his abandoned glass and tossed back the contents. Then, I made my way out of the lounge and up to our room.

I was a mess waiting for them. I paced the small but nicely kept hotel room, unable to sit or stand still. I turned on the gas fireplace but then turned it off. Finally, I went to stare out the window at the street below.

By the time Arys opened the door, I was gripping the window sill so hard my clawed nails left gouges in the wood. I whirled around to face him. I hadn't sated the bloodlust in days. I wasn't sure how much more I could take. He had wanted me to be pushed to the breaking point. It was nearing quickly.

"Alexa, this is Roxanne. She was supposed to meet a blind date in the bar, but lucky us, she has agreed to keep us company." Arys flashed me a smug smile and a wink. He ushered Roxanne into the room and locked the door. She didn't seem to notice.

She stared at me with a big smile plastered on her pink lips. The spellbound expression she wore was unsettling; I didn't like it. The vampire in me thought back to something Kale had once said. He preferred it when they knew it was coming, when they begged and screamed. If this mesmerized complacency was the alternative, I'd prefer the screams, too.

No sooner had that thought crossed my mind than I wondered what it would take to make Roxanne scream. My fangs filled my mouth, four brutal points that I ached to sink into her. I moved toward her, and Arys stepped in between us.

He must have seen the intent in my eyes because he smiled and shook his head. "Patience, my love. This is about satisfaction through control, not weakness because of the loss of it. Follow my lead."

Roxanne stood there like a human doll, waiting for us to play with her. It was disturbing to see someone so completely lost in the thrall of a powerful vampire. I hated that I kind of liked it.

"Roxanne, sweetheart," Arys purred, taking her hand and bringing it to his lips. "We won't keep you long. Just a little taste, alright my dear?"

She didn't even speak. Gazing up at him with those glazed eyes, she merely smiled timidly and nodded. Arys kissed his way up her bare arm, and she giggled. I waited for jealousy to hit, but it never did. I wanted to watch him in his element. The seduction and the hunt, that was Arys at his best, and I wanted to see it.

He took his time, making his way from her wrist to her neck. Her eyes closed, and her head fell back. Desire flowed from her, tantalizing and hot. My grip was slipping, and I knew I couldn't cling to sanity much longer. The bloodlust was a powerful master, and once again, it had made me its slave.

His lips on her skin, the scent of her growing desire, and the sound of her heart beat growing louder in my ears, it all came at me in a rush, driving me into a frenzy. Arys, being the incubus he was, manipulated her sexual response to him, encouraging it to flow freely as he fed upon it.

The energy in the room became suffocating. I snarled, baring my fangs. Arys lifted his head to find me on the edge of the abyss, about to step past the point of no return. He gripped her forearm, and with a sudden aggression that spoke to the wolf in me, Arys bit into her wrist.

Blood spilled forth, and I was ravenous. I lunged at them, willing to knock Arys aside to get to that glorious red stream. He held me back with a hand on my throat, cutting off my air supply just enough to shake some sense back into me.

"You can't bite her, Alexa. You'll turn her or kill her. That's not what you want."

I wasn't listening. I was staring at the blood that ran down Roxanne's hand to drip off the tips of her fingers. It was all I could smell, all I could focus on.

Arys sat Roxanne on the end of the bed. Her eyes fluttered open and then closed again. She sighed softly. Gripping both of my arms tightly, Arys forced me to look into his eyes.

"It will always be part of you, but it doesn't have to own you. You can control this." He shook me when I growled at him. "Stop giving in so easily. You're stronger than that."

Then he slapped me.

It was startling. The sound of his hand hitting my cheek was loud in the quiet room. I laughed. It earned me a glare.

"Let me have her. Just this once." I was detached, hearing myself talk but not fully aware it was me.

The power flared between us as Arys struggled to get through to me. "You will master this or else it masters you. Got it? Is that what you want? To be just another killer?"

"Why not?" I snapped. "It seems to be good enough for you."

Arys dragged me close and pressed his forehead to mine. His eyes closed, and I felt the warm push of calming energy. It filled me from head to toe, bringing me back to myself. I hovered precariously in that awkward place between who I was and what I had become.

His voice low, almost a whisper, Arys loosened his grip. "You are the light in my darkness. I can't watch you become something you will grow to hate."

Something in his tone struck a nerve deep down. I blinked a few times, and the bloodlust cleared from my vision. "Arys..."

Opening his eyes, he gazed deep into me, and then he released me entirely. Together we approached the bed where Roxanne sat in a deep thrall. I could do this. I had to. I was stronger than the bloodlust.

Arys watched me as I sat on the floor before her and took her bloody wrist in my hands. The scent of her blood filled my lungs, and it tore at my fragile control. I ran my tongue over her smooth, lightly tanned skin. The urge to rush into the kill was strong, but I wasn't giving in this time. I slowly licked the red rivulets that dripped into the palm of her hand. No words could describe the way it felt; *orgasmic, pure bliss*, they didn't even come close. Tasting her was like finding a peace I never knew existed. It felt right, like I was finally whole. And, I knew it was all a lie.

As I drank the blood from Arys' bite, I saw it all so clearly. We were all creatures in unbearable pain, always seeking escape from something, even if we didn't know it at the time. Every one of us found our moment of peace in something dark and twisted. This was mine.

On the bed, Arys knelt beside our victim. I could see them from where I sat. He bit into her neck, and she gasped. Or had it been me? I wasn't sure.

A roar filled my ears as the power Arys and I shared grew to an explosive level. He reached out for me, his hand seeking mine. I surrendered it to him, crying out when a hot jolt of electricity burned my skin where it touched his.

Blood in my mouth and Arys' skin on mine stirred my longing. Heat flooded my loins as I watched his lips against her skin, his tongue running over the wound. It wasn't enough. The hunger grew, and my moment of peace was shattered.

Arys must have felt me slip because he stopped me from doing something I would deeply regret. With a snarl, I bared my fangs, craving the sensation of having them buried in flesh. The blood wasn't enough. The need to tear into Roxanne was driven by more than the bloodlust. Caught up in the throes of power and hunger, my wolf struggled to break free.

I was on my ass across the room before I had a chance to hurt her. Trapped by Arys' energy wall, there was a sense of déjà vu as I remembered how recently this had happened in the bathroom at The Wicked Kiss. One day, Arys wouldn't be there to save me from myself.

With a hand on Roxanne's face, he got her up on her feet. Her eyes were open but unfocused. Stuffing some cash into her hand, Arys spoke slow and clear. "Go downstairs, get into the first cab you see and go straight home. You won't ever tell anyone anything you might remember because they would never believe you. There is no such thing as vampires."

She nodded and allowed Arys to lead her to the door. I was intent on the barrier he'd thrown at me. Like the last time, I was certain I could bend it to my will. Instead of fighting it, I concentrated on pulling it into me and making it mine. A strange, almost sick feeling hit my stomach as the barrier broke. I couldn't breathe as it rushed into me, becoming one with my power.

It was easier than I'd expected. It also proved what I'd suspected for a while. Arys and I could turn our power on one another, but we could also take that power into ourselves. His power was mine, and therefore, he couldn't truly harm me, not if I took the control back from him.

Free of his hold on me, I lunged at the door as Arys closed it behind her. Astonished but alert, he reacted quickly. Arys shoved me back, blocking my path to the door. I wanted her, and he had just let her go.

"Come on, Alexa." He taunted me, curling a finger in invitation. "You have some aggression to unleash. Let's have it."

He was right. I had a burning need for violence and gratification. Licking the blood from my lips, I advanced on him with a wicked yearning clawing at my insides.

The fire in Arys' midnight eyes brought a naughty smile to my face. Pressing my body against his, I grasped a handful of his hair and pulled his head down to mine. I licked his bottom lip before nipping it with my upper fangs. Sucking it into my mouth, I delighted in the spicy taste of his blood.

I kissed him, seeking to feel his tongue on mine. It was a hard and bruising kiss. I wanted to devour him. Arys groaned, his hands sliding to my waist. Our power was heightened, creating a dizzying storm that I could feel both in and out. Urgency gripped me.

I clawed Arys' arms and chest in my haste to tear his shirt off, leaving bloody scratches behind. I wanted him, and I didn't want to wait. I ran a finger through a crimson smear on his abdomen, pausing to taste it. It fueled my desire for him.

I slipped my underwear down from under my skirt, kicking them off. "I need you now."

A wolf-like growl came from Arys. He grabbed me roughly. His fingers dug into my arms as he slid my top up and over my head. Undeniably, he felt it, too, the rabid need that drove me. Shoving me on the bed, Arys pressed his face into the swell of my cleavage and bit into my left breast.

I made a pained noise that fed his voracious appetite. His mouth was hot and wet against my sensitive flesh as he sucked at the bleeding wound. Blood seeped from the bite, escaping him to stain the soft material of my white bra.

Arys pushed my skirt up, exposing me to him. In our struggle for dominance, he pinned me to the bed with strong hands on my hips before lowering his head to the cleft between my legs. The velvet touch of his tongue had me quivering.

Riding the high of the bloodlust and power, my every sense was amplified. Arys attacked me with a wild passion. The sharp sting of fangs on the inside of my thigh was shocking splendor. I reveled in the way his head of silky hair felt nestled between my legs.

With a hungry fervor he consumed both my blood and my pleasure. Arys eagerly fed from my lusty energy and the blood that flowed from his bite. I found myself spiraling into that wonderful state of bliss where both mind and body was his to command. I writhed on the bed as he brought me to a glorious climax.

It did nothing to sate my desire for him. I was just getting started. Impatience gripped me when Arys paused to remove the last of his clothing. I couldn't calm the beast inside me that, when paired with the hungers of the vampire, knew no restraint.

I was sticky with blood. It decorated me in splashes of scarlet, like crude body art. The scent of it was heavy on the air. I reached for Arys with the intent to spill his, too. I wanted to bask in every part of him.

Capturing one of my bloodstained hands in his, he turned me around and forced me up on my knees. I was pressed against the headboard so my back was to him. Lifting my skirt so it bunched up around my waist, he held firmly to my hips and entered me from behind.

I cried out as he thrust roughly into me. Every stroke was ecstasy. I hated that I couldn't look into his eyes, but I loved the raw, carnal way in which he took me. I braced myself against the wall above the headboard, my fingers slipping to leave bloody handprints.

Our lovemaking grew into a high-paced, tense fervor. The metaphysical power we created broke free of our hold. It seemed to feed upon the both of us. The lights dimmed to almost complete darkness before surging again. I felt the effect ripple throughout the entire hotel.

I waited until I was sure Arys was close to the peak of pleasure, and then I turned slightly so I could shove him off me. I forced him down on the bed, straddling him but careful not to give him what he wanted. Not just yet.

Raking my claws down his chest, I delighted in the red ribbons that blossomed in my wake. I dipped my head to glide my tongue along a fresh scratch as I rubbed my groin against his. Tauntingly slow, I took him inside me just enough to make him groan before releasing him from the warmth of my body.

He grabbed my hair in a grip that was excitingly painful and threw me down so that I was beneath him. "You little tease."

I laughed, a throaty sound that was laced with a growl. Forcing my legs apart, Arys took me again. Buried deep inside me, he unleashed any hold he might have maintained on rationale and control. With eyes flashing dangerously, he bit deep into my neck, hard enough to make me shriek.

I felt the telltale warmth of blood trickling down my shoulder to the bed below. I held tight to Arys, blood pooling beneath my nails as we moved together as one. The power we commanded was like a steadily growing wind whipping through the room. In the distance, I heard thunder, and I wondered if we'd somehow caused it.

The bed was a mess of blood. When at last we lay entangled among the blankets, exhausted and fulfilled, I groaned as the euphoria ebbed and the pain set in. My head spun, and my mouth was thick with the taste of blood. Nobody had ever loved me the wild, crazed way that Arys did. I adored every moment of it.

I lay curled in Arys' warm embrace, basking in the afterglow. Maybe it wasn't the right time to bring it up, but I wanted to take advantage of having him in a position where he couldn't dodge my questions.

"So now seems like a good time for you to shed a little light on what Maxwell said. I think I deserve to know, Arys."

"Really?" He groaned and rolled his eyes. "You want to do this now?"

"I do. Start talking. No lies and no avoidance. Tell me what he meant when he said that I was the one you'd been waiting for."

"It's a long story. Too long to go into right now."

I fixed him with a fierce stare. I was not going to let up on this. "Scratch the surface."

Arys forced a dramatic, exasperated sigh and propped himself up on one arm. "Here's the quick version. A little more than a century ago, I was told by a witch that she could see my other half. She could see you, the one who would complete me. Lena was right when she told you we were two souls cut from the same magical cloth. We were always meant to be one. I didn't believe it until I met you. Actually, I didn't even let myself believe it then, not until it became impossible to deny."

"And, you never thought to tell me this? There has to be more to it. Keep talking."

"It's rare for a connection like ours to actually be made. If I'd lived and died as human, we never would have met. Most people bound the way we are never meet." His expression grew dark, and I got the feeling he would have done anything to avoid having this conversation. "Yin and yang. You know how that works? Well, that's us. Two sides of the same coin but neither alike. Together we create something new, something powerful."

My thoughts raced as I tried to piece it together. "Alright. That fits with a lot of what Lena said. But still … what does it really mean? And, why didn't you want to tell me?"

Arys reached to take my hand with his free one. "That's exactly why I didn't tell you. I don't know what it means. All I know is that I am the dark and you are the light. And, it's only a matter of time until my darkness consumes you. When it does, we both die."

"No way." I sat up quickly, tossing the bloodstained blanket aside. "There has to be more to it than that. There has to be a reason for it all."

I couldn't believe what I was hearing. I could see in Arys' eyes that he really believed what he'd said, which explained why he'd been unwilling to share it earlier. Still, something didn't add up. It didn't entirely make sense.

"I'm sure there is a reason," Arys offered, attempting to provide some comfort. "We have only just begun to realize what we can do together. We were bound before you were even born. Nothing was going to change that. But, I have to admit, sometimes I wish I hadn't blood bonded you. It's tainted you with parts of me that you should never have to deal with."

"Is that why you were so adamant about tonight? Controlling the bloodlust didn't work out so well." I caught sight of my reflection in the mirror on the bureau, and I cringed. I looked like hell with blood and bruises covering more of me than unblemished skin. "If you didn't bind me to you, someone else would have. You know that. Things would be worse if we hadn't done it. Don't waste time on regrets."

"Alexa, be careful. Shya knows about us. That's why he wanted me, too. You have a role to play there, but don't let him exploit you."

My head was starting to ache. I needed a shower, but the questions wouldn't stop coming. "I still think there's more to it. What aren't you telling me? And, how did Maxwell know about this?"

Arys stroked a hand down my cheek before pulling me back down beside him. "Harley made him, too. We were close at one time. Don't worry about this stuff, ok? We're strong together. I'd walk into the sun before I'd let anything happen to you. But, if you still have questions, read the journal I gave you. Then if you still want to, we'll talk further."

He hugged me close, an action that silenced my further questions. Arys believed we were made for each other, and he believed it would destroy us both. Rather than push the subject the way I wanted to, I clung to him in quiet contemplation.

I couldn't stop thinking about what I'd just heard. Pieces were missing, I was sure of it. I needed to read Arys' journal sooner rather than later.

Replaying the events of the evening in my mind, I was faced with the raw truth of what had really occurred. Arys' intent had been for me to develop control, to conquer the undeniable call of the bloodlust before it devoured me. I had failed.

I should have been content to be there with him in that moment, but I was worried. Arys had stopped me from killing more than once. I couldn't always rely on him to fix my mistakes before I made them.

This was bad. I was slipping further into the clutches of a weakness I now knew we both feared. I couldn't let it claim me, but I was running out of time. Every time I gave in to the welcoming splendor of the bloodlust, I lost a bit more of what little humanity I had left. Arys' words echoed inside my head. *Master it or it masters you.*

Epilogue

It was as close to normal as I was going to get. I had the house to myself, a rarity. I didn't like to think about it much, but I still wasn't comfortable being in Raoul's house alone. With an episode of *Castle* on television and the scent of pizza permeating the house, I curled up on the couch with a coffee in hand.

My laptop sat next to me on the middle cushion. I glared at it and clicked a few things randomly. Though I hadn't had much time to break my way into Veryl's files, I wasn't having any luck. At all.

Setting my mug on the coffee table, I took a bite of pizza before typing "open password protected files" into Google. The results were repetitive. Sites trying to sell me software or the same bits of information that were getting me nowhere. I needed to find a professional to do it for me, one who would keep his or her mouth shut.

One thing at a time.

I glanced at the old, leather journal where it sat on the far end of the coffee table. I hadn't opened it yet despite how badly I wanted to know what was inside. It felt good to sit on my couch and watch TV like a normal person. I didn't get to do this enough. I wanted to savor it. The moment I opened that book, it would all end, and I'd be faced with reality again.

I laughed at a quip on the show, glancing up to re-immerse myself in the fictional on-screen world. I couldn't look at the television without my gaze straying to the large, framed photo above it. It felt surreal to stare into my own eyes without recognition.

The gift I'd received from Kylarai and Zoey had been a photo of Shaz and me. Kylarai had captured it with her camera early one morning as we'd been trotting through the farmer's field to her backyard.

In the picture, I was staring off into the distance while Shaz leaned into me, his face rubbing alongside mine. It was really weird to see myself as a wolf. I never did, not like this. Shaz stood out brilliantly next to me with his bright green eyes and white fur. My ash blond fur and dark eyes weren't quite as striking, but I had to admit, together we looked good. Maybe even beautiful.

It was one of the most meaningful gifts I'd ever gotten. I'd cried a little when I first saw it. It symbolized a side of me that I saw less frequently these days. It also made me ache for Shaz.

I was expecting him close to dawn. Until then it was just me, my locked files and Arys' journal. More than enough to keep me busy.

While munching on pizza I made a few more feeble attempts at busting into Veryl's files. I didn't want to give up, but I was getting nowhere. I was also using it as a way to procrastinate on the journal. Whatever was in the files could wait; I couldn't access it, and anything inside had been hidden from me for a while now. Arys' journal was right there, waiting for me to open it.

Since our night at the hotel a week ago, he had done all he could to avoid talking about it further. He thought he was going to destroy me, thereby destroying us both. I understood his concern, but I was skeptical. I'd come close to death enough times to know that it could never be so cut and dry.

So some witch had been able to see that Arys wasn't a lone soul? So what? It didn't mean we were destined to self-destruct. Lena, too, had been aware there was something big between us, but she'd never spoken of doom and gloom, although she had been full of warnings.

I missed her. It hurt to think about her, flashing back to the night she died. I still wished I could have made Maxwell suffer. However, I had a renewed confidence since I'd killed him. I'd said that if anyone had a right to Harley's place in Vegas, it was me. Knowing that to be true, I didn't fear anyone or anything coming out of Sin City now. If they came, I'd be ready.

I couldn't say that I missed Veryl. He was one individual I simply couldn't mourn. If that made me a bad person, then so be it.

Since his death Lilah had taken over the office. We hadn't spoken about it much. I didn't know whether or not the information he had on her had been leaked. I didn't ask.

Everything else functioned like usual. Jez was back at it, hunting the newborn vamps and Weres that I'd tired of. She enjoyed it, and someone had to take care of that stuff. Kale, like me, had joined Shya's personal team. I had yet to hear from the demon since the last time I'd seen him. I was still reeling from that night.

I didn't trust Shya. At this point, I had no reason to. But, I couldn't shake the feeling that working with him was the right thing to do. If there were forces out there, other supernaturals that were working to expose us all on a grand scale then I had to be involved. My own ass was on the line.

Jez had been going out of her way to avoid Kale. I'd suggested that they talk about it, but she'd declared she wasn't ready and might never be. When I'd pushed her on it, she had promptly asked if I'd be on her side if she had been the one in love with me instead of Kale. I let it go. I felt bad for Kale, but he'd really fucked up. Jez would either come around or not.

Abandoning my laptop for the night, I clutched my coffee cup in both hands and watched the rest of the show. It felt weird to just sit and do nothing. I couldn't help but feel like I should be looking over my shoulder for danger or babysitting the assholes at The Wicked Kiss. Being in the comfort of my own home, doing something other than sleeping, felt really nice. I needed more of this.

The pizza was good, but it wasn't what I really wanted. The bloodlust lurked deep inside. It would be unbearable within the next night or two. I didn't intend to let it reach that point. When Shaz arrived, I would take blood from him. I'd done it before. He could defend himself from me in ways a human couldn't, a relief, but it wasn't enough. I still hungered for the kill.

Once I started thinking about it, my moment of normalcy was over. Arys feared the darkness he saw growing within me, his darkness. I had to win this battle.

With a sigh I set my coffee aside and reached for Arys' journal. Having a written account of events from his life before me was almost too good to be true. What I found inside could open the door to memories locked in my subconscious. I remembered enough of Arys' memories to know that some were better left hidden from my conscious mind, but it was too late for that. We were part of one another.

I ran a finger over the plain cover. It had worn thin in places and bore the marks of decades of wear. I was nervous and had to laugh at myself. Part of me was afraid to open it and see what was on the first page.

Curiosity and the need to know won out. So much lay ahead. I had to be prepared to take on whatever came our way. Reading this journal could help me do that. Swallowing my hesitation, I bit the bullet and opened the cover.

The first page was written in faded ink. Arys had done a remarkable job preserving it. The date at the top of the page was October, 1849. My gaze fell upon the first line, and my heart dropped.

I saw her again in my dreams, the wolf.

I was shocked, so much so that I had to pause before I could continue. It was almost too much to wrap my mind around, and I'd barely begun. The fact that Arys had never told me this said more about him than I think he'd ever want to admit. He had a vulnerability, and I was it.

I held the journal carefully, as if it would crumble to dust if I gripped it too hard. Taking a few calming breaths, I leaned back on the couch and began to read.

About the Author

Trina M. Lee has walked in the darkness alongside vampires and werewolves since adolescence. Trina lives in Alberta, Canada with her fiancé and daughter, along with their 3 cats. Trina is a big fan of indie movies, books that make her cry and her Dodge Charger. She loves to hear from readers via email or Twitter.

For news and information regarding the next book in the Alexa O'Brien Huntress series, please visit:

www.TrinaMLee.com